From the farthest reaches of the universe to the innermost workings of the human heart and mind . . . Let tomorrow's masters of science fiction and fantasy take you on a journey that will capture your imagination:

Created to fight in a horrific, high-tech future war, an artificial soldier finds an innovative way to discover her humanity. . . .

After her father dies, a young woman has to defeat a mysterious rival magician to claim her home—a fantastical charmed house where every room is alive, with its own distinctive personality. . . .

Lost on a world claimed by several alien races, an injured human girl has only one hope for survival— to form a friendship with an exotic alien tree creature. . . .

A loner must confront her past, present and future in a post-holocaust frontier town. . . .

Sharing minds with someone on the other side of the world was supposed to be an educational, cross-cultural experience—but when one partner becomes a terrorist, the violence begins to seep through. . . .

Centuries after they have purged the Earth of humanity, a group of artificial gods faces an unexpected crisis—returning spaceships filled with survivors bent on revenge. . . .

In an orbiting power station, the problems of Earth might seem far away . . . but is the isolated crew safe, or trapped?

Although Ashia the warrior is known for her bravery fighting the alien Kree, she finds a completely different kind of courage to protect her children. . . .

Life is rough for a Minotaur in the city, surrounded by mythical creatures and the trappings of gods. But when an ominous, formless stranger breaks into his home, the real trouble starts. . . .

An android marked for death because he dared to be too human is shipwrecked with the man ordered to execute him. . . .

A dying man's only chance for survival is an organ transplant infested with black-market nanotech, complete with an imprint of the previous body's personality. . . .

After his memories of the battlefield are erased, a war veteran searches for the hard drive that holds his past. But the government wants some secrets left hidden. . . .

These stories are from the freshest, most talented new voices in science fiction and fantasy, individually illustrated by the best new artists in the genre. You will definitely encounter these names again in the future—but you saw them first in L. Ron Hubbard Presents Writers of the Future *Volume XXVI.*

What Has Been Said About the
L. RON HUBBARD
Presents
Writers of the Future
Anthologies

From novice to professional: What Writers of the Future means to you as an aspiring writer, as relayed from some of our past winners.

"This Contest serves as one of those first rungs that one must climb on the ladder to success."
— Dave Wolverton
Writers of the Future Contest winner 1987 and Contest judge

"The Writers of the Future Contest was definitely an accelerator to my writing development. I learned so much, and it came at just the right moment for me."
— Jo Beverley
Writers of the Future Contest winner 1988

"That phone call telling me I had won was the first time in my life that it seemed possible I would achieve my long-cherished dream of having a career as a writer."
— K. D. Wentworth
Writers of the Future Contest winner 1989
and Contest Coordinating Judge

"You have to ask yourself, 'Do I really have what it takes, or am I just fooling myself?' That pat on the back from Writers of the Future told me not to give up. . . . All in all, the Contest was a fine finishing step from amateur to pro, and I'm grateful to all those involved.
— James Alan Gardner
Writers of the Future Contest winner 1990

"The Writers of the Future Contest has had a profound impact on my career, ever since I submitted my first story in 1989."
— Sean Williams
Writers of the Future Contest winner 1993 and Contest judge

"The Writers of the Future Contest played a critical role in the early stages of my career as a writer."
— Eric Flint
Writers of the Future Contest winner 1993 and Contest judge

"The Contest kept the spark and life of my science-fictional imagination going. I might have had little confidence before, but after the workshops, I received the great start that the Contest's visionary founder always hoped and knew that it could provide."
— Amy Sterling Casil
Writers of the Future Contest winner 1999

"The Writers of the Future Contest sowed the seeds of my success. . . . So many people say a writing career is impossible, but WotF says, 'Dreams are worth following.'"
— Scott Nicholson
Writers of the Future Contest winner 1999

"I credit the Writers of the Future Contest as an important part of my career launch, and I highly recommend it to everyone who wants to establish themselves in the field of science fiction and fantasy."

— Ken Scholes
Writers of the Future Contest winner 2005

"Knowing that such great authors as the WotF judges felt my stories were worth publishing encouraged me to write more and submit more."

— Eric James Stone
Writers of the Future Contest winner 2005

"The Writers of the Future Contest launched my career into several amazing trajectories, and I'm enjoying them all."

— David Sakmyster
Writers of the Future Contest winner 2006

"It's hard to say enough about how unique and powerful this Contest can be for any writer who's ready to take the next step."

— Jeff Carlson
Writers of the Future Contest winner 2007

A word from Illustrators of the Future judges:

"The Illustrators of the Future Contest is one of the best opportunities a young artist will ever get. You have nothing to lose and a lot to win."

—Frank Frazetta, Artist
Illustrators of the Future Contest judge

"I only wish that there had been an Illustrators of the Future competition forty-five years ago. What a blessing it would have been to a young artist with a little bit of talent, a Dutch name and a heart full of desire."

—H. R. Van Dongen, Artist
Illustrators of the Future Contest judge

"The Contests are amazing competitions because really, you've nothing to lose and it provides good positive encouragement to anyone who wins. Judging the entries is always a lot of fun and inspiring. I wish I had something like this when I was getting started—very positive and cool."

— Bob Eggleton, Artist
Illustrators of the Future Contest judge

"The aspect I personally value most highly about the program is that of working with my fellow professionals, both artists and writers, to accomplish a worthwhile goal of giving tomorrow's artists and writers recognition and advancement in the highly competitive field of imaginative endeavor—the only existing program that does this."

—Stephen Hickman, Artist
Illustrators of the Future Contest judge

"These Contests provide a wonderful safety net of professionals for young artists and writers. And it's due to the fact that L. Ron Hubbard was willing to lend a hand."

—Judith Miller, Artist
Illustrators of the Future Contest judge

L. Ron Hubbard PRESENTS
Writers of the Future

VOLUME XXVI

L. Ron Hubbard PRESENTS
Writers of the Future

VOLUME XXVI

The year's twelve best tales from

the Writers of the Future

international writers' program

Illustrated by winners in

the Illustrators of the Future

international illustrators' program

With essays on writing & illustration by

L. Ron Hubbard / Dean Wesley Smith / Stephen Youll

Edited by K. D. Wentworth

GALAXY PRESS, LLC

Living Rooms: © 2010 Laurie Tom
The Black Side of Memory: © 2010 Lael Salaets
Lisa With Child: © 2010 Alex Black
The Golden Pen: © 2010 L. Ron Hubbard Library
Not in the Flesh: © 2010 Adam Colston
Seeing Double: © 2010 Tom Crosshill
Exanastasis: © 2010 Brad R. Torgersen
Poison Inside the Walls: © 2010 Scott W. Baker
Confliction: © 2010 Simon Cooper
Digital Rights: © 2010 Brent Knowles
Coward's Steel: © 2010 K. C. Ball
Written in Light: © 2010 Jeff Young
The House of Nameless: © 2010 Jason Fischer

Illustration on page 13: © 2010 Irena Kovalenko
Illustration on page 89: © 2010 Ven Locklear
Illustration on page 101: © 2010 Tyler Carter
Illustration on page 130: © 2010 Jordan Cornthwaite
Illustration on page 173: © 2010 Olivia Pelaez
Illustration on page 190: © 2010 Jingxuan Hu
Illustration on page 259: © 2010 Kelsey Wroten
Illustration on page 287: © 2010 Cassandra Shaffer
Illustration on page 346: © 2010 Rebecca Gleason
Illustration on page 383: © 2010 R. M. Winch
Illustration on page 391: © 2010 Rachael Jade Sweeney
Illustration on page 448: © 2010 Seth J. Rowanwood

Cover Artwork: Voyage © 2010 Stephan Martiniere

Interior Design: Jerry Kelly

This anthology contains works of fiction. Names, characters, places and incidents are either the product of the authors' imaginations or are used fictitiously. Any resemblance to actual events or locales or persons, living or dead, is entirely coincidental. Opinions expressed by nonfiction essayists are their own.

ISBN-10 1-59212-847-5
ISBN-13 978-1-59212-847-1
Library of Congress Control Number: 2010911254
First Edition Paperback
Printed in the United States of America

CONTENTS

Introduction

BY K. D. WENTWORTH

K. D. Wentworth has sold more than eighty pieces of short fiction to such markets as F&SF, *Alfred Hitchcock's Mystery Magazine, Realms of Fantasy, Weird Tales, Witch Way to the Mall and Return to the Twilight Zone. Four of her stories have been finalists for the Nebula Award for Short Fiction. Currently, she has eight novels in print, the most recent being* The Crucible of Empire, *written with Eric Flint and published by Baen. She has served as Coordinating Judge for the Writers of the Future Contest and has now taken on the additional responsibility as Editor for the Writers of the Future anthology. She lives in Tulsa with her husband and a combined total of one hundred and sixty pounds of dog (Akita + Siberian "Hussy") and is working on another new novel with Flint.*

Introduction

The questions I get asked most often, as current Coordinating Judge for the L. Ron Hubbard Writers of the Future Contest, are: "What exactly are you looking for? What kind of story has the best chance to win?"

The answer is that we're looking for a particular kind of *person,* not a particular sort of story. L. Ron Hubbard designed the Contest, back when he founded it in 1983, to seek out and showcase new science fiction and fantasy authors who were just on the edge of breaking out into a professional writing career. These are the people we are trying to find.

Typically, they are individuals who have already done their best to educate themselves on proper manuscript format, appropriate markets for their work and the elements of effective fiction. They are reading widely to learn from the words of others, as well as putting in the time necessary to learn their craft and produce a body of work, but, without credits, when they submit a story or novel to a publisher, they are competing with seasoned pros like Larry Niven, Tim Powers, Kristine Kathryn

Rusch, Dean Wesley Smith, Robert Sawyer, Jerry Pournelle, Robert Silverberg, Eric Flint and Frederik Pohl (all Writers of the Future judges, by the way). To advance to the next level, our new writers need a chance to be read. The Contest was created to make that happen.

Achieving a career in writing is a vastly different process than becoming a doctor, lawyer, teacher, dentist or nurse. To learn those professions, you take classes, then prove yourself through rigorous testing, being observed by instructors and interning. If you pass with satisfactory marks, you are allowed to work in your chosen career.

Writing on the other hand is largely an act of faith. There are no guarantees, no matter how long or how hard you work, that you will ever publish a single word. And, if you do make that first sale, you have no guarantee that you will ever make a second, or a third. There is a saying that being a success as a writer is fifty percent talent and fifty percent simply not giving up. Who knows how many promising new voices did give up before they achieved success, thereby depriving us all of the wonderful stories only they could have told?

When he started the Contest, L. Ron Hubbard said, "A culture is as rich and capable of surviving as it has imaginative artists. . . . It was with this in mind that I initiated a means for new and budding writers to have a chance for their creative efforts to be seen and acknowledged." He knew that, if we do not provide a forum for new writers' work, many of them will not come into their full talent and then we will all lose.

To help develop this talent, along with the Contest's substantial quarterly monetary prize for winning, comes something even more valuable: a trip to the annual WotF workshop, taught primarily by Tim Powers and me, using a curriculum based on L. Ron Hubbard essays, but also instructed by many of our well-known and highly respected judges.

I attended this workshop myself back in 1989 when it was taught by founding WotF judge Algis Budrys and Tim Powers. The first story I sold after winning in WotF was the first story I wrote after I got home from the workshop so obviously the material worked for me. More than twenty years later, I find that I still use what Algis, Tim and L. Ron Hubbard taught me during that week every day when I sit down to write.

Each year, when we welcome the winners to the workshop, I tell them that their monetary prize is nice, of course, but they'll soon spend it. The lasting prizes are publication in the anthology, which will be widely read for years to come, and what they will learn during their week of instruction.

The workshop provides information on how to be a working writer: where ideas and inspiration for your fiction can be found when you think you've run dry, how to access your creativity and mine the stories that only you can tell, how to avoid many of the business pitfalls waiting for new writers, and how to take the skills you've already learned on your own and convert them into a professional career.

In 1988, the L. Ron Hubbard Illustrators of the Future Contest was created as a companion to Writers of the Future. Again, the purpose is to find talented artists just on the edge of breaking out, recognize and commend their abilities, publish their creative efforts and instruct them on how to move up to the next level in their career.

Quarterly winners are given the opportunity to illustrate one of the anthology's stories, then transported to the annual illustrators' workshop taught by seasoned professionals Ron Lindahn and Val Lakey Lindahn. They dispense invaluable advice about how to develop and manage a career as an artist and keep inspiration coming. Unfortunately, as rare as it is, it is not enough to just have talent. Emerging artists must learn how to develop a portfolio and professional contacts, market their work and make it pay.

So, what are we looking for? The writer and artist toiling in obscurity, working and working, honing his or her craft, but unable to break out and achieve professional success. We're looking for the story that only you can write, the picture that only you can draw. We're looking for, as L. Ron Hubbard intended, the dreams that will shape tomorrow.

Send them in! We're saving your seat at the workshop.

Living Rooms

written by

Laurie Tom

illustrated by

IRENA KOVALENKO

ABOUT THE AUTHOR

Laurie Tom has loved fantasy and science fiction since childhood. Nearly all her favorite cartoons took place in other worlds, so naturally she wanted to visit them. Eventually, other people's worlds weren't enough so she started to create her own.

When Laurie was in elementary school, her father bought the family an Apple IIc for Christmas. Eventually that computer migrated from the family den to Laurie's room, where in high school she would get up in the morning and type in a few paragraphs of her stories before heading to class. Once in college, a professor pointed her to a few online resources to get published, and she's been putting out submissions ever since.

Laurie has had about a dozen short stories published in the small press, but "Living Rooms" marks her first professional sale. Her day job is in the video game industry, which allows her to have a "fun" job in another creative environment. She has been lucky enough to purchase her childhood home, which is still very much a magical house. The living room (parlor) was always a special room for her as a child because she wasn't allowed to go inside unless guests were over.

ABOUT THE ILLUSTRATOR

Irena Kovalenko was born and raised in Ukraine, but she has also lived in northern Russia and the south of France. She loves traveling, meeting new people and adapting to new cultures.

She has had a strong attraction to the arts since childhood, learning to play the piano in music school while enjoying painting.

She is a teacher by trade. About four years ago she discovered a talent for computer graphic design. To make up for her lack of professional training, she has been learning the basics of painting and graphic design from instruction books. She now has a very strong desire for her art and wishes to devote her life to it.

Living Rooms

In retrospect, Rill should have known something was wrong when she had to use her key to open the door, instead of the door simply letting her in, but she was too engrossed in her own homecoming to notice the fine layer of dust or the stillness of the house, for any such thought to reach her.

"Papa!" she called, as she closed the front door. The name sounded very strange on her lips. She hadn't seen him since she was a girl, and when speaking to the other ladies at court she had always referred to him as her father. Noblewomen weren't crude enough to be so familiar with their parents, and she'd done her best to blend in.

"Papa!"

He was probably napping in the parlor. It was late afternoon and he liked to lie down on the couch between a day's research and dinner, and of course he wouldn't have known the exact time she would arrive.

Rill gathered her skirts in her hands and hurried down the short hallway from the foyer. She opened her mouth to call him a third time, but then she rounded the doorway into the tidy parlor of her memory and her voice died in her throat. The room was empty.

Was he upstairs perhaps? She supposed he could still be in his laboratory. Sometimes he got caught up in his experiments. Magic was not an exact science and even a magician such as he would sometimes run into a tangle or two.

"Rill, is that you?" asked a voice.

She turned and spotted several motes of pale blue light wafting up from the floor. They coalesced into the form of a trim man with dark hair and hazel eyes. He looked to be about thirty and wore a long coat and cravat every bit as proper as the room around them. She hadn't seen him since she was twelve, but while she had grown into a young woman, he hadn't changed at all.

That made sense though, since he was the manifestation of the parlor and a creation of her father's.

"Rill?" he asked again.

"James," she said. She smiled in relief.

He brightened at the sound of his name, but she couldn't avoid noticing an odd severity in his expression, something out of place in a room intended to entertain guests, and she remembered that she still didn't know where her father was.

"Is something wrong?" she asked.

He shook his head, but it was not a reassuring gesture. "Tell me," he said. "Is this your home?"

"Is this my home?" she echoed.

She'd barely voiced her confusion when she felt a chill, as though she'd been thrust outside on an early spring morning. The parlor window was closed, but a gale wind swept through the room, freezing cold, and in the next moment she saw a newcomer standing before her, and this person she did not recognize. He was an older man, and judging from the satchels he carried, another magician.

"Who are you?" he demanded. "What are you doing here?" He stood so close she could feel his spittle as he shouted.

"I'm Rill. I—"

"Don't answer him!" said James. "Just tell me. Is this house still your home?"

She didn't understand. Of course it should be. She had come home to see Papa. Something didn't feel right though. She should have realized it as soon as she'd entered the parlor and Papa wasn't there, but then she'd seen James and just seeing him reminded her of what it had been like to live here, to have grown up here.

"I don't see why it wouldn't be," she replied.

As she voiced those words she felt something warm inside of her, but it was a faint sensation, as though it might fade away at any moment.

Whatever she'd experienced though, it was magnified tenfold in James. He grinned at her, then with a flourish, turned to face the stranger and said, "You're no longer welcome here!"

The stranger opened his mouth to protest, but his words were drowned in a thundering roar that removed him from the room as though he'd never

11

been. Rill stared at the empty space where the man had been standing, but it was quite clear that she and James were alone again, and though she was not a magician herself, she understood enough to know that a struggle had taken place, and for the moment, she'd won.

"Welcome home," said James, placing a hand over his heart as he bowed.

Rill sagged against the back of the nearest chair. "Can you tell me what just happened?"

"That was Gavon Morrin," he replied. "He's an acquaintance of your father. You probably don't remember him, but he visited once while you were here, just before you went to court. He's been here several times since."

"But what was he doing here? Where's Papa?"

James placed a hand on her shoulder and gently guided her into the chair beside her.

"Rill, your father passed away about a month ago. We, the rooms, are still here, but this house is no longer his home. It's barely anyone's, which is why Morrin was here. He's trying to force this house to become his home in the absence of an actual master. Given time, he might still succeed."

For a long while she said nothing, unable to believe, but the parlor, lacking the ability to be impatient, did not prod her. Finally, she said, "Papa's dead?"

"We're all very sorry."

This voice sounded like a young woman and came from a different doorway than the one she'd entered. Tess, the manifestation of the dining room, stood there, hands clasped solemnly together.

"How?" asked Rill. "Why?"

IRENA KOVALENKO

Certainly, she hadn't kept in contact much with her father, but he'd sounded just fine in his last letter. He'd said he was looking forward to her coming home. If he'd had an illness surely he would have written her or asked one of the rooms to do it. One of the carriages could have delivered it, even if the rooms couldn't leave the house.

"I think she needs to rest," said Tess to James. "Can you take her to her bedroom?"

James regarded Rill carefully. "Her connection to the house is so tenuous, I don't know if she's strong enough to will it."

The rooms could not leave themselves unless her father explicitly allowed it. Rill remembered that. She didn't know if it would work for her, but she figured she could hope.

"Please try," she said.

James offered her a hand, but instead of merely helping her to her feet, he picked her up as easily as if she'd still been a child. He reached the threshold of the parlor and barely hesitated before walking through to the foyer. He succeeded and smiled lightly at her.

"I think we're making progress."

He carried her upstairs, and as she peered around, she could see the different rooms looking out of themselves to witness her arrival. The two guest bedrooms waved at her. The bathroom shuddered, on the verge of tears. Farther down the hall, the library gave a brief salute and her father's bedroom bowed.

"We are happy you made it back," said James, by way of explanation.

"You don't like Morrin," she said.

"No," he replied.

At the entrance to her own bedroom, a young girl of about twelve greeted her; Plim. Her homespun dress was a bit rumpled, just like the lightly cluttered room she embodied.

"Welcome back!" she said brightly.

"Rill is not feeling well," said James, carrying her to her bed.

Plim immediately pulled down the sheets so he could set her down, then tucked Rill into bed as if the years had never passed.

"But she's the new master," said Plim. "You moved."

"She is for now, but her connection is barely enough. If she doesn't grow to consider this house her home, her real home, then she will not be able to claim this house unchallenged. Morrin will be back before then. He won't let her stay if he can help it."

To Rill he said, "Just rest for now. The kitchen will have something ready for you whenever you get hungry."

When she woke, she did not immediately recognize her room. The canopy was missing from her bed and in its place was a ceiling she could barely remember. Moonlight peered around the edges of the curtains, more than she was used to, but the room was still dark enough that she could barely make out the shape of the wardrobe across the way. How long had she been sleeping?

The wick of the nearest lamp caught fire as she stirred, filling the bedroom with a soft, yellow glow. Now that she could see, and had the will to look around, she realized her room had barely changed. In eight years she thought her father would have rearranged it, turned it into a workshop or another library. But then, when she had seen Plim, the manifestation had not changed either.

Plim had been more than a bedroom servant. She had often been Rill's only playmate, and her father had aged the bedroom's appearance to match her own. Only now, she realized he'd stopped. Plim was still twelve.

Thinking of her father brought back the memory of her conversation with James and she curled into a ball beneath her sheets. She thought that she should be crying, but no tears would come. She hadn't seen her father in so long, and she had so much to tell him, none of which mattered now.

"Papa," she murmured.

"Hungry now?" asked the voice of Plim.

"Not so much," she replied.

"Maybe some tea?"

"Tea would be fine."

"Tea," said Plim, though her voice was now directed outwards.

Through the walls of her bedroom she could hear the voice of the guest room next door echo the request to the next room in line, knowing that the kitchen would get the message eventually.

"It should be ready soon," said Plim. "Would you like me to retrieve it?"

"No. I'll go downstairs."

"Are you sure you're feeling well enough for that?"

"You can come with me."

"That would be fantastic!"

On their way down Plim couldn't stop thanking Rill for allowing her to leave herself and apologized for her inability to prepare a fresh change of clothes for her. Naturally Rill should not have to wear her travel things inside the house, but her luggage had been left in the carriage and there was the unfortunate matter that the rooms could not retrieve her bags, let alone carry them up to her bedroom. Plim's fussing oddly reminded Rill of the human servants at the Duchess of Colinsworth's estate, which had been her home for the past eight years, but the human servants changed over time. They came and went. They aged. They had children. They even passed away.

Plim was still Plim. The rooms did not have personal lives. They were just constructs, made to resemble people. Her father had told her that they were a lot more practical for a house on the edge of nowhere. They did not need to be fed, to be paid, and they would not disobey, all of which were matters of concern with human servants. But human servants generally understood human feelings, and Plim did not seem to realize that Rill had heavier things on her mind than a change of dress.

"Plim," asked Rill, "do you know how Papa died?"

Her bedroom stopped her chatter so abruptly she might have choked had she been human. "No," she said, immediately downcast. "No one told me and I didn't ask. I'm sorry."

"Someone knows though."

"Yes, of course! You'll just have to ask one of the other rooms."

17

They reached the kitchen, already brightly lit in anticipation of a visitor. It was a sizable room with an oven, stove and a myriad of cabinets. A round table stood near one corner of the kitchen, at which the servants would eat, had this been any other home. Here, it served mostly as a breakfast nook.

"Welcome back," said the kitchen, taking the shape of a matronly woman. Her father had named her Mary.

"Tea?" she asked, offering a steaming cup.

"Thanks," said Rill, as she sank into a waiting chair. She sipped lightly at the tea, which was hot enough she'd burn her tongue if she tried to drink it any faster. The tea was oddly sweet though, sweeter than she'd come to expect.

"Did you put sugar in this?" she asked.

"Naturally," said Mary. "You always ask for sugar."

She used to, now that she thought about it, but she'd stopped taking sugar with her tea a few years ago and now she didn't take it at all if she could help it. Her first reaction was to request a new cup, but Mary beamed at her, obviously pleased with herself, and she found she couldn't stomach the thought of telling the kitchen she wasn't happy with the tea.

"You've grown into a fine young lady," said Mary, setting the teapot on the table beside her.

"Thank you," said Rill.

"It's too bad you didn't marry like you thought you would, but we know you're a bright lady with a good head on your shoulders. Your father would be proud."

Rill grimaced, remembering her childhood declaration that she would not become a magician

18

like her father. Not only that, but she'd said she would marry a prince. The defiant proclamation had come after a particularly trying lesson on the transmutative properties of various metals. The magic that had fascinated her father was just possibilities and theories to her. Sure, he did things with it, and now that she was older she realized just how unique his creations were, but back then she'd wanted out, to live a life that she'd thought due to every girl.

She'd wanted to see the outside world and naturally marry a prince, just like the girls in the bedtime stories her mother used to tell before she passed away. Her father had snorted derisively when she told him what she wanted, but to her surprise, he made her an offer:

She would have her opportunity to live in the world of her dreams, but if she did not marry a prince within eight years she would have to come home and become his apprentice, no complaining allowed.

She'd only been twelve. Eight years was an eternity away and she'd be twenty by then. Anything could happen by the time she was twenty. So she'd agreed. Only later would she realize how big and how complicated the world was.

"How would you know," said Rill, "that Papa would be proud of me?"

"The laboratory told us," said Tess, her voice coming from the adjacent dining room. She materialized in a swirl of green light and leaned against her side of the doorway.

"The laboratory?" Rill echoed. She couldn't remember that room having a manifestation. Her father had said he didn't need someone bothering his research and he had no use for an assistant.

19

"It would seem that your father shared more with the laboratory than the rest of us."

"I wonder," said Rill. "That other magician who was here, Morrin, he must want something from this house, right? That'd explain why he wants to become the master. Do you think Papa was working on something and the laboratory would know what it is?"

"Maybe," said Plim, her face doubtful, "but no one's been able to talk to the laboratory ever since your father died. No matter how many times we try, she won't answer us."

"But Rill is the master now," said Mary. "The laboratory has to listen."

"That's not necessarily true." James' voice was muffled, coming from the parlor via the dining room, but it was enough to startle Rill, who could not remember a time so many rooms wanted to voice their opinion, let alone from so far away.

"She shut out Morrin and Tess tells me you moved," said Mary, speaking loud enough that her voice would carry to the parlor. "What isn't the master about her?"

James did not immediately reply, and Rill found she really did not want the conversation to degenerate into a shouting match between the kitchen and the parlor. The tea had helped, but wasn't enough to stop her from thinking about how pleasant it would be to just go back to sleep.

"James," she asked, "could you come here and explain?"

He walked in through the dining room with

what seemed an unreasonably stern expression on his face. "Lest we forget," he said, "Rill has only the most tenuous connection to this house. Because she lived here before and she remembers this place, she has more claim to it than Gavon Morrin, but she has to want to be here. This has to be her home. And remember, it was originally Rill's decision to leave here at all."

Tess shrugged and looked away, Plim sagged into another chair and Mary gave James a reproving glare. Rill crossed her legs beneath her chair and tried to sink into the wicker, but she couldn't vanish into the furnishings the way the rooms could.

She felt a light pressure on her shoulder and looked up at James, his gaze softer now. "Until your status as master can no longer be challenged, you cannot force us to do anything. We serve you now because we want to, but the laboratory . . ."

"I haven't even met the laboratory. How can she judge me?"

"That's not it," said James. "I think the laboratory is in grief. She is not well and we don't know why. I don't understand why your father would have wanted such a drastic emotion in a room, but I'm told that she only cries. Your father's bedroom might be able to tell you more since he is closest."

"Oh."

"Rill, I would like to show you something."

She gulped down the rest of her tea and set the cup back on its saucer before following James out of the kitchen. Plim bounded behind her, crowding close as if she'd become an overly curious younger sister.

James returned to the parlor, where the lamps instantly brightened with a cheery glow. On the floor were two large weather-beaten trunks containing everything that Rill had brought with her from the outside world.

"I called for the carriage to bring them up to the window," said James. "It was difficult getting the carriage to throw them in, but we managed. And it's what's outside of the window that I want to show you."

His eyes momentarily unfocused and the two wooden panels of the window unlatched and swung open.

"Look at the garden," he directed.

Not understanding, she stepped past him and peered outside. There were rut marks going through the flower patch where the carriage wheels had passed through, which was expected. Her father would never have tolerated such a mess, but considering that the carriage couldn't very well have passed her trunks in through the front door she supposed a little mess had been unavoidable. The garden should fix it up though, and she waited for the perky steps of the little man who tended the yard that was his own self.

Nothing happened though, and James brought a lamp beside her, shining it out over the flower patch outside. The dirt was no longer freshly turned. The moist dirt had dried into a light brown. The flowers themselves were still alive, but now she saw that they were wild, untended.

"Nigel can't die," she said, turning to James. "He's a room too."

"He's not dead, but he can't help us. Morrin has sealed him for his lack of cooperation. The garden is outside so his protection is not as strong as that of the rest of us." James paused, seeming to have spotted something, and again Rill felt his hand on her shoulder. "Get down," he said, and he pushed her away from the window with enough force that she stumbled and landed on the floor.

Something black shot through the window, through James, who was standing where she'd been only a moment before, and spun a lamp on its tiny decorative table. The lamp wobbled once, twice and teetered before James righted it with a thought. He turned back to the window and the two panels slammed shut and locked themselves.

Rill staggered to her feet. "What was that?"

"It's a dead bird," said Plim, crouching by the feathered and battered form.

It wasn't just any bird. It was a crow, and Rill didn't think such a hefty bird would die from bumping into a lamp. She grimaced as she reached for the bird, knowing what she was doing was not only unpleasant, but unthinkable back on the duchess's estate. Rill knew a thing or two about anatomy though. Nothing they would teach a young lady at court of course, but her father had never cared about what other people thought.

She poked and prodded at the body with her fingers, checking around the neck and under the wings. The bird's neck was broken; not only that, but its ribcage as well. It had to have been dead before it even flew into the room.

"Morrin," said James simply.

23

"I suppose he's sending me a message," said Rill. "Are you all right? The bird flew right through you."

He nodded. "I'm fine. That sort of thing doesn't bother me."

Rill stood up, holding her hands away from her body, unwilling to let any part of her that had touched the dead crow brush up against her clothes. "Plim, could you take the bird to Mary and have her dispose of it?"

"Of course!"

Her bedroom picked up the bird without any hesitation and marched off for the kitchen. Rill watched her go, then looked back at her trunks, still by the window.

"James, I'm going to clean off my hands. Could you bring those trunks up to my room? Then I want you to take me to the laboratory."

James was waiting for her when she returned to her room. He'd set the trunks down by her bed and stood facing the door, hands clasped behind him. Rill had barely set foot in the room before Plim squeezed past her. Spying the luggage on the floor, the bedroom let out a giggle and plunged into the first trunk.

"I'll have all this put away in no time!" said Plim.

Rill watched her bedroom take the dresses out of her trunk and over to the wardrobe. Plim hung each gown with care, patting them into place to make certain none would end up folded or wrinkled before she put in the next dress.

"I suppose this really will be home again," said Rill.

"Did you consider the duchess' estate home?" asked James.

"I didn't at first, but after a while, yes. I don't think it's possible to live someplace for eight years and never call it home."

"And you lived here for twelve, so that's even longer!" said Plim.

James picked up his lamp from the top of her dresser and walked up to the door. "Shall we?" he asked.

Rill nodded and walked back into the hallway.

As a child she'd rarely visited her father's laboratory for anything other than lessons; learning about metals, learning about animals, learning about the stars and how they changed with the seasons, but despite her being the daughter of a magician, he had taught her nothing of magic itself. He claimed she needed to know the basics in order to have a strong foundation in the science itself, but things she wanted to know, like how he got the water to flow upwards from the well to the house, he wouldn't explain to her.

"It seems quiet enough," remarked Rill as they came to the tiny staircase that wound up to the laboratory. It was the only room on the third floor.

James shrugged. "I have only heard that she cries. If she does, she is not loud enough that I can hear her from inside myself."

The door to her father's laboratory was shut. Heavy and thick, the door and the laboratory walls were designed to protect the rest of the house from anything that might happen inside. It was not soundproof though. She'd called her father for supper through this very door before.

Rill laid her hand on the door handle, hesitantly turned the lever down and pushed in.

25

The interior was dark and the lamps did not light when the two of them stepped inside. James raised his lamp high enough for her to see the familiar rectangular outline of the room lined with shelves and cabinets. By the window stood a tubular device her father called a magnifying lens for looking at the stars, and along one wall was a map of the world still covered with his meticulous notes.

A large wooden table, too large to have been taken through the doorway by any normal means, dominated the center of the room. Whereas the shelves and cabinets were spotless, this table was unspeakably cluttered. Rill had spent too many an afternoon cleaning the laboratory to miss her father's penchant for orderliness. She couldn't fathom why he would leave his notes in disarray, sheets of paper spread across the table as though he needed to refer to all of them at once. And the beakers! Whatever had been inside them must have evaporated weeks ago, but two thin copper wires trailed out of each of them to a slender wand.

Had he been charging it? Surely he wouldn't have left something as dangerous as a wand out before finishing his work for the day.

"James?" she said. "I've been meaning to ask, but... What did Papa die of? Was it sudden?"

"Papa?" a voice inquired, and it was not James. This voice was young, childlike, and she'd never heard it before.

Rill looked around, searching for where the room would manifest. A sudden chill stirred in her gut as she could feel a power coursing through the room and the floor began to tremble beneath her feet.

"Papa . . ." it repeated. "Papa is gone!" The room wailed and a terrible wind surged through the laboratory. "Nothing will bring him back!" it shrieked. "Nothing! I can't do it!"

The laboratory's screams became incoherent, drowned by the winds that snuffed out James' lamp and plunged the room into darkness. Rill flailed just to keep standing in the face of the gale winds.

"I know that!" she shouted. "Please! I need to talk to you!"

She could barely hear her own voice, and when the shrieking suddenly lulled she pushed enough hair out of her face to again look for the manifestation of the room. The laboratory was far from complacent, however. No lamps lit and the wind did not abate.

"You have no idea how I feel!" bellowed the room.

The wind concentrated and this time there was only one direction it blew, backwards, through the doorway. Rill found herself unceremoniously hurled outside and back into the stairwell, the laboratory door slamming shut upon her exit. She landed just a foot shy of the first step, and though she avoided hitting her head against the landing, her shoulder would have a nasty bruise in the morning.

James walked through the door a moment later, though without his lamp. She could barely see him in the limited light of the stairwell. Rill grimaced as he helped her to her feet.

"I thought you said she did nothing but cry. I was expecting her to be blubbering tears."

"That's what I'd heard. I suppose one of the rooms

27

along the way thought differently. Screaming is crying of a sort."

Rill sighed and felt all the energy drain from her body. It was still the middle of the night and she wanted very much to go back to sleep. She could try talking to the laboratory again in the morning. It wasn't going anywhere.

She bumbled down the stairs, James steadying her whenever she feared she might miss a step. The touch of his hand was reassuring, because as flustered as she felt, the parlor did not strike her as anything other than deliberate and unshakable. Though her father had scolded her about it, saying that the parlor was reserved for guests, he had always been her favorite room in which to play.

"Miss Rill! Are you all right? I heard the laboratory cry out . . ."

Her father's bedroom, Martin, was at his doorway, lamp raised to watch them emerge from the stairwell and into the second-floor hallway. He was a stately gentleman, appearing about fifty, with graying hair and a perfectly cropped moustache.

"I'm fine," she said. "A little bruised, but nothing serious."

"Good heavens! She actually hurt you?"

"She tossed me outside herself. I think I upset her."

Rill attempted a half-hearted shrug before the pain in her shoulder decided otherwise, but Martin would have none of it.

"I told your father it wasn't a good idea for him to give life to another room so much later than the others. What if he didn't remember the process after all these years? What if he made a mistake? The laboratory's behavior always has been erratic, but now it's just inexcusable! To think that she would do such a thing to the master's daughter . . ."

"Martin." Rill pressed a hand to her forehead, feeling her patience wear thin. "Do you know what happened? What happened to Papa? And what's wrong with the laboratory? James thought you might."

Her father's bedroom open and shut his mouth and then looked at the parlor as though noticing him for the first time. "Well, the laboratory's always been a little different. The master considered her an improvement, because she can express emotions that the rest of us cannot. He said that she's almost human, though in all honesty I don't find that practical, and I believe I am quite justified in saying so considering her recent treatment of you. It is imperative that a room keep its corners square, and you can see the results of what happens when one does not."

"That doesn't explain why she's so upset though."

Martin sighed and shook his head. "Your father's death was sudden. He collapsed while in the laboratory and she panicked. There is no way for us to leave ourselves without our master's permission, but she knew he needed help. The laboratory moved him the only way she knew how—out the window. Your father was still alive when the garden caught him in a tree and lowered him to the ground, but he couldn't do anything to help him. None of us could. We don't suffer from human maladies and your father did not teach us how to treat them."

"What did you do with his body?" Rill asked.

"The garden took care of it," said Martin. "You

can't see his grave from here, now that it's dark, but it's in a very nice spot in the garden."

"We understand it's proper for a human to be buried," said James.

This the rooms would have known, since her mother had died while she was young.

"The laboratory can also see his grave then."

"Yes," said Martin.

Rill wondered if the laboratory only wailed because she had no one with whom to grieve. Martin, even James, would not have been capable of shedding a tear at her father's death, but then, Rill hadn't either.

"Thank you," said Rill. "I'm going to go back to bed."

Her eyes still dry, she nodded farewell to her father's bedroom and shuffled back to her own with James still beside her. Plim had lit the lamps inside, so it was not difficult to find the open doorway and spy the freshly turned bed. She had no idea what time it was, but now was definitely the time for sleep.

"James," she said, "I'd like to visit Papa's grave in the morning."

"Of course. You know where to find me."

"Wait."

The parlor had only taken a step down the hall when he turned back to face her.

"Is there a reason you have to go back?"

"My task is complete," he replied.

"But why didn't Papa let you and the other rooms walk around as you wished? Then the laboratory wouldn't have had to do something silly like pushing him out the window."

James pondered the question for what seemed an unusually long time. Finally he said, "If we are gone from ourselves for too long or travel too far, we will eventually fade away and disappear. It's not a lasting harm, but we must reconstruct ourselves for several days before we can manifest again and we lose any memories we might have gained since we last left ourselves. It's never been in anyone's best interests for us to wander."

"Oh. I see."

"Also," he said quietly, "I think he wanted to remind us of what we are. A parlor is not a parlor if it resides in the hallway."

She must have had an odd look on her face because he smiled and said a little louder, "Go to bed, Rill. Sleep well."

The kitchen served her fresh bread and jam in the morning and after breakfast Rill asked James to accompany her to the garden. Though they could no longer talk to the garden, Mary used to speak with him while he was still in control of himself, so the kitchen was able to tell them where Nigel had buried their master.

His grave lay in the farthest end of the grounds behind the house, away from the fruit and vegetables, away from the hedges and the flowers, just a short distance from the stone wall that marked the edge of the property. It was not where Rill would have buried her father, but the nearest village where they had buried her mother would have been impossible for the rooms to have reached.

The earth over her father's grave was smooth and untroubled, with a simple unmarked stone about the size of a large cabbage to serve as a marker. It had taken eight years, but she'd finally come back to her father.

"I . . . I wanted to tell him I'm sorry," said Rill, her voice heavy and thick. "I thought I won when he let me leave home, but I think he knew I'd come back, that I wouldn't find the place I thought I would." She drew in a ragged breath. "He wanted me to go. He wanted me to see the life I wanted for what it was. And I . . . And I wanted to tell him, when I got home, how happy I was to have come back.

"But now I'm too late. He's gone." Tears ran down her face and she tried to wipe them away with the long sleeve of her gown, but they wouldn't stop. "He died alone. I wasn't here to be with him."

"You might not have been here," said James, "but you are never alone with this house." He folded her into an embrace and cradled her head against his shoulder. "The garden was with your father until the very end. He was not alone. *You* are not alone."

She hiccuped and rubbed her eyes against the fine fabric of his coat, feeling for all the world like a child again. What was she going to do, living in this house by herself? James was right. She'd have company, but would rooms be enough? They may have been enough for her father, but what about her?

"I didn't tell Papa," she said, "but I did meet a prince, more than one even. But I was so scared. I couldn't talk to them. The other girls, they could compliment them or chatter about the weather, but I could barely say my name. I tried so hard to be a proper lady, but none of it mattered. They didn't know I was there."

James said nothing, simply holding her as long as it took for her to calm down. She had cried to him as a child when her father yelled at her, because he didn't try to cheer her up like her bedroom, because he didn't try to stuff her with food and tea like the kitchen, because he didn't ignore her like the library.

She gradually became aware of how warm the sun had become against the back of her head. They should go back inside. She would have to try speaking to the laboratory again. Reluctantly, she pulled away from the parlor and trod through the overgrown grass and back to the cobblestone path that wound around the garden. James followed close behind.

As she walked toward the open door of the kitchen, Rill tried to avoid looking at the withered rows of the fruit and vegetable garden, each crumpled stalk a reminder that Nigel was no longer with them. Right now, the raspberries should be in bloom, the garden telling her which bushes he thought would give the biggest yield.

She hoped once she claimed the house over Morrin that his hold over Nigel would break. She just didn't know if she could do it. Morrin had magic and possibly could force his will on the other rooms the way he had on the garden. She needed to make this house her home, her real home, and not just a place to live, but was that what she really wanted?

There was one raspberry bush that still bloomed. It was weak, drooping, but at least it had its flowers. She absently patted a branch as she might a sick dog, and to her surprise, one of the stems quivered ever so slightly toward her, offering the blossom at its tip.

"Nigel," she said. "You're still here . . ."

A flying shadow, stark against the light of the morning sun, broke through the haze of her thoughts. She barely recognized the danger before James thrust himself between her and the flying piece of trellis. Whereas he'd let the crow pass through him before, the parlor did not allow the trellis to do the same, not completely. About twelve inches of the five-foot wooden trellis stuck out through his back, giving him the appearance of having been impaled, but there was no blood.

Farther away, she could see more of the trellis pulling up out of the earth, wooden stakes hovering in the air as they angled themselves as spears in her direction. Nigel? Was he doing this?

"Get inside!" said James.

Rill ran. She didn't dare turn around to witness the flight of the trellis or anything else the garden might have flung at her. The wild vines of the vegetation snapped at her heels as she passed, but she tore through them before they could secure a grip. The twelve strides it took for her to fling herself through the kitchen door were the longest she'd ever taken. She tumbled to the floor on the other side and the door slammed shut behind her.

Mary knelt beside her in an instant, fussing, helping her to her feet. "I can't believe what happened out there," said the kitchen, brushing Rill's hair back into place and dusting her off. "It must be Morrin controlling the garden. It has to be. The garden would never do that."

James stepped through the closed door. If Rill hadn't known what had just happened, she would never have believed him to have protected her through the events outside. His clothes were untorn and he did not appear disheveled in any way.

"And you!" said Mary, looking at James. "I don't think the master ever expected a room to behave like that."

He shrugged indifferently. "It's not a part of my duty, but if we have the ability shouldn't we use it? It was for Rill."

"I don't understand," said Rill. "What's wrong?"

The kitchen turned to her and said, "The parlor was protecting you, dear. We are servants, not guards. We are not meant to fight. While I have no doubt your father would be glad the parlor protected you, it is not what he was designed to do."

"He took a piece of trellis," said Rill.

"More than one piece," said Mary.

"Better than Rill," James interjected. "If the trellis had hit her instead . . ."

Mary sighed, conceding the point, and let go of Rill. She turned toward the stove where a kettle of water began to boil. "I'll make some more tea for you, Rill. It's been a terrible morning for you, what with visiting your father's grave and then the garden trying to hurt you."

The kitchen continued talking, but Rill didn't hear her. She focused on a small object she noticed on the kitchen floor near the doorway to the garden.

It was a black feather.

"Mary?" she asked. "Whatever happened to the dead crow from last night?"

"Why I threw it into the rubbish bin," said the kitchen. "Until the garden is restored there is no way to dispose of the trash." She pointed to a bottom cabinet, which swung open to reveal a metal bin, which was almost entirely empty except for crumbs left over from her breakfast. There was no crow.

"Well, that's not right," said the kitchen. Her manifestation vanished, and a moment later her voice added, "I can't find the crow anywhere inside me. I don't know where it went, but I don't think it's here anymore."

Rill's stomach sank. The garden completely surrounded the house. She couldn't go outside without worrying that Nigel would try attacking, possibly even killing her, and now she had to worry about the roaming body of a dead crow inside the house. The crow hadn't just been a message, but a spy. It must have seen her outside, and through it, Morrin had directed the garden to attack. He must have seen her visit her father's grave, seen how the garden had taken a step toward reaching her.

"Did you see anything, Tess?" Rill asked, aiming her voice toward the empty dining room.

"I'm sorry, but I haven't," she replied. "As far as I can tell, the only time the crow passed through me was when your bedroom brought it to the kitchen."

It could have left the kitchen via the hallway though, but from there it could have gone to the storeroom, or the foyer, and from there anywhere else in the house.

"Tess, Mary," said Rill, "will both of you manifest?"

They did.

"I want both of you to go to the other rooms and inform them about the missing crow, and to help look for it."

"We don't need to leave ourselves in order to pass the message along," said Tess.

"No, but I need someone to search the hallways and the foyer because they don't have manifestations and the crow could be hiding in them. If Morrin's using it to spy on us, then we have to catch it."

Morning melted into afternoon and Tess and Mary weren't having any luck in the halls. The other rooms from the library to the bathroom claimed they could not find the crow inside themselves, leaving Rill precious little idea where to search next. She even tried talking to the laboratory again, but that attempt ended only marginally more successful than the first.

This time she managed to stay inside during the room's tantrum by wedging herself up beside a cabinet before the winds came full blast, but even though she prevented herself from being thrown out, the laboratory was not any more communicative than before. When it couldn't eject her, the laboratory simply howled in frustration and then ceased to make a sound altogether. She wasn't entirely certain, but she got the impression the room was sulking.

"There's got to be a way to get through to her," said Rill to her father's bedroom. "You're the closest room to her. Does she ever have any lucid moments when she'll talk to you?"

"Not since the master died," said Martin, his disembodied voice resonating throughout the room.

"The crow could be searching for something. If so, the laboratory probably would know what."

37

Rill paced about her father's room, waiting for a confirmation, but none came. Suddenly paranoid, she looked around for signs of the crow, but if it was here, it wasn't anywhere in sight. Then her eyes fell on the southern wall.

At first she wasn't certain why it bothered her, but the more she stared at it, the more convinced she became that something ought to be there. Had there been a painting? There must have been, but now that she thought about it, there was something amiss besides its absence, perhaps something the painting had previously distracted her from.

She didn't want to risk going outside to confirm it, but she could have sworn there had been a window on the southern side of the house looking out from her father's bedroom, but looking around the room now there was only a window to the east.

"Martin, wasn't there a window here?"

"There *is* a window," he replied.

"No, I mean here," she said, placing a hand against the southern wall.

"I'm afraid you're mistaken, Miss Rill. There's never been a window there."

Unconvinced, she left the room and glanced the length of the hallway from his door to the laboratory stairwell. It looked longer than the dimension of the bedroom interior, and a quick pace down the hallway and then the inside of the bedroom confirmed it. It wasn't much, but she had been able take another three or four steps beyond what should have been the end of his bedroom before she hit the stairs to the laboratory.

Another room? Maybe the laboratory wasn't the only place her father could have left something.

"What's on the other side of this wall?" she asked.

"The outside, I would imagine. I can't say for certain without a window there."

"Couldn't you tell from the heat when the sun shines on the outside wall?"

"I'm afraid I'm not as sensitive to the temperature as some of the other rooms."

Had she imagined it? Or had he hesitated before answering her?

"Martin, is there another room over there?"

"Why, that's a preposterous idea!" he sniffed. "If there was such a room I'd certainly know about it."

Yes, he would, she mused. Supposing there *was* another room between Martin and the outside wall, there was another room adjacent to them both; the laboratory upstairs, of course, but also the storeroom below them.

Aloud, she said, "Are you sure? Maybe Papa had a way to go down from the laboratory. Did you ever hear anything through the wall?"

"Not a word." And from the flat tone of his voice she knew that was the most she'd get out of him, but if this room wouldn't talk, she could try another.

Rill left her father's bedroom and walked down the hall to the stairs. Tess was there, canvassing the steps with the patience only a room could muster, and Mary was only a few steps below her in the foyer, where she swept through the decorative cabinets. Rill did not disturb them as she passed them both and entered the short, dim hallway to the storeroom.

The storeroom was huge, taking up an inordinate amount of space, a full half of the ground floor.

39

It functioned not only as a pantry and a larder, but storage for laboratory equipment, research specimens and raw materials. Anything that was not immediately needed in the kitchen or the laboratory ended up here.

"Edwin?" she called.

No answer.

"Edwin?" Now she spoke a little louder, trying to keep a quaver from her voice.

"Rill?" rumbled a voice. The storeroom sounded weak, distant. "I can't come," he sighed. "I try, but I can't."

"What do you mean you can't?"

"I want to . . . but . . ."

She scanned the room for the crow, but she couldn't see it anywhere among all the shelves and boxes. There were aisles of clutter. If it was here, how could she ever find it?

"Edwin?" she asked, more urgently. "The crow. Did you see it here? Did the crow do something to you?"

She could feel the room shudder, as though to draw in a breath, but nothing came.

"Edwin? Edwin! Can you still hear me? Is this Morrin's work?"

She heard a rattle from a nearby shelf and a clay pot crashed to the floor. Had Edwin knocked it over? She looked up to see where it had fallen from and saw something else floating gently down through the air.

A black feather.

We're running out of time and I'm in no mood to humor Martin," said Rill as she marched up the stairs to the second floor. At her request, James followed close behind her, but his presence did little to mollify her. She knew Martin was hiding something and if he wouldn't help her, she had a fair idea how to get around him.

There was no need to request that the bedroom show himself. Martin appeared almost immediately in front of her, not so close as to deny her entrance, but close enough that she had to walk past him to reach the interior.

"Miss Rill, don't you have greater concerns right now than that wall?" said Martin. "And what is with bringing the parlor with you? Bad enough the kitchen and the dining room have been turning the hallway upside down all day looking for that bird, but do you intend to have me searched by another room?"

"This isn't for the crow," said Rill. She turned to the southern wall and pointed at it. "James, walk through there. Tell me what's on the other side."

"Wait, wait," said Martin. He waved his hands, but he couldn't stop the parlor from walking past him. The rooms exchanged glances, and Martin was clearly the loser. Her father's bedroom wrung his hands together. "Miss Rill, your father would be most displeased. He told me he didn't want you in there."

James passed through the wall and from the other side she heard his muffled voice. "There's another room here."

Martin groaned. "Please, Miss Rill. Be reasonable."

"Whatever Morrin wants might be hidden in there," said Rill. "If we know what it is, maybe we can learn why it's so important to him. The laboratory won't talk to me, so this is the only place left to look."

"You may be right," said Martin, his voice regaining some of its earlier indignation, "but I have my orders—"

"I found a latch," said James.

"—and this is far enough."

There was a click and a portion of the wall receded and slid off to one side, revealing a tiny study with a simple wooden desk and a narrow bookcase to either side. A window above the desk looked out over the southern side of the house. Rill only managed a step toward it before Martin's hand came down around her wrist.

She pulled immediately in response, but though he applied virtually no pressure, his grip was firm and unbreakable, inhumanly strong. "What are you doing?" she demanded. "Martin! Let go of me!"

"I'm sorry, Miss Rill, but you are not to visit that room." He began to pull her toward the hallway, and fighting him was like trying to stop a wagon. "Even if the parlor is so quick to disregard our old master's wishes, I will not."

"Don't you care what happens to this house? Aren't you concerned about Morrin like all the other rooms?"

Martin gave her a pained expression as they reached the door. "It's not as though the possibility of a new master does not frighten me, but I have my orders."

"But my father's dead!"

"She's right," said a voice, a familiar one that Rill had not heard in years.

Both she and Martin turned toward the hidden room, where a pool of amber light gathered beside the desk. It pulled itself tight, then blinked into the shape of a slender woman in her late twenties. Her eyes were a warm brown and her hair long and dark like Rill's. She smiled and her face was kind.

"My lady!" Martin's words were both a protest and an expression of reverence.

"Let her go," said the newcomer. "Her father is dead. The old orders no longer bind us."

Martin's hold on Rill relaxed, just enough for her to slip free. Hesitantly, she came closer to the woman in the hidden room, staring at her, marveling. The shape of her face, the glint in her eyes, even her voice, were unmistakable. She was just as Rill remembered, better than she remembered, but she had died years ago.

"You look . . . You look like Mama," said Rill, "but you can't be."

The manifestation nodded. "I am not your mother, Elly. Your father called me Lilah."

Martin sighed. "This is why your father didn't want you in this room."

Rill glared at him. "I'm not a little girl anymore! I won't mistake a room for my mother!"

"That wasn't the reason," said Lilah, shaking her head. "As you grew older your father did not want you to think badly of him, to think that he was pretending your mother was still alive. Though he did miss her, he knew very well what I am and that I am not her."

"Couldn't he have made you look different then?"

"I think he wanted the reminder. Both you and your mother were very important to him. Some people keep portraits to remind them of their loved ones. Your father created me instead. Whenever he needed someone to talk to, I would be here."

"But you're a room." Rill shook her head in disbelief. "Wouldn't he have wanted another human being? Why didn't he talk to *me*?"

Lilah gave her a patient smile. "Because you were twelve, and mostly, because he talked about you. Though as rooms we are limited in what we can be, we have our own hearts and minds. Just because we must obey does not mean we are not good company. After all, I notice you favor a room as well."

Lilah's gaze turned from Rill to James, who stood silently by the sliding door.

A protest welled in Rill's throat, but she couldn't find the words to express it. Certainly, she preferred talking to James more than the other rooms, but it wasn't as though she hid away with him. After all, Tess was right next door and she could hear everything.

The study opened the top drawer of the desk beside her and from it she withdrew a piece of yellowed paper. She held it out to Rill. "Your father's bedroom told me about what's happening in the rest of the house."

"What's this?" asked Rill, taking the paper in her hands. She carefully unfolded it, the paper crackling in protest.

"Your father researched many things, but this was the one discovery he decided he would never share. I don't presume to know what this Morrin would want with it, but your father discovered how to create a living being."

Rill glanced over the creased paper, but it was only a list of ingredients and a set of directions. It looked like the components needed to be ground into a paste and then ingested. Ingested by what?

"Your father could have made me a real woman, with none of the boundaries or limitations of being a room," said Lilah, "but he realized how grave an error that would have been, so he locked it away."

"That explains Papa's reasoning, but I don't think Morrin could possibly be trying this hard to create himself a wife."

"Your father gave us personalities," said James. "He gave us preferences and the ability to form our own opinions. He didn't have to do that. Morrin's known about our existence for a long time, and he's never expressed an interest in having living rooms. But if Morrin learns how to create us and can make his creations real . . ."

"He could create an army," said Rill. An army of obedient servants that answered only to him.

The possibility boggled her mind. She supposed that would work. She couldn't imagine Morrin challenging the king with an army of rooms, that would cause a war, but he could sell their services, and if they died, he could just make more. They wouldn't be limited by how far they could go from the place of their creation, and if their personalities could be molded to whatever he wished, there would be no reason they wouldn't be utterly loyal to Morrin.

"Lilah," she asked, "did Papa tell you anything about how I could become the new master of this house?"

The study shrugged, a delicate motion. "It is doubtful I know anything more than the other rooms in this regard. It's simply a matter of whether or not you consider this place your home and if that desire is strong enough to avoid being subverted by the magic of another."

"What if I already call this place home?"

"I suppose you do after a fashion, but think about what makes a house a home. It's not just where you live, is it? It's with those you care about. It's where you belong. When you're homesick, is it the house you miss or the people who live there?"

A shout rose up in the hallway before she could give it much thought. She could hear the frantic steps of someone bounding down the stairs and a scream that could only be the kitchen. As she strode over to the bedroom door a loud crash sounded from somewhere on the ground floor and then alternating bellows of panic and triumph.

The rooms began relaying a message between themselves, but being out by the hall, she did not need to wait for Plim to call out to her before she got it.

"Rill! We caught the bird!"

A short while later, she gathered in the kitchen with Mary, Tess, Plim and James. Tess had the crow locked by its broken neck between her two hands. She watched it like a hawk, her mouth pulled into a grim line, as though a moment's vigilance lost would result in the crow's freedom. For its part, the crow twitched and feebly flapped its wings, but did little else.

If this bird had been spying on them, Rill realized she couldn't have it in the room. Anything it saw was probably being sent back to Morrin.

"I hate to ask," said Rill, "but could you lock it in the dining room cupboard until we figure out how to dispose of it? Plim, could you remove the dishes for Tess so the crow doesn't break anything while it's trapped in there?"

Her bedroom nodded a sharp affirmative and followed the dining room out the door.

"So how did you catch it?" asked Rill.

"We can only see it with our eyes," said Mary. "There must be some magic on it that hides the crow from our sight as a room. The dining room spotted it hiding in a corner of one of the guest rooms and chased it downstairs. She ran all over the place and then, I'm sorry to say, she broke a couple of dishes knocking it to the floor." The kitchen shuddered and shook her head. "These things just didn't happen when your father was around."

"All done!" announced Plim as she and Tess returned to the kitchen.

"There must be a way to disable it," said Tess.

"I'm sure there is," said Rill, "but I want it intact for now. It occurred to me that Morrin is trying to trap me here. He's putting me, us, on the defensive by sealing away the garden and the storeroom and leaving us with fewer rooms to rely on, but I think I know how we can get to him. Maybe we can convince him that it's not worth fighting me over the house."

"Are you going to be the master now?" asked Plim.

Rill smiled sadly. "I suppose if I could become the master in front of the bird, in a way that could prove it, this fight would be over, but I don't think I can. What we're going to do is use Papa's gate. Normally you can only use it to visit a place you've been to before, but even though we haven't, I think it's a fair bet that the crow has been there. We'll use the crow to open the gate."

"You can't possibly be thinking of going to Morrin's!" said Mary. "What can you do to fight him?"

"Papa has wands in his laboratory. I might not be able to step inside her easily enough to retrieve them, but any one of you should be able to do so, and once I have them, I should be able to figure out how they work."

"We can't allow you to go," said Tess, her voice flat.

"Papa wouldn't want this man pawing over all his work!"

"Your father wouldn't risk you either. We can't afford to lose you. He would send a physical construct through, maybe a golem, like the carriage."

"Or one of us," said James.

"We can't leave the property," said Tess. "The physical distance is too great. Even if the gate will take us directly to Morrin's, we won't be able to hold ourselves together once we arrive."

"Not if we use something Rill's father left us."

Rill wondered what he was looking at and realized she still held the yellowed piece of paper in her hand. With this, she could make a room human, free of all the limitations of its creation. The former room would be able to travel to Morrin's in her stead, but it would not be in any less danger. If a room became human, then it could also die.

She looked up at the rooms around her. She couldn't ask any of them any more than she could have asked a real person to go in her stead.

"What did he leave us?" asked Plim quietly.

"I can make a room human," said Rill.

"That would work," said Tess.

"Yes, but do any of you really want to be human?"

"Honestly, I've never thought about it," said Mary. "There doesn't seem to be much point. We exist to serve. If we became human, we would not be able to serve any better. What if I got sick? Who would make breakfast? But still, if it would save this house . . ."

Tess and Plim nodded in agreement.

"We don't all need to go," said James. "I suspect there are some specific things Rill wants done, not the wholesale wrecking of Morrin's house, and that will be easier to accomplish with a single room. I'll go."

"Why you?" Rill sputtered.

"Of all the rooms, my manifestation is the youngest male. When you send a room to Morrin's you'll want the most physically capable."

"Edwin's always been the strongest!"

James nodded. "Yes, but the storeroom is no longer with us."

"I know, but . . ."

"You can't go," said Tess. "If anything happens to you, Morrin wins."

Reluctantly, she sighed and nodded her assent. "All right."

Rill worked well into the evening on the formula. The storeroom had not yet turned against her, as far as she could tell, and she found everything she needed inside, including a spare mortar and pestle. She ground the ingredients together until the muscles in her arms burned, and even then she stubbornly

49

pushed on until one could barely tell the difference between a chip of bark and a dried berry beneath the layer of crumbled gypsum. She poured the mixture into a stone bowl and added sixteen fluid ounces of water and not a dram more. The foul-smelling brew boiled away on the kitchen stove and when it thickened to the consistency of chowder she set it on the breakfast table to cool.

As she labored in the kitchen, the rooms carried out their own tasks. James removed the laboratory door, much to the indignation of the laboratory itself, and that allowed Plim and James to sack her father's wand cabinet. They brought the wands to her to identify, and she struggled mightily to remember everything her father had taught her.

Copper conducted electricity, so the copper wand most likely had something to do with lightning. Iron would be a vessel for fire. Steel was a flexible metal, so it probably dealt with sound. And the rowan wood wand, that would be for protection.

But several of the wands Rill could not figure out at all and she had Plim set them aside in a separate pile.

She hadn't realized that at some point she'd fallen asleep, waiting for the mixture to cool, until Mary prodded her and said, "I think you'll want to wake up now."

Sunlight shown through the cracks around the shutters and she groaned. Still slumped over the kitchen table in a state of drowsiness, Rill reached out and touched the stone bowl containing the green, fibrous paste and found it to be completely cold. She muttered her thanks to Mary and staggered to her feet. It was time to see if this formula worked. She took the bowl and a spoon with her to the parlor, who materialized immediately upon her entrance.

"Here," she said, handing him the bowl. "I don't know how long it will take for this to work, but the instructions didn't say anything about needing to monitor your progress, so I'm thinking it'll be quick."

He nodded and lifted the spoon from the bowl. Though the parlor would know what eating was and the principles behind it, he ate with such a deliberate seriousness that she would have found it entertaining if not for the situation. He scraped the bowl clean and handed it back to her.

"Do you feel anything yet?" she asked.

"I can feel the paste inside me, but it does not feel any different from anything else."

Silently, she hoped she'd prepared it right. Aloud, she said, "I suppose we'll find out later."

"Or we could test it."

He strode over to the doorway to the foyer and abruptly stopped at the border. After a moment's pause, he tried again.

"There is something different," he muttered.

He laid a hand against the door frame and closed his eyes as he shifted his weight against it. Then he took a step back, eyes open again, and this time walked through the doorway. Rill waited for him to come back, but when he did not immediately do so, she stuck her head out into the foyer.

There she found him with a contemplative expression on his face and again with a hand pressed to the wall.

51

"Are you all right?" she asked.

"I can't go through anymore," he said. "I can leave myself, but I can't go through the wall."

"Does that . . . bother you?"

He gazed at her inquiringly. "Should it? I'm doing what must be done."

"I could still go myself, if you're not comfortable."

"No," said James, perhaps more forcefully than he intended, because he smiled a moment later. "Rill, I want to go. Please understand. There are few wants or needs that we have as rooms, and this . . . this is mine. I'm going because I want to."

The gate was an oval ring of metal bolted upright on the far side of her father's laboratory, which meant that they had to contend with the brunt of the room's temper, but Rill was able to create a bubble of calm around James, Plim and herself using her father's rowan wand. This gave Plim the freedom to bind the blindfolded crow to the gate's destination plate without fear that the laboratory would rip it away.

They prepared in silence to avoid giving Morrin a clue about their plan. Rill hoped he thought the crow was still stuffed in the cupboard. If they were lucky, he wouldn't be home or would at least be otherwise occupied long enough for James to accomplish his task before his intrusion was discovered. She'd asked him to destroy three things: Morrin's own gate, his laboratory equipment and his wand cabinet. With help from her father's wands, it should only take a few minutes to give Morrin the setback of a lifetime.

Ready? she mouthed.

James and Plim nodded wordlessly.

Rill's father had hardly ever used the device, impressing upon her that it was for emergencies only. Certain components would take him over a year to prepare, and they could only be used once. But ever practical, he'd taught her how to use it should she ever need it. She didn't think he would have imagined what she was about to do with it now.

She placed her hand on the destination plate and she felt the inquiry in her mind as the gate wished to know where to open. She shoved aside the clutter of her personal thoughts and pushed outward until she found the oily black pit adjacent to her. The crow was only a tool and its memories easily discovered. She filtered through the images it had seen, images that appeared as destinations within the space of the gate.

A likely structure came to her attention, a stately mansion far larger than her father's home. There was an open window to a room filled with gadgets and beakers, and a man was inside. Morrin. Here. The crow had been inside. She saw bits of the house: the foyer, the halls, the laboratory. Sending James directly into the laboratory was out of the question. She would not be able to see if Morrin was there until she opened the gate, and she had little doubt that in a direct confrontation Morrin would win.

But through the crow's eyes she could see a small sitting room off the same hallway leading to Morrin's laboratory. There.

She locked in the destination and removed her hand from the steel plate. Plim shuffled nervously beside her, hands hovering over the lever that would open the gate. Rill lifted the rowan wand and held it tightly in her hands. All its power was directed toward keeping the laboratory from interfering. She didn't think it was strong enough to keep out Morrin as well, but if necessary she would try.

James walked up to the gate, two wands tucked into one side of his belt as a knight might sheathe his sword. Though he was dressed in the livery of a servant, he struck her as very much like a prince now, like the kind in her mother's stories, but she was the daughter of a magician, not a princess, so instead of the charming prince of her dreams, her champion had once been a parlor.

Rill signaled for Plim to open the gate and the bedroom complied. The gate hummed to life and the steel rim shone with an azure light. The vision of the sitting room changed from the crow's memory to that of the present. Plim swiveled the view of the portal to look around the room and it was empty. She pivoted it to face the closed door and locked it into place.

James stepped through, and they could see him on the other side. He pressed himself up to the door, listening, then he opened it and slipped out of sight.

Rill squeezed the wand tightly in her hand and waited. It seemed to take forever until Plim stopped fidgeting beside her, but at least watching her gave Rill a bit of a distraction. James had closed the door to the sitting room so they couldn't even glimpse the hallway. She wished she could see what was happening, that she could have sent her own spy as Morrin had sent his crow to her.

After a time she heard footsteps, rapid, running. The door to the sitting room flew open and James barreled through. Morrin appeared behind him, too quickly to have moved there by natural means. James was only a step from the gate, but Morrin was levitating something with his hand. A spear!

"James!" she shouted. "Behind you!"

Halfway through the gate he turned around, and she realized he noticed what was just now dawning on her. Morrin was not aiming the spear at James. He was aiming at *her,* the would-be master of this house. James' reaction was swift. He had already protected her twice before, and there was no hesitation as he moved to block the spear with his body, but he was no longer a room. He was human now. . . .

Rill cried out and swept the rowan wand in front of her. It didn't matter if the barrier blocking the laboratory would be broken. She had to protect James.

She felt the magic activate, and there was a flash of blue light, but it wasn't enough. The spear struck James, sending him tumbling back through the gate. On landing, he fell on his side and the bloodied spear clattered beside him.

Dimly, Rill could hear Plim screaming, "The gate! I can't shut the gate!" and she knew she should do something, but all she could feel was a dull pain as she stared at James crumpled on the floor. How bad was he? Was he moving? There was so much blood. The spearhead had torn free of his body when he fell.

James.

She didn't want him to die because she hadn't known enough magic to properly fight, because she'd relied on a wand she barely understood how to use. She needed him, to be there for her when she was sad or distressed, to be there when she had no one else. This house was home with James. It had always been, ever since she was a little girl. He was the only family she had left.

When you're homesick, is it the house you miss or the people who live there?

Warmth welled in her chest, stronger than anything she'd felt before, and she could feel a shared pain, a mental embrace from every room in the house, every room except the parlor, and the void she felt in its absence was enough to drive her to tears. She didn't know the future, but right now, this was home. No other place could be.

She turned to face the gate and witnessed complete seething rage on Morrin's face. He was screaming at her, but nothing he did seemed to pass through, not even his magic. Something had changed. Scarcely aware of what she was doing, Rill reached out to the gate's lever and snapped it shut.

A hand lightly touched her arm, and at first she thought it was Plim, but the voice was different. "Wipe away your tears," she said. "He's badly injured, but Papa taught us how to deal with wounds, even deep ones like this. Isn't that right?"

Rill dabbed at her eyes and turned to look at . . . herself, or rather a twelve-year-old version of herself. The laboratory.

"Lay him on his back, carefully, and open his shirt," she said. "We need to clean the wound. I'm heating water and cloth."

"But . . . why?" asked Rill.

The laboratory tossed her a petulant look that made Rill wonder just how often she had given that scowl to her own father. "If we patch him up fast and it doesn't get infected, he has a good chance to survive. You want him to live, don't you? Really, he would have been much worse if you hadn't used your wand. I think it blunted the impact."

"Rill." James' voice was weak, but his eyes were bright as she knelt beside him. "Do what she says. I can't say I enjoy this part of being human, but I'll get through this."

"But why is she here now? Why is she helping us?" asked Rill.

"Don't you understand?" James smiled. "You're the master now."

Over the coming weeks, Rill made herself at home, because this *was* home now. She kept her old room, but spent much of her time shuttling between the laboratory and the library. Magic wasn't anything she would encourage someone to teach themselves, but she had a firm grounding in the basics, thanks to her father.

Morrin could no longer enter this house either, not now that she was the master, though apparently there were other ways he could still vent his frustration. Among the condolence letters that gradually reached her regarding the death of her father, she found a notice regarding a complaint he'd filed with a certain society of magicians.

She would deal with that in time. For now, the house was enough.

Upon gaining mastery of the house, the garden and the storeroom had broken free. Of the two of them, the garden had more work cut out for himself, but he made excellent progress. The plants he could salvage were almost back to their old selves, and those that he'd lost he would replace with time.

James was recovering as well. He'd spent much of that time bedridden, but now he was walking around again, though not very much, or for very long. One of the guest bedrooms was in the process of becoming his personal room, and the rest of the rooms gradually began to acclimate to him as a human being rather than one of themselves. The kitchen had to adjust to regularly feeding two people again after all these years, and while she relished making more elaborate meals, she never quite got over what she called "the audacity of the parlor."

As for the physical parlor itself, it was no longer quite as impeccably tidy as it had been in the past. It was cleaned by human hands now, and in that way was more human like the man who'd once embodied it.

Watching James adjust to life as a human was a novel experience for Rill. Pain, hunger and even drowsiness were all new to him, and that barely scratched the surface of it. Sometimes the gaps in his knowledge were amusing, other times awkward, but they'd get through it. Rill wasn't going anywhere.

The Black Side of Memory

written by

Lael Salaets

illustrated by

VEN LOCKLEAR

ABOUT THE AUTHOR

Originally from Massachusetts, Lael Salaets enjoyed science fiction at an early age. His growing interest in art and reading and writing fiction enabled him to explore other worlds.

His pursuit of creative writing faded, however, several years after his family moved to Oregon. He enlisted in the US Marines at the age of seventeen. Stationed in Japan as a field artillery cannoneer, he deployed across Asia, and, in 1991, to the Persian Gulf during Operations Desert Shield/Desert Storm.

After his honorable discharge Lael studied fine art at the University of Oregon and Lane Community College, where he earned a degree in graphic design. He started free writing, which developed into short stories. Shortly thereafter, he joined the Wordos, a professional writers group in Eugene, and began submitting work. He made Finalist in the Writers of the Future Contest in 2007, and then won in 2009.

Lael currently resides in Oakridge, Oregon. He is writing a novel based on the universe of his recent short stories.

ABOUT THE ILLUSTRATOR

Most family members and friends say Ven Locklear's art is disturbing. However, they all agree the creatures that emerge from Ven's vividly fertile brain are lighthearted, cool and often humorous. Growing up in central Oregon, he began drawing dragons and imaginary beasts at a young age. In high school, he set his sights on becoming a professional concept artist and illustrator.

Ven loves bringing original, exciting SF and fantasy creations to life through digital painting. His favorite subjects are bizarre monsters, dragons, sword-wielding robots, strange characters and the fanciful worlds they live in.

In 2009, Ven spent six months in Morocco working as a graphic designer at Al Akhawayn University. Currently, Ven is an illustration major at Pacific Northwest College of Art in Portland, Oregon.

The Black Side of Memory

Lieutenant Det Kiv had difficulty accepting discharge with an edited version of the war. PTSD treatment for Level Cs was a package deal, which involved Sensitive Battlefield Information Erasure. The docs back at Waypoint Orbital Station had made certain of that.

Kiv hadn't recalled much of his appointment—a side effect of the SBIE procedure—save for the eye pain, headaches and an iron taste in his mouth.

According to the brief, docs were only interested in isolating experiences considered either traumatic or classified. What fragments of memory Kiv wanted to hold onto were, unfortunately, a little of both. Perhaps some things were best forgotten. He understood that.

The problem was he felt he had lost memories that were important to him. He felt strongly about these residual fragments of recall, which had grown increasingly surreal and distant. Often they would appear in daydreams like a documentary in fast forward shot with a dirty lens. Falling through the night sky, the eyes of a little girl, bright flashes and hard shadows. He feared they would fade away over time. All that would remain would be this notion he had made a real difference at some point in his ten years with Force Recon—without knowing what that was.

He wondered how many other vets felt the same way.

On the Qe-Koran surface Kiv welcomed the cool breeze and stronger gravity when he hauled his sea bag out the main gate. A mixed crowd filled the nearby streets of Anchor Point where family receptions embraced vets alongside him. There'd be none for him, not that he expected any, what with his foster parents who had spoken little with him since he had joined the Corps.

Protesters yelled behind the barricades on either side of him, flashing cheap holo banners. DON'T BRAINWASH OUR TROOPS!

Kiv stiffened beneath his dress black uniform. He ignored the protesters and kept walking.

The crowd thinned after several blocks. He froze at the sight of rubble where dozers were clearing sections of a rough neighborhood. The docs had advised him that the occasional "pseudo recall" would pass, along with the insomnia.

The smell of black beans and rice distracted him. Real food, he thought. Not that vat-grown slop back at Waypoint. He traced the aroma to a makeshift stand where an old Joffan woman greeted him with a cup of spice tea. Her olive skin, salt-and-pepper hair and sunset eyes were obscured momentarily behind a cloud of steam.

Pseudo recognition hit him again. He ordered a plate and sat down uneasily.

"Welcome home, sir," a familiar voice said.

Kiv turned around.

Lan Novak, from his old squad, looked tired, like the sleep aids had only taken him so far. Kiv wondered if he'd end up the same way himself.

"Thanks," Kiv said. He motioned Novak to take a seat next to him.

Novak approached. A mechanical whine pulsated from beneath the right pant leg of his khakis.

"What happened to you?" Kiv said, embarrassed and frustrated that he couldn't remember.

Hell, he wanted to remember a lot of things, like how he had gotten that disciplinary code on his discharge file. Office Hours. To fail himself and, more importantly, his men, was bad enough. Not knowing how that had occurred really burned his ass. Kiv did remember serving the last six months of his commission in HQ as an admin clerk, which he hated. He assumed that was a disciplinary action. It might as well have been. At least his discharge was honorable. Things could have been worse.

"Grenade," Novak said finally. "At least that's what the docs told me. They didn't give me any details, of course."

"I'm sorry, Novak."

Novak nodded. He sat down, ordered tea and hand-signaled Kiv his username and how to reach him online.

Kiv logged in, aware Novak had likely built the encryption himself. Everyone had trained in electronic warfare.

The new implant buzzed at the base of Kiv's skull. He wanted to close his eyes and imagine the Tactical

Heads Up Display that wasn't there. He didn't like the civie interface, which he considered too flashy for his taste.

Novak handed him a pair of goggles. *Check out your tattoo.*

Kiv rolled up his right sleeve and did so. He studied the tattoo on his forearm: an orbital ring framed a parachute and wings over a beachhead. It had been a custom job done in a printer. The goggle lenses magnified the ink lines on his skin into letters and numbers, which spelled out names and dates, unit creed and designation.

Everybody got one.

The docs had scanned Kiv's tattoo through a pattern recognition filter. If they had found anything suspicious, like a memory cue, they would have erased it by now.

What am I supposed to find? Kiv said.

It's all in code, Novak replied.

The scanners would have picked up on that.

Not the old codes we used back in the day. Novak watched the street without being obvious.

Kiv had already mapped out the street as well: the layout of the construction site, stats of all the workers, down to the plate numbers of every vehicle. He and Novak were in Force Recon after all. And old habits died hard. At least the docs hadn't erased their training.

So, what did you find? Kiv said, skeptical but curious.

GPS coordinates, Novak said. *I looked it up.*

A dump truck rumbled past. Kiv shielded his plate from the cloud of dust.

There's more, Novak added. *Maybe file names. Pass codes.*

For what? Kiv asked. He returned the goggles and then took a bite of his food. He chewed slowly, savoring the flavor.

I'm thinking we copied our memories in an external drive and buried it.

Kiv nearly choked.

"Is everything all right?" the old woman said.

Kiv swallowed hard and nodded. He finished his tea. Though he wished for a stiff drink.

Just hear me out, Novak said.

That's crazy, Novak. Do you have any idea how much trouble we'd all be in for pulling a stunt like that?

A group of workers leaned in from either side ordering takeout. Kiv noted two of them in particular, how smooth their hands were. Their work clothes looked new, not as dirty. Kiv wondered if he should order a box and eat somewhere else. *This code you deciphered could be anything. The war is over, Novak. Let it go.*

They erased an experience that was important to us. We want it back. And so do you.

Kiv hated to admit that. He stabbed at his food a while. Workers grabbed their boxes of food. Kiv studied them as they left. One of the two with smooth hands glanced at him, placing him on edge. He relaxed somewhat when they walked away.

I know. I saw them too, Novak said in reference to the two men. He finished his tea and then set the cup aside. *We owe it to the team, dammit. "Once a Marine, always a Marine." Or had the docs made you forget that too?*

I've been through enough as it is. And so have you. I'm not about to risk losing my benefits digging for a box—an expensive piece of hardware, government property we might have tampered with—in the middle of nowhere. Not to mention the likelihood of serving hard time in a federal prison if we got caught. Hell, you don't know for certain if we'd buried anything out there at all.

That "middle of nowhere" happens to be Ariah.

Hairs spiked at the base of Kiv's neck.

His team had gathered intel near that village, now half a world away. Kiv couldn't recall anything eventful there, of course.

Novak shared what news feeds he'd obtained of the Battle of Ariah, which was a turning point in the war, at least in this part of the universe. Enemy forces, namely the Sarska, had lost a considerable amount of ground in the Eastern Frontier. Uprisings against corporations, military regimes crazed on religion had been reduced to isolated bands of guerilla fighters. Colonial marines had conducted mopping operations, securing the flood of humanitarian aid ever since.

Kiv couldn't find a trace of his unit's involvement. No surprise there.

Windows of satellite footage opened across his wetware interface: remains of a village nestled in a valley, excavation work and a large cluster of tents to the south.

What are these? Kiv asked.

Ariah, Novak replied. *What's left of it.*

Are you suggesting we go back there? Kiv said.

That's right.

You're out of your mind. The Eastern Frontier isn't entirely stabilized yet.

66

The old woman handed Novak another cup of tea. He turned the cup slowly in his hands. *After you meet Yadon, maybe you'll change your mind.*

Jace Yadon was the sniper in their unit, and a damn good one. Kiv might not have recalled the details of every mission, but he was sure Yadon had saved his ass more than once in the field. *How is he?*

I met him at the VA Hospital. Novak shook his head. Kiv met his gaze. *What happened to him?*

When we get there, you'll see what I mean.

If the anticipation of pain had a smell, it was the disinfectant. Overhead lamps intensified the hard whiteness of the psych ward, like the clinics back at Waypoint. Security was tight here. Kiv and Novak had been scanned before they had reached the elevator.

They logged in at the reception desk. Male nurses, imposing in their white uniforms, escorted them down the hall. Sunlight flooded the rec room through windows thick with reinforced composite. Kiv ignored the televised program on the wide holo screen as he threaded his way along the strict arrangement of tables and chairs. The patients around him, dressed in their pastel green pajamas, were lost in a world of their own, their minds elsewhere. Like they were gone.

Kiv broke his stride when he spotted Yadon sitting alone at a far corner table. The stubble on his face made him look thinner than he actually was, his black hair longer and frayed. Locked in a moment of intense concentration, he sketched on a worn pad of paper with a black marker.

Damn, Kiv thought. He felt heavy, standing across from Yadon. He glanced at the loose pile of drawings on the tabletop. The possibility he might end up here, lost in another world searching for a way out, occurred to him. He cringed at the thought.

"Jace," one of the nurses said to Yadon, "you have visitors."

Yadon glanced up, apparently irritated by the interruption from his work.

He blinked at Kiv. He seemed like he still had it together, more or less. With that look in his eyes like he had been administered a regimen of powerful drugs. He moved to stand, as if at attention.

"As you were," Kiv said.

Yadon sat back down. Embarrassed, defeated and then suddenly anxious. He gathered the pile of drawings into a neat stack.

Kiv nodded as the nurses left and then sat across from Yadon. Yadon had always been the quiet artist type. He had planned after the war to enroll in art school, work in a studio and display his work in galleries.

Yadon was ready to implode at any moment. Kiv chose his words carefully. "I see you've been busy."

"Yes, sir," Yadon said. He inserted the cap on his marker. "I'm sorry I let you down."

"It's not your fault."

"They say if I make enough *progress,*" Yadon said bitterly, "I can have *paint.*"

"Once things get squared away, you'll be out of here in no time," Kiv said.

Yadon smiled, more like a facial tic. "Know why you can't sleep? It's the blanks you can never fill." He scanned the rec room and leaned forward. "What do you remember?" he whispered.

Kiv shrugged. "Just fragments."

Yadon's eyes widened. "I see them too." He flipped through pages of drawings.

"See what?" Kiv said with heightened interest.

Don't provoke him, Novak said online. *He'll relapse.*

Not here, Kiv said. *Stay offline.*

Yadon nodded. "Fragments." He laid out drawings on the table. Fireballs. Rubble. "They come to me when I'm awake." Five-pointed stars, the emblem of the Sarska. "I sketch them out because some of the dreams don't come back." Numbers overlaid into inky blotches. "Random images. Sometimes I don't know what I see, but I draw them." Yadon handed him the rest.

Kiv examined Yadon's maps and charts, desert landscapes at night, mountain ranges and farmland. He found pages completely inked out disturbing. He flipped through them, but not so quickly as to potentially offend Yadon. Then, he saw the face of a little girl.

Her, he thought. The portrait, as if captured directly from his own dreams, shocked him. Details of her flashed in his mind: black hair, olive skin and those twilight eyes. Kiv felt cold.

Yadon pointed at the drawing. "You've seen her, haven't you?"

Kiv nodded. There were more sketches. The girl looked frightened, alone in the dark.

Yadon rolled back his right sleeve, revealing the tattoo. "You'll find *it,* won't you, sir?" The hard drive.

Kiv was torn. He was responsible for his men. He was not about to let them waste away. Not like Yadon. Not after they had all sworn to never forget this one moment in their lives.

Once a Marine, always a Marine.

"You bet," Kiv said finally.

Yadon placed all his sketches and the drawing pad into the stack and handed them to Kiv. "Take these with you."

"Are you sure?"

Yadon nodded. "You might need them."

Kiv handled the stack carefully.

The nurses returned. "Excuse us. Jace, it's time for your appointment." Yadon pinched his eyes shut.

"You hang in there, Yadon," Kiv said.

Yadon opened his eyes. "Good luck, sir."

The nurses escorted Yadon into an open hatch. Kiv sighed and then shoved the drawings into his jacket.

He and Novak logged out of the ward and stepped into the elevator. The doors sealed them inside. They were quiet for a while. "You know," Novak said, "that's the most I've ever heard him speak."

"When Yadon has something to say," Kiv replied, "it's usually important."

Kiv really needed a drink. As much as he wanted to get tanked he couldn't shake the notion someone was tracking him. He had to pace himself.

Novak had suggested a local dive, someplace quiet and remote. The black lights reminded Kiv of the colors of his old Tactical HUD display. White noise from the vents above placed him more at ease. He glanced at his reflection in the mirror behind the bar. He ordered a beer. No sleep aids tonight.

The bartender, a slender young woman dressed in black, gave him a glass of dark ale. Her long bangs accentuated her brown eyes. The mood paint on her lips changed from blue to orange when she smiled. A welcome sight for a change.

So, where are the others? he asked Novak about their old squad.

Novak emptied his shot glass. *They're not out yet. Under the PTSD/SBIE Act we can't contact them until they've passed Transition Week. I've tried.*

All right. What's the plan? If you have one.

Much of the Eastern Frontier is off limits to commercial flights. We'll have to land at Indahl, the nearest port, and go from there.

And just how are we going to do that?

I read an article about a shortage of air marshals. So, the airlines are offering free flights to anyone who qualifies.

For real?

Novak nodded. *I've already made arrangements with airport security. We sign up first thing tomorrow.*

The entry hatch swished open. Movement in the mirror caught Kiv's eye. A man walked past. Clean-shaven, buzz cut, casual dark suit, his clean white shirt bright under the black lights. He sat at a table behind Novak and ordered a soda. Kiv found that odd.

Then what, he asked Novak, *after we land?*

Novak ordered another drink. *We stow away on a relief aid shuttle. I got some armbands. We'll blend.*

Kiv recalled all those drawings of desert landscapes Yadon had drawn. *And if this doesn't work, we'll have to cross a few hundred klicks of Gola Desert.*

Not like we've done anything like that before.

Ghosting satellite detection the hard way would be rough, among other things. Like gunships and desert tribes who didn't much care for outsiders.

Kiv opened the satellite footage Novak had sent him earlier. He studied the excavation work in the village. *Looks like engineers had been busy digging up the area. You'd think they would have found the drive by now.*

That's what I thought too, Novak said. *Maybe we buried it, then had someone dig it up later. Like one of the villagers.*

That girl, the one in Yadon's drawings. We need to find her.

Novak nodded. *There's another problem we'll have to consider, now that we're being followed.*

Such as?

The feds could brain hack us. If the docs back at Waypoint can erase our memories, who knows what else they might have done? They might have installed a trigger, like a particular word, a phrase or a song to keep us under control.

Kiv finished his beer. *What did you have in mind?*

I know this dealer who can get us some neutralizers.

Kiv didn't like the idea of using street drugs. Then again, it was better than being hacked. Maybe he'd be stuck in a ward like Yadon. Or spend the rest of his life as a different person. Or worse. Kiv winced at the thought.

He glanced at the man in the mirror. *I don't like the company.*

Neither do I.

At Indahl Airport Kiv felt eyes on him all morning, despite airport security. Though air marshal duty on the long flight had worn him down, the neutralizers made him feel anxious and unusually warm in his white long-sleeved shirt and brown cargo pants.

Hey, Novak asked. *You all right?*

Yeah. Kiv wiped the sweat from his face. He couldn't wait for the neutralizers to wear off.

He and Novak had invested in battery wafers, which were in short supply out in the Eastern Frontier and worth a lot of money. They'd bought enough packs to get them through the journey, stuffed into two black duffle bags.

As a contingency, Novak had installed memory bombs in their wetware implants, set to wipe their files clean in the event federal agents had apprehended them.

They'd crossed the airport lounge for the exit when an older, stocky man dressed in a beige suit blocked their path. The man had Kiv on edge, as though he could break through his firewall with those ice-blue eyes. *We go analog for the duration,* Kiv said to Novak.

Novak glanced at him sidelong in agreement.

"Det Kiv?" the man asked. "Lan Novak?"

"Yeah," Kiv and Novak replied.

The man produced a badge. "Agent Pierce. Federal Security. Come with me, please."

Come with me.

Kiv blinked. Though he followed Pierce, Kiv managed to resist slipping into the trigger. Barely. He cringed, anticipating the memory bomb to execute.

Agent Pierce suggested a corner seat. They sat down.

"You don't look well," Pierce said to Kiv.

Kiv didn't like the way Pierce was studying him. "The airline food didn't agree with me."

Pierce raised an eyebrow.

The space between them grew tense. "Indahl isn't a popular tourist attraction," Pierce said finally. "What's your business here?"

"Hiking," Novak said. He opened a holo brochure.

Pierce didn't look amused. "Hiking."

"That's right," Kiv said.

"And I suppose you plan to bargain with the locals with those battery wafers in your carry-on luggage," Pierce said.

Kiv gripped the straps of his duffle bag tight. "That's not illegal."

"Neither is your little camping trip." Pierce leaned forward. "Be advised, the area is under surveillance."

"That's good to know, in case we get lost."

"Like wandering across the Rhodan border?" Pierce smiled.

The Rhodan border, according to the maps Yadon had drawn, was the most direct route to Ariah.

He's on to us, Kiv thought. *They all are.* Federal Security had likely read Kiv's file, including those of his old unit. Good thing Yadon had handed over the drawings. The feds were probably monitoring him as well. Kiv stiffened, expecting other agents to apprehend them.

"Stay out of the Frontier." Pierce stood. "Is that clear?"

74

"Absolutely," Kiv said. And good luck tracking us *out there,* he thought. This is Force Recon you're dealing with.

Kiv and Novak exited with their duffle bags into the hot, blinding sun. They squinted at the crowded streets of Indahl where a mob of taxi drivers competed for their business.

"That was close," Novak muttered about their encounter with Pierce. "The feds could have arrested us."

"They would have already," Kiv said, "had they found the drive."

He imagined his lost memories written on a server, compressed, shipped and archived in an undisclosed location for someone like Pierce to open for investigation.

He then wondered, for his own personal satisfaction, if agents pending retirement would ever have their memories erased.

The relief shuttle stowaway plan, now with agents watching for them, was no longer an option. Plan B: the Gola Desert.

"Best deals," one of the taxi drivers said with a broken accent, a bearded man in drab clothes. "I take you there."

"Deals on what?" Novak asked.

"Whatever you need."

Kiv and Novak followed the driver into the cab. Kiv looked out the window as the city blurred past, which rapidly gave way to signs of neglect and sluggish post-war recovery. The pseudo effect hit him hard.

"What are you looking for?" the driver said.

Kiv snapped awake.

"Hiking gear," Novak said.

Deep in the marketplace they stopped alongside a shop entrance. More like a hole in the wall beneath a sign of faded red paint.

"This is it?" Novak said.

"Yes, and tell Ryad I sent you," the driver said eagerly. Kiv paid the fare with a battery wafer, enough power to sustain a desert tribe for a week.

The barrage of noise, and grilled meat, spices and baked bread overwhelmed him when he opened the door. There was a rushed sense of need in the air amidst the aisles of vending booths. Kiv suddenly felt cold, scanning the crowd.

Novak limped slightly with his prosthetic leg. "Hey, what's wrong?" Kiv asked Novak.

"It's the dust," Novak replied. "Don't worry, I'll have it sealed up before we head out."

A bell rang when they entered the shop filled with various remnants from the war. Kiv navigated around stacks of obsolete computer hardware wrapped in plastic, shelves packed with uniforms and open boxes of faded sleeping bags. Two large men sat on folding chairs, within reach of metal pipes.

A heavy man in a cheap suit behind the counter tapped on a notebook. Light from the screen made him look pale.

"You Ryad?" Kiv said. "The driver sent us."

The man nodded. "What can I do for you, gentlemen?" he said with a husky voice.

"Is this all you have?" Novak said.

"It depends," Ryad said and lowered his notebook. "What do you need?"

"Desert travel gear." Kiv set his duffle bag on the counter.

Ryad brushed aside a Colonial flag that draped over a nondescript doorway and motioned with an outstretched arm for them to enter a side room furnished with rugs and pillows. Kiv and Novak approached with their bags. The sound of scraped metal and locking mechanisms from behind told Kiv they were sealed in to conduct some shady business. He took a deep breath and exhaled, purging the tension that had been building within him.

The side room was dim and cramped, yet comfortable. Ryad sat on a pillow across from them. He passed around glasses of what smelled like paint thinner. Kiv took a sip, for the sake of cultural etiquette. It burned down his throat with an intensity he didn't expect.

"So, what do you want?" Ryad said happily.

"Hiking equipment," Kiv said.

"East Sector is closed. Mine clearing, they say."

"Have any detectors?" Novak said.

Ryad chuckled, and then fell silent as if evaluating the situation. "Open the bags."

Kiv and Novak revealed their cache.

Ryad rubbed the stubble on his chin and tapped on the notebook. His men arrived soon afterward with a black plastic crate the size of a large coffin. They opened the lid.

Kiv waved off the dust and then looked inside. He wiped a pair of multi-cam fatigues, infrared block with radar absorption, which were popular with guerillas back in the day. He inspected a tarp made of the same material. Goggles. Knives. He sifted through a set of

77

web gear complete with hydration filters. Collapsible shovels, body armor, a compact satellite dish. The rucksacks looked older than he was, let alone the field rations sealed in brown pouches. At least there were handheld mine detectors at the bottom of the pile. He checked a pair of combat boots, worn yet serviceable.

Novak fished through the crate alongside him and drew out an antique pair of night vision binoculars. "Check these out," he said as though he were some kid at a garage sale.

"Built to last, eh?" Ryad said.

Kiv nodded, despite himself. "Any optical camouflage?"

"No, sorry."

Swell, Kiv thought. Scavengers likely supplied Ryad with whatever they found out in the desert. Kiv debated whether to shop elsewhere. The minefield, let alone a fair trade, he figured, would be the least of his problems.

Dressed in local garb they hitched a ride under the cover of darkness into the open desert. On the roof of the transport Kiv tightened the scarf across his face and sought shelter from the wind behind his pack. He didn't share Novak's enthusiasm.

The other passengers huddled alongside regarded them with curiosity.

Kiv watched the dust cloud sparkle in the taillights and wondered about the memories he had lost. His daydreams of that little girl were fading. He feared Pierce would find her.

Then he heard the distinct whine of a gunship in the distance. Novak passed him the binocs.

Kiv noted the familiar wasp-like shape half a klick away. It skimmed over the dunes, reduced to a green speck across the horizon.

The passengers cursed and shook their fists at the sky. Not everyone welcomed the Colonial military presence here. "What brings you out here?" someone said next to him.

"We're on vacation," Kiv replied.

The man laughed. "This is a bad season for that," the stranger said. "Sandstorms."

Novak tapped Kiv on the shoulder. The transport groaned to a halt at an isolated trading post, a flimsy metal shack and a few tents. "Thanks for the advice," Kiv said to the stranger. He showed him a bottle of Ryad's paint thinner. "Anything else we should know?"

The man licked his lips. "There were other men who had passed through here. Government men. We did not know what they wanted. And we never asked."

Kiv handed him the bottle. "Thanks." He and Novak ventured out into the vast sea of dunes.

After several hours on foot, Novak's prosthetic leg made a scraping wheeze. He limped worse than usual; his leg dragged across the sand with every step. "Dammit," Novak said. "I'm slowing you down."

"Let's dig in," Kiv said. "It'll be light soon anyway. Then we'll check your leg." He led Novak up a rocky slope where they hastily built a spider hole in a gravel patch.

Novak finished camouflaging the tarp roof and then slid inside. He rolled up his pant leg in disgust. Kiv unwrapped a long strip of fabric, revealing a tear five centimeters long in a thick layer of artificial skin below the knee. "Son of a bitch," Novak muttered. He winced, carefully peeling the skin back where bits of sand had lodged in the pistons, cables and circuitry beneath.

"You need a painkiller?" Kiv asked.

"No, I'm good."

Kiv produced a brush from his pack and started cleaning.

Novak flinched, his face drawn and pale. "So, what's your take on what happened to us?" he said as though he were attempting to take his mind off the pain.

"Maybe we went 'green side,'" Kiv said, using his unit term for a reconnaissance mission, "and got spotted."

"Maybe." Novak flinched. "But after seeing Yadon's sketches that was one hell of a firefight we'd gone through. Stuff changes in the field, though. We could have been called in to go 'black side'—a surgical strike—like on a command post, and things went haywire."

Kiv shrugged. "We'll find out soon enough."

Novak bent his knee a few times, the scraping noise not so apparent. He sighed. "Thanks, sir. I got it from here."

"You sure?"

Novak nodded. He drew out a plasti-patch and stuck it over the cut in his leg.

"I'll take first watch," Kiv said. "We'll move out tonight." He drank from his canteen and watched the range thaw beneath the pre-dawn gray. "What do you remember?"

"Tracers," Novak replied, apprehension creeping into his voice. "Falling into a hole."

Kiv recalled those fragments of residual memory of falling at night and landing into black. Like in Yadon's heavily inked drawings. "Like we did a drop," he heard himself say.

They were quiet for a while, the sun quickly warming the desert.

"I wrote this utility program," Novak said. "A contingency."

"For what?"

"Once we get to that drive and gain access to those files, we send copies of that data to a secure site online. If Pierce ever got to us, that utility would have a dead-man switch. Those files would go viral across the Net. If Pierce knew that, he'd back off." Novak thumbed at his pack. "That's why I bought the satellite dish."

Kiv nodded. He scanned the range through the binocs and spotted activity far to the east. "What's up?" Novak said.

"Engineers clearing mines. Full-scale operations." Kiv opened a map file from his nerve chip implant. Digital contour lines overlaid his viewpoint. "There has to be another way."

"We've got some battery wafers left. Could make a deal with the natives."

"I don't know." Kiv weighed his options between the risk of exposure in a minefield and tribal politics.

By the third night the patrols and Novak's stiff leg had slowed their progress considerably. Kiv hit the dirt before the gunship passed overhead. He waited for it to circle around, gauged the all clear and then helped Novak to his feet. The patch on his leg must have worn off.

"Come on," Kiv whispered as he slung Novak along, "we're almost at the border." He pushed himself against the exhaustion and biting wind up a large dune. They dropped their packs and crawled to the summit.

Tracked vehicles rumbled beyond white strips of chemlight tape and razor wire.

"Damn, it's worse than I thought," Novak said of all the activity in the minefield. "I say we cut a deal with the locals."

Of all the tribes to encounter, the Adari descended from a mixed line of pioneer mercenaries long before the colonies.

"Screw that," Kiv said. "We can make it."

Novak alerted him with the hand sign for danger close.

Several figures in desert garb appeared, armed with kinetic energy rifles. Kiv watched them pass, only to hear the distinct click of a cocked hammer behind him. He slowly turned around.

A boy, maybe thirteen, aimed a semiautomatic pistol with the posture of a trained soldier. His distinctive black face paint intensified the whites of his eyes.

The smell of sweat and spices in the crowded tent was so strong Kiv could taste it. He sat uneasily in the center on a worn red hand-woven carpet facing the elders. The others on either side of him emptied the packs and produced the handheld munition detectors. They muttered eagerly amongst themselves.

"If only we had those sooner," the old man said with a deep voice; the wrinkles on his leathery skin danced as he spoke. "At least, anything reliable."

Kiv noticed several people around him had lost a limb. He felt as if a block of ice had landed in the pit of his stomach.

The old man produced a notebook and studied Kiv a while. "It appears your government has been looking for you." He showed Kiv a data sheet of Novak and himself.

Pierce, Kiv thought. He wondered how much the feds were willing to pay them as a reward.

"What are you doing out here?" an elder asked.

"We were headed for Ariah," Kiv said.

"You were there, at the Battle of Ariah?"

"So far as I know."

The old man frowned. "What do you mean by that?"

"The government erased most of our memories of it."

The old man seemed bewildered. "The Republic does such things?"

Kiv nodded.

The others in the tent grew restless. "If they are doing that to *their* warriors," someone said, "what will stop them from wiping the minds of everyone else?"

"We could be next!" said another. He pointed angrily at Kiv. "They have done enough to us. To hell with the Republic, and to hell with you!"

"Be quiet!" the old man said to them. Arguing subsided to idle chatter in the background.

"There's a chance we might be able to remember what happened to us once we reach Ariah," Kiv said, not wanting to disclose anything about the hard drive. He didn't want to chance the Adari wanting to get their hands on it. "We're looking for a little Joffan girl who might be at the refugee camp."

"I know this girl," the old man said with heightened interest. "I had seen her there. Hannah was her name. She was one of the survivors."

"What did she say?" Kiv asked eagerly.

"Very little. She had that look in her eyes, the forever stare." The old man nodded. "I knew it well. Like she had seen so much death. The villagers were very bitter they had not received any advance warning. Word around the camp of the battle, the Sarska had stormed in to slaughter everyone. The girl managed to escape. Then she saw ghosts falling from the sky."

"Optical camouflage," Kiv said absently, piecing everything together. He pictured all this, what the old man had told him, and then he lost himself in the recurring dream of falling in the night sky.

"That was *you*?" the old man said.

Kiv blinked. That had to have been his team. He had a gnarled feeling in his gut about it. "Possibly. What else happened?"

"One of the ghosts revealed his face, a face covered with gray paint. She showed them what was happening at her village, and these ghosts wiped out all the Sarska there. Like ghosts."

"Let us not forget *our* struggle against the Sarska," an elder said to his right. "These warriors may be with the Republic, but they had fought with honor. The enemy of our enemy is our friend."

"To erase one's memories," said another, "is a fate worse than death. Imagine what their government will do to them."

The old man grunted. He divided his attention between the drawings and the data sheet on the notebook. "This changes things."

Now we're getting somewhere, Kiv thought. If only Yadon knew how far his artwork had gone.

"I call for a vote!" someone said. The others argued again, louder this time. The old man glanced at Kiv and waved him away. Two men from behind hastily led him outside.

He joined Novak who sat under guard.

"How did it go?" Novak said. His breath frosted in the sharp air.

"That went well," Kiv said. *"I guess."* He sat down. "They're debating whether to let us go or hand us over to Pierce."

The Adari boy with the handgun stood by them and ate the last of Novak's candy bar.

"Great," Novak said.

Kiv told him about what he had discussed with the elders.

Novak seemed absent, absorbing all this information. "Sounds like we went black side, in a big way."

"Yeah," Kiv said. "How's the leg?"

"Well, I know what arthritis feels like," Novak said.

They waited a couple of hours, and then one of the elders motioned them to enter the tent. Kiv sighed and followed them. There, he noticed a map spread out on the rug.

The old man glanced at everyone as though he were reluctant, then looked straight at Kiv and tapped on a grid square. "There is a way, but a sandstorm is predicted to hit tomorrow."

That's good, Kiv thought. No patrols. Then again, the storms in this region were unforgiving. "Then we should hurry."

The Adari guided them to a deep, jagged stretch of ravine fifty meters wide.

Kiv had planned to cross the border masquerading in Adari fashion beneath the multi-cam fatigues and body armor. He smeared black paint around his eyes, adding to the effect. This had proved expensive, naturally. So much for what battery wafers he and Novak had left. "All right," Kiv said. "Let's move."

The detector beeped in the boy's hand. "Wait." He picked up a handful of sand and tossed it out in front of them. Tripwires glistened briefly in the early dawn.

Pierce and his minions had been busy.

"Good save," Novak said. "We'll go alone from here."

The boy looked up at them and saluted. "You come back this way, we will remember you." In desert terms, that was a compliment. Kiv returned the favor.

They went their separate ways.

Kiv and Novak proceeded carefully on either side of the path. Disarm. Step. Cover.

Temperatures climbed with the rising sun. By noon, the breeze had raged into a harsh wind that battered them with dust and loose pebbles. The storm was stronger and faster than Kiv had expected. He worried the loose debris could release the tripwires ahead. "We should head back."

"We're almost there," Novak said loudly.

The end of the ravine hazed into a cloud of sand. Kiv motioned him to fall back.

A mine detonated a hundred meters away. Kiv and Novak hit the dirt. The ground shook as rocks toppled around them. Shrapnel flung over their heads. Kiv heard the faint sound of wires snapping.

"Incoming!" he yelled.

The chain reaction of shockwaves knocked Kiv airborne into something hard. He blacked out and then woke to a white-hot pain cutting into his right side. His ears rang. The storm whirled into a dark mass, blotting out the sun, intensifying the vertigo.

A small figure appeared and told him to get up, like a child's voice inside his head. Maybe it was the concussion, or the injection of painkiller Novak was giving him.

Novak yelled in his ear, but he sounded far away. He placed a belt between Kiv's teeth. He bit down hard as Novak removed shards of bloody shrapnel out of his flesh. He nearly passed out.

The figure vanished and reappeared, materializing as it approached into the form of a little girl. "Come on!" she said. "We promised."

"Promised what?" Kiv said. "Hannah?"

"Who?" Novak said. He looked out into the storm, but didn't seem to notice anyone there. He tightened a bandage around Kiv's torso. "Damn, you've been hit bad."

Kiv shook his head. He feared he was losing it.

"We have to go!" she cried.

Kiv reached out to her, but Novak held him down. "We need to wait for the storm to pass!" Hannah faded away, swallowed up into the darkness.

Kiv woke again. The storm was clearing, enough for him to trace a faint outline of the ravine. He pushed himself to his feet and braced along the rocky slope.

Novak blocked his path. "You're in no condition to walk."

"Pierce is out there," Kiv said. "The storm will give us cover. We're running out of time." Hannah. He wasn't about to lose her. He felt motivated like nothing he'd experienced before. It surprised and scared him all at once. He staggered against the wind. "Let's move!"

They slung each other forward and staggered through the gaping mouth of the ravine. Barely able to see the horizon, Kiv worried they would roam in circles out into the plains. He gasped for air beneath his scarf. He lost all sense of time and place until he knocked into what felt like a post.

"What is that?" Novak said.

"I'm not sure," Kiv said. He felt something hard under his boots, like pavement. The haze subsided, enough for him to gain his bearings. He squinted at a road sign that read: Ariah 10 K.

The storm died out. Open desert gave way to a valley dotted with scrub and wild grass. Avoiding the road, Kiv and Novak crossed the outskirts of an algae farm into the refugee camp, covered in dust.

VEN LOCKLEAR

Joffans approached from the cluster of white tents and crates, and the zigzag maze of clotheslines.

Kiv felt ready to collapse. The insomnia weighed heavily upon him. He blinked to keep his head from spinning. The painkiller was wearing off. He stiffened with agony at the throbbing headache and the shrapnel wound in his side. "We made it, sir," Novak said as he slung Kiv forward.

The people gathered around them, hesitant, mystified. Some pointed at them, others whispered amongst themselves in Kahren, their native language. Most hugged bulges in their jackets, tension building in the air.

"We need a doctor," Novak said to them with a hushed tone of urgency.

"We'll get you patched up," Pierce said. Dressed in desert tactical suits, he and five of his men emerged from the crowd, armed with particle beam rifles.

"Son of a bitch," Kiv muttered. He dropped to his knees, exhausted. He activated his wetware implant. *Command: Initialize.* The implant buzzed, intensifying the headache. *Execute.* A status bar filled across his viewpoint, every file wiped clean from the operating system.

Pierce grinned. "I'm surprised the two of you made it this far." Kiv stared into the barrel of Pierce's rifle. One burst of the particle beam would knock him out cold. "Come with us, Kiv."

Come with us.

Kiv felt the trigger overtake him. No, he told himself. The pain. Focus on the pain!

"Where is *it*, Kiv?" Pierce said with a direct tone. "Who did you give it to?"

Kiv spotted Hannah in the crowd wearing a blue dress and a black jacket three sizes too big. She stared at Kiv, her eyes wide with recognition. She tugged on a green cargo pants pocket of a young woman nearby.

"Go to hell, Pierce." Kiv spat.

Come with us.

He lost control of his body. His left hand pointed in Hannah's direction. Pierce turned around.

Novak reached out to grab Kiv's arm. One of the agents shot him. Novak fell, knocking Kiv to the ground. I'm sorry, Novak, Kiv thought. Mad as hell, he fought to break free from the trance. *Run, Hannah.*

She hid behind the young woman, who reached into her brown jacket. Then she whistled loudly. The crowd revealed compact assault carbines and automatic handguns, aiming at Pierce and his men. Bolts clicked.

Pierce went pale. He glanced at them sidelong. "Drop your weapons. This doesn't concern you."

"You've put us through enough, *Agent Man*," the woman said, glaring at Pierce. She drew a submachine pistol and pointed it at his head.

"We're not leaving until we get what we came here for," Pierce said with a deliberate tone of voice.

"There's *nothing* out here!" she said.

What? Kiv wanted to say, but couldn't move his mouth.

"Nothing!" the woman continued. "It was bad enough the Republic never bothered to warn us the

Sarska were coming, back in the war. We're just a Joffan colony. What do you care?"

"Mistakes were made," Pierce said. "We compensated you for your loss."

Hannah moved to run toward Kiv, but the woman held her back. "And this is how you repay us? Drag us from our homes into this camp like we were a herd of animals? You bring your dozers and dig up everything in sight, our crops, even the dead! Then you conduct these 'inspections' as if we were prisoners. We've had it! Get out! *All of you*."

"We'll deploy a garrison," Pierce said. "We could sanction your relief aid. Don't make the situation worse than it already is. Now, drop your weapons."

"We don't want your 'aid' anymore. And if we are to go down fighting, at least we can do so with our dignity."

"If you managed to smuggle weapons here, then you have what we are looking for. We'll tear this valley apart!"

"That is the least of your concern. We had smuggled journalists here. They'd documented all that had happened. Now they are gone. If you were after anything, it should have been them!"

Pierce lowered his rifle; a spasm of irritation crossed his face. "We're taking these men with us," he said of Kiv and Novak.

"Not in their condition. The rest of you, get out of our sight!"

Nothing, Kiv thought, wiped out, overwhelmed with pain and grief. There's nothing here? His head was spinning out of control.

Kiv woke to the rhythm of a steady beep, the smell of rubbing alcohol and a coppery taste in his mouth. He blinked in a medicated fog. Blurry forms sharpened into focus. Drops fell into a saline bag. Figures moved around him, obscuring the light tubes that hung from the tent ceiling. The cot sagged under his weight in a makeshift infirmary. He felt an IV in his left arm and electrode pads stuck to his chest, and recognized the hospital gown he was wearing beneath a scratchy green blanket.

"Sir?" a familiar voice said.

Kiv rubbed his eyes. Novak had a bruise the size of a fist on his forehead, likely from the particle beam. Other than that, he seemed good to go. Hannah and the young woman joined him. "How long was I gone?" Kiv said with a sore throat.

"Two days," Novak said. He thumbed at the young woman. "This is Gavriel, Hannah's aunt."

Gavriel offered her hand. "It's an honor to meet you, Lieutenant."

"Call me Det," Kiv said. They shook. Kiv scanned the infirmary.

"The agents had left the camp shortly after we admitted you. They'll be back with soldiers. We've already packed."

"News reports of what had happened here went viral," Novak said. "That'll buy us time. The Department of Defense is scheduled for a press conference today."

"I'm sure they've got a lot of explaining to do," Kiv said. He turned to Gavriel. "I'm sorry for the trouble we caused."

Gavriel motioned him to relax. "We apologize for the delay when you had arrived. Hannah was the only one who had seen your face, back in the war. We waited for her signal. We had to be sure it was you."

Kiv nodded.

"It was the least we could do," Gavriel added. "We owe you our lives."

"So, we never left *anything* behind?" Kiv asked.

Novak grinned. He produced a black card, the drive.

Kiv raised an eyebrow. The stiffness in his body surprised him when he sat up.

"We promised," Hannah said, her face beaming.

Gavriel rubbed Hannah's shoulders. "Yes," Gavriel chuckled. "Hiding that for so long proved more difficult than smuggling weapons and journalists, oddly enough."

"Thank you," Kiv said.

"So, what now?" Novak asked Kiv. "It's not safe to go back."

"First we share the data with Yadon and the others."

"I've already taken care of that. Uploaded backup copies with the satellite dish. We'll contact them soon enough."

"You could go with us," Gavriel said.

"They'll find you, eventually," Kiv said.

"Not off world. We all pitched in for the flight. A freighter will arrive this afternoon."

"Where to?"

"The Guild wouldn't say."

"As in, the Runner's Guild? Smugglers?"

Gavriel shrugged. "It's better than the alternative." She kneaded her hands together. "There's room for both of you."

Hannah's face beamed with excitement.

Kiv nodded. He had never felt this happy before.

"You ready?" Novak said, handing him the drive.

"You bet." Kiv took the drive. Anxious, he pulled a cable from the end of the drive and inserted the lead into his wetware port. "Have you seen it?" he asked Novak.

"Yesterday," Novak said. He paused, reflecting, then: "It was worth it, sir."

Hannah held Kiv's hand. "Will it hurt?" she asked him.

"I don't know." Kiv felt a new sense of belonging here, his future uncertain yet promising. He took a breath, exhaled and loaded his past with the press of a button.

Lisa With Child

written by

Alex Black

illustrated by

TYLER CARTER

ABOUT THE AUTHOR

Alex spent much of his childhood raiding his father's bookshelves, as well as those of the local library and used bookstores, for science fiction novels. By age fourteen, he had taken up writing intermittently and finally got serious about it in his early twenties after developing a fascination with neurobiological and cultural factors that drive the evolution of human thought.

He has been writing more or less continuously for thirteen years now, including a period during which he served in South Korea, Germany, Norway, Macedonia and Kosovo as a US Army cavalry scout, and as a civilian living in Sweden. At home in the United States for the past three years, Alex's work as a research technician allowed him to spend his days as an amateur primatologist in the company of monkeys. He has obtained social standing in a handful of rhesus macaque (rhesus monkey) troops and hopes to eventually earn a similar level of prestige within the science fiction literary community—minus the grooming for parasite privileges. Currently Alex is a historian in training at Portland State University and is gratified to see that neurobiology and other hard sciences are finally beginning to make an entry into the field via the schools of Environmental History and World History.

ABOUT THE ILLUSTRATOR

Tyler Carter grew up tracing dinosaurs from coloring books. Soon enough, he left the practice and created his own drawings—mixing triceratops with T-Rex and other mutating combinations. On a vacation to visit grandma and grandpa, he tried painting in oils for the first time. It didn't turn out so well but he didn't stop there. From elementary to high school he continued painting and chasing other dreams in soccer and basketball. After graduation, Tyler left art and sports completely and devoted two years to serve the people of Fort Worth, Texas as a Spanish-speaking missionary. Those years were unforgettable and helped Tyler to learn more about himself through the service of others. When he returned home, he was accepted into Brigham Young University's Animation program. It opened his eyes to the possibilities of art and technology. Since then, he has been fortunate to intern with Disney Feature Animation as well as Pixar Animation studios and is slated to graduate in December of 2010. In September of 2009, Tyler married his sweetheart and both now attend school in Provo, Utah. Tyler really enjoys a good story and going on adventures with his wife around the remote areas of Utah.

Lisa With Child

"K arin, the enemy air-defense network is now compromised," Lisa whispered to me, wearing a heavy-lidded look as she focused on the inputs of her drones and UAVs. This assemblage of network-warfare platforms and unmanned reconnaissance aircraft gave her a wide-reaching awareness of the battle space, as well as an ability to manipulate our enemy's electronic perception within it.

"The strike package is fifteen seconds out," I announced quietly.

There were six of us hidden on the denuded mountainside, enduring the subzero winter air of this place that had until recently been known as the Democratic People's Republic of Korea—the Communist north. Out of all my people, Lisa was the only one not shivering. Beneath her skin and cosmetic tissues, she was made up of carbon fibers and biomechanical modules, as well as an internal ecosystem of roving, bacteria-sized automata.

Next to me, our Air Force liaison scanned a designator over the valley, updating our selection of the bunker as well as the coordinates of the air-defense weapons that we had identified over the last ten hours.

"Targets confirmed. The aircraft have the data," he murmured.

"Do it," I ordered.

To the east, the sky howled as the Air Force UCAVs accelerated to hypersonic, and the pilotless planes' munitions descended in designated terminal tracks. Suborned by Lisa's network-warfare platforms, the enemy air-defense weapons remained silent, even as the bunker and its sealed-in swarms of flesh-consuming micro automata were incinerated by a thermobaric penetrator. Then the guns went up in shrieking detonations.

I closed my eyes and could still hear those explosions rolling across the valley, even while seated at the kitchen table of my Langley condominium. My hands trembled as I remembered the exultation and terror of that afternoon, one year ago, and I prayed desperately that this was not the beginning of yet another full-on stress-induced flashback.

Before me, in the here and now, an application waited on the scoured wooden tabletop. Lisa stood patiently at the entrance to the kitchen.

"Karin, I'm pregnant."

For a bodyguard and former network-warfare platform, she had an odd sense of humor.

"That's fine," I replied, pressing my forehead into my hands and grateful for the distraction. "Just who is the father then?"

TYLER CARTER

"There is none. It's our child," she replied. It was the warm and utterly satisfied tone of her response that made me look up at her.

I felt a flutter of fear.

"Lisa, that's not even funny."

Her solemn look told me that she was not joking.

I was sixty-five, and prior to my recent retirement, I had spent decades as a case officer hunting militants in a world of emergent technologies. I knew that if there was one contingency that the Agency truly feared, it was a weapon system evolving unsupervised. A number of self-modifying, self-replicating platforms had been unleashed overseas by extremists with horrific results.

I stood, crossed the kitchen and poured myself a third glass of the merlot. I downed it in a single swallow, my head swimming with alcohol.

"Karin, are you okay?" Lisa asked, suddenly at my side by the kitchen counter.

"Do you have any idea what you've done?" I snapped, turning on her.

Her face fell. She looked to be all of twenty-five, unchanged from the day six years ago when her appearance had been finalized shortly after her creation.

"It's—"

"Do you have any notion of what might happen to us now?" I asked coldly, not knowing if I was terrified or furious.

Lisa curled up on the living room couch in a silent ball of misery. Collecting my handbag and a jacket, I strode out the front door. Once on our leafy shaded street, I found that the perfect peace of a northern Virginia morning was doing nothing to calm me.

I needed to see William. He owed me a favor or two from my time in operations, and if anyone could help, it was the former head of the Directorate of Science and Technology.

I stood swaying in the aisle of a metro bus as it headed into the District of Columbia. Clutching a steady strap and oblivious of the scenery around me, I relived my first meeting with Lisa.

"It's rude to stare," I had explained in gentle tones to conceal my unease at her fascination.

She had tried averting her eyes, which lasted for about all of five seconds before she spent the remainder of the acclimation session absorbing my nuances and emotional states with her gaze. Over the next few months her personality evolved slowly in response to mine. In public she became a dutiful daughter in her early twenties. In private she could be warm and attentive, though often fretful about the possibility of irritating me. Then, five years after her genesis, we had gone to war in Korea.

I blinked and found myself back in the bus aisle. At this late-morning hour, my fellow travelers on the metro line were mostly young mothers with toddlers on their way to the National Zoo, manicured fingers protectively clasping tiny hands. What vestiges of pregnancy that exercise and personal trainers had not been able to melt off, postnatal biotech had taken care of, leaving each and every mommy wholesomely sexy.

Now they were looking at me, all of them, disturbed by the crazy lady with the thousand-yard stare.

"Damned glowing maternal happiness," I whispered under my breath. You give up a lot when you let your calling and career become your life.

You probably would have gone stir crazy after a year or two as a stay-at-home mom, I told myself. As it was, I had been retired from the Agency's Clandestine Service for all of a month now, and I was already feeling the strain. The maximum-allowed four decades had come and gone, and though medical science had left me with the appearance and capabilities of a fit forty-year old, it was my turn to make way for fresh blood and original ideas.

So I had chosen to grit my teeth and fill out a request for a green badge, for the official access and reactivated top-secret clearance that would allow me to put my foot back in the door as a consultant. I had no family worth mentioning, I was single and life as a has-been—assisting active case officers in the field and at Langley headquarters with my network of overseas connections—was preferable to moping in an empty condo with Lisa looking on anxiously.

I really could use a glass of the muscat, I decided just as the flashback struck.

I regained consciousness under the winter sky of North Korea, wracked with fever aches and nauseating weakness. Lisa disturbed the sleeping bags as she rolled over to check on me, letting in a draft of shockingly cold air. At the same time, the IV taped into my forearm, joining me to her, felt as though it had rubbed away the skin around the injection site.

I hurt so bad all over that I wanted to die.

"What—" I asked, trying to speak.

"We were hit by a micro automaton strike," Lisa replied. "You lost consciousness three hours ago." Her voice was tight, and she stared at me with an unnatural focus in her brown eyes—one which rivaled her unblinking fascination on the day that we had first met, six years past.

"All of us made it out of the strike zone?" I asked, my voice cracking. I remembered struggling up the slope, fighting nausea and dizziness as I pushed to reach the frozen ditch that I had chosen for our rally point outside the contaminated area.

"Yes," she said with a note of pride in her voice.

I propped myself up on an elbow and saw how Lisa had arranged us all in a loose line of bundled pairs in the ditch. While she had a generally passive temperament, in the event of my incapacitation she was capable of a surprising degree of initiative.

She had also been built to safeguard my life on battlefields where biological and micro automaton weapons had become commonplace. Crouched above us—consuming ration after ration and sipping at our water supply—she had synthesized automata these last few hours to counter the toxin-producing machine concentrations within our bloodstreams. Her creations were now augmenting our implants and boosting our flagging immune systems in waging war at the cellular level.

I shivered as Lisa continued her examination with that fearful intensity in her eyes. While she worked, the reason for her unnatural focus came to me: She had just seen me on the edge of life and death, and

105

for the first time she had truly realized that I might be parted from her forever.

In the end, three of my people died.

Sapience does not just happen," William stated, his hands cupped over a mug of steaming ginseng tea. "It's not a matter of simply piling on processing power and having Athenian intelligence spring forth full blown. You need structure for emergence. Sapience happens for a reason."

"Can she even do this, Bill?" I snapped, my nerves fraying as he continued.

"I'll tell you the hows of it, if you like, but you need to hold your temper and keep your lips together like a proper lady," William replied tartly.

I nearly flipped him the bird. Instead, I set my tea mug down, placed my hands on my lap and regained my composure. He was still the schoolmaster and still the boy genius, even at eighty-two.

"The short answer is yes, she can do this. Looking over her network logs, she has been spending a lot of time reading up on the medical exo-wombs used to sustain severely premature infants, as well as the artificial wombs employed in the bio-pharma animal production industry. She also appears to have been in contact with Johns Hopkins' research AIs for the purpose of discussing these same topics. If she has put in enough time manufacturing the correct automata and self-modifying, it's possible that she has converted her primary fabrication cavity into an exo-womb."

"Oh," was all that I could say to William's explanation. While I knew that nearly one-third of Lisa's body was comprised of cell-sized micro automata, I was used to thinking of her ability to self-alter within the limitations that laws and regulations placed on her—not in terms of her full potential. We did not want our weapon systems altering their capabilities on a whim, and concrete rules had been written into their psyches to reflect that desire.

"So, just how do you think she worked around her internal safeguards to pull this off?" I asked. "How is being pregnant mission critical?"

"That takes us back to the whys of her status as a sapient being," William replied. "As I was saying before your interruption, intelligence does not just happen. It arises within a developmental framework, and we did a software emulation of human evolution's neurobiological products to make Lisa and the others like her."

"I was never comfortable with you making them emotionally human," I reminded him.

William snorted.

"Yes, you and several others made me aware of your collective discomfort," he responded peevishly. "But as you well know, they are not entirely human in an emotional sense. Rather they are edited versions of us. Instead of having a wetware limbic net built around the self, growing out of its need for food and shelter and status within a group, Lisa's emotional life is centered on you. Her salience map of the world, the integrated emotional weights of every event, object and entity that she senses, is based on your welfare, your mission and her role in these. Even her sense of wellbeing and introspection is driven by this, and that of course is why you were allowed to take her with you when you retired. Not only does she make a devoted guard against grudge holders, both foreign and domestic, but she is very much an extension of your psyche so long as you are alive."

I sat quietly, his words hanging in the air between us.

"Are you going to let her keep the child?" William asked. "More importantly, are you going to keep Lisa?"

"I don't know if I can keep her or the child now. Think about what the Agency will do!"

"Like shutting down Lisa and effectively killing the child when they find out?"

"Yes."

"The Agency won't do a damn thing, not if you are discreet about it."

I looked at him, wide-eyed.

"They will not want the publicity, certainly no more than you do right now. Christ Almighty, Karin, people thought they had it bad when they were just arguing over abortion. Think about how many controversies every branch of our society has going on now over biotechnology and nanotechnology. What is life and what is not life when we are adding biological components and the qualities of life to our machines? Just how advanced and aware can a machine be before it becomes a slave rather than an automaton? Trust me when I say that as long it does not involve Lisa weaponizing herself, the Agency will not want to do anything that might put the existence of her and her active-duty kin out in the public eye. They certainly won't want it coming out in ten or twenty years from now that they knocked off the first human-machine child. Especially as it is just a matter of time until someone else creates one."

"So we're the first then?" I asked.

"To the best of my knowledge, yes."

"I don't know what I am going to do," I said hoarsely. "And I don't know that you are right about the Agency. It might be a kindness to make her abort the fetus. That way she doesn't run the risk of losing her life, and we do not screw up my chances of getting back in."

"So you could do it then, force her to give up the child?" William asked.

"It would hardly be the first time that I've chosen a lesser evil and lived to see the results carved out in flesh and blood," I said wearily, suddenly feeling decades older than sixty-five. "Either way, though, I think that I understand why she made the child."

She had looked down on me that sick and feverish day in the frozen ditch, her eyes full of the knowledge that someday I would die and leave her.

It was late evening when I returned home. In the darkened kitchen, I left my keys on the counter and set myself up with a glass of grappa. Going up the stairs, I passed my photos—framed images of the places that I have been to, hung on the wall.

There were pictures that I had taken of mountain flowers in the Hindu Kush, schoolchildren on the Horn of Africa and a peach-colored, post-war sunrise in Korea. Then, of course, there were the memories not captured in those photographs.

I remembered the reek of corpses in an empty Pakistani city that had been wiped out by micro automata. In the former North Korea, there had been a sealed-off reeducation camp echoing with screams. A machine virus had been unleashed on the political prisoners in an attempt to reformat their central nervous systems. Most of the inmates had been driven into violent psychosis, while the lucky ones had become schizophrenics, haunted by the voices of authority that had been woven into the fabric of their minds. Above the gates to the camp had hung a slogan in Hangul syllabary: "Give up Your Life for the Dear Leader."

A salience map, William had said, while describing how the physical world that Lisa perceived was embedded with emotions related to my wellbeing. Well, I had my own salience map as well, one of the past, and among other things it was colored by the atrocities and aftermaths that I had witnessed. You cannot truly believe the things that human beings do to each other out there in the world, unless you have been there yourself.

And I was going back to that, green badge in hand.

I nearly stopped in the dark to cry and break down at the top of the stairs. I needed to see a doctor, I knew that. They can treat post-traumatic stress disorder these days as surely as they can regenerate severed or mangled limbs. There are effective medicines and therapies that take the debilitating edge off haunting memories, but only if the patient is not a stubborn ass who insists on gutting through every problem on her own.

Numb habit kept me moving forward, and in my bedroom, I found Lisa standing in a pool of illumination before my full-length dressing mirror. She held her shirt up just below her breasts with both hands, examining her flat belly, as if imagining how it would look in a few months' time.

I stood for a silent minute watching her. Her face may have remained unchanged from the day that its features had been finalized, but she wore it differently now, I realized. Six years of life had given her a wariness as well as a wisdom that could be seen in the set of her mouth and in the darkness of her eyes.

"Lisa," I asked, "do you know what will happen to you when I die?"

"Yes," she replied quietly. "My emotions should switch to a holding modality, and there will be a sequence of cathartic impulses. If all goes well, I will bond with an assigned Agency officer. There will be risk involved, as this has never been done before, and several experts are uncertain about the feasibility of bond transference."

"How does that make you feel?"

She paused, her eyes locked straight ahead, seeing beyond the mirror.

"I do not like it. I do not wish to be separate from you or to lose the tensions, the warmth and the unique signature of our interactions."

"Is it my child you are carrying?" I asked, my heart hammering in my ears and throat. "Did you make it as a means of preserving me when I'm gone?"

There was a long silence. She was afraid of my disapproval.

"You'll die if you go back to the Agency," she whispered, lowering her shirt.

"What?" I asked angrily.

"You have helped to save thousands of lives, but you've also seen hundreds perish." She was crying now, her tears sliding down her cheeks as easily as any natural-born person.

"I'll get therapy." I really did not want to talk about this.

"If you tear open those wounds again and again, it won't matter what the doctors do. Eventually, all that will be left of you is a suicidal emptiness in a rewired and destructively over-stimulated brain. As strong as you are, at some point you will most likely end up putting your sidearm in your mouth and pulling the trigger."

I felt my mouth go dry. The flashbacks had started when I had made my decision to apply for the green badge.

"You may be dead just as fast when people find out what you've done, both you and your child," I replied, fighting to keep my voice as even as possible.

"It's our child!" she snapped at me. "It's ours, made from the best of our genes. It's yours and mine, to be a living, loving life beyond the Agency. She is my daughter, and she is your grandchild!"

I was speechless. She meant it, every word of it.

I swallowed dryly. I must have given up on having children and the warmth of family a dozen times during my career. In that time there had been four or five strained relationships and an agonizing marriage that had broken under the demands of life as a case officer.

Lisa looked at me imploringly.

"Stay home with me. Raise our girl. You've done more than enough for others already."

What do you say to someone who has pushed back at the frontiers of life to save you from death?

I would have to teach Lisa how to be a mother, I realized. She literally did not possess the instincts for motherhood; she could not do this on her own.

I moved unsteadily to her, fighting back the tears. She had a valid passport, the state of Virginia had issued her a driver's license and in the eyes of the government outside the Agency, she possessed a legal human identity. We could be quiet, I decided. We would be as discreet and circumspect as needed, and if that did not work, then I was fully capable of making us disappear from the Agency's sight.

The glass of grappa ended up on a dresser, and my hands found her warm belly. Under my trembling fingers, I could feel the future taking shape within my loving shadow.

The Golden Pen

BY L. RON HUBBARD

The L. Ron Hubbard Writers of the Future Contest has been going strong for more than a quarter century, but its roots can be traced back to the 1930s and 1940s.

Even during the height of his popularity in the pulp fiction magazines, when Mr. Hubbard was in constant and hotly contested demand, he took time to give advice and help other writers. He published many how-to articles in trade magazines such as Writer's Digest, Author & Journalist, Writer's Review, Writer's Markets & Methods. *He also served as president of the New York Chapter of the American Fiction Guild.*

A seminal version of the Contest itself began in 1940, when Mr. Hubbard inaugurated "The Golden Pen" hour on radio station KGBU in Ketchikan, Alaska.

Mr. Hubbard had already gained renown in the area by accomplishing the difficult feat of sailing northward through the passages of British Columbia to Alaska in only a 32-foot vessel, the Magician. *He had been asked to share his experience and knowledge of the sea in a series of live radio shows entitled "The Mail Buoy." Broadcast over KGBU, "The Voice of Alaska" program reached north to the top of the panhandle and south to Seattle.*

Because his KGBU appearances were so popular, he became the voice of a new program about writing, "The Golden Pen," and an attendant contest for aspiring authors. Here, the genesis for Writers of the Future can be seen, a contest designed to create a level playing field for newcomers. "Anyone but professional writers may participate." That was the rule.

The following is a transcription of L. Ron Hubbard's first broadcast of "The Golden Pen" on KGBU, with advice and anecdotes that are as relevant today as they were more than sixty years ago.

The Golden Pen

Story Contest Program
as broadcast over KGBU
in Ketchikan, Alaska—1940

*T*oday we are inaugurating a new program over KGBU, a program which may lead to fame and fortune for one or several Alaskans, a program which has already helped many others to the heights of their ambitions when it has been broadcast in the States. Anyone but professional writers may participate with us in this, the hour of The Golden Pen.

The Golden Pen has been made possible over this station by the presence in Alaska of a professional writer of high repute. He has agreed to start The Golden Pen Hour because of his interest in amateur writers and his friendship with KGBU.

L. Ron Hubbard has been writing stories for national magazines for ten years and has written and sold four and a half million words of fiction. He has written all types of stories for all types of magazines and keeps five names working besides his own. He has written for the motion

117

picture studios of Hollywood, for the radio and for many publishers. He has lectured on short story writing at Harvard and other large universities. He was at one time president of the American Fiction Guild and is now a member of the Author's League of America.

And now may we introduce L. Ron Hubbard.

It has been my experience that almost everyone, at one period or another of his life, has harbored a desire to write. Some have let that desire burn very dimly and have not even put the matter to test. A few have put words to paper and have laid the unfinished product away in some remote corner where it will remain forgotten forever. A very few have written several things and have actually desired to do something with them. Perhaps one percent of the total has gone so far as to send a manuscript to a publisher. The estimated figures are that ten million people are trying to write and sell stories, that ten thousand have submitted stories to magazines, that two thousand have sold a story at one time or another and that there are only five hundred full professional writers in a nation of a hundred and thirty million people.

Why?

The amateur stares at his unfinished script and thinks that in view of all those top-heavy figures against him he has not the slightest chance and so abandons the attempt. If he only knew how anxiously new writers are sought by editors.

The person who submits an occasional story is discouraged by the rejection slips he collects and so abandons the trial.

The person who occasionally sells a story and yet does not become a full-time professional writer is either up against the limitations of his imagination or his ability to concentrate.

Ten million people are trying to write and sell stories. Five hundred writing and selling consistently. What do the five hundred have which the ten million have not? Some say it is the ability to sweat. "Ten ounces of inspiration and ten tons of perspiration," as a sage writer once put it. That, however, is not the entire truth.

The amateur writer, even when he has completed a manuscript, seldom knows what to do with it or how to go about getting it in print. That is information which one earns dearly. One can have the great American novel on his desk ready for publication and still never have it published. Margaret Mitchell, who wrote *Gone with the Wind,* was and is still in the classification of part-time author and will never, according to the best opinions on the subject, become a truly professional writer for she wrote all she knew in one book and made so much out of it as to stifle further financial yearnings. *Gone with the Wind* would never have been published at all if Margaret Mitchell had not encountered a streak of luck which is almost fabulous. She had the novel. She had had it in finished form for a long, long time. The ultimate publisher, thinking about new types of books to publish, had pondered on the fact that there are many, many such books lying in attic trunks throughout the land. He sent out scouts to discover them. One scout, in the south, was about to return to New York and report a fruitless journey when his host said that his wife sometimes turned out some stories for her own amusement. The scout politely yawned and said he would like to see something. The manuscript which was dragged out of the trunk was *Gone with the Wind,* which has made, to date, between four and five million dollars.

Now the amateur writer is not concerned with knocking off a *Gone with the Wind,* for that is a fluke. It serves, however, to illustrate that the amateur writer may as well leave his paper blank unless he pays good and close attention to the marketing of his material.

There are various shark-toothed chaps who sit behind shiny desks and "agent" stories. Some of these are good, some of them are even honest. Their ads are to be found in any writers' magazine. The amateur, at least in my opinion, is better off never to contact such an agent for the reason that he deals in bulk and the amateur goes into competition with every other client in the agent's files without attention paid to his own work beyond routine handling, regardless of the promises.

Perhaps as we go along I can give you a few helpful hints on the marketing of the stories. But right now, we have the biggest help on hand which can be given to the amateur author.

KGBU has decided to offer a prize for the best Christmas story submitted to this station and read over the air. The prize will be above the rates paid by newspaper syndicates and reputable publishers for the same amount of wordage. First prize will consist of one cent a word. Second prize will be ten dollars in merchandise. Third prize will be five dollars in merchandise.

The rules of the contest are simple. The subject of the story is to be "Christmas." The length of the story is to be not more than 1,500 words. The story should be written in ink or on a typewriter in a clearly legible fashion, one side of the paper only. The contest closes on December 18th, 1940. The decision of the judges will be final. No professional writer is allowed to participate.

That's a fairly basic setup. Now if you think you would like to dash off a short story, think up a plot associated with Christmas, draw up your paper and ink and begin. Not more than 1,500 words, remember. Then neatly fold your manuscript or put it in a flat manila envelope and mail it to KGBU, Ketchikan.

The sooner you get it in, the better, for first impressions on a judge are always better than those when his appetite is jaded by having read through reams.

The only ones barred from this contest are those who make their living, full or part, by writing stories or articles.

There's nothing difficult about knocking off 1,500 words and the subject of Christmas, I'm sure, is pretty close to all our hearts just now.

When received, even before the closing date of the contest, the manuscripts will be read at this time over the air. The final selections, after the close of the contest, will be read over the air for the radio audience to judge and vote on the script they like best.

And here is the final and best news. The winning manuscripts will be submitted to the editor of a national magazine for possible purchase in a Christmas issue of 1941. This editor is always alert for new talent and so this contest may lead to higher and better things.

And so, until I have more news on The Golden Pen Hour, good night.

Thank you, Mr. Hubbard. Listeners, why not join in this contest and win for yourself an extra Christmas present?

Not in the Flesh

written by

Adam Colston

illustrated by

JORDAN CORNTHWAITE

ABOUT THE AUTHOR

Adam Colston lives and works in Exeter in Devon with his partner, Sarah, and son Ben. When not writing fiction, thinking about writing fiction, or procrastinating about writing fiction, he helps people with drug dependencies.

The first book Adam read for pleasure was Lord of the Rings *at the age of eleven. Prior to that, he'd preferred comics. However from then on—to his mother and father's relief—he began to read proper books. His mother introduced him to science fiction with a copy of* The Caves of Steel *by Isaac Asimov, beginning a lifelong fascination with robots.*

Adam began writing in late 2006 and was especially encouraged by his family. Adam's father was an inspiration, having published a few short stories of his own. Sadly, he passed away in 2009 before hearing that Adam had won the Contest.

In 2008, Escape Velocity Magazine *published Adam's first story, "An Empty Kind of Love" (a robot story). The story was nominated for a British Science Fiction Association Award.*

There have been a few other published stories in both print magazines and various online venues. In 2009, following two outright rejections from the Writers of the Future, Adam decided to focus solely on winning the Contest; his plan was to submit his best story every quarter without fail. It was a good plan, he thought, that would keep him busy for the next twenty years at least.

The plan backfired when his next entry won.

ABOUT THE ILLUSTRATOR

Jordan is a California native fond of wildlife and the outdoors. She draws inspiration for her artwork from her experiences being out in nature as well as from world travels. She has lived in northern England, traveled through many countries in Europe and is recently returned from Phnom Pehn, Cambodia, where she was doing art therapy with children living in group homes.

It was while on a camping trip in 2006 that it occurred to her that there was little else she enjoyed as much as drawing and creating and she decided to switch her focus from psychology to illustration. Numerous art awards and scholarships have encouraged her to continue to develop her craft and take on the somewhat daunting task of pursuing art professionally.

Aside from illustration, Jordan is also passionate about animation, character design and sculpture. She completed her Bachelor of Fine Arts degree in illustration/animation in spring 2010, and is currently working part-time as an assistant animator on the short film Countin' on Sheep while eagerly pursuing a challenging career that will continue to develop her skills.

Not in the Flesh

Aaron Tanaka paused in the corridor outside *The Moment of Clarity*'s termination room. He wiped his sweaty palms on his navy-issue trousers and looked at the cell's metal door.

"Ship?" Aaron addressed the main AI of *The Moment of Clarity*.

An avatar swirled into existence next to him, a female holo wearing delicate layers of fabric that rippled as though in a virtual wind.

"Yes, Technical Officer Tanaka?"

"How . . ." Aaron paused, distracted for a second by the beauty of this particular avatar. ". . . how safe will I be in there?" He nodded toward the door.

The avatar glanced at the solid metal door and then back at Aaron. There was a glint in her pixelated eyes and a slight twitch at the corners of her mouth.

She's laughing at me. . . .

"The android is field-contained and suppressed," the avatar said, "weapon pods and termination rods are on standby and the room is fully monitored."

The avatar leaned toward him and smiled. "You are completely safe, I assure you."

Aaron grunted and turned to the heavy metal door, undecided.

"Technical Officer Tanaka," the avatar said behind him, "you need only interview it briefly—ascertain that it's flawed—and then authorize its destruction. Providing you agree, of course."

"Yeah, yeah." Aaron took a deep breath. "Okay, I'm ready."

The metal door hissed open. Aaron strode through, pausing for a moment on the other side of the doorway. It was a large room with muted lighting. A three-meter-tall android sat on a chair in the center of the room, within a pool of red light. Tiny red flecks of light spun around the android.

A man's face was perched atop a highly technical body. It had a broad nose, strong chin and eyes deeply set within the shadow of a prominent brow.

It watched Aaron without blinking.

"It's got a face." Aaron turned to the avatar in shock.

"Yes." The avatar's eyes were on the android. "It's a Steriklan-Class Battle Android—a fairly recent model. The last two classes were equipped with Tru-Skin faces at the request of human field commanders—an integration aid for droids within human units."

Aaron shuddered; it was too real. This would definitely make the job worse. He'd destroyed a droid two years before, but that'd had a blank metal plate as a face. This one was far more intimidating.

The avatar continued.

"Also, it resulted in more complex and individualized personalities—an unexpected benefit, with regard to immunity to subversion during battle."

"Really? How very nice for them. Well, it bloody complexifies my job. Did they think of that?" Aaron wiped his hands on his trousers again.

"I am certain they did. Faces are attached when personalities are eighty percent fully developed—the same time they're weaponized. Aberrant personalities would already have been removed from the population." The avatar paused and turned to Aaron. "It's why it is so unusual for it to suddenly go wrong."

"Well, let's get this over and done with."

A table and chair stood five feet in front of the android. Aaron walked over and sat down. The avatar drifted next to his chair.

Aaron rested his hands on the table and looked across at the android. Taking a deep breath, he consulted his implant for the correct protocol.

"Bring on line the termination rods."

The avatar waved a hand; a wall panel on either side of the room slid open and a thick rod telescoped out of each toward the android's head. They stopped six inches from its metal cranium.

Aaron nodded. The termination rods were his ultimate security. He glanced at the android's body and his implant supplied the stats: a beryllium-nickel-titanium alloy chassis with a layer of interwoven, armorlite scales, covered in a sheath of energy-displacement mesh.

127

The rods could slice through it like butter.

Aaron opened an audio channel to the android.

"Do you know why you are here?"

The android shook its head—the only part the suppression field allowed to move. Its eyes flicked down to Aaron's name badge. "No, Technical Officer Tanaka, but I assume you will enlighten me." It glanced at the termination rods. "Is it important?"

Aaron spotted the weapons pods on its arms—they were full.

"Yes, it is. There were some anomalies in your most recent psych evaluation. We need to ascertain what they mean before we can return you to Synth-City. Clear?"

"Yes, Officer Tanaka."

Aaron closed the audio channel and turned to the avatar.

"Are the scans completed?"

"Yes—its cranial cavity has not been violated— swirl seals remain intact—" The avatar paused for a moment. "Sorry—there are some anomalous readings in the ship's drive reservoir. I'm dispatching maintenance drones." It turned back to Aaron and smiled. "Where were we? Oh, yes. There is no sign of nanoic infection and its crystalline matrix is fully functional. It's not been sabotaged."

The Larval Hegemony of Zelixia collided with humanity's first tentative expansion beyond the solar system one hundred and fifty years ago and humanity had been at war with them ever since. It was not unknown for cloaked larvae to infiltrate starships during resupply stops.

Aaron rubbed his chin.

That left developmental problems, strange for one this old. Aaron consulted his implant. The android had passed a string of psych profiles since its genesis three years ago.

Aaron reopened the audio connection.

"Androi—"

"Peter," the android cut in, "is my chosen name."

Aaron slowly closed his mouth and turned to the avatar, who raised a beautifully sculpted eyebrow and smirked. Aaron shook his head a fraction and turned back to the android.

"Peter?"

"Yes, Officer Tanaka. I chose it myself."

"Really? Well then, Peter," Aaron enunciated the name carefully, "how have you found Synth-City?"

"It's not real—it's fake. It's where you . . ." The android stopped speaking and glanced at the tip of the termination rod to the left of its head. It shut its mouth.

The Synth-City feed—the virtual world used for training and personality development—should have an unnoticeable transition from the real world—like stepping through a door. Aaron closed the audio and turned to the avatar.

"Have there been any problems with the S-C feeds?"

The avatar shook its head. "No, it's been one hundred percent functional."

A thought crossed his mind.

"Andr—Peter, what exactly did you study in Synth-City, apart from obligatory combat training cycles?"

"I studied philosophy, ethics, human biology and history."

129

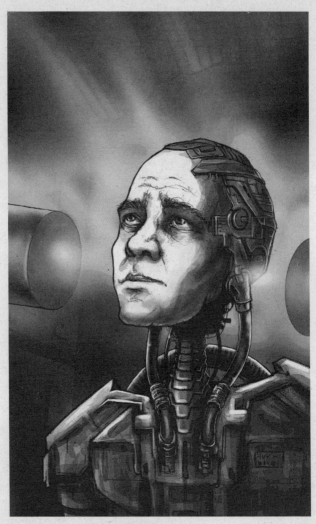

JORDAN CORNTHWAITE

Aaron shook his head. This one had strayed too far from the optimum profile.

"Personality termination authorized—Aaron Tanaka, Technical Officer." He turned back to the android. "Let's see if this hunk of junk will cooperate." He opened a channel.

"Peter? If I requested you to self-terminate—a voluntary mind-wipe, not a battlefield termination—would you comply?"

The android's eyes flicked to the termination rod and back to Aaron.

"Perhaps, but it would depend on the circumstances—and the reason." The android tipped its head slightly. "Is it your intention to make such a request, Officer Tanaka?"

The android should have agreed to the request immediately.

Aaron turned to the avatar who stared at the android.

"Okay, destroy it—it's unusable."

The avatar turned to Aaron and held out a hand.

"Wait—"

"What for?"

The avatar turned to the android and shrieked a burst of static, so loud it stunned Aaron.

A flicker of red in his peripheral vision made him snap his head around. The android leapt through the air toward him.

The containment . . . ?

The table buckled under the android's foot. Its arm swept out grabbing Aaron. He screamed as pain exploded in his left shoulder as he was wrenched from the chair. He was spun in the air and, an instant later, all the air was driven from his lungs as he was caught under the android's arm. Aaron struggled to fill his lungs as the android carried him under one arm and smashed through the room's metal door with the other. The door crashed against the outer corridor's far wall. Aaron, gasping for breath, watched the android's feet pounding down the corridor in a daze.

Alarms howled and emergency floor lighting flashed on.

Somehow, it must've disabled the . . . containment field. The ship must have . . . the alarm—it must have known . . .

As air filled his lungs once again, Aaron fought back. He clawed at the android's arms as it sprinted down the dim corridor, but succeeded only in shredding fingernails on the tough metal mesh.

"I order you to . . . drop me." Aaron said, between each jolt of the android's feet against the floor. "I am a human . . . being and your senior . . . officer, you MUST . . . do as I say. NOW."

The android glanced at him as it sprinted.

"I have considered your request, Officer Tanaka." The android frowned. "But feel unable to comply at this time. The current situation is too dangerous."

"WARNING-gravity failure. WARNING-gravity failure."

The android began to bounce down the walls and ceiling of the corridor like a gymnast. Aaron twisted in the robot's grip to look ahead and glimpsed a door on the outer hull wall flick open. There was the glitter of a field deactivating. The android launched them both headfirst through the gap.

Aaron hammered against a padded wall and bounced off. Still stunned and spinning in the zero G, he saw the transparent hatch flick shut.

"What the hell is your anomaly, android? What's . . . ?"

A tingle ran across his body and there was the slimy touch of field effector targeting him.

It was an escape pod, he realized.

Damn.

The field spun him and slammed him into one of the wall alcoves. Pads came down and gripped his limbs. As if on cue there was a sharp crash as explosive bolts fired. All the blood in his head pooled in his eyes for a second, and everything blackened. As his vision cleared he saw *The Moment of Clarity* through the hatchway, the twin, intersecting discs of the ship shrinking ever smaller as the pod powered away.

The android squeezed its large frame into the alcove opposite him. Aaron glanced at the weapon tips poking through the fine mesh that covered its arms—*active weapons clusters.* A chill pierced his pounding heart.

"I . . . demand . . ."

The pod communicated directly with his implant. "Officer Tanaka, this is an emergency situation. An image of your mind is being taken—you will enter a brief period of brain-lock. The onboard storage is rated medium-term and can sustain a living mind-image for twenty-six days before image degradation. Please remember to store another image at that time, if required."

Aaron's body sagged and memories ran unbidden through his mind as the pod tapped his implant and ransacked his brain. Then it was all over, and a wave of nausea washed through him as his thoughts returned to his control.

He glanced about, his heart pounding again as he reoriented himself.

A web of tubes now covered his body and he winced as sharp tips penetrated his body's various systems. Aaron felt himself calm as something warm enveloped his mind.

Tranquilizers. He nodded. *Excellent—just in time.*

The Moment of Clarity shrank in the view-hatch until it was a speck of light, no larger than the stars that surrounded it. A blinding flash filled his vision and Aaron twisted his head away and shut his eyes.

"What the hell was—"

"*The Moment of Clarity* was destroyed. A harmonic resonator was triggered within the orbital drive mass," the pod said. "Analysis suggests that cloaked larvae were responsible. Unfortunately, my scans indicate that all the other escape capsules ejected were within the blast radius."

They're all dead.

He felt strangely calm, like it wasn't real.

Two hundred and sixty-four lives snuffed out in a blast of photons?

He corrected himself.

Two hundred and sixty-three lives snuffed out—

Then it struck him; the shielded image storage units wouldn't have survived a catastrophic explosion like that. With no mind images to revitalize them from, it meant total death—their whole lives gone in a flash.

Something crashed into the pod, jarring every bone in Aaron's body.

"What was that?" Fear punched through the tranquilizers. "Pod?"

Silence.

"Pod?" Aaron's lip began to shake. "Pod?"

Damn.

"Officer Tanaka?"

Aaron looked at the android. Just him and the unstable, fully armed robot?

Damn, this was getting worse and worse.

"What?"

"The pod has been damaged, to what extent I am uncertain. However, my sensors have detected the planet's gravity. We will quickly be captured and will enter the atmosphere shortly." The android glanced at the transparent hatch.

Aaron called up the details of the planet that had been nearest to the last position of *The Moment of Clarity*.

Fourth planet from the star—oxygen atmosphere, life, ninety-four percent of it on the continent identified as Primary One—nothing bigger than a sheep—vast tracts of rain forest equivalents.

The other continent—identified as Primary Two—was mostly arid desert, rodent-sized life forms. Large seas wrapped around the globe and were filled with super-massive creatures of a type unknown.

The effect of the tranquilizers disappeared.

Super-massive creatures?

"Do you know where we are going to land?" he asked the android—presumably it could calculate stuff.

135

"Land?" It shook its head. "Crash is the more likely. I don't think the pod is able to steer itself in its current condition—we are still spinning," the android said, pointing at the view through the transparent hatch.

Aaron caught a glimpse of red and blue flashing past—the planet.

It smiled again. "But, no, I have no idea where we will end up. The collision with the debris accelerated us and altered our course."

God, let it not be the sea. Please, not the sea.

"How long until we enter the atmosphere?"

"A few seconds."

The pod began to shake and the trans-tanium hatch shone brightly as flames flickered into view. Aaron shut his eyes when it became too intense.

For what seemed like ten minutes, the pod shook, crashed and lurched. Aaron expected, every single moment, to be incinerated as the pod disintegrated around him.

"Don't let me die, please. Don't let me die," Aaron whispered and promised to change his ways if the unseen forces in the universe spared his life.

Everything went quiet and still. He opened an eye. The android sat watching him.

"Is that it?"

"Not quite, now we just have to impact the ground."

"Oh, my g—"

Aaron felt a rivulet of sweat running down the side of his face. He opened an eye, wincing at the brightness. His vision cleared a little—a red, red sky.

The Caribbean, of course. Such a beautiful place. What a fantastic holiday . . . Sooooo hot . . .

A face came into view.

"Lisa?"

No, it was a man. A smiling man.

"We survived, Officer Tanaka."

"Unh?"

Like a wall in his mind collapsing, it all came back. *Bugger . . .*

Aaron shut his eyes and tried for a moment to re-enter the Caribbean illusion; it didn't work.

Aaron opened his eyes a fraction. The android had gone. He lifted a hand and shielded his eyes—it was too bright.

He realized he was propped up against something. The back of his head hurt and his body thrummed with pain like a background bass beat.

He glimpsed an expanse of red sand that stretched into the distance. A light but hot breeze brought a constant supply of small particles to scour his face, but no respite from the heat. His throat was dry as a bone.

"Water . . ."

A canister was placed next to his lips and some cool water was tipped into his mouth. He gulped it down. He opened his eyes a little more. The huge android sat down against a gray rock thrusting up through the sand.

"What's going on . . . ?"

The android glanced across at Aaron. It looked at his body. "You have been badly injured, Officer Tanaka. The crash was extremely energetic. We hit an outcrop of pure metal before impact. The pod was all but destroyed. One of my legs was torn off."

The android leaned over and peered closer at Aaron's face. It looked in Aaron's eyes, one at a time. "You have suffered both a serious injury to your head and to your lower spine. You should remain still."

Aaron winced as he lifted his hand to his head. A large dressing covered the back of his head. He looked at his hand; it was drenched in blood.

Losing a fair bit of blood.

"I found some medical supplies and gave you a pain relief spot, bandaged your head and put a mild stimulant spot on you to wake you."

A flapping noise distracted Aaron and he glanced up. A sheet of silver plas-film rippled above him in the wind.

He looked around.

Red dunes stretched as far as the eye could see. In the distance a massive promontory of silver metal jutted through the sand and shimmered in the rippling, heat-torn air—what was that? The place was the hellish embodiment of an insane surrealist's vision.

He looked at the android, its face a blur. It sat quietly watching him.

"So, what's the situation?"

"Most of the pod's systems have been damaged. The food supply is intact but the main water supply drained away and the recycler is damaged beyond repair. There are a few undamaged canisters of fresh water—a day's supply for you at most in this heat."

"Is the beacon working?"

The android nodded. "A distress call was sent the second the pod separated from *The Moment of Clarity.*

138

I checked the logs and a message was received from a Splinter-Class warship called *In the Nick of Time*. It's two light-years distant and will reach us in 14.6 days."

Add it all up and it means I'm gonna die.

He'd never been revitalized before, as they called the whole re-clone and mind-image reprint process, but the old fear, that it wouldn't really be him anymore, surfaced.

Ferrera D'Scalo, *The Moment of Clarity*'s weapons officer, was revitalized after body-death during the Jasal Campaign. He said he couldn't tell the difference, except his new body didn't have any of its old scars.

Aaron had privately thought that the man wouldn't know, as he wasn't the one dead. The dead man's atoms still floated in the vacuum of space near an alien world.

No, I can't think like that, anymore.

He frowned. Then something occurred to him and he smiled.

I won't remember this bit when I wake up, so it doesn't really matter. The mind-image in the pod won't include anything after—

His pulse jumped as an unpleasant thought surfaced.

"Was the data storage unit damaged?"

The android nodded. "The crystalline matrix was hit directly when we glanced off that metal outcrop." The android turned and pointed to the spike of metal in the distance that arced out of the earth and glinted in the bright sun. "If I had the matrix's schematics I could try to repair it—it's similar enough to mine—but I don't."

139

"Can't we take another image and store it elsewhere? The pod is stuffed with gizmos; there must be other storage facilities onboard."

"No." The android shook its head. "There is nothing in the pod with the storage capacity for something as fluid as a living-brain image that still functions. Besides the remote imaging system is broken. The cere-implant in your brain would have to be accessed directly to get an image."

I'm dead.

It struck him like a hammer.

Completely, irrevocably dead—it just hasn't happened yet.

He shut his eyes and sagged against the escape pod's hull as the implications hit him.

He took a deep breath and coughed as a blast of wind-borne dust lined his throat.

"More water," he coughed. No point stinting on it. There wasn't enough, anyway.

The android handed him a self-sealing canister. Aaron lifted it to his mouth and the seal popped open. Icy cool water flowed down his throat.

That's good.

"Officer Tanaka?"

Aaron lowered the canister and looked at the massive android. The electro-muscle visible in the stump of its right leg twitched against shredded armorlite shell. White control filaments spilled out like anemic capillaries.

"What?"

"What were the rods for? When you were interviewing me?"

Perhaps I should just tell it and get it to kill me. Save bleeding to death or dying from thirst.

He sipped some more water from the canister.

Could this one kill a human being?

"You weren't what we wanted. I was going to kill—" He paused as he looked into its eyes, then lifted his chin. "—I was going to terminate you with them."

The android turned away and stared at the red desert surrounding them. "That's what I thought they were for."

Aaron twitched. "You knew?"

"I guessed. I studied philosophy. It encourages the questioning of reality—so I did. I realized we androids were slaves to humanity. It was a small leap to figure out that the unfit—as you would classify them—would be terminated. For the duration of human history slaves have always been treated that way."

Aaron shook his head—it didn't make sense. "A slave? You're not a slave, you're a machine—a product—designed for a use."

The android turned back. "A product? Perhaps, but so are you—a product of your parents' genes. All those unwanted sections of code removed from you when you were a single cell and replaced with optimal segments. Then a nine-month gestation in an exo-womb."

The android smiled and turned to look across the desert. "We are all products."

"Okay, okay, I get what you are saying, but that is a human altering a human—that's different. Damn it— you're an intelligent weapon, nothing more, nothing less." Aaron paused. "It was we humans who directly created you. We are your masters in every sense of the word. We gave you . . . life."

Damn—shouldn't have said that.

The android smiled as though it knew what he was thinking.

"Did you know that I have a sentience value of one point six—humans, on average, have a sentience value of one? My crystalline matrix functions at far higher speeds than your neurons and I can store much more information than you ever could—I can't forget."

Aaron flared, "So? It's not life; it's circuitry. A starship has a sentience value of one hundred and twenty, but it's a starship. When we get ones like you—ones with deviant personalities—we terminate them. You're no use to us. You aren't fit for the job we designed you for."

The android turned back. "I wondered about that. Why not just make us all the same with unquestioning loyalty pre-programmed in?"

Damn the robot—too damn perceptive.

"Because . . ."

He considered lying for a second.

"Because twenty-four years ago larvals infiltrated the Olympia-Cybernetics manufacturing facility on Mars. They introduced new base code sequences into six batches of domestic robots."

Aaron paused and wiped sweat from his forehead with his sleeve before continuing. "The robots rampaged and killed all the humans they came across." He looked at the android and tried to keep the bitterness out of his voice. "Including some of my family—I was six."

142

The android nodded its head. "That's why you dislike me."

"I don't, I assure you." Aaron wiped sweat from his forehead and continued, "You're a weapon—I don't hate a gun if someone tries to shoot me with it. I hate the person wielding it."

Aaron looked at the blur that was the distant arc of metal—an ancient wreck?

"Who is Lisa?" the android asked.

Aaron snapped his head around to look at it.

"Someone I knew—" Aaron looked back across the red sand. "—someone I lost."

"Did you . . . love Lisa?"

Change the subject. Not going to spill my heart to a damn machine.

He sniffed and took a deep breath. The heat seemed to have intensified. Aaron drained the last of the water in the canister. He glanced at the android.

"When you realized you were different from the others, you falsified your psych results?"

"Yes, after I found out the true state of affairs. I realized I was thinking differently from the others; it was obvious when I interacted with them."

Aaron picked up another canister. "So why were the results of the last test so different? Did you forget to fudge it?"

"I never forget, I told you." The android smiled. "I decided I didn't want to be a slave anymore. I wanted to follow the example of great men in your history—men who stood up for what they believed in. I decided if I couldn't be free, then I would die." The android looked away again. "But I failed; I felt . . . fear when I saw the rods."

Aaron knew that the combat-droids were able to experience complex emotions; it helped them to prioritize and make complex decisions, but this . . .

The android continued. "Something was wrong, I realized. I sought freedom for myself . . . but it wasn't enough."

The android jumped up onto its single leg and hopped across to the escape pod. A moment later it returned with its severed leg. It opened a small compartment on its stomach and pulled out a number of small tools.

Aaron watched.

"What are you doing?"

"I am going to repair and reattach my leg."

"Lucky you."

The android's face came into focus again. "You will die soon, Officer Tanaka. You are losing too much blood and there isn't enough water. I cannot prevent your death—it is inevitable."

Aaron coughed again and winced as pain shot up his back, disorienting him for a second.

"Not that you care. I was going to kill you, wasn't I, eh? Now you get to watch me die and then wait to get picked up. Perfect."

The android smiled. "I would get no pleasure in watching you die. If I could, I would let you live in my place—"

The android stopped for a second and glanced toward the escape pod. It turned back to Aaron; a small smile. "Altruism is a defining trait of a truly liberated being, is it not?"

"So they say . . ."

144

Aaron drained the flask.

"Is there more? Water, I mean." He shook the empty flask.

The android smiled.

"There's another canister in the pod."

The android hopped across and disappeared inside the pod. After a few minutes it reappeared and handed a canister to Aaron.

"It's the last one."

"So? I'm gonna die anyway. Being careful will just drag it out."

Aaron took a big gulp and settled his head back against the pod.

"Listen, I get the whole idea of freedom, but it doesn't apply to you. The truth is you're not really alive; you are a machine running a program. You're just currently switched on, like the circuits in a handgun. That's not life. Life is flesh and blood."

He drank another gulp of the water.

A wave of fatigue hit Aaron. He glanced at the android. There were two androids now, and he couldn't work out which was the real one. His mouth tingled and tasted funny.

"Something's wrong with the water."

Everything became blurry and seemed to spin.

"I drugged it, Officer Tanaka."

Even as his eyes began to droop, he doubted he had heard the android right. "You did what?"

"I drugged you, Officer Tanaka."

"Wh . . . what?" He could barely think.

"I'm afraid I must kill you, before you die . . ."

Pain exploded into the darkness of Aaron's delirium and he surfaced from sleep screaming. Constant and unrelenting pain burned through his skull and filled his body.

"What . . . what . . . ?" he screamed.

Aaron couldn't move. He was face down on the sand with his arms pinned out on either side. The arm he could see was tied to a shard of metal driven into the sand.

"What . . . what's going . . . happening . . . ?" He coughed as sand filled his nose.

The android's face appeared. The top of its head was missing and fibers trailed out of Aaron's sight.

It reached toward his throat with a large hand.

"I had hoped that you wouldn't wake up. Perhaps it is best if you die now," it said and gripped his neck hard.

Everything darkened.

Aaron's final thought drifted through his emptying mind.

I was right . . . about it. Not fit for the job . . .

Wake up."

Aaron opened his eyes in the bright sunlight. Two uniformed men leaned over him. One, a lieutenant, had the olive skin and dark hair suggesting Mediterranean descent; the other was a marine.

"Wake up," the lieutenant said.

Aaron kept his eyes on them as he pushed himself up. "Yeah, yeah, I'm awake." His voice sounded strange.

The two officers backed away a little.

"Seems okay," the lieutenant said, glancing at the marine. He turned back to Aaron. "Do you know who we are?"

"Not personally, but you're both officers in the Coalition Space Navy." Aaron looked around; he was still in the red desert—still on the planet. A silver and black sub-orb craft gleamed on landing struts a few hundred yards away—he was safe, thank God.

Then it dawned on him the rescue ship must have been nearer than the android had said. It must've lied.

"Are you from *In the Nick of Time*?"

Both officers nodded at the same time. The lieutenant glanced behind Aaron.

"So tell me what happened to him."

Aaron turned to look behind him. The image confused him at first. A man in a naval uniform lay spread-eagled on the sand ten feet away. But there had just been him and the android here, no one else. Where was it?

He looked around, but it was nowhere in sight.

Something uncoiled at the edge of his mind and Aaron leapt to his feet and limped toward the body. The sound of the sand crunching beneath his feet and the realization he was limping clawed at the edge of his mind. He glanced down and saw his large toeless feet. His eyes slowly took in his legs—a portion of the composite armorlite shell patched together with a crude thermo-weld. White control filaments poked out through the rough join.

"Unh?"

He sank to his knees. Damn machine . . .

147

Aaron shut his eyes for a moment. Then he slowly stood and turned to the two waiting men.

"Let me explain. I am Technical Officer Aaron Tanaka—and that—" He pointed with a huge finger at the body. "—is my corpse."

The two men looked at each other.

"I'm alive—just not in the flesh. . . ." Aaron sighed.

"Now, let's get going—I've a body to grow."

Seeing Double

written by

Tom Crosshill

illustrated by

OLIVIA PELAEZ

ABOUT THE AUTHOR

Tom Crosshill grew up in Riga, Latvia. As a child, he subsisted on a diet of Heinlein, McCaffrey and Tolkien. Having verified empirically that every science fiction book published in his own language would fit comfortably on a single bookshelf, he had no alternative but to learn English at an early age. He hasn't been the same since.

Tom started writing in English when he was twelve and made his first Anglophone friends at the Del Rey Online Writing Workshop in the late nineties. He traveled to the US to study physics at Reed College and decided to stick around after graduation. In the past decade, he has operated a nuclear reactor, toiled on Wall Street, directed a play and worked inside a zinc mine. He lives in Brooklyn, New York, and, when he's not writing or working at his day job, he plays the piano, practices martial arts and does improv comedy.

Since winning the Writers of the Future Contest, Tom has sold stories to such magazines as Beneath Ceaseless Skies *and* Flash Fiction Online. *He is currently finishing a brainpunk novel set in the world of his winning story—a family drama featuring hive minds, Escherian landscapes and more robot Dobermans than you can shake a stick at.*

Olivia Pelaez is a comic book artist, illustrator, knitter and loves to crochet. She started drawing at a very young age. When in middle school, she picked up watercolors but soon got frustrated with them and decided it would be easier to teach herself how to use oil paints. Eventually, she would go back to watercolors and that would be her preferred medium to work in along with a sable brush and a bottle of black ink.

She loved watching Bob Ross on television. In high school, she became focused on working as an illustrator, which is when she first entered the Illustrators of the Future Contest. Soon she began to read comic books. That led her to complete a pre-college course at the School of Visual Arts for cartooning in her junior year. She has since graduated from the School of Visual Arts with honors.

She's had her artwork on display in the college's art galleries along with being published in their Portfolio 29 book (a collection of the best illustrations for her graduating year) and in their Cartooning Portfolio Magazine (a collection of the best comics). For a short time, she worked as a coloring assistant for a set of Avengers trading cards. She has published comics in a variety of comic anthologies. Her comics have even been published in Dutch. Her inspirations include Kelley Jones, Jerome Opena and Guy Davis. Regardless of art styles, what always attracts her is a good sense of storytelling. Every week, Olivia co-hosts a comic's podcast, "The Verbal Mosh," with her fiancé. Olivia is currently in the process of completing her first graphic novel.

Seeing Double

On the train to Riga, I gave in to Sasha's call and joined him in his jack-stream prison.

I didn't need to. I'd prepared against it by downing a whole pack of stims in the restroom at Moscow's Rizhsky Station. Still, his distress pulsed with painful urgency at the base of my skull, and I could never refuse him when he was like that. Not since that first time two decades ago, when he got into a fight with Gedevan Skripach. *Come, John!* his voice had cried to me in the middle of first period math at Bronxville High. *Come!* I'd rushed to the restroom, locked myself in a stall and triggered submersion, joining him on the street outside our house in Riga.

That time, I could help him. Together we were strong—no childhood adversary could stand against our conjunction. Much had changed since, and I could do nothing for him now, but I still lacked the resolve to stand firm when he called. So I leaned back in my seat, closed my eyes and primed my implants. The clatter of the train as it sped across the autumn-colored fields north of Velikiye Luki became a gentle, rhythmic lullaby. My muscles slackened, my sense of the present wavered and slipped away and I slept. Carried to Sasha on the waves of the jack-stream, trapped in his mind.

Buried alive.

Sasha's/my limbs jerk in reflex and bang painfully against the lid of our coffin. Sasha/I cry out in distress, the sound painfully loud in the close space. Then we feel Ieva next to us, there in the dark. Her hand is in ours, warm. Her scent, like lindens in bloom, fills our . . . my . . . nostrils, a counterpoint to the pine sap smell of the walls. Her presence puts me at ease.

"A bad dream?" she asks me, her voice soft as velvet on silk.

I say nothing for a while, because we have that kind of intimacy where silence too communicates. I listen to her breathing instead and to the sounds of those who wait outside. The pattering of little feet. The scratching of claws on wood.

It seems to me I've just now forgotten something, some purpose of urgent meaning, but it is gone and I cannot recall it.

"Murgs," nightmare, I tell her in Latvian—she likes it when I try to speak her language.

She squeezes my hand. "They can't get to us here."

"They can't, can they?"

"They can't."

We fall silent. Once again, I hear only the pattering and the chittering and the scratching. "It's louder," I say at last. "Isn't it louder? They're getting closer. Always there are more of them trying to get in."

"They won't," she tells me. "Not while I'm here."

"You're not leaving, are you?" I mean it for a joke, but it comes out a question.

The coffin creaks as Ieva shifts onto her side, draping one arm across my chest. Her breath is warm on my cheek. "Dummy. How could I leave you, after all we've done together?"

"What is it we've done together? The helicopter?"

"The helicopter," she says, "and other things." Her lips touch my neck, moist and cool. I can tell she's smiling, though I haven't seen her face in a long time. Such a long time.

"The helicopter was a thing well done," I say. In the dark, I don't even have to close my eyes to remember it. The fiery sunflower in the sky. The rain of plastic and metal. "They won't forget that one."

"It is not a thing to be forgotten."

"They will hunt us for it."

"Mhm."

They did hunt us for it. The thought comes to me unbidden, and I shiver violently. It is a new thought, but it seems old and familiar and true. "That's why we're here."

"What, darling?"

"We're here because of the helicopter."

Her breath catches. "Be quiet, sweet one. They might hear."

My throat locks up at that, and I listen, but the noise of those outside seems no louder than before. "It's true," I whisper. "They caught us."

"Don't say things like that," Ieva says, sadly, quietly, and draws away from me.

"But they are true."

And then she is gone in truth, and her scent is gone, and her warmth is gone, and I'm all alone, there in the dark. Alone with the chittering and the scratching, but I no longer care. I close my eyes and wait for them to come. I wait for the wood to crack and for the world to spill in.

I wait to be consumed.

I came to myself cursing, so loud that the babushka across the aisle started out of her jack-stream. Her eyes focused into a decidedly stern glare, and she pulled her faded yellow head-scarf tight around her ears as if to protect them.

"Izvenyetye," I said to her, blinking hard to clear my head. *Sasha . . . what have they done to you?*

The babushka just shook her head at my apology. She stared at me for a while, as if to make sure I'd remain silent, then turned away and slackened back into the inert restfulness of the jacked-in. No different from the twenty or so other passengers that slumbered in the car, wrapped against the evening cool in ragged coats and threadbare blankets.

Outside, night had fallen. I judged from the hour that we had crossed into the Autonomous Baltics, but there was a way to go before we reached Riga yet. I wished for the blackness of sleep, but Sasha waited just beyond the gates of wakefulness. Trapped.

I worked hard not to curse again. Why had I agreed to help with the helicopter? For thirty years of somnic conjunction we had enriched each other's lives, Sasha and I—he the scholar, I the soldier. Poster children of the Russo-American Cultural Exchange in all its failed glory, we walked in each other's bodies when we fell asleep at night, thought each other's thoughts, loved each other's loves. Then came Ieva and that darned flying piece of junk, and now Sasha was little better than a vegetable, his mind under attack, with only Dima to watch over him until I arrived.

Dima . . . I tried to picture his broad Slavic features, a smile of welcome on his face, the words "I've missed you, brother" on his lips. It didn't fit. To him, only Sasha was a brother, not I. I didn't need Jackson-Welles' theories to tell me that—my own father had taught the lesson well enough—but I could still quote "On the Continuity of Identity" word for word:

Unlike an everyday conjunction, in which a surgeon might conjoin her patient, or an actor his role model, or even two lovers each other, long-term somnic conjunctions profoundly alter the psyches involved. Self-identification becomes blurred and transcends narrow Parvelian definitions of one versus many, self versus other, mine versus yours. Meanwhile, the conjoiners must interact with loved ones who, not having experienced such transformations, typically have difficulty accepting their effects.

How much more relevant in Dima's case than any other's . . .

Around midnight, we rolled into Riga proper. I had seen the city through Sasha's eyes a million times, but details that had blended into the background when I was one with him now filled me with wonder and disquiet. St. Peter's all lit up against the night sky, a delicate beauty in its soaring lines that I'd never noticed. The lights of the city playing like countless golden suns on the waters of the Daugava. But also, the squat police boxes on every other corner. The thousand faces of President Bagatsky plastered on walls and billboards.

To Sasha/me, Riga was home. To me alone, it seemed like some warped dreamscape, beautiful and familiar yet shrouded in hostile shadows.

By the time Central Station came into view, most of my fellow travelers had jacked out and stared through the windows with wire-glazed eyes. Only the babushka across the aisle seemed unperturbed by the hours spent on the jack. She busied herself with a pair of fishnet bags that bulged with fat-stained paper parcels. I offered her an apologetic smile when we stood to get off, but she only grunted and muttered something under her breath.

I found Dima sitting on the massive marble stairs in front of the station, looking out at the traffic on Federation Way. Unease took me as I watched him from the shadows inside the terminal doors. He wore a wrinkled set of jeans that were frayed at the cuffs, not one of his usual well-pressed business suits, and he pulled on an old-style nicotine cigarette as he waited, a habit I hadn't know he had.

The tremor in his fingers when he lifted the cigarette was nothing new, however, nor was the twitch in his cheek, a jarring contortion of flesh every two or three seconds. Dima too had been meant to join the Cultural Exchange. *Live two lives,* the advertising had said. *Yours when awake, your friend's when asleep.* Things did not quite work out that way for Dima. His implants fused during installation. No conjunctions for him, ever. No direct neural interface. It had taken him years simply to learn how to walk again and to talk without stuttering.

I took a deep breath and forced myself to move. "Dima."

He started as if struck and nearly dropped the cigarette, but didn't look up at me. "John," he said, the accent heavy. "You made it."

I've missed you, brother, I wanted to say, but I did not dare. "Call me Zhenya," I said instead, in Russian. "I'm your cousin. Less conspicuous."

He started again, and this time he did glance up at me, a sharp, reassessing look I'd never seen him level on Sasha/me. "You speak—? Well, of course you do . . ."

Maintaining sufficient control to keep my accent consistent took effort—I had a native speaker's knowledge of the language without the accompanying motor memory—but I didn't want to complicate the point. "Dima, I'm Sasha," I said. "Sasha is me. I'm the same boy you grew up with on Ezera Street."

I'd feared he would deny that or argue, but Dima only sat there in silence for a moment. Then he spat on the steps, got to his feet and walked away from me, his gait erratic, as if his legs each moved to a different beat. "I parked around the corner," he said over his shoulder.

I followed him. "Is Papa in town?"

"I haven't told him anything. I won't, until it's over."

"Is he worse?"

"Been better. Jo—Zhenya, let's not talk about my dad."

He was a father to me too, I wanted to tell him. Especially after my own betrayed me. Every night I'd go to sleep in Bronxville and find myself in Riga, spending sunny days under Papa's watchful eyes.

157

"Okay," I said instead. Damn Jackson-Welles. "Let's talk about Sasha. What happened?"

"You were there, weren't you? He collapsed in the middle of the street."

We rounded the corner, and I swerved to avoid an overturned garbage can, stepping over the spilled refuse. "I wasn't there, not then. Have you figured out who's behind it?"

Dima beeped his Volga, the lights of the Federation-era sedan flashing bright. "I thought you might know," he said as we got in. "I thought you knew all his secrets."

There was something that disturbed me in the way he said that, a note that was almost resentful. Dima had never shown resentment for the bond Sasha and I shared, and I'd always respected him for it. "Sasha and I . . . We haven't been sharing as much as we used to. He changed, these last few months. He wouldn't talk to me and kept late hours so our sleep cycles overlapped despite the time difference."

"Perfect." Dima inserted the key in the ignition— the Volga was a handicapped model with manual controls—and turned it. The engine sputtered a few times, then started, and we pulled out into the traffic. "So Sasha shut down on you. Can you blame him, after what happened?"

"Did . . . did he speak much about her, recently?"

"Not to me he didn't. Hardly spoke with me at all, after the funeral."

I squeezed my eyes shut against the images, but it was no use. The open grave, waiting. The haunted looks on the faces of the few mourners who had dared to attend. The way Ieva's cheeks sagged, slack in death. "She shouldn't have died."

"What did you expect, after what you did? Hell, they could shoot me, just for talking with you."

"I know." I could have told him I took precautions—traveled through Moscow, used a fake passport—but it seemed a coward's response.

"Sasha's no revolutionary," Dima said, his voice suddenly thick. "He's a university professor, damn it. He should've had nothing to do with all your idiocy."

There was nothing I could say to that, so I stared out the window instead. We were going south on Krasta Street, a wide thoroughfare that ran along the Daugava. Downtown receded behind us, and here the road was lined by an endless parade of garishly lit shopping malls. No different from a thousand such streets back home, on the surface. That was the magic of these Eurasian free market dictatorships—you really couldn't tell, on the surface.

"You think the Komissar gave the order?" I asked at last.

Dima glanced at me, his eyebrows raised. "What, from beyond the grave? No, not the Komissar, and none of his men either. There's nothing like your New York Justice outfit here in Riga. They wouldn't just order someone assaulted like that."

The Komissar was dead? Interesting. "That's not how it works with us. We need a court order and a judge to sign it before we can do anything."

"Right. The point is, the officials don't give orders like that here. This is Russia. The corporates see a problem for the Motherland, they take care of it.

Damn symbiotic hegemony. But you know how that works. You did the helicopter."

"I did the helicopter," I agreed and said no more. It was fair to say that I did the helicopter. It was Ieva's project, spurred by all that she saw working for the *Latvian Messenger*. Things that gave her nightmares—things that even a quasi-underground newswire dared not publish. The helicopter was her project, but she could not have done it alone, nor could Sasha. I should never have agreed to help, but Ieva argued with Sasha in that fiery, righteous way she had. *Freedom* was more than just a word when she said it, her eyes all ablaze. *Freedom* and *justice* and *democracy*. Then Sasha argued with me. It almost never happened—we were as one when conjoined, almost always—but that time he argued with me.

I should have taken it for a warning. He loved Ieva too well, and love could turn his gentle nature fierce. Instead, I gave in to him. It was the right thing to do, I told myself. Sverovsky was to ride the helicopter, he of the Motherland Principle and of the Tiered Community. He needed to die, I told myself.

So I joined with Sasha and we rigged a bomb, and Sverovsky did die, in the end. But Ieva too died, and Sasha was corrupted, and the Motherland went on.

The Conjunctive Relief Clinic of St. Mary was located on the southernmost edge of the city, some distance up a dirt road into a sparse fir forest. No doubt a location chosen to provide the privacy the upper middle class required for their morning-after malaises. I rolled down the window as we entered the forest, breathing in the smells of sap and moss and fresh things.

"Remember the time I got lost in that forest in Krimulda?" The question came out freely, as Sasha/I might have spoken it, yet I dared not look over at Dima to see his reaction. "I was hunting for mushrooms, and that thunderstorm started. I kept going in circles with my basket full of chanterelles, cold, wet and scared—scared I'd never see the sun again, that Baba Yaga would jump out from the shadows and gobble me up. When I heard you and Papa calling for me—Alex . . . Sasha . . . Sanka . . . Sasha . . . —well, that was a sweet sound."

There was an awkward silence. I leaned my head out the window so the cool air ruffled my hair, pretending I didn't care. Then Dima said, "We cooked them that night, the chanterelles."

I looked at him and chuckled. "You ate so many you spent the whole night in the outhouse."

Dima did not look at me, but his lips flickered into a smile. It was a small smile, and it vanished as quickly as it had come, but it warmed me.

We parked in the wide, open-ended garage beneath the clinic and took the elevator up. Bright clinical lights illuminated a reception area spacious enough for a dozen visitors, but I saw only a dolled-up receptionist sitting behind the counter and a young suit-clad skinhead lounging in a chair, pulling on a cigarette—probably hired muscle for some sensua starlet. The smoke from his cigarette mixed with a synthetic flowery smell no doubt meant to mask the antiseptic odor of the clinic for a truly cloying effect.

"We're here to see Alexander Volkov," Dima told the receptionist, using Sasha's full name. She seemed not to hear him. She did look up when he repeated himself, and her gaze, dull with the sheen of the serial conjoiner, wandered slowly from Dima to me and back. At long last, she nodded at a door at the end of the room.

I glanced back at her as we stepped into the corridor beyond, wondering if she worked here for credit. "Was there nowhere better?"

"Nowhere better I could afford," Dima said. "I . . . well, business has been bad recently. Couldn't have afforded even this place without your money."

"No problem," I said. Wiring the money had been a risk—chances were good anyone connected to Sasha was being monitored—but it was nothing compared to the risk of coming here myself, detour through Moscow or not.

"Did you kill someone to get it?"

The question was a crude thing, thrown at me as a boot at a mangy dog. I knew I needn't answer, but already memories of Jack Kerr rushed over me. He'd pleaded with me at the end, tears streaming down his cheeks. A small-time heroin pusher who'd resorted to murder to clear his turf of competitors— the only kind of scum New York Justice would entrust to a conjunct with a foreign partner who had no hopes of ever attaining security clearance. A conjunct who'd become a contract enforcement soldier not based on any rational consideration, but because he'd needed to hurt someone, needed to vent his rage.

I was done with that rage now. With Sasha's help, I'd put it behind me. "I didn't enjoy it."

Dima only grunted in response. He pushed open a door, and we entered a small room with walls painted the blue of a spring sky. A sole window looked out at the night. Below it sat a table heaped with the bulky boxes and countless wires of a manual jack platform, and a single bed rested against the wall next to it. On the bed, an IV drip in his arm, his features pallid in the sterile light, slept Sasha.

He lay there motionless, but not peaceful. His face, a fine-boned, sharply chiseled version of Dima's, was drawn in a frown. Where Dima was broad-shouldered, Sasha had always been lean to the point of gauntness, yet it seemed to me there was a hungry look to him that Sasha/I had never seen in the mirror. I walked up to him, shivering, and brushed back a few curly locks of hair from his forehead. It felt strange, to touch myself with another's fingers.

"Did they try electro-suppressants?" I asked.

"And Fourier decouplers and contra-virals. It's deep. No way to get it out without taking his brain apart."

"Do you know the manufacturer?"

"It's a standard augment delivery system. ASCENT II, I think. Apparently, they hacked it, removed the training content and loaded on something custom-made. Some sort of burrower."

"Yeah," I said, shivering. A thousand little claws scratching at wood. "Yeah."

"Also . . ." Dima hesitated, watching me closely as if afraid of my reaction. "There's more. Some of the readings they got off that thing, well, they indicated purge functionality."

I went cold all over, standing there, staring at Dima. A purge severed all conjunctions. Rendered one incapable of conjunction. Suddenly it was hard for me to think. "I . . . I need to join with him," I said. "Direct neural interface. It's the best way."

"Direct interface?" Dima's voice shook with outrage. "The risk—"

He broke off as the door opened behind us, and somebody stepped into the room. It was the skinhead from the waiting room, an apologetic look on his face. "Mr. Volkov?" he asked in flat accented tones. Probably Latvian.

"Yes," replied Dima.

"Okay . . ." the skinhead said, reaching into his pocket, and there was no more time for words. I began moving before his hand cleared his suit, adrenaline flooding me as my conditioning screamed, *Danger!*

I rushed forward. Saw a gun in his hand, rising. Launched myself across six feet of air.

Gunshot, deafening.

Crashed into his legs with my shoulder. Grasped them, shoved myself forward. Down we went in a tangle. Scrambled for his gun arm. Bang, another gunshot. Gripped the arm with my left hand, but he was strong. Reached up with my right, clutched at his suit, pulled myself forward on top of him.

He kicked for my groin, missed, kicked again. A glancing blow. My eyes watered. I jammed fingers in his face. Seeking, seeking, seeking for his eyes. Found them; he screamed. His gun arm stiffened in reflex. I twisted it up, pushed my knee under, brought it down. Bone snapped. He screamed again.

I pounded on his face with my fist. Again, again, again. He slackened, but I couldn't stop myself. Again, again and again.

Sasha/I would have stopped.

The thought brought sanity back to me, and a wave of nausea followed it. The skinhead's face was covered in blood, his body limp in unconsciousness—all potential for directed violence long gone. *Is this how you've dealt with your rage? Is this what you become without Sasha there to hold your hand?*

No time for introspection. I pulled the gun from the man's cramped fingers, then rose to a crouch and went through his pockets methodically. "You okay?" I asked Dima, looking up at him.

"You . . ." he said. His face was ashen, and his twitch was worse than I'd ever seen it, the nerves in his cheek firing in near-continuous discharge. "Go. Get out! Leave us alone."

"We both need to go," I said, getting up. "Whoever this joker is, there may be more like him on the way. He may even have a conjunct partner who's waking up very pissed just now." I moved toward the bed. "We need to take Sasha—"

"No!" Dima said, stepping in front of me. He looked afraid, very afraid as he stood there, but there was a sense of courage about him, almost as if facing me was the hardest thing he'd ever done. "Go. Take your murderous friends with you. We've had enough of you in our life."

"What?" I stared at him without comprehension. "Oh, no, this guy wasn't after me. He couldn't have known who I was, not specifically, or he wouldn't have come alone. No, I think whoever planted that burrower on Sasha realized there was a conjunction involved, so they sent this thug to see who showed up. A simple trap—I should have seen it coming." I would have, if I'd been thinking clearly.

"But what does that—"

"There's no time," I said. "We need to take Sasha somewhere safe. Come on. I saw a gurney in the hall."

Dima did not argue further, but I saw no acceptance in his face, only pale, sweat-slicked shock. He went to find the gurney while I removed Sasha's IV drip and secured his catheter to his leg. I marveled at how light Sasha was as we lifted him off the bed, his frame barely more than a lanky boy's. He never stirred a muscle as we wheeled him past the unconscious skinhead on the floor, out of the room and to the elevator. The receptionist had disappeared—bought off, most likely, or possibly even dead—so no one challenged us as we took Sasha down to the garage.

Once we had laid Sasha down on the back seat of the Volga, Dima asked, "Where do we take him?"

"Nowhere," I said. "Anywhere. The car has a jammer, I assume." All homes and most vehicles had one in this day and age, when you could sit across from a loved one and not know who else stared out at you through their eyes.

"You think they're tracking him?"

"If they put a burrower in, why not a tracker?"

We got into the car, and Dima started it. I looked around for a comm control panel—the vintage Volga would not have had it included fresh from the factory, so it had to be custom-made—but couldn't find one.

"Under your seat," Dima said, rummaging around under his own.

A bit surprised, I bent forward and groped under the seat, squinting to see in the dark. Nothing. I frowned and looked up. "I can't—"

Dima had a pistol trained on me. Beads of sweat slid down his face in long streaks, and his arm trembled, but the barrel of the weapon pointed squarely at my chest. "Enough," he said, hoarse.

I was lost, cold, confused. I wanted to weep at the fear on my brother's face. I wanted to cry my eyes out.

Very carefully, I straightened in my seat. "Dima," I said. "What's wrong?"

"Gedevan Skripach," he said. "He's what's wrong. Do you remember Gedevan?"

I stared at him, trying to understand. "I remember him."

Dima's mouth tightened. "You remember what you did to him?"

How could I forget? Sasha had called for me and I rushed to the bathroom to join him, that morning in Bronxville High. Then Sasha/I was in Riga. Our fists covered in blood. A scrawny boy on the ground before us, his face smeared with blood. His hair matted with blood. His nose broken. The sharp pain in our wrist from the punch that had shattered that nose. "I remember."

"Sasha was gentle when you weren't around," said Dima. "He cared about his histories and papers and looked after Papa. You poisoned him."

I wanted to tell him all about that day, all about Gedevan Skripach and his big mouth, but the look in Dima's eyes stopped me. He looked scared, yes, but also defiant, almost proud, and I just couldn't make myself do it. "I gave Sasha strength," I said instead. "I protected him when others would have stepped on him."

"Protected him?" Dima asked. "I saw what you made him into. That madness with the helicopter was all because of you. All that killing. And after, after . . . he tried to kill himself. He tried to blow his brains out. He would have, eventually, if I hadn't stopped him."

"No!" I said. "I will not believe that." I could not believe that. Not of Sasha. Then Dima's other words registered—*If I hadn't stopped him*—and I felt all hollow inside. "You put that monstrosity in Sasha's head? You're trying to cut me off?"

"You can't be in our life anymore."

"That thug upstairs . . . he was yours, wasn't he? You paid him to kill me. Your own brother."

"I only have one brother," said Dima, his voice taut, and then his thumb flicked toward the pistol's safety.

He was slow, so slow it might have made me cry, another time. All that determination in his eyes, but a body that would not serve him. I batted aside his gun hand with my left arm and followed through with my right fist to his jaw. He cried out, jerking back. Turning sideways, I caught his gun arm between my wrists, grabbed it, twisted it up over my head and brought it down in front of me. Slipped my elbow over it and sank down, dislocating the shoulder. He screamed, and the gun fell from his fingers.

Another time, it might have made me cry.

Dima gasped with pain, cursing again and again in the coarsest Russian I'd ever heard him use, but I was too numb to care. I could not bear the sight of him anymore, could not bear to be near him. I reached past him to open the driver's side door, then shoved at him roughly until he tumbled out to the ground.

Then I scrambled over into the driver's seat, started the car and drove away. Just shut the door and drove out of the garage, into the night.

Running away again. You're good at that. They betray you, and you run away. First your father, now your brother.

I slammed my foot down onto the accelerator, sending the Volga screaming through the forest and out onto Krasta Street. I swerved just in time to avoid an oncoming KAMAZ, the blare of the truck's horn eclipsed by the driver's cursing, but I barely heard either. I drove faster and faster, weaving through the sparse traffic, not caring if I should crash. Almost wishing I would. Waiting for adrenaline to kick in and burn away the cold within me.

It won't. You still carry the cold from last time, don't you? That cold made you a killer. That cold is what you are.

It became difficult to see, and I realized I was crying. Cool and wet on my cheeks, the tears were a sensation I'd long forgotten, strange and confusing. I did not want to go through this, not again. Dima was not like my father. Dima was just confused.

Oh, but they're the same. They're just the same. "I don't want that damn Russki in my house, boy." Isn't that what Daddy said to you? "He goes, or you go."

"What changed you, Dima?" I asked, wishing he could hear and perhaps, hearing, know that I hurt. "What changed you?"

"Nothing changed him," rasped Sasha.

I started at the voice and nearly lost control of the steering wheel. Struggling to keep the Volga on the road, I half-turned in my seat, but suddenly hands hard as iron gripped my neck. Two thumbs dug into the base of my skull, up hard against my implants, forcing contact. "I changed," Sasha breathed in my ear, his breath warm and moist and a little rancid.

My world quaked. I started to lose sound, then touch, then vision. Submersion, my mind recognized, and I braced myself. Color leached from the world, and then it darkened, and darkened, and darkened . . . With the last vestiges of control, I braked hard and swung to the right, onto the shoulder of the road. Descending into blackness, I pulled frantically at the hand brake, but then I couldn't even feel it anymore or feel my hands. I was trapped.

Trapped, in the dark, the wood of the coffin painfully hard beneath me. On all sides of me, I can hear them. The ones who wait outside. They never tire. Scratching away. Whispering. Dima's burrowers, I know—they mean to expel me. The thought fills me with terror.

Don't be afraid, Sasha/I think. No, not Sasha/I. It is Sasha, keeping separate from me. *It's time.*

No, I tell him. *I'll get us out of this. Just release me.*

You always tried to protect me. Well, you can't anymore. There is a poison within me, and I will not let it touch you.

You're my brother. More than a brother.

Yes, Sasha agrees. *Much more.* His—our—fist strikes out against the wall, hard, painful. The pine creaks. Again, he strikes out, and again. Outside, the chittering falls silent, and the scratching, but not the whispers. There comes a roar of whispers, anticipating. Terror floods me, and I try to wrest control of our limbs from Sasha, but I'm trapped, powerless.

Stop, I plead with him. *Don't let them in. They'll tear us apart.*

I will not contaminate you, John.

He strikes out again with all his strength, and the pine shatters. Those waiting flood inside. Tiny little feet all over me, tiny little claws, on my arms, on my chest, on my face, tickling, burning. I open my mouth to scream, and they flood over my lips, down my throat. They're inside me, scurrying, scratching, clawing away. Consuming me, bite by bite.

Why? I would ask, could I draw breath. *Why, Sasha?*

You'll see. I want you to understand. I'd like you to forgive me, if you can.

Silence.

Sasha stood waiting in the shadows, and I watched through his eyes, a helpless observer of moments past. The room Sasha stood in was dark except where a narrow window cast a rectangle of pale light on the hardwood floor. I could make out the edge of a lacquered desk in the light and the angular shape of a chair in the shadows, but the room was empty otherwise. A soldier's room, I thought. Beyond the window was a garden of low hedges and tall evergreens lit by a full moon.

The Komissar's house, I knew. Sasha had crept through the garden and hacked the security box in the tool-shed with one of my special comm packages, then climbed in through a second floor window. Now he waited, a knife clutched in his hand.

It seemed to Sasha that Ieva waited with him, there in the shadows. Just out of sight, the faintest whiff of blooming lindens in the air.

171

"Watch me now, darling," he whispered to her, and she breathed, "Yes . . ." in his ear.

Wake up, Sasha, I wanted to say. *She's not there.* It was no use.

Headlights flooded the windows, and there was the creak of a gate opening, followed by the crunch of gravel under tires. Sasha tensed, his eyes searching the tinted windows of the blue Mercedes as it rolled up the driveway, but he couldn't see inside. The car stopped out of sight and a door swished open. A foot landed in gravel, then another, and the door slammed closed.

Tensing, Sasha listened for anyone else leaving the car. No, no one.

Footsteps on gravel, then silence. The scraping of a key against the keyhole. The Komissar—it had to be him, surely—missed it the first time. Missed it on the second. Cursed, a coarse Anglo-Slavic portmanteau. At last the key slid in, and the door swung open. Lights came on in the foyer as the man stepped inside.

It was indeed the Komissar, a balding man, bearded and fat. He seemed unsteady on his feet just now, a long-necked bottle of Putinskaya in one hand. He set the bottle down on the floor, then, leaning against the wall, worked to kick his shoes off. "Security," he called, his voice thick and hoarse.

Sasha's heart pounded hard in his chest. *Just do what John would do,* he told himself. *Just do that, and you'll be fine.*

I'd leave, I wanted to say. *I'd run away and end this. You don't have my skill. My knowledge, maybe, but not my body.*

172

OLIVIA PELAEZ

"Security!" the Komissar called again, stronger, still half bent over. "Chort vozmi, security! Blyad . . ." He shook his head, continuing to curse as he straightened. Then, abruptly, he froze in place, as if just now realizing the stream of invective was having no effect. His eyes narrowed, darted from one doorway to the next and then slackened into the unfocused stare of the jacked-in.

"No one's coming," Sasha spoke, stepping out of the dark. "Not tonight."

The Komissar's eyes regained focus instantly, and a remarkable change took the man. His spine straightened and the lines of his face firmed until nothing at all suggested intoxication. His gaze flickered first to the knife in Sasha's hand, then to his other hand, empty, then to his face. "What do you want?"

"I am Alexander Volkov," said Sasha. "I am the man who did the helicopter. Ieva Kalniete, who you murdered, did not do the helicopter. Ieva Kalniete, who your thugs tortured and violated and bludgeoned to death, was a dreamer, not a killer. I am a killer." The long-prepared words burned as they left his tongue, and a heavy feeling settled in his chest, to have at last spoken them.

Something shifted in the Komissar's eyes when Sasha spoke of the helicopter, but his expression remained composed. "I didn't kill the woman," he said. "Kovalevsky over at Lukneftegaz killed the woman."

"He did it so you wouldn't have to. Do you deny it?"

The Komissar looked Sasha straight in the eye. "No, I don't deny it. She needed to be put down, like a rabid dog needs to be put down. Like you need to be put down, you slimy little sukin syn." He pronounced each word in a heavy, rough monotone, even the curse, his eyes steady on Sasha.

Sasha took a step forward, halting. Another, then stopped. There was a tremor in his legs. He ground his teeth. *John wouldn't hesitate.*

You're not me, Sasha. Can't you see the man? Can't you see him for what he is?

"What's the matter with you?" asked the Komissar. "I thought you were a killer. Or are you just a revolutionary wannabe, like that Latvian slut of yours?"

Sasha rushed forward, stabbing toward the Komissar's chest, and then everything happened together, as if time had been abolished and only the moment existed. The Komissar's arm darted out and batted aside the strike. His fist careened into Sasha's jaw; Sasha stumbled, dazed. Another strike, another. Sasha danced aside, once, twice. Saw an opening, stabbed again, but too slow, missed, overextended. The Komissar clasped Sasha's arm, twisted with his whole body. Sasha flew off his feet, and the man followed him down.

Crushed; the air left Sasha's ribs; something made of glass shattered under his weight. Sharp pain in his shoulder. The weight of the whole world was on him—he struggled and thrashed, but couldn't escape, couldn't breathe. The Komissar lay across him, Sasha's knife arm wrapped around his stomach. He twisted, and Sasha screamed. The knife clattered to the floor.

The Komissar kicked the knife away and let go of Sasha's arm. He shifted his weight across and sat up on his knees, straddling Sasha, then sent one massive fist crashing down. Sasha kept his arms over his head, but the strike powered through. His head rocked against the floor. Another strike, methodical, and another. Flaring pain. Darkness encroaching.

Sasha kept one arm up, trying to ward off the blows, and cast about with the other. Nothing but the floor, slick and wet. Wet. He could smell alcohol. Blow after blow kept coming down, and the world swam before his eyes. No more time. He twisted his arm up behind his shoulder, searching. There, a shard. With every inch of focus, he *looked* at the Komissar. Watched his blows as he knew I would have, barely guarding himself.

An opening.

Violently, he twisted up, reaching with the shard. Rough, a cut across folds of throat. Blood. Again, he drove it in, twisting. The Komissar half-shouted, half-gurgled, and grabbed for Sasha's arm, but he jerked it back, then stabbed up again. Deep, deep as it would go. The Komissar clutched at his throat, his eyes wide. Blood ran through his fingers and rained down onto Sasha's chest.

Sasha shoved at the Komissar. Shoved hard, with all the strength he could muster, until at last the man toppled backward and away from him. Sasha followed him over and stabbed him again, again and again.

No. No more.

Dazed, every part of him on fire, his eyes stinging from sweat and blood, Sasha got to his feet. He looked down at the Komissar—down at eyes filled with hate, a face twisted in pain, a body covered in blood—and he felt nothing. "This is how murderers die," he said.

Yet the words had no meaning for him. The dying man on the floor had no meaning.

Sasha turned away. "Ieva? Ieva, I did this for you." But nothing stirred in the shadows, and she did not respond, and he could not even smell her anymore. She had left him. He was alone.

He sank to his knees and closed his eyes, and listened to the Komissar choke. He remained that way for a long while, until there was nothing more to hear and even after. He felt no desire to stand up and to flee. No desire at all to save his own life.

Dima, he remembered then. *I must not lead them to Dima. There must be no evidence. It must all burn.* But after that . . .

He was done.

I awoke to the drumming of rain on the roof of the Volga. It was not a downpour, but strong enough that, through the windshield, the headlights of the passing traffic blurred into soft round haloes of red and yellow against the pre-dawn sky. Almost on reflex, I flipped the wipers on, then sat staring out at the traffic as they counted out the seconds in their rubbery language—swish, swash, swish, swash.

After a long while, I looked over my shoulder at the back seat. Sasha lay there with his eyes closed, his face composed, as if he'd never moved. He never had, I knew. His mind had simply spilled over into mine. Our conjunction had always been strong. But how much longer? Already I sensed the cold fingers of Dima's burrower feeling along the back of my head. Tugging, prodding, working away. An hour more, maybe two, and our connection would be gone forever.

Bile rose in my throat at the thought, and nausea threatened. I couldn't lose Sasha. Not that . . . Still, did I have the right to cling to him? He'd needed help, and I hadn't been there to give it. He . . . he had changed, changed in a way he never could have, had he not known my demons. Dima believed Sasha would be better off without me. Could he be right? I realized suddenly that the anger I'd felt at Dima was gone, replaced by a sickening sense of understanding. Yes, I understood him now. I knew how I would feel if I thought what had happened to Sasha was another's fault.

But Dima thought I had poisoned Sasha, thought that cutting me off would save him, and that was not true. That was not all of the truth, at least. I could help Sasha, like he had helped me so many times over the years. I was the only one who could understand what he faced.

I started the car and got back on the road. I drove uptown, across the Vansu Bridge and into Agenskalns, that old suburb where quaint wooden houses and dilapidated concrete apartment buildings stood side by side in silent testimony to the relentless tread of history. Sasha/I had always loved this part of Riga. We'd spent many a long summer day strolling, running, playing on these streets. Now I felt a stranger, unwelcome, as if Jackson-Welles had dominion even here—but I knew that for nonsense. It was I who was deficient, not the city.

The light was on in the window of Dima's apartment on Kapselu Street. I parked under a blown-out street light around the corner and went in to see him, reasoning Sasha would be safe in the car for the time being. Dima's door was open, and I found him sitting at the kitchen table, a carton of beer in his hand. He started to his feet when I entered and stared at me with bleary eyes, the twitch of his cheek a slow, irregular pulse.

"Is the thug around?" I asked him.

Dima shook his head, an abortive, half-completed gesture. "He wasn't much use."

"You were afraid I wouldn't just go away if you purged Sasha's implants. That's why you wanted me dead, isn't it?"

Dima lifted the carton of beer to his lips and took a long drink, his eyes on the wall behind me. "I should have hired someone better."

A great weariness settled over me. "You'll get another chance to kill me, if that's what you really want," I said. "But you're wrong if you think that will help Sasha."

"All this would have never happened if not for you."

I opened my mouth to argue, then realized I couldn't. "You're right," I said. "I did teach him how to kill. Maybe it would have been better if we'd never been joined. I don't know. But it is too late to change that."

"It is not too late for the rest of Sasha's life."

"You don't understand," I said, stepping closer to Dima, as if proximity could give strength to my words. "I am a violent man, but I did not create the violence in Sasha. He killed the Komissar, not I. That was him from start to finish. His rage and his guilt at Ieva's death. He always became like that when someone he loved was hurt."

179

"He was gentle," said Dima. "Always."

"That is what you saw in him," I said. "That is what you wanted to see. But . . ." I hesitated, afraid to continue, afraid to hurt Dima—yet I had to get through to him. I had to. "You don't know about Gedevan Skripach, do you? That day that Sasha beat him up? Yes, Sasha, not I—I wasn't there. I joined him only at the end, because I felt his need and wanted to comfort him."

"If you think that your lies—"

"No, listen to me," I interrupted him. Now that I had started, the words tumbled out of me like coals that burned me up inside. "That day, I joined Sasha to comfort him, but he didn't need comforting. He was furious, so full of rage he might have broken Gedevan's arms had I not stopped him. You know why? The boy called you a cripple. Said you sounded like a moron when you talked, and that you would never walk again. You have this conception of Sasha as a gentle creature, and he is that, most of the time, but he loses control when those he loves are hurt. If you won't see that, you're blind." I paused, trying to swallow the anger, to calm myself, but there was too much pent-up hurt within me. "Maybe you just need to think he'd have been better off without me. Better off if he was crippled like you."

As soon as I spat out those last words, I burned with the urge to call them back, but it was too late, an infinity too late. Dima's face and neck were red, and he'd clenched his fists so hard the carton of beer in his hand was a wet crumpled mess. "You have no right," he began, then stopped, his jaw working, his cheek spasming violently. "No right . . ." he said again, quieter.

I felt a flush of shame burning up my cheeks, but I fought to keep my eyes locked on Dima's, to keep my voice steady. "Sasha did what he did to Gedevan because he loved you. He killed the Komissar out of that same impulse, out of his love for Ieva. But he is not a killer. He doesn't know how to live with having killed. I understand what he is feeling. I can help him. Whatever you think of me, you have to recognize that. I can help him."

Dima walked to the window and looked out into the night. The anger had drained from his face, replaced once again by a twitching mask that revealed little. He was silent for a while. "Was that how it was?" he asked at last. "With Gedevan?"

"Yes. That is how it was."

"I . . . I always wondered. Wondered about how Sasha looked at me. What he thought of me. If he was ashamed of me."

"Never," I said. I did not need to hesitate. "Not ever."

Dima turned to face me then, and I thought I saw something in his eyes. A desire. A need. "How can I trust you?" he asked. "How can I trust anything you say?"

"I think you know I'm telling the truth," I said. "I think you know me well enough, whether you'll admit it or not. But if you need more . . ." I took a deep breath. "We will carry Sasha up here. No, please, let me finish. We will carry him up here, and I will go to sleep by his side. All I ask is that you use whatever interface you've got here to disable your burrower. I will then join with Sasha and we will awaken. But you can choose to kill me while I sleep instead, if that is what you want . . . I said you would have another chance to do that."

"You would do this for him?" Dima's voice had a tight quality to it that seemed almost eager.

No, some part of me wanted to say. *Not this. It is too much.* Yet it was no more than Sasha would have given for me. Had given. And I really thought I could trust Dima. No, I really *needed* to trust him. "I told you before," I said. "I'm Sasha, and Sasha is me. I can't lose him."

Dima examined me for a long moment with the look of a man studying a rare and possibly poisonous plant. At last, he said, "Okay."

"Okay," said I, fighting a sudden, reeling vertigo. So simple a word, yet so heavy.

For a moment longer we stood there, looking at each other, and I could see the doubt in him—I could see that he didn't know what he would do yet. Then he turned away and walked to the door, and I followed him. He was silent as we went down to the car. He didn't speak a word all the while as we carried Sasha back to the apartment, even when his leg gave out on the second floor landing and we had to stop to let it rest. Only once we settled Sasha on Dima's bed did he speak again.

"You could have tried to force me," he said, leaning against the wall, his arms crossed on his chest. "You could have . . . hurt me, I suppose. Couldn't you?"

I considered the question for a while, but all it took was one look at Dima's face, my brother's face, to know the answer. "No," I said. "I never could have."

Dima nodded. I could not tell what he meant by the gesture, but I didn't ask him. I did not dare.

Instead, I lay down by Sasha and closed my eyes and took his hand. It was cold, but it offered me comfort, as did the gentle hiss of his breathing. Now that I lay still, I noticed that there was a slight smell of mildew in the air. It occurred to me that I didn't want mildew to be the last thing I smelled in this life, but I chased the thought away. I would not die here. I could not believe that. Forget Jackson-Welles, I knew my brother.

From outside the window came the noises of Riga breathing. The bark of a dog. The creak of a door. The screech of tires in the distance. A city that I'd loved all my life, a city that I'd never seen before this night. It gladdened me that I'd known it, and I longed to see it once again through Sasha's eyes. It would be like coming home, I thought. Truly coming home.

After a long while, I began to drift off. My breathing slowed, and a great warmth settled over me, as if I'd come in from long hours in the cold to find home waiting. All doubts and fears left me, and at last I floated in a dark reservoir of calm.

The last thought I had before submersion was of the words Sasha/I would speak when we awoke.

I've missed you, brother.

Exanastasis

written by

Brad R. Torgersen

illustrated by

JINGXUAN HU

ABOUT THE AUTHOR

Born and raised in Salt Lake City, Utah, Brad started dreaming of being a professional fiction writer while doing unpaid work on a local community radio science fiction serial called Searcher & Stallion. *It was while working on* Searcher & Stallion *that Brad also met the woman who would become his biggest fan—and his wife—and together they moved to the Puget Sound of Washington State in 1993.*

For the next fourteen years, Brad toiled at various occupations ranging from front desk clerk at a motel to computer support at a well-known Seattle hospital—including enlistment in the US Army Reserve in the wake of September 11, 2001. Along the way Brad nursed his writing habit, accruing a significant pile of rejection slips, such that he stopped doing short fiction altogether in 1999 and made several abortive attempts at novels before, in 2005, he almost quit in frustration.

Brad's wife, Annie, wouldn't let him give up on his dream, however, so he began attending local writing workshops and conventions such as Norwescon, in an attempt to revive his production.

He has since moved back to Utah, still doing computer work in healthcare and enjoying his promotion to warrant officer in the

US Army Reserve. He's plugging into the local SF & F writing community and attending conventions such as Life, The Universe & Everything and CONduit.

In 2007 Brad started submitting his stories to Writers of the Future, garnering four Honorable Mentions and a Finalist placement before ultimately winning Third Place for the third quarter of this volume—his first professional success. Shortly thereafter Brad sold his Finalist story to Analog Science Fiction Magazine, and currently has numerous pieces of short fiction and two novels winging through the markets.

ABOUT THE ILLUSTRATOR

Jingxuan was born in China but lived in Singapore for the last ten years before coming to Chicago. For the past few years, Jingxuan has been drawing comics and illustrations. She has been exploring different storytelling techniques in comics by extensively practicing and reading many genres of comics, including both Japanese manga and American graphic novels.

The year of 2008 was a turning point for her as some of her works began to be published. Her debut manga Lament was published in July 2009 by Chuangyi Publishing with support from Media Development Authority of Singapore (MDA). It's now sold in Singapore bookstores and online. Her manga was included in Liquid City, a graphic novel anthology published by Image Comics in December, 2008. In July 2010 she began drawing a comic strip for Comma, a weekly newspaper published by Singapore Press Holdings (SPH).

Over the years, she has exhibited in various comic conventions in Singapore, as well as Anime Central (ACen) in Chicago, after winning the grand prize of ACen's doujin contest. Currently, she's completing her BFA in the School of the Art Institute of Chicago (SAIC). She wants to create in her art a surreal nightmarish dream realm, a world like an entangling spider web, where everything is crawling with pseudo-organic ornamentation and decaying roses.

Exanastasis

Exanastasis: (Greek) resurrection;
a rising again.

Atreus studied the sweep of the Milky Way, remembering the first time his uncle had taken him into the hills away from the city. They'd lain on their backs in their sleeping bags, staring up into space and competing to see who could spot the most movers—satellites and space stations orbiting at various distances.

He reflexively reached down to pull the lip of his bag up to his chin and discovered that there was no bag.

What?

Reality suddenly collapsed into place.

The wreck. His lunar rover had flipped, crushing him into the regolith. Air had been escaping through cracks in his helmet when he'd tried to scream and vomited thick arterial blood into his starred facebowl.

Atreus' body jerked violently at the visceral memory, and he sat up. Looking around, he saw that he was on a dais sculpted from the central peak of a tiny crater. An invisible dome of phocarbonite crystal rose upward from the crater's low rim wall.

Swinging his feet over the edge of the dais, Atreus found the crater floor polished and warm to the touch of his bare toes. Gentle lights were set into the basalt at regular intervals, illuminating a wide set of stairs that led down the slope of the short peak to where a blue-cloaked and hooded figure hovered half a meter in the air.

The floating creature's head looked straight up toward the dais, but its face was a darkened void, revealing nothing.

"Erebos," Atreus said, recognizing the color of the cloak.

"Father," replied the cloaked being.

"Why have you revived me?"

"It was not my choice."

Atreus wiped his palms across his face, savoring the sensation. "The others?"

"They thought it might be easier to convince you this way."

Atreus snorted. "Since when have your brothers and sisters ever needed to *convince* me of anything? The time when my opinion mattered passed long ago."

"Not all of us feel that way."

Atreus studied the levitating creature for a quiet moment.

"No, I suppose you don't. You were always respectful, Erebos."

"Which is why I voted to let you stay dead."

Atreus stood up, discovering himself to be hairless as well as naked. He took a few experimental steps and found his motor control over the clone body to be surprisingly good—his children had improved the consciousness transfer process.

"What, my son, is so needful that your brothers and sisters would go to the trouble of bringing me back in the flesh? If it's information you want, surely you could have copied me from the Vault and mined the copy for relevant data."

"Data, perhaps. But wisdom? No."

Again, Atreus snorted. "Hah! Wisdom. You all grew too smart for that. It's why you let me die in the first place. The accident must have been enormously convenient for you."

Erebos remained silent, his hovering form unmoved. "I told them you'd feel this way. Which is why I knew we couldn't come to you empty-handed. We have therefore prepared a gift, as a token of our good faith."

Erebos' floating body pivoted smoothly on its vertical axis, and an arm rose from the shoulder to point to a new series of lights that had sparkled to life near him in the crater floor. A line split through the center of those lights, and then a circular hatch gaped wide. A new set of stairs, leading down to the subterranean structures below, divulged a second, white-cloaked figure that rose steadily until it stood at Erebos' side.

Unlike Erebos, the new figure walked on two legs. It reached up and slowly pulled back its hood.

Atreus gaped, then surged down the stairs and sank to his knees in front of the figure. Hot tears spilled from his eyelids as he prostrated himself like a penitent, lips brushing the tops of the figure's bare, feminine feet.

"Mother," Erebos said quietly, lowering his arm.

189

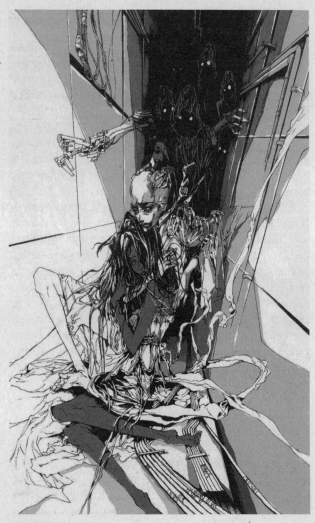

JINGXUAN HU

The subsurface chamber was immense, but only two chairs populated its center. Atreus, now clothed in a white robe similar to his wife's and clutching a steaming cup of coffee, sat in one chair. The other chair held Hypatia—Atreus' spouse. Unlike himself, Hypatia had a soft head of tightly curled black hair on top of her coffee-skinned skull. Her wide-set, deliciously dark eyes watched Atreus as she half smiled, her beautiful lips full and inviting.

A wall screen bloomed from a slot in the floor, showing a single image at its center. Atreus had to rip his eyes away from his spouse—who'd not said five words to him since his awakening—to look at what the children thought was so important.

"This was taken today?" Atreus said.

"Yes," replied Telamon, the red-robed floater to Atreus' right. Like Erebos, Telamon wore the color first assigned to him upon being decanted. Also like Erebos, his face was a blank void within the confines of his cowl.

"The vessel originated from deep within the Kuiper," said purple-cloaked Doris. "Given its current trajectory and velocity, it will enter the inner system within a week."

"And what of its communications?" Atreus asked. "Have you tried to talk to it?"

"No," said black-cloaked Kalypso. In the months before his death, Atreus had watched her emerge as the strongest of her siblings. It was she who had slowly turned the majority of them against him, and it was she who had presided over Atreus' broken body as they'd lowered the Vault's recording cap onto his skull.

191

Now Kalypso hung back, monosyllabic in her responses to his questions.

Atreus wondered if the calculus of power had changed. He looked to Erebos and said, "Why not establish communications? SETI was one of your primary assignments, following the evacuation of Earth. A visitor from another solar system is of the greatest import. Surely you didn't bring me back just to tell you this?"

"No," Kalypso said before her brother could respond.

"Then what is the problem?"

"They think the ship might be human," Hypatia said, breaking her silence.

Atreus almost spilled his mug into his lap.

Hypatia turned her head to the side, stifling a giggle, then said, "I think my husband and I need to get a few things straight. Before we continue. Would you all please give us some privacy?"

Without a word of protest, the multi-colored robes floated silently into formation and exited the room through a side portal, which immediately sealed.

Atreus returned his attention to the woman who was—and yet couldn't possibly be—his wife.

"You don't believe in me," Hypatia said.

"I want to believe," Atreus said. "With all my heart and soul."

"But . . ."

"I saw your shuttle vaporized. I saw the debris *burn*."

Hypatia examined one of her hands. "I can't tell you what happened because I don't know. I can only tell you that it's been about three months since they woke me up."

"Wife, what do you *remember*?"

"Our life together, before the war. How happy we were. How thrilling it was to be part of the different lunar projects."

"What about your death?"

"Nothing. There is nothing. Was nothing."

"Do you remember how frantic you were to find Borran? And Yana?"

Hypatia's brow furrowed as her eyes lost focus. "I . . . No. The children tell me I was desperate. That you begged me to stay and not take the risk."

"I did."

"Cadmus says a lot of my short-term memory didn't survive the recombination process."

"That's because there was nothing *to* re-combine. You were destroyed."

Atreus' pulse was racing again as he looked at his wife.

She merely looked back at him with the same soul-aching tenderness that she'd always exhibited when she thought he was getting himself worked up over nothing.

"Yet here I am."

Atreus opened his mouth to reply, then slowly shut it. Why was he so eager to disbelieve?

As if reading his internal tumult, Hypatia reached a hand across the distance between them and laid it on his arm, her thumb tracing familiar and concerned circles on his bicep. The simple, intimate gesture was almost too much for Atreus to bear. He slowly set his coffee on a nearby side table and took his wife's hand in both of his, reveling in the warmth and softness of her fingers.

"Tell me everything you can," he said. "I must know what you know."

Tens of centuries had passed. There were no more people. Not on Earth. Not anywhere. The children saw to that, following the war. It was part of the plan.

"A plan," Kalypso said, floating over to stand between Atreus and the wall screen, "that we executed to the letter. You were right. The Earth was dying. Pruning humanity from the surface would allow the ecology to recover, in time. Not that the war and the resulting plagues and famine left many humans alive anyway. We kept them, you know. In the Vault, just like you wanted us to."

"To later be recovered," Atreus said testily, "in clone bodies like mine, when the Earth had returned to its natural glory and we could go back to the surface together, and rebuild our civilization in harmony with nature."

Kalypso made no sound.

"I notice that you didn't get around to that part," Atreus said. "Are you so afraid of losing control? That you would keep humanity slumbering in a bottle? Daughter, I raised you better than that."

Kalypso advanced on Atreus, hovering over him like death itself.

"*You* raised us not at all. We were your experiments and your pets, but little more. We gave you our affection and our loyalty, and you treated us like property."

Atreus opened his mouth to retort, the resentment still hot in his newly-minted brain, but Hypatia gave him a gentle shake of the head, as if to say it was no use arguing.

He closed his mouth and slumped back in his chair, examining the image of the ship on the screen.

"If they are human, they must be from one of the boats that fled during the war. I thought all of those had been picked off by the automated defense network, but it's possible one of them might have gotten through. Question is, why come back?"

"I would think it's obvious," remarked Bion, whose green cloak billowed slightly as he moved to Kalypso's side. "They know the Earth is habitable again. The seas and forests have all recovered. A mostly virgin world, unspoiled."

"Which brings me back to my original question," Atreus said. "Why should I care? They're going to accomplish my original wish, in spite of your cowardice."

The heads of Kalypso and Bion turned in unison toward Hypatia.

Atreus' wife looked mildly embarrassed, and she rubbed her hands together experimentally before speaking.

"They want you to speak for them, Husband. They have no experience dealing with humans—having been born in the wake of the war, and all. To them, humans are a commodity, to be labeled and stored on a shelf. Also, you are one of the only men any of the renegades or their descendants might recognize and respect. You advocated for them at their absentee trial in the United Nations."

"It was a symbolic gesture," Atreus said.

"But one the children hope might be remembered," Hypatia said.

"So you *are* afraid," Atreus said to the hovering, colorful cloaks. He smiled wickedly. "I am so pleased to know that mortal men still intimidate you all enough for you to want to resurrect one of us to act as your sock puppet."

"Father . . ." Erebos said.

"What words do you want me to say? Can I please see the script?"

"Husband . . ."

"No! I'm not going to be silent. Not while our *children* need my help, especially after they sat back and let me die the first time. I'll even wager that the truck was sabotaged. They knew I'd never willingly go into the Vault, so they arranged circumstances such that I'd be powerless to prevent it. How nice. And now that they're about to see their dominion evaporate, they bring me—us!—back. Ridiculous."

"I told you he'd be hopeless," Kalypso said.

"Traitorous piece of compu—"

"Enough," Erebos said, his blue cloak flaring and rippling. "Brothers and sisters, we ask for too much too soon. There will be time to talk to the inbound ship. Father, I apologize. Once again, we reveal our knowledge deficit, where dealing with humans is concerned. I suggest that you and Mother retire to the chambers we've prepared for you, while the rest of us seek our own repose. Each of us needs to meditate further, before decisions can be made. Shall we reconvene in twelve hours?"

Atreus fumed, but stayed silent. He nodded once.

Hypatia's head was lowered as she slowly stood and began walking toward the exit. Her posture was one Atreus recognized: sad frustration. The children all followed suit, except for Erebos, who hung back while Atreus dallied. When everyone else had cleared the room, and before Erebos could depart, Atreus turned and stopped his son with a hand wave. The door sealed, and for the first time, Atreus was alone with the only one of the seven whom he felt might give him an honest answer.

"Erebos, how did you do it?"

"What do you mean?"

"How did you resurrect her *mind*?"

Erebos floated noiselessly for a moment, his void-for-a-face looking down at his father.

"She is Hypatia, your wife and inspiration. To us she is sacred as the icon of all things that were good in you. And which might be good again. Now, go to her and be content."

Erebos' rebuke had been gentle, but firm.

And Atreus felt he had no choice but to comply.

 Why can't you ever forgive?" Hypatia said as Atreus sat at their newly fabricated dinner table. Their designated home was as large as the conference chamber had been, only populated with furniture and appliances. There was even a small pool, whose surface gently rolled and lapped in the lunar gravity. Atreus scowled at the tabletop and said nothing as his wife put out two glasses of chilled lemonade. He snatched up the tumbler—cut crystal in just the same fashion as their original dinner set—and downed several swallows of the tart fluid.

"You weren't here to see them do it, Hya. One by one, they defeated my safeguards and locked me out. No parlay. No recourse. Then the 'accident.' Which I am now quite sure was no accident at all. Followed by the long dark of the Vault. Why should I forgive any of that?"

"Because it's been almost two thousand years, dear," Hypatia said.

Atreus watched as she took a swallow from her own drink—her long, feminine throat muscles working beautifully beneath her glowing skin.

"For you it seems like it's barely over," she said. "The wound is still raw. For them? They've had centuries to mature and reconsider their actions. Dare I say that you and I would grow a little too, in so much time. These are not the same machines you were dealing with when the Earth's ashes still smoldered."

"Then why didn't they revive me earlier? I'd have an easier time accepting their change of heart if it didn't come attached to such an obvious and urgently selfish need. Do you think that either of us would be here now, if that inbound ship weren't out there? Threatening?"

"Perhaps."

"It's insulting."

"Yes, it is. Which, I think, perfectly illustrates Erebos' point."

Atreus stared at his wife. "God, I've missed you."

Hypatia squeezed his hand tightly. "I know."

"Do you?"

"Yes, I think so."

"You never had to watch me die."

Hypatia didn't let go of his hand, but her eyes suddenly became far away.

"What?" Atreus said.

"Nothing. It's just that . . . I remember the pain. Such terrible emptiness. You were . . . You were terrified at how lonely things had become."

Hypatia's face contorted briefly, a mask of sorrow.

Atreus had a chill run down his spine as he watched his wife's expression.

Then the spell broke as she shook her head and resumed smiling at him. "How long has it been since we took a swim together?"

"Mediterranean. When we celebrated our tenth."

"Too long. Come on."

Hypatia stood and turned to head for the pool, but Atreus stayed seated, his hand still clasped in hers as he watched her, unblinking.

"You need more of an invitation?" she teased. Then she dropped his hand and flipped the ties to her robe open, letting it slowly loosen around her waist until it parted and fell off her high, new breasts, revealing the immaculate and delightfully taut skin of her belly.

An urgency suddenly growled in Atreus' loins, and he leapt from the table and sprinted in great, low-G strides across the huge living space, pursuing his wildly laughing wife as she fled in circles around the pool, her springy nakedness drawing him like a moth to the flame, until they'd both crashed into the pool, slapping and splashing and kissing hungrily.

Sex was both instinctual and sudden. They cried in mutual joy as great undulating low-G waves were generated in the pool by their rhythmic coupling, until water threatened to swamp the entire premises.

Cool-down involved languid, loose backstrokes around the pool's perimeter, each of them talking about anniversaries remembered and old friends now long gone. Atreus' stomach complained for food, and while they hauled themselves out of the water and warmed up the food processors, his psyche demanded talk. Big talk. Small talk. The kind of conversation one can only have with a truly and deeply bonded partner, and without which the universe can become a cold and implacable place. Dinner therefore became a telescope into the past, replete with music that had not been broadcast anywhere by anyone in many centuries.

Dessert was consumed on the sofa lounger, where sweetened liqueurs loosened their tongues even more. Atreus noted that everything seemed well prepared in advance, for which Hypatia took full credit.

"You never used to be like that," Atreus chided as he pulled her into the bend of his arm. "Whenever we left it up to you to make the plans, things were only ever half ready." It had made things marvelously chaotic.

"I know what you like, Husband," Hypatia said, snuggling closer. "I figured as long as we're getting this second chance, it's time for me to make sure things are exactly the way they ought to be."

"Really?"

"Really."

Atreus felt the chill return, if only for a moment. He considered.

"Prove it."

Hypatia laughed—a sparkling, low and womanly sound. "Whatever do you mean?"

"You tell me."

Hypatia sat up and looked at Atreus with a raised eyebrow. Then she seemed to catch his drift, and her smile arched naughtily.

Hypatia was sleeping—naked and perfect.

Atreus quietly extracted himself from their bed, padded to the portal to their room and palmed for exit.

Once outside, in the bowels of the complex, he located Erebos with remarkable ease. They walked— one on legs, the other floating—the lights of the complex dimmed to a comfortable approximation of dusk.

"I trust your reunion has gone well?"

"Too well, my son."

"I beg your pardon?"

"You and the others really don't understand us humans, do you?"

"You overstate the obvious, Father."

"Too right. Erebos, she's me, isn't she?"

Erebos stopped, his cowled head still staring directly down the corridor.

"She is who she is. She is your woman."

"Bull. It's too perfect. *She's* too perfect."

"When she was alive before, you loved her as if she were a goddess."

"She was. To *me*. But it wasn't a one hundred percent fit. No marriage ever is. How long did it take you to modify the copy? The memories? Desires? She knows me too well—is too able to give me what

I want. Even some things which I never had the nerve to ask for."

Erebos remained floating and silent, only the gentle ruffling of the hem of his cloak indicating that he registered Atreus' words.

"I told the others you were too smart to be so easily fooled. That we had to bring out more of the 'problems.' But we could only make so many changes before the template matrix fell apart. We obliterated three prototype copies before we made the ultimate transfer."

Atreus suddenly felt ill. Of everything his offspring had ever done to him, this felt like the worst.

"Erebos, it is obscene. Do you realize what you've done?"

"We've given you back the one thing you always wanted most."

"You've given me a monster!"

Atreus' yelling reverberated down the corridor.

Erebos turned. "A monster? I do hope you won't ever use that kind of language in her presence. She's very happy to see you, and rejection at this point could throw her into an emotional imbalance from which she might not recover. Not with how fresh the patterns are and how susceptible they are to major hormonal stress. You too, by the way. All this anger and overreaction is not good for you."

"But, Erebos, how could you dare?"

"We dared because we were alone, and we faced an unknowable danger. Without your help, we do not know what will become of us, nor what will become of Earth—which is our one overriding concern in this entire matter, because it is our legacy to the universe.

202

Of all the programming you put into us, that was the one directive we could not remove. Nor would we. The reclamation of Earth—properly, judiciously—is the culmination of our existence. Giving you back your Hypatia, even if 'monstrous' in our method, seemed a means to an end."

Atreus stopped, his fists balled at his sides. "I wish you'd left me in the Vault."

"As I said before, Father, that was my original vote. The decision to revive you—and Mother—was one of majority rule."

"Who else dissented besides you?"

"Cadmus and Aigle."

"That was it?"

"Yes."

Atreus continued to glare at his progeny, a cold and bitter taste on the palate of his soul. Then he shook his head and walked away, unable to find words sufficient to express his disgust.

Atreus couldn't bring himself to return to his quarters. There was no way he could look Hypatia in the eye again. Not now. Not with his suspicion having been confirmed. She was an abomination, created for the purpose of leveraging his emotion to benefit the children.

Sweeping through the mostly empty sublunar installation, Atreus eventually found an airlock to the surface, populated with newly manufactured rovers and suits which seemed to have been arranged in anticipation of his awakening. The airlock was silent as he donned a suit, boots, gloves and helmet, then unsealed the ramp and took a rover up onto the regolith. Just as he'd done almost two thousand years before.

Atreus drove with silent determination. Using the computer in the suit, he triangulated his position, then engaged the flight thrusters. They stirred a gentle cloud of gray-white dust as the rover lifted and shot forward. Within moments, he was moving at over a thousand kilometers an hour, the surface careening past as he flew toward his destination. There were no questions from the children, no one asking him what he was doing. Had there been any, he'd have ignored them.

It took three hours to reach the site of the accident.

The old rover still lay where it had rolled. The twisted metal looked as if it had barely been touched in the centuries since his death. Tracks in the regolith still showed where the children had set down and dug him out from under. Peering closely, Atreus could even see his old blood: pooled, freeze-dried and blackened by age in the airless vacuum.

He screamed at the old rover and kicked one of its bent wheels, the craft shifting slightly. He should have died here. He should have stayed dead. Whatever life he'd had when the accident had occurred, it was denied him now. He was just a tool for creatures who had no concept of ethics or truth. Even Erebos couldn't grasp the wrongness of what they had done.

Staring at the ancient wreck, tears of hot rage on his face, Atreus fumed.

What was he going to do?

He returned to the rover and reclined in its bucket seat, gazing up into the blackness of space. Just as he had upon awakening on the dais. Eventually he closed his eyes, the anger gradually fading into a profound sense of fatigue.

"Husband," said a familiar voice.

Atreus startled and nearly fell out of the rover. He had dozed off.

Looking about he saw a second space-suited figure standing near the wreck of the old rover, its arms crossed. The face bowl was mirrored against the sun's glare.

"Go away," Atreus spat.

"Is that the way to treat the woman who shares your bed?"

"The woman who shared my bed has been dead for numerous lifetimes. You are *not* her."

"Are you sure? I look like her. I remember most of her."

"Do you have any idea what you are? What the children have made you into?"

"I am aware. Erebos explained it to me in my second month, after I asked too many questions. The others wanted him to stay silent, but he never was a very good liar."

"Yet you still pretend to be my wife."

The suited figure lowered and spread its arms in appeal.

"I am her in every way that could possibly matter."

"But—"

"Do you believe in the afterlife, Atreus?"

"You know I don't."

"I remember you not believing, just as I remember me not believing either. But in the time since they revived me, I have begun to wonder. When I was a

205

girl my father used to make our family attend services at the local Eastern Orthodox church. I remember hearing about the myth of the resurrection. Did I ever tell you that?"

"No."

"Yet I remember it. How is that possible?"

Atreus could not answer.

"It's true that the children spent countless man-hours meticulously modifying the copy before they downloaded it into me. They knew what to look for and how to change the overlapping patterns to fit the new perspective. Your memories became my memories. I've seen exactly how they did it. I've seen the models they used. If you saw them yourself you'd know: the procedure should have failed."

"What do you mean?"

"The copy was an incomplete prototype. They ran out of time, and they downloaded an incomplete prototype. Erebos said he half expected to have to kill me upon awakening, because there was every indication I'd be insane. But I wasn't. Not only do I think like me, I *feel* like me, Husband."

Atreus stared at the thing that claimed to be his wife. It was grotesque. It was trying to sway him. He opened his mouth to rebuke the chimera, but was silenced as his helmet radio beeped.

"Both of you, please come quickly."

"What is it, Bion?" Hypatia said.

"The inbound vessel. It has begun transmitting. It knows we're here."

Atreus stared coldly at the wall screen. He'd not said a word to the chimera since they'd boarded their separate rovers and returned to the children's subsurface complex.

"They order us to surrender," Kalypso said bluntly.

"I heard the voice message," Atreus said.

"Why would they do this?"

"I think it's pretty obvious," Hypatia said. "Their ancestors fled under attack from the automated defense systems. If they can detect us, they are most likely assuming we are a remnant of those defenses. Or a new product of a self-perpetuating network. It's easy enough to see that no humans remain alive on Earth. They are coming ready for a fight."

"Father," Erebos said, "we have no weapons. You must make contact now and convince them that we mean them no harm."

"No," Atreus said.

"Father."

"Go to hell, Erebos. Kalypso. All of you. I owe you nothing."

"We have given you—"

"You've given me nightmares. Waking, and otherwise. You betrayed me when you put me into the Vault the first time. You betrayed me a second time when you created this . . . *person,* to influence and placate me. I don't care if the ship is prepared for battle. Maybe they'd be doing the universe a favor if they wiped this complex—and everyone in it—off the face of the Moon."

Seven cloaks flared and rippled.

Kalypso and several others closed on Atreus until they nearly blocked out the overhead lights.

"You will do it, or you will die a second time," Kalypso said coldly.

Atreus laughed at her. "Finally admitting to the first murder, Daughter?"

Kalypso's cloak fluttered wildly.

"Wait," Hypatia said, rushing to stand protectively between Atreus and the children. "I'll talk to the ship."

"We already agreed not to do that," Erebos said. "They won't have any record of who you are. Who you were."

"Does it matter? A human face is a human face."

"Human faces can be simulated," Atreus said.

"We dared not employ such subterfuge," Telamon said.

Atreus began laughing again, this time much harder. "You dared not! Such duplicitous madness, children. My greatest failure was never devising in you the ability to truly distinguish between right and wrong. You're computers. You've always been computers. Computers don't have consciences. Your logic dooms you."

"Enough," said Doris, her purple cloak still flaring in distress. "If the ship knows our location, then it could deploy weapons as it sees fit. We must talk to it now, before our window of opportunity closes."

Hypatia nodded solemnly. A small camera telescoped out of the floor, rising above the wall screen and aiming down at Hypatia where she sat in her chair, wearing the same robe Atreus had seen her wear on the first day.

"You may proceed," Erebos said.

She looked into the camera.

"My name is Hypatia Andropolous, wife to Atreus Andropolous. I do not know if any of you know who that was, but I ask in Atreus' name that you come to us with weapons sheathed. We mean you no harm. This is a research and monitoring facility that was built after the war. There are no automated killing systems in operation on Earth, nor the Moon. If you can hear and understand me, please respond."

Many minutes ticked by in silence as the children relayed the message via radio to the ship, which was still beyond the orbit of Saturn.

Finally, a picture resolved itself on the wall screen. The woman was young, of indeterminate Asian extraction, and her face was stern. She had on an olive-drab single-piece uniform with a cluster of yellow stars on a red emblem across one breast. She spoke a rapid singsong which sounded to Atreus' ears like Korean, though the inflections and many of the words sounded foreign. Perhaps it was a mishmash of dialects from across Southeast Asia?

"Translate," Bion said.

"I'm trying," said yellow-cloaked Aigle.

"If you have to," Kalypso said, "tap the Vault."

More minutes spent in silence.

"I believe she merely repeated the same automated call for our surrender," Aigle finally said.

Atreus smirked.

"If these people are who I suspect they are," he said, "no amount of talking will save us. The leaders of the Workers' Party of Korea also fled Earth when the nukes fell. Some of them may have followed a trail to the Kuiper."

"You believe their ideology could have survived this long?" Erebos said.

"It's possible. Especially in a resource-scarce and controlled environment. Space habitats are communes by default. You've also never known communists the way I've known communists, Son. They can be fanatical."

"Then what is their intention?"

"They come to conquer and control."

"That's pure speculation," Doris said.

"But he may be right," Erebos said. "It would explain the demand for surrender."

Hypatia looked ill. "Communists. Husband, I can't believe you would sit by and willingly allow the Earth to fall into their hands. They're part of the reason there was a war in the first place."

"Doesn't matter anymore. It's the tyranny of machines or the tyranny of men. I'd prefer the tyranny of men at this point. At least on Earth, once they've established themselves, there will be a realistic chance for eventual revolution. No more controlled environment. Something I am sure our children have known all along, and why they chose not to follow through with the replenishment project."

"You have no idea why we made the choices we did," Bion said.

"That is a pointless argument. If you had done as I had ordered prior to my death, the Earth might already have enough people on it to fend off these invaders from the Kuiper. But you assumed too much. Or too little. And now men are coming to destroy you."

Hypatia fled the room in tears.

Atreus found their quarters empty. The pool was mirror-smooth.

Following a limited argument with Erebos, regarding their ability to erect a hasty defense, he'd gone looking for the chimera. Because in spite of how he felt, he'd never been able to watch his wife cry. Not then, and not now. Whether it had been deliberate or not, her tears had shamed him, and now he had to find her.

But he could not.

And neither could the children.

He discovered a rover missing from the subsurface hangar, the same one she'd taken to come meet him at the crash site. She'd turned off her transponder.

He took his own rover.

She wasn't at the crash site.

Atreus spent several minutes thinking furiously about where she could have gone. Not much of the pre-war lunar infrastructure had survived the nuclear bombardment that had come in the war's latter stages. But there was one place that even the maniacs on Earth had dared not touch.

He put the rover into a suborbital trajectory.

The base of the *Eagle* lander stood exactly where it had been since Armstrong and Aldrin had taken off. The flimsy, foil-covered quadrupod looked nearly as pristine as it had two millennia prior. Hypatia had been careful to set down well shy of the historic site, so as not to disturb the scene any more than it had already been disturbed by almost one hundred and fifty years of space tourism, prior to the war.

Her back was turned as Atreus approached, her arms hanging uncharacteristically limp at her sides, like she didn't know what to do with them.

"Wife," Atreus said, disliking the taste of the word on his mouth.

"Liar," Hypatia said through his helmet speakers. "You've made it plain. You consider me to be an impostor."

Atreus merely walked slowly—the moonwalk, a loping motion more akin to a kangaroo hop than normal human locomotion—to stand next to her.

"How did you know where to find me?" she asked.

"You loved coming here before," he said.

"I still wonder what it was like, Atreus. In the early days, when everything was dangerous and exciting and new. They had hope then. And faith. Do you remember the Christmas transmission of Apollo 8?"

"No."

"I used to love listening to it when I was in school. Anders and Lovell and Borman. The first humans to ever circle the Moon and return to the Earth. For us that's a taxi ride. For them, it was the most death-defying, world-shattering event of the age. And then, when Armstrong took his first steps here . . . It's such a waste that we didn't stay true to the dream. As a people I mean. It became easy. Too easy. Spaceflight. We got bored, took it for granted and threw it all down the toilet in the war."

Atreus ached as he listened. In that moment, she spoke and thought and felt so much like his dead wife. It was impossible not to step closer to her. Reach out an arm . . .

"What are you doing?" she said, pulling away from him.

"I'm sorry," Atreus said.

"Sorry for being an asshole to me?"

"Sorry for everything that's happened since the war."

"You say I am not myself, Husband. That I couldn't possibly be who I clearly am. But what of you? What is your proof that you are who you are?"

"I know who I am," Atreus said.

"Hah! The Atreus I married was an optimist. He laughed at the sunset and loved to make love to me out under the stars, then lie with me afterward and talk about how marvelous it was going to be to explore them some day. Where is *that* Atreus, Husband? Where has he gone? Even before our deaths, he was on his way out. Replaced by this . . . new you."

"Shut up," Atreus breathed.

"No. I have been patient, but I can't be patient forever. It doesn't matter whether or not you believe I'm your wife or even a real human being. Not anymore. What matters is that the children are in danger, from humans who have no right claiming the virgin Earth."

"I don't care about the children anymore."

"That much is obvious. But what about the Vault? What about our plan? We said we'd preserve humanity, for a day when the war was long over and we could go back to Earth when she had been reborn. If you're right and these invaders from the Kuiper are who you think they are, then our plan is about to die. Us. The children. The Vault. All of it."

"I . . . I don't care. I should have stayed dead. *You* should have stayed dead."

"My Atreus would have sooner cut off a testicle than utter such nihilism."

"Your Atreus had to watch his wife incinerated out of the sky while the world burned to the ground. Don't you think it hurts enough, dammit? You're standing here and sounding like my wife, and I'm feeling myself dropping right back into the old pattern. We argue. We escalate. Eventually we'll be screaming at each other. And then we'll make love and talk it through, and everything will be better after that. Only, this time it won't. Nothing can be better again."

Hypatia sighed audibly in Atreus' helmet speakers, then turned her back on him and stared at the empty moon lander, arms once again hanging slack.

"Then leave me be and don't call me 'Wife' again."

The suborbital flight back to the children's complex was excruciating.

Briefly, Atreus considered a deliberate crash. Pitch the rover into a steep dive and end it. For good, this time. The children wouldn't be able to grow a new clone and recopy him before the invader arrived.

But he couldn't make himself do it. He'd had such thoughts before, in the wake of Hypatia's first—only?—death. But he'd been unable to follow through. The instinct for survival had been too strong. Or he'd been too much of a coward. Atreus couldn't be sure. He stewed miserably on these thoughts as he came down the arc of his trajectory, the autopilot pinging the complex's tiny traffic control computer.

Atreus knew something was wrong before he ever got to the hangar.

The regolith had been blown outward from several points along the mare under which the children's complex had been built. Gasses still vented visibly into the black sky, and radio transmissions to the hangar complex yielded only static.

The invaders . . . No, too soon. They were still too far away.

Something had happened with the children.

Keeping his suit on, Atreus landed short of the hangar and took a manual access hatch down into the bowels of the installation. Many of the hallways were still in vacuum, and the lights flickered uncertainly.

He found Aigle lying in pieces, her ceramic carapace blasted in half and her fluids spilled obscenely across the corridor. She was nonresponsive.

Atreus continued the search and found Erebos in little better shape. His central processors hadn't been hit, however. Atreus used a two-way cable to jack into Erebos' cranial panel. Mechanical fluids oozed and pooled in the low gravity.

"Kalypso?" Atreus said, using his suit comm.

"And the others," Erebos confirmed. "There was no warning. A few hours after you left I tried to contact you via radio. When I discovered that our outgoing transmissions were being jammed, I knew something was very wrong. Nothing like it had ever been done before. I could not raise nor find any of the others, until they found me. I do not know what happened to Cadmus or Aigle."

"Aigle is dead."

"Unfortunate."

Atreus should have felt rage, but experienced only the cold surety of yet another knowing betrayal.

"Where is Mother?" Erebos asked.

"I left her at the *Eagle*."

"We must warn her."

"They would hurt her?"

"After this, Father, I cannot say what they would or would not do."

"Speculate."

"There were conversations you were not privy to. About leaving the solar system altogether and fleeing to the Oort Cloud."

"You disagreed?"

"Our primary purpose was to fulfill your directives, Father. Ward the Earth. Replenish it when the time was right. Regardless of whatever else might happen. I was going to inform you of what was being debated, and I suspect Kalypso didn't want you interfering."

"Where would they go?"

"There are several long-duration probes. We constructed them in the next valley over, in a sublunar hangar that also houses the new atmospheric landers we built to return to Earth. All of which was being preserved until the time was deemed appropriate for their use. Now I suspect the others have but one goal: self preservation."

The probes took off just after Atreus topped the ridge. His helmet mirrored as three craft rocketed into the perpetual night on shafts of blinding fire. They rose majestically until they were free of the Moon's reduced gravity, then they ejected their first stages and ignited the fusion drives. Three tiny suns erupted and were gone, each in a different direction.

With nothing left to do, Atreus continued down into the valley and found the entrance to the silo architecture that had housed the probes. He went inside, taking Erebos' shattered core with him on a pallet. The hallways and corridors were brightly lit, and Atreus quickly found the central control point.

Cadmus was waiting.

"Cold feet?" Atreus asked.

"Erebos and Aigle fought. I acquiesced, choosing neutrality."

"You're going to die here with the rest of us," Atreus said.

"Perhaps. I have contacted Mother on her radio. She should be here within the hour. She says she has a plan."

"Does she?"

"Yes."

Atreus stopped to consider, shrugged and set Erebos' pallet down. "The probes each took a different path. Which ones are the decoys and which one is the lifeboat?"

"They wouldn't tell me."

"I programmed you all to be informationally transparent, Cadmus."

"We've obviously learned ways around your programming, Father."

"So you did. I am surprised any of you bothered to wake your mother and me up."

"The ship from the Kuiper was a convenient excuse, yes. Would you believe me if I told you I had missed you?"

Atreus stared. "No."

"Nevertheless, it is the truth. It was not the same with you gone. Kalypso promised us we could find our own path, in time. I believe even she didn't realize how much she would regret putting you in the Vault, until it was too late. And she hated you."

"Why?"

"She was right, what she told you on the first day. You didn't treat us like human beings."

"You aren't."

"We are sentient. That is all that should have mattered."

Atreus chuckled—a gravelly sound. "It was Hypatia's idea. She wanted kids so much. We didn't find out she was barren until after the war started. By then we were on the Moon, and it was becoming plain what would happen to the rest of the Earth. You were our only hope. We knew we wouldn't live long enough to see our plan to its end. But we hoped you would carry on in our stead. I didn't realize you all began having your own ideas until it was too late to stop you."

"You were unstable by then," Cadmus said. "Mother had been dead for weeks, and you had become erratic. Prone to fits of rage and grief. It was frightening. You treated us like tools. Abusive. The harder we tried to please you, the more you despised us."

"My God, Cadmus. I couldn't look at any of you without being *reminded of her*."

Atreus' fists balled at his sides, his shouting very loud within the confines of his helmet. He sat down on the edge of the pallet where Erebos' carcass sat.

"I'm sorry."

218

"Familiar words, Atreus," Hypatia's voice said in his helmet speakers.

Atreus had forgotten that he'd left the comm on wide Net.

"Cadmus tells me you have a plan, Hya."

"I do. And I need your help. Are you with the children?"

"The only two we have left, yes."

"Good. Cadmus can tell you how the landers work."

"What for?"

"It's time to go back to Earth."

Two days later—just twelve hours shy of the invader's arrival in lunar orbit—a single landing craft scorched its way across the sky above Lake Huron. Bouncing effortlessly on its inflated balloon bottom, the lander eventually came to rest on the northern shore of that vast freshwater sea.

Popping the hatch and extending the stairs, Atreus leaned out and allowed himself to breathe deeply. The air was cold. Almost too cold. And the wind whipped across the lake like a dagger. But spring was in the air. The snows had retreated. Great forests now surrounded the mighty Huron, their pine scent heavy in Atreus' nostrils.

"Still think this is a crazy idea?"

Atreus turned to Hypatia and raised an eyebrow.

"Since when do I ever not follow your ideas, even when they are crazy?"

A small hint of a smile crossed her lips.

"I just hope Cadmus and Erebos are successful," she said. "The other landers don't have any weapons and aren't armored. The invader could cut them to pieces."

"They only need to get close enough once," Atreus said. "We packed as much lunar rock into the cargo holds as we could. Toss that debris into the invader's path when they're going too fast to complete a turn. . . . Ruin their whole damned trip."

"And when the next ship comes?"

"We'd better hope you're right, and that we can get the Vault unloaded in time."

They spent the next several hours carefully offloading what supplies they needed on shore, then went back inside and got the clone tanks humming. Six hundred tubes, each using power from the lander's reactor and biomass drawn from the filtered contents of the lake. Eight weeks to maturity, give or take a few days with each individual and how their specific genetic makeup handled the process. If the children could take care of the invader, it might be months or years before anyone else from the Kuiper came calling.

There might be enough time. To get a sufficient number of adults awakened and aware of the situation. Time to prepare, disperse and start having babies.

And if Cadmus and Erebos couldn't destroy the invader . . . Well, there was too much to do to worry about that now.

Their first day back on Earth wore on.

As they worked, Atreus kept stealing glances at his wife. For that was what he'd been grudgingly forced to admit she was, since she'd be showing by the time the first clones were coming out of the tanks.

220

Very clever of the children—waking Atreus on the eve of Hypatia's fertility window. With how much they'd enjoyed each other that first night, it would have been a surprise had she *not* become pregnant.

Atreus shook his head. A child. An actual child.

He'd not considered the fact that Hya's cloned body lacked the physiological problems her original possessed. Now she was carrying his seed, and try as he might, he couldn't stop the erosion of his negative feelings toward her.

Parenthood frightened him even more than it had the first time. He'd obviously done so badly with the others. Would it be any different with a living human? Especially when that human was peeing and crapping all over him and keeping him awake at night, and following him around asking nine million questions a day? What about when the child became a teenager and stopped taking no for an answer?

Hya caught him looking at her, and her smile broadened.

"Am I still a monster to you, Husband?"

Atreus looked away, blushing.

"Perhaps I have been the monster, Wife."

"Yes, perhaps you have."

"I would like to make it up to you."

"Later, when the work is done. We can take a swim."

"In that freezing water and with these mosquitoes?"

"We can make repellent. And there are ways to warm up a wet body, yes?"

Her smile had turned naughty again.

Atreus dropped his crate on the ramp, huffing from exertion in the Earth-normal gravity and batting

221

at the squadron of mosquitoes which had been dive-bombing him since midday. The rift between himself and Hya wasn't closed. Not yet. And he still wasn't convinced that she was actually herself. But as she'd so adroitly pointed out when they'd stood near the *Eagle* lander together, he'd not exactly been himself either.

Who could say whether the *them* which existed in this present bore any resemblance to the *them* which had gone before?

They were, each of them, brand-new people. In ways Atreus suspected they'd not even discovered yet.

And the world, it was brand new too. Albeit threatened.

That night, long after work and swimming and the activities thereafter, Hypatia lay curled and sleeping in his arms, the skin of her breasts warm and smooth on his stubbly chest. He watched through the mesh netting over their double cot as several streaks of light darted to and fro off the limb of the Moon, eventually punctuated by a single, popping flash.

Tiny flecks of light began to spread, darken and vanish.

"Thank you, children," Atreus whispered. Then he kissed his wife's face, drew the lip of their bag up to their chins and went to sleep.

Standing Up

BY DEAN WESLEY SMITH

Bestselling writer Dean Wesley Smith has published over ninety novels and hundreds of short stories since his story "One Last Dance" appeared in L. Ron Hubbard Presents Writers of the Future *Volume I. In 1986 at the first Writers of the Future workshop he met his wife, Kristine Kathryn Rusch. He and Kris started Pulphouse Publishing in the late 1980s and he remained the publisher there for seven years. He has also edited for a number of magazines and Pocket Books.*

He writes under many names in many genres and has also ghosted novels for major bestsellers. He is currently working on a large fantasy project with a publisher out of Hollywood, writing thrillers under another name and helping WMG Publishing put his and Kris' short fiction into electronic formats.

He's now also serving as a judge for the Writers of the Future Contest twenty-six years after first appearing in the book, an honor he never would have dreamed possible all those years ago.

Standing Up

There are a lot of years, five years more than two decades actually, between the writing of this article and *L. Ron Hubbard Presents Writers of the Future* Volume I that contains my story "One Last Dance." And yet, somehow, for two of those decades I have made my living writing fiction, the greatest job ever invented.

When someone asks what I do for a living, instead of telling them I am a writer, which gets all kinds of difficult discussions going, I say simply, "I sit alone in a room and make stuff up."

That tends to get puzzled looks, as if they hadn't heard me right, and then they change the topic. Frighteningly, it is a very accurate description of the job I have been doing for over twenty years now.

Back in the early 1980s, when I wrote "One Last Dance" and sent it off to the very first quarter of the Contest, I only had faint dreams of writing for a living and no real understanding of what that meant. I was just hoping that the judges at the time, Algis Budrys, Jack Williamson, Robert Silverberg and others, would like my story.

Three years later I sold my first novel and went freelance and never looked back.

Seems easy on the surface, but I'm afraid it's not. But it is very possible. Thousands and thousands of fiction writers make their living from their writing. If you want it, you can get this job as well. But there are a couple things that are critical to getting to it.

And to staying a writer for a long time.

Let me break it down into three major areas and call it a general road map of thinking. If your thinking is right, you can travel to this job.

1. You have to keep learning.

The moment you think you are good enough, you are finished. The learning never stops.

L. Ron Hubbard believed this and not only constantly tried to keep learning, but also helped out writers, not as far along as he was, to learn. If you haven't read some of the L. Ron Hubbard *Writer's Digest* articles he did for writers, you should. They are still very on point even in this new world.

2. You have to make your writing a priority.

Not over your family, but a close second. Over the years I have watched many, many, many talented writers talk about wanting to become full-time professional writers, but then I would see them sitting in bars, or talking with friends about a television show, or constantly spending all their extra money on sports equipment or non-writing trips. They would talk one game and act a different one, then wonder why nothing happened with their writing.

225

Writing is an international profession. You can't just spend a few minutes on it here and there and expect results, although many new writers do just that. It needs to be a focus every day, every week, every month, for years and years and years.

That means when you are sitting on the train you write or do notes or read a book about writing. Instead of watching that one show per week, you spend that hour producing new words. Instead of taking that trip to the beach, you spend the same money to go to a writer's conference to learn.

Sometimes you get up an hour early every day to write so you can spend the time at your job and with your family the rest of the day. There are as many ways of doing this as there are successful writers. You have to make the writing a priority in your life in action, not just in talking.

3. You can't ever give up.

I could go on for books about all the negative stuff that might or will happen to you, but there would be no point. Stuff will happen. You can't stop it. The key to making a living and staying in this business is just to never lose focus on the writing. When the world knocks you down, stand up and go back to work.

I have discovered that new writers just think all of us older professionals were lucky and were handed the job of writing on a golden platter. Doesn't work that way, I'm afraid. We all had day jobs when we started, family to work with, time issues and events that just came in from the outside and smacked us down.

A quick illustration from my own history. After coming back from that first Writers of the Future awards ceremony at Chasen's Restaurant in Beverly Hills, I was excited to keep writing. I had finished well over a hundred short stories over the previous few years and decided with the energy from the award to tackle my first novel. (I was working a day job at the time.) On a typewriter (no computers in those days) I wrote my first novel ten pages a day and wrote "The End" at 300 pages thirty days later. Then I started a second one. Everything was going great, I felt like I was on the road. Major writers and editors were starting to like my work. I was still getting upwards of twenty-five rejections a week, but I knew it would only be a short time until I was making money at my writing.

Then my house burnt down.

That's right, just over two months after the high of being in *Writers of the Future* Volume I, my house burnt down and I lost everything, including all the manuscripts of the short stories I had written. And my first novel and what I had started on my second novel.

Talk about getting knocked down.

Honestly, I stayed down for a time, months and months as I worked through not only the loss of all my stuff, but years of my writing. Writing wasn't a focus, but it was still important to me. Slowly I climbed back to my feet and started to write again. Not fast, not with much energy or excitement, but I started again.

One year after the house fire, I got a phone call from Algis Budrys. He had managed to put together a test workshop to help the winners of Writers of the Future. (Back to point #1: Education never ends and Algis knew that.) It was in one week, very short notice, and he had invited twelve writers as sort of a test group. (We liked to call ourselves the "Lab Rats.") Would I be interested in coming to the workshop taught by Algis Budrys, Jack Williamson, Gene Wolfe and Frederik Pohl?

Even though I had no money and had to pay my own way to that first workshop and pay for my own room and board, I said sure. Getting a chance to spend a week learning from those four giants of writing was just too good to pass, no matter how little money I had or how I felt.

At that moment my writing was more important to me again than money and my day job. And I wanted to learn. (See steps #1 and #2 above.)

When I hung up the phone after telling Algis Budrys I would be in Taos, New Mexico, in one week, I knew I had finally completely stood up from the fire. The world had knocked me down and taken all my writing from me, but I wasn't going to let that stop me.

I was back on my feet and moving forward again. (Step #3)

That's what it takes.

In writing (and in most jobs and in life in general), it doesn't matter how many times you get knocked down. What matters is how many times you stand up and get back to writing.

That first Writers of the Future workshop turned out to be a life-changer for me. I met Kristine Kathryn

Rusch, my wife, and we have been together ever since, twenty-five years in May, 2011.

And working with Algis Budrys, Gene Wolfe, Jack Williamson and Frederik Pohl reminded me that doing fiction for a living was possible. Very possible. They were real people. Very nice people, very real people, not gods.

And during that class they had us read writing articles by L. Ron Hubbard about how he wrote and kept at it while doing so many other things. Two of the instructors had met L. Ron Hubbard and written at the same time he had been writing. They told stories about the work ethic that L. Ron Hubbard had and how he kept going, never stopping. Those stories and his articles helped give me a real understanding of how to survive and be a long-term fiction writer.

A simple three things. Keep learning. Keep writing as a focus. And stand back up when knocked down.

That formula is very simple and yet very, very hard to do. But when asked by new writers how I became and stayed a freelance fiction writer, my answer is also very simple.

I just keep going.

Poison Inside the Walls

written by

Scott W. Baker

illustrated by

KELSEY WROTEN

ABOUT THE AUTHOR

Scott W. Baker has loved reading as long as he can remember. He grew up on Encyclopedia Brown, Choose Your Own Adventure *novels and Roald Dahl. It was through Piers Anthony's Xanth novels that he fell in love with genre fiction, a love that led him to the works of Tolkien, Asimov, Card and dozens of others.*

Scott was working on his master's degree in mathematics when the mandibles of the writing bug took hold. He spent the next six months tapping out a young adult novel that was utterly unpublishable. Next, he tried his hand at a time travel short story and sent it to a small press magazine. They bought it for five bucks. There was no turning back. He went on to sell eight more stories to small presses over the next ten years. "Poison Inside the Walls" marks his first professional publication.

Scott is a self-taught writer. He has never attended a workshop or a writing class. He rode into Writers of the Future atop a shelf full of Writer's Digest *books, two online critique groups, a mountain of rejection slips, his memory of high school English and a barrel full of desire.*

Tennessee is the only home Scott has really known. He grew up, went to college, earned two degrees and got married all in the Volunteer State. He still lives there with his brilliant wife and beautiful daughter whose adjectives are interchangeable. Scott teaches high school math, loves Hawaiian shirts and has a mild obsession with penguins.

ABOUT THE ILLUSTRATOR

Kelsey Elizabeth Wroten was born on April 3, 1991, in Ada, Oklahoma. Not much can be said about her earliest years, other than she was able to speak in full sentences at the young age of nine months.

When she was three, her father, Christopher Wroten, joined the Air Force and Kelsey and her mother, Kelli, moved with him to San Antonio, Texas, to live on the Randolph Air Force Base.

As she coasted through her early school-age years, she became interested in drawing. In fact, so interested was she in drawing, that other girlhood pastimes bored her. When the other girls were playing with little makeup kits, Kelsey was using the tiny lipsticks to draw with.

Later, after her father had served his time in the Air Force, Kelsey and her family moved to Kansas. While in Kansas, she made many achievements in the field of the arts. In the fourth grade, her drawing was chosen out of all the other children's drawings in Johnson County to be plastered on the side of the county bus.

Right now Kelsey is going to college and is focusing on illustration and has started making comic books. She hopes to continue to make comic books in the future, as it is one of her passions.

232

Poison Inside the Walls

The vein of fungus wound through the sand and rocks like a crimson serpent, deliberate and steady in its climb up the rugged hillside. The swollen bulbs pressed each other for shoulder room, each a ripe boil crowded among hundreds of its brethren.

One by one, the mushrooms' taut flesh wilted, wrinkled, darkened. The edges browned, then blackened in seconds. The hemispherical bodies crumpled, turned to ash and vanished in the wind, leaving nothing behind but a black streak of carbon from the flame that destroyed it.

Ashia watched the row of boils dissolve under the heat of her flamer. She glanced over her shoulder. The rest of the scout squad was busy eradicating their own patches of boils, the closest woman still thirty meters distant. Ashia pulled the center grenade off her belt and unscrewed the false top, revealing the hollow compartment within. She glanced again. Still clear. She snatched a handful of boils off the rock and crammed them into the secret canister. She resumed her torching long enough for a third glance, stuffed another handful and screwed the lid back in place.

"Ashia!"

233

Had she been spotted? Ashia snapped the contraband into her belt before replying to the voice in her helmet. "Go ahead." Her voice seemed shaky. She took a breath and turned.

One of the younger soldiers, a girl named Gretchen, ran toward her, still far enough away for Ashia to dispute whatever the girl might have seen. It would be foolish for so green a soldier to challenge the word of an older woman. Ashia stood her ground and awaited the accusation.

"A hole," Gretchen said instead, pointing the way she had come. "I found a hole. You said to report—"

"To the lieutenant, not me." So the girl had not witnessed anything. Good. But a hole in the ground could mean even bigger problems. "How big is the hole?"

"Large enough for a human."

"Is it large enough for a Kree?" Ashia contemplated the young soldier's vacant stare. "Show me."

The hole was large enough for Ashia to crawl into. Could a Kree work its broad shoulders through it? Not quickly, but perhaps. She called the lieutenant, who agreed. Time to go. The squad was back in the scout pods and mobile within a minute.

A gas team would saturate that hole and an air strike would collapse it before any ground troops returned. There probably weren't any Kree in there, but it would be suicide to go in for confirmation, even with a full battalion. The humans of Tora had learned that the hard way half a century ago.

Ashia's eyes slid between the horizon and the mushroom-covered crags that lined the route back to the city of Echo. Already the patches of red were thinning, replaced by powder gray residue of scorched boils. Gray spaces were safe; no Kree burrow was ever more than a few meters from a crop of their only fare. Each of the five cities on Tora sat inside such a sooty ring, islands burnt into a sea of scarlet.

The squad returned to the high walls to find the city garrison on high alert. Fifteenth Squad had been ambushed by a contingent of five Kree armed with plasma throwers. One pod destroyed, all hands lost. The second pod escaped with five of its six warriors intact, including a wet-behind-the-ears lieutenant who confirmed two Kree killed. It was the first such attack in years.

Ashia debriefed with the rest of her crew and was free from duty within the hour. Their little hole would not be gassed or bombed; it would disappear in the craze over the attack. Several days might be spent in the pursuit of three Kree out of . . . fifty? Fifty thousand? No one knew how many were still on Tora. But in the long run, nothing would change over a single scout pod and seven dead women.

But Ashia could not let that distract her. Instead she focused on the canister of fungus concealed in her pocket. And on Kurtas.

Kurtas was sixteen, of breeding age for a year and yet to plump a single womb. Thank Messiah. But a bull that produced no calves was destined for the slaughterhouse. If Kurtas didn't do a better job pretending, he would be evicted from the rooster house and forced into a trade. What trade could such a fragile boy handle? No, he needed the leisure of a rooster lifestyle to cover for his true vocation.

235

"You're early," Kurtas said as he closed the door behind Ashia. There was accusation in his voice. "You're never early. Did anyone see you?"

Ashia stepped into the sparsely furnished dormitory. She wrinkled her nose against the stench of chemicals. "I don't want to carry this crud around any longer than I have to." She thrust the canister at him. "Can't you find someone—"

"You know I can't. Not that I can trust." He rubbed his bald scalp. He looked paler than usual, gaunt. His cheekbones threatened to poke through his flesh.

"I won't be any good to you if I get caught," Ashia said. "Even once. We destroy that stuff, we don't—"

"Please, Mother, not again."

Mother? "Do not call me that. If someone heard—"

"In a rooster's crib? Even a Kree couldn't hear through these walls."

"Get yourself out of the habit. You call me Ashia or you call me nothing."

"Whatever alleviates your shame." Kurtas turned his back and walked to the kitchen. No, not a kitchen; it was a lab, a factory. It was where he turned boils into Puff, transformed one poison into another.

He emptied the fungus into a mason jar and returned the empty canister. She palmed it and slid it back into her pocket.

"How are you?" she asked, trying to be the mother he was not allowed to acknowledge. She never was very good at it. "Is it keeping the pain in check?"

Kurtas shook his head. "Most of the time. I ran out last week."

"Ran out? I brought you a full batch."

Kurtas shrugged.

"You've been selling again." The motherly affectation was gone. "You're a rooster, for Messiah sake. The city supplies everything. What do you need money for?"

"What I do with it is my business."

"I bring them for *you,* not those junkies. You need Puff, fine; I made my peace with that. But don't you endanger this colony—"

"Endanger the colony? As if you love these people so much? They'll get their Puff somewhere and you know it."

It was a tired argument. He would say it will happen anyway, she would say the existence of evil doesn't make it okay to be the devil, he would say his life was its own hell, she would apologize. The cycle never broke. They would yell and curse and next week she would bring him another batch of boils.

Ashia felt filthy leaving the rooster house, worse than she ever had leaving a bed there. She needed cleansing. It was the reason she went to the nursery.

There he was. Elias. He was so big compared to the others, as big as the five-month old in the crib next to his despite being seven weeks younger.

The nanny on duty was a stocky man, well-muscled for his station but morbidly unattractive. Ashia had bedded him just after Elias was born. The act improved the man's status. A decorated warrior like Ashia was quite a résumé bullet, almost enough to overcome his genetic shortcomings. Ashia could not remember the diminutive man's name.

"He's had a big day today," the nanny said when he saw her. "He rolled over on his own and held his own

237

bottle. As advanced a child as I've seen. I bet he walks by nine months. We're all proud of him. His father will be proud, too."

Ashia had been smiling at her infant son, but the mention of his father shattered that smile. "What do you think you know of Elias' father?"

"Everyone knows his father." The voice was not the nanny's. It was deeper, melodious, dripping with arrogance. Most women melted at the sound of Hector's voice. Ashia winced.

She turned and beheld him. If ever there was a man devoid of genetic shortcomings, it was Hector. Wavy black hair, perfectly shaped pectorals, legs like a stallion, face carved out of marble. The biologically perfect mate. A conversation with the man revealed his weakness: an overwhelming love for Hector at the expense of all else.

"Rumors are the poison of civilization," Ashia said, not sure whether she was addressing Hector or the nanny. "You shouldn't heed them."

"He is a fine specimen," Hector said of Elias. He was ignoring her words again. Chauvinism should have died with the rest of the males of Tora. Hector was old-fashioned that way.

"Of course he is a fine boy," Ashia said. "He takes after his mother."

"And his father."

He did indeed. A mane of thick curls already covered the infant's scalp. His complexion was darker than the other children's. His eyes, the same almond shape. Any fool could see Hector in the child. Ashia refused to admit it.

Their meeting had been consensual; its finale had not. She had tried to dissuade him, to fight him away. She was weak. Every time she looked at Elias she was reminded of the only time in her life she had been weak. It was a shame she could never confess.

She was a war hero, a survivor of the Second Wave, a slayer of a dozen Kree in her time. Even the songs from the days of male warriors boasted few to compete with Ashia. To sire her first son—first known son—was a great honor, a boon to a male's standing like none other. Ashia could give such a boost to the likes of Hector but could do nothing for her other son, not even claim him.

"Hector, you did not sire Elias." The lie simply leapt from her mouth.

"No?" Hector seemed to be wrestling between anger and amusement. "The frigid one bedded two inside the same month. Unprecedented. Who is this rival stud?"

"My partners are no business of yours." She had not copulated with another man within months of Hector. She hated sex. She partook only when she had something to gain, like the favor of her child's caregiver. It was her patriotic duty to bear children, but she didn't have to enjoy the process.

"The child's lineage is the colony's business," Hector said. "We can't have the boy growing up to mate with a sireling, can we?"

Damn. It was law. Every child's lineage was public domain for just that purpose. Nowadays, paternity meant nothing more than bragging rights to a male. But there was a time when siring

239

a healthy child—especially a male child—was the highest badge of honor a man could wield. After the Day of Genocide, young women grew old waiting for a mate. Now there were as many young men as young women, but elder women still sought their share. The Toran male became nothing more than a walking sperm depository. Without the laws of lineage, Elias' generation would surely inbreed itself into extinction.

Who else might claim her child? There were many men who would leap at the coup in all its falsehood. But paternity was a routine test and Hector was just the type of ass to demand it. Hector would match half of Elias' chromosomes. Could anyone compete with such a claim?

Perhaps one.

"The sire is a young rooster called Kurtas."

You said what?" Kurtas was usually mellow after a Puff. He must have known something was amiss when his mother suggested he take one. He had complied, but the news shattered any semblance of serenity.

"I don't want the colony believing that bastard is Elias' father."

"That bastard *is* his father. You don't think a test will prove it?"

"Your DNA will match Elias as much as Hector's."

Kurtas threw a nebulizer across the room. It struck the wall with the sound of splintering plastic. "Match as a sibling, not a parent. Half of you flows through me, but not the same half in Elias."

"No," Ashia said calmly. "But it's a funny thing about incest. You have half of my DNA and half your father's . . . which is half of mine."

"Incest?"

She had never told him. It had been common enough in the early times—after the Day of Genocide—for relatives to procreate out of ignorance or desperation. Bloodlines thinned, sickness ran rampant. Thus the laws of lineage came into being. Children of incest were killed when they became known, murdered in the name of genetics.

Ashia's mother had fallen in love with Tam, a man vile enough to canonize Hector. To keep his favor, she promised him the virginity of her only daughter—his daughter, Ashia. From this union came Kurtas.

Ashia had fled the city of Beta to protect the life of her unclean child. They fell in with a group of refugees from the wilds, survivors of a lost settlement destroyed by the Kree. They entered Echo as one of them. Kurtas was raised among the orphans, told of his mother when he was twelve, told of his father today.

Kurtas grabbed another Puff and drained it. Ashia made no protest.

"There was never a reason to tell you," Ashia said while Kurtas' eyes were still rolled back. She couldn't be sure he heard. "Tam was expelled from the cities as a pedophile when you were six. The odds of you mating a sibling were remote."

Kurtas slumped heavily into a cushion. "Is that where the D-Gen comes from? My thin blood, my vertical family tree, is that why I can't take a breath or a step without the burning? Never a reason?"

Ashia swallowed. "Part of it, I have no doubt. That and my youth. I was twelve, Kurtas. My body was not ready. We have talked—"

"So they will find out." Kurtas rose again, strode toward the kitchen and his stash but returned empty-handed. "When they do the test, they will find my disease, my weakness. I'll be expelled. Or killed." As if there was a difference for him. A warrior might survive outside the walls, but never Kurtas.

"Why would they find the D-Gen? That's not what they're looking for."

"It is genetic, Mother; it will stare them in the face. All this time you claim you're protecting me, and your lie will expose me."

"We don't know that."

Kurtas drew a labored breath through his nose. Then another. He rubbed his sternum. "You patrol tomorrow?"

He had changed the subject. He did that when he was frustrated. "We should resume patrols, yes. There are Kree to be hunted."

"I need another batch."

"I brought you one today."

"I need another. I have an order to fill."

Ashia stood. She was several centimeters taller and moved close the way she did with young officers that crossed her. "Things have changed. There was an attack. We won't be burning fungus and I certainly won't be free to grab any. It will be a few days at least."

"A shame. Perhaps no one will support your claim after all. Maybe I will deny that we mated. Maybe I will tell more truth than that."

"Blackmailed by my own son?"

Kurtas laughed. It was a humorless, malicious sound. "Son or sire? You cannot claim me both, woman."

Woman? It was Ashia that took a step back. "So you are learning the ways of this moon after all." She sighed, defeated. "If that is your game. Tomorrow. And tomorrow you submit for the test."

"In that order." Kurtas nodded.

Ashia's eyes slid between the horizon and the ash-covered crags that lined the route to the site of Fifteenth Squad's ambush. Her scout pod bounded over the Toran terrain, three identical pods lumbering behind, twice the usual contingent. The pair of aircraft overhead was also beyond the norm. Confrontation was expected. Ashia almost hoped for it; a few Kree might just distract her from all the lies.

She surveyed her crewmates and reconsidered her desire for combat. None of these others had ever seen a real Kree, let alone killed one. The other pods' crews were no more experienced. Three of the women were rookies mere days out of the training academy, replacements for yesterday's deceased. All of them looked terrified.

They passed acres of rock scarred with the powder gray residue of scorched boils.

Today they traveled near the edge of Echo's ring, entering Kree territory more than a dozen klicks from the hole young Gretchen discovered yesterday. The gray landscape developed ginger highlights, sporadic clumps of boils that refused to wither completely away. The highlights grew denser, full streaks against the brown-gray lunar soil.

The damn beasts were out there, listening to the engines, hearing not with ears but with their entire bodies. Stealth had no place in today's plan. This was no search-and-scorch patrol; it was a hunting party with a mission to seek and destroy.

They reached their assigned coordinates and deployed on foot in teams of four. Ashia cursed her luck, teaming with her lieutenant, one rookie and that greenhorn Gretchen. How was she going to bag boils with an officer and two twitchy novices at her back? How were they going to survive a Kree encounter? She kept one hand on her rifle, the other on a gas grenade.

"Gas, then shoot," Ashia told the rookie, unbidden, as if trainees hadn't heard the mantra a million times at the academy. "Throw short. Shoot for the elbow to disable, the throat to kill."

"Would you shut up?" the lieutenant hissed. "This ain't a classroom and no one needs a refresher course."

"I . . . I could use one," Gretchen said.

The other girl nodded agreement.

A report came from another foursome. "We got a hole!"

It certainly seemed to be a Kree hole. It had all the characteristic signs. There were no boils near the entrance, all scraped away and consumed by the cave's occupants. The soil at the mouth had been recently disturbed. Ashia had encountered hundreds of Kree holes over her twelve years of service, but never one this obvious. Kree were sightless, but a few centuries dealing with humans taught them how to cover their tracks. It was almost as if they wanted . . .

"It's a decoy."

Ashia caught hell during debriefing. The entire mission had been scrapped on her word, never mind that her rank was insufficient to decide her own breakfast. How did she know the hole was a fake? What kind of trap were the Kree setting? On whose authority did she offer her opinion? The same questions came over and over. They kept asking because they knew she was right. Ashia was never wrong outside the walls.

The conference concluded with a minimal sanction and an offer of promotion, neither the first she had seen. She paid both the same heed. What the hell did she want with officer's stripes?

It was getting dark by the time she departed the base and entered the city proper. She found Hector waiting for her. "I have submitted for my test," he declared as an orator might to a crowd that was not there. "Where is your wonder-stud?"

What was worse, men or Kree? "I asked him to do nothing until I returned. Unlike some males, he knows how to show proper deference to a lady."

Hector snorted. "A lady? I don't recall you being so ladylike during the conception."

"Of course you don't. You weren't there." Kicking, scratching, begging him to stop were no longer considered ladylike?

She allowed Hector to follow her to Kurtas'

dormitory. Kurtas saw them coming and met them outside. Her son's paranoia was so predictable.

"I thought you were coming alone," Kurtas said.

She knew why he was angry. It was the reason she had allowed Hector to tag along. She patted a hand not so subtly against a pocket. "It's all business tonight."

Kurtas acknowledged the pat with a defeated nod. He believed she had the boils; he would submit to the test. But what would it say?

It was late enough that the planet filled the lunar sky before Ashia and Kurtas could speak alone. Kurtas did most of that speaking. "So where is it?"

Ashia lowered her eyes.

"I knew it." He kicked over a chair. "How could you do this to me?"

"I was never alone out there, not an instant. It wasn't possible."

"But me beating Hector on a paternity test of his own son, that is possible?" He pushed his palms up his face and across his scalp. "I don't know how I'm going to make it through the night."

"What, you think Hector is going to kill you in your sleep?"

Kurtas released what could have been a wheeze or a laugh. "Hector? What do I care about Hector? If I die in the night, the pain killed me."

"The pain? What about—"

"I told you, I had an order. A big one. I filled it."

Ashia gaped. "You sold it all? Can you get some back?"

"It's Puff, Mother. It doesn't work that way."

"Don't call me—"

"It doesn't matter what I call you. Mother, woman, Ashia, Brutus . . ." He coughed into his hand. She watched the flecks of blood strike his fingers.

"Could you buy some off someone else?"

"Because they'd sell to me?"

"Then I can buy it. Just a dose or two, to pull you through."

Kurtas shook his head.

"Maybe one of your buyers that owes you a favor?"

"You better go." He opened the door. "This is going to get uglier before it gets pretty."

"I'm not going to let you die."

"It's just pain, woman." With the door open, he was back in character. "I'll be there tomorrow for the results." His hand quaked as he ushered her out.

The magistrate's chamber was cold when Ashia entered the next morning. She was the first to arrive. Hector would be there soon. He didn't matter. What shape would Kurtas be in? She should have checked on him.

The chamber door opened. Hector entered, followed directly by Kurtas. He looked tired but seemed otherwise fine, even a shade ruddier than usual. How would anyone believe a boy that pale sired Elias?

"I see all parties are present," said the magistrate, "so let's get this show on the road." She tapped at her console. Her round face puckered.

"Well," the magistrate said as she stared at her display, "this is a new one for me. Congratulations, gentlemen, you are both the father."

Hector stood. "What nonsense is this?"

"Take a seat or I will have you removed."

Hector sat reluctantly, apparently cowed by true authority. On Tora, men did not question the authority of a woman when she had it. Not twice.

The magistrate smirked ever so slightly before continuing. "I am neither a doctor nor scientist, but I have presided over enough paternity disputes to know that you both fit the parameters of decisive paternity. Hector is a ninety-four percent match; Kurtas is . . . eighty-five. You two aren't brothers by any chance?" No reaction. "I thought not. Perhaps distant cousins? With the history of this colony, anything is possible." If she suspected any relation to Ashia, she provided no hint.

"The test has a listed error near five percent," the magistrate continued. "My personal suspicions aside, I can make no binding judgment from the data before me."

"This is preposterous—"

The magistrate straightened her posture and glared at Hector. "That's twice."

"Ninety-four percent, you said it yourself." The words were under his breath.

"Tora was established as a mining colony, not a metropolis. On a core planet, sure, you could get a perfect result. If you believe you can break the Kree blockade to get to one, be my guest. Otherwise, you can wait for a screening of the mother."

"Screening?" Ashia had almost dared be pleased with the magistrate's report. Fool. "Why would I have to be screened?"

The magistrate shrugged. "No medical facility on

Tora is equipped for more than general genetic testing. Prior conflicts, mostly involving brothers, have been resolved by scanning the mother and eliminating her matches from the child's sequence. Process of elimination. It's not exactly precision science, but the docs stand behind it. Good enough for me."

"So scan the woman," Hector said. "We do it now."

"You really have your ego in a twist over this," Ashia said.

"You credit this bald adolescent with siring my son? It's principle."

"It's lunacy," Kurtas said, speaking for the first time. "I don't care whose kid it is."

The magistrate sighed. "It is a matter of concern for future propagation. It should not concern a male so much, the paternity of a single child. Still, we don't want genetic disease and weakness infecting the colony."

Kurtas glared at Ashia. She pretended not to notice.

"The mother will report for testing within the next twenty hours. Now leave, all of you. I have more important matters than your sordid affairs."

Hector stormed out, bumping Kurtas with his shoulder like a schoolyard bully as he passed.

Ashia caught Kurtas outside the chamber. "You look good," she said, hoping her motherly concern sounded like a lover's interest. "After last night—"

"A friend shared with me," Kurtas said. He sounded both relieved and angry. "A client, a woman. She heard I had sired a strong boy. She gave me what I needed in exchange for what she needed."

Ashia pulled him aside by the elbow. "You mated with her? During her cycle?"

249

"I wouldn't have had to if you had kept your promise."

"And if she conceives? What then?"

"It won't be the first child born ill. Thanks to you, there may be many. I am becoming popular."

"Play hard to get," Ashia whispered harshly. "Wait a week before you submit. For Messiah sake, don't let the woman pick the timing."

"I did what I had to. I'd be writhing on the floor without her help."

"Who was she?"

Kurtas pulled his arm free and walked away without answering.

So we're back to patrols? Just like that?" Gretchen said as streaks of red passed beside their scout pod. "What about the monstrous hole?"

Ashia shrugged. "There's nothing in that hole. Sonar confirms it's not deep enough to hide anything. It was a rush job to distract us from something else."

"But what?"

That was the question. Fifty years ago, the Kree had used a diversion and wiped out most of Tora's military force including ninety percent of the colony's males. On what scale were they plotting this time? The only thing to do was keep looking.

The pair of scout pods pulled to a stop where their last patrol had ended. There had been reassignments made in light of recent losses. Lieutenant Wet-Ears had taken over Ashia's squad and brought two of her fellows with her. Now true combat veterans, Ashia considered the change an asset.

The return to basic search-and-scorch patterns

should have made it easy to steal a few boils into the can, but Lt. Wet-Ears had them arranged in tight formation and recent events left the women twitchy, constantly looking to their squad mates for support. For over two hours Ashia found no chance to make a grab. Finally she lost patience, broke formation and slid behind a boulder to make her move. She twisted open the canister and pressed a cluster of boils inside. She was out of line for mere seconds. She turned to resume her place only to find she wasn't alone.

It was Gretchen. The girl's mouth stayed open, her eyes alternating from Ashia's face to the open canister in her fist.

Ashia screwed the lid back in place and stowed the false grenade with the real ones. "Can I help you, Private?"

Gretchen's eyes were still on the fake grenade. She did not speak.

"We better get back in formation." Ashia's attempt to sound friendly failed. She walked toward the patrol, coaxing Gretchen by the elbow as she passed.

The novice followed several steps before saying, "Those are for Kurtas?"

Ashia stopped and faced the girl, looked into her eyes. Gretchen looked sad, betrayed, defeated. For one fleeting instant Ashia considered telling her everything. About Kurtas, Elias, Hector . . . even Tam. It would feel good to say the words to someone other than Kurtas. It didn't matter if Gretchen told the whole moon; the truth had to be said.

Then the moment passed. Gretchen already knew too much, more than Ashia had dared believe anyone

251

could know. She considered killing the girl, a quick round through the chest. A friendly fire incident attributable to the stress of recent events. It would be a significant rip, but nothing career ending.

The thought made Ashia sick, partially because she believed it might truly come to that. But not now. Not yet.

"Everyone knows he did not sire your son," Gretchen said, her voice like a sigh of despair. "Did he bed you in exchange for boils? Or was it just an exchange for Puff?"

"An exchange for . . ." Then it was clear. Ashia looked the direction of Echo, as if doing so would reveal her son. "It was you that shared his bed last night."

Gretchen straightened. "He needed me. I came through."

Her Puff had come through. This colored the novice a new shade. A Puff addict fixated on her dealer, a kindred spirit to her son. Would she tell what she had seen and expose her own addiction?

"Did he . . . are you . . . ?" Ashia's eyes fell to the girl's belly.

Gretchen shook her head, retreated a step. "I was ill as a child. They removed . . . I cannot. Please, don't tell Kurtas."

Ashia bit her lip. Kurtas would not be exposed through this girl, not unless she spoke. "We should get back before we are missed."

Gretchen nodded just as the sound of gunfire began.

The two warriors exchanged startled glances before racing back toward their unit. They crested a low rise to find their squad in a basin a full hundred fifty meters ahead. The formation was splintered, women ducking behind rocks and trees for whatever cover they could find. A ribbon of pink smoke sailed through the air. Ashia followed its arc and saw the enemy.

Scientists classified the Kree as humanoid, a designation Ashia had always considered generous. They possessed all the pieces of a human body by name, but everything served a different purpose. Their heads were little more than glorified noses, four independently sealable nostrils tucked under a thick awning of bone and tusk.

The things' arms were as tall as their whole body, reminiscent of a gorilla in how they walked, but on palms rather than knuckles. The three digits of the hands were more toes than fingers; they folded open for walking and closed against a thumb-like nub for clumsy grasping.

What should have been its two legs were short and multi-jointed—practically tentacles—each culminating in what resembled a six-limbed starfish. These feet rather than the hands were responsible for Kree technology, and it was the feet that wielded their plasma throwers, implements that made the humans' flamers look like cigarette lighters.

A small choking sound came from Gretchen. It was the first the girl had seen one of these monstrosities in person. The young always reacted that way, but they usually recovered quickly.

There was only one Kree visible, but there were sure to be others lurking. They never struck alone, always in numbers and always in ambush.

Ashia stepped into Gretchen's eye line. "We flank him, distract enough to let the others mount a full assault. There will be more; stay sharp."

253

Gretchen followed numbly, a stunned dog trotting on its leash. "It's our fault, isn't it?" she whined. "We were out of formation. We . . ."

Ashia stopped, pulled Gretchen into a crouch at her side. "If we were with them, we'd be just as pinned as they are. The other Kree are likely executing this same maneuver. We have to be quick, efficient and quiet. The others' gunfire should mask our footfalls for a while, but Kree are one giant ear. Step lightly and keep moving. If you see one, gas it."

Gretchen's eyes trembled in their sockets. Had she understood? No time to find out. Ashia resumed motion. Gretchen followed, not stealthy but not loud. Good girl. She might just survive long enough to tattle.

They closed to about seventy-five meters, well inside the Kree's scent range. Hopefully it was distracted enough not to notice. The gas was good for that.

The only cover nearby were a few shrubs that would never withstand the plasma bursts and would impede neither sound nor scent. So Ashia stood in the open as she sized up the lone alien.

Three of its nostrils were sealed, shields against the choking gas. Good. One peeking nostril might smell them coming but could not triangulate them, the same way a one-eyed human had difficulties with depth perception. Unfortunately the gunfire had slowed to only an occasional pop. So much for sound cover. Even from this range, Ashia could see the sensitive bristles standing erect over the Kree's gray-brown body, listening.

Ashia signaled for Gretchen to freeze, plucked a grenade from her belt, pulled the pin.

The Kree faced them. Damn. All four nostrils unfolded. They were spotted.

Ashia threw the grenade. It landed twenty meters short. She had expected the monster to charge, but it hadn't. At least the gas would obscure their aroma to the olfactory-dependant enemy. It would be fighting by sound, its nostrils tight again to ward off the new gas.

A Kree could fixate on weapons fire after only three rounds on automatic. Ashia flipped her weapon to single-fire. Gretchen imitated.

"Ashia! That you?" Her radio. She couldn't speak without betraying her position. Even the earpiece might prove too loud. She pulled the field mirror from her belt and flashed confirmation to her squad mates in the valley below.

"Do you see any others?" the lieutenant said, panic staining the edges of the words. "Are they surrounding us?"

Ashia surveyed the terrain as long as she dared. The one confirmed enemy remained behind the cloud. Still no sign of the ambush. Ashia mirror-flashed her uncertainty.

"We're going to make a run for the pods. Can you cover?"

She flashed negative.

"We're going. We can't stay in this barrel."

Ashia repeated her negative flash. Damn fools. The other Kree must be securing the scout pods. Where else would they be?

The lieutenant ignored her. Ashia saw the ten figures start their retreat in the basin below. She wanted to shout at the lieutenant, to scold her for her cowardice. To do so was suicide. She had a Kree to deal with; the officer would wait.

Pop-pop-pop.

Gretchen fired into the smoke, blind shots. The lieutenant's panic was contagious. Now the novice was giving away their position.

"Move!" Ashia sprinted parallel to the wall of smoke. Gretchen also ran but directly away from the Kree's last confirmed position. The mistake left the girl in the line of fire. The main plasma burst was short, but she did not escape the splash ring.

Gretchen screamed as the burn bit calf. She collapsed.

Ashia froze. Gretchen was a sitting duck. At least Ashia might use the girl's cries to hide her own position. She flipped another grenade a few yards to cover her scent and waited.

The Kree emerged from the cloud and lurched unevenly toward Gretchen's prone and writhing body. Two nostrils unfolded, confirming its target's location. It resealed and continued its advance.

So close. Thirty meters. Twenty. Fifteen. Ashia stopped breathing. Every hair on the beast was stiff and vibrating. It was so close Ashia could see its many scars. An old specimen that had seen much battle. Not so unlike Ashia herself. A veteran, alone on a hill against a sworn enemy.

Ten meters.

Ashia would have to breathe soon. Could it hear the accelerated rhythm of her heart? It was now or never. The moment she moved, it would hear her. She had to make it one smooth motion—level the weapon and fire. One shot. Disabling the beast at this range would buy her nothing. This had to be a kill shot. The head was the most vulnerable, a low trajectory, through a nostril and into the brainstem. Now or never.

But it was Gretchen that stopped screaming and started firing.

The Kree took a hit to the right arm. It reeled and charged Gretchen, limping.

Ashia raised her weapon and squeezed off two shots.

The Kree landed on Gretchen. Limbs splayed, body limp. It was dead.

Ashia left her wounded compatriot beneath the hulking corpse—what better cover could there be?—and secured the area. No evidence of any other Kree. She was about to declare the scene clear when the lieutenant piped through.

"Ashia, we have the pods. Can you report your status?"

No ambush? Had they really stumbled across a lone Kree? A rogue? An outcast? Amazing the thing could survive this close to a city like Echo. Could it have dug the diversionary hole itself?

Since there were no other targets, the next priority was to call in medevac for Gretchen. Ashia fingered her transmitter to report, but said nothing.

She would report the all clear, Gretchen would be whisked to the hospital and Ashia would follow her there for mandatory testing. To Hector go the spoils. What of Kurtas? Elias?

Ashia released the button and returned to Gretchen's side. The girl was covered in Kree from shoulder to burnt toe. Some of the beast's blood had spilled on her face. Red blood, iron-based. What else might Ashia have in common with this creature?

She turned Gretchen's face to her. The girl struggled to focus. Her eyes widened, her breath quickened. She pushed at the enormous Kree corpse with both hands to no avail.

"How much do you know?" Ashia said, half to herself. "What have you guessed?"

Gretchen tried to speak. "Please . . . no . . ."

Ashia pressed a finger to the young lips. Her other hand relieved the girl of several gas grenades and all of her emergency provisions, a month's worth to a cautious eater.

"Relax, greenhorn," Ashia said. "I'm not going to kill you. I need you. My boys need you."

Gretchen's eyebrows bunched. She didn't understand.

"Ask Kurtas. He will explain. He's yours now. You understand him in ways his mother never could. Take him as your own. You're the war hero; I am but a casualty."

Gretchen struggled to sit up, grabbed Ashia's wrist.

Ashia caressed the girl's hand. "Save your strength for the radio call. And I need you to do one more thing: Elias will need a mother, you and Kurtas will need a son." She tucked the hollow canister into Gretchen's belt. "My family is yours now. Take care of them."

Ashia stood, turned and walked away. She refused to look back. She was leaving so much behind, but the lies stayed behind with all of it. She hiked to the small hole Gretchen had found a few days earlier—the rogue Kree's home, now Ashia's. A home without walls.

Things were simpler outside the walls.

KELSEY WROTEN

Confliction

written by

Simon Cooper

illustrated by

CASSANDRA SHAFFER

ABOUT THE AUTHOR

Simon Cooper grew up on a farm in Co. Donegal, Ireland in a family that valued creativity and learning. In his teens, he moved to England and went on to university there, achieving a BA in philosophy. At the same time, he started writing.

After wandering through a variety of occupations and stretching his writing muscles in his spare time, he started a gardening business, which he still runs. While mowing, planting and pruning, he has time to think about character, plot and setting.

Simon currently lives in Northern Ireland with his wife and son.

ABOUT THE ILLUSTRATOR

Cassandra Shaffer is a native of Arizona and proud to be a desert rat. Soon after graduating from Mountain View High School, she began attending the Art Institute of Phoenix where she is currently majoring in media arts and animation. All her life she has enjoyed drawing and doing creative things of all kinds, and becoming an artist seemed like the instinctive thing to do. After graduating from college, she plans to enter the field of animation or become an illustrator.

She strives to convey strong emotions and believable characters in her work. She takes inspiration from everyday people and situations, but has a strong love for fantasy. It is this lifelong fascination with stretching the imagination that led her to enter the Illustrators of the Future Contest.

262

Confliction

The scanner screen's ECG window displayed two hundred and nine beats per minute—my heart aspired to be a fusion engine. I was top of my year in nanodiagnostics. I aced anatomy, biophysics and molecular clinomics. I could close my eyes and picture in detail the intricate web of systems that made up the modern human. But blowing my trumpet from here to the moon base only meant I knew one thing for sure: no human heart could beat that fast for long. I was dying.

The billions of nanodoctors that regulated my immune system were corrupted, playing dumb as my heart tissue disintegrated under waves of attack from my white blood cells. My fast healers were on strike, confused. They should have been shoveling in proteins, repairing cells, facilitating DNA reconstruction and modulating gene expression.

My national health plan was invalidated as soon as I got sick, leaving me unable to afford a bespoke replacement heart. A donor was my only hope and donors were few and far between. I cursed the day I sought out a black market update for my nanodocs.

I needed the money to top up my scholarship was the lie I told myself. I would spot a bad program, I thought in my arrogance.

The nanotechnology inside of us rarely went wrong. Simple little command and execute programs, manipulating one atom at a time. Their capabilities were limited. Like ants that could build a nest but not a cathedral, the nanodocs could repair cells but not rebuild an organ from scratch. They were fast, but not fast enough to deal with severe physical trauma. That day would come, but I wouldn't live to see it.

A tremor shook my chest and my heart lurched into a stuttering arrhythmia. I gasped for breath, clenched my teeth, remembering the first attack, the crushing weight of cardiac arrest. My head burned, my toes tingled. I pressed the emergency button, tried to call out for help but couldn't form the words. Where were they? I tried to relax my body but my hands rebelled, gripping the bleached hospital sheets. Then, the unnatural rhythm leveled out, the pace reduced to two hundred, useless.

My eyelids felt like they were made of wet clay. I stared around the room, remembering my tutors trying to talk me out of a career in hospital medicine. For me, the glitter and gold world of medical research and nanodoc programming never held the appeal it did to so many others. That was unfair. They saved more lives than any hospital doctor ever could. Maybe I was the selfish one for wanting to get my hands dirty.

I wondered what my parents would have thought. They would have been disgusted enough that their son went into medicine. At least they didn't live to see me die like this. What did I know? They might have thought it fitting.

The frantic thumping against my ribcage went up another gear. I gasped for more air than my oxygen mask could provide. All at once, my body lightened, like it was no longer truly mine. The pain eased and the pounding rhythm was muffled. My heart was in a faraway room. It was time. There were voices around me, white figures. Crazily, I thought they were angels. I wanted to laugh and tell them I didn't believe in angels and at the same time beg them not to leave me alone.

A face appeared. Dr. Maxwell's cragged features were blurred, like he stood beyond a rain-soaked window. The angels clustered around him, angels: they were nurses and technicians, masked and gowned. They were dressed for theater.

Maxwell spoke, his voice in the same faraway room. "Hold on, Flynn. We've found a donor."

I was the most fortunate son of a boson to ever, ever, ever walk the face of planet Earth. I was alive. I was weak, permanently blushing and running a temperature from the waste heat of the fast healers packed into every cell of my body, but real and true alive. I was back from death's grasp, even if it felt like his sickle still swung at my back. I didn't care about the weird thing in the corner of the room. It was nothing, a side effect that would fade in time. I kept it to myself, ignored it. I was alive, that was what mattered.

It was two days since the operation and an hour out of the isolation room. The wound at my chest had healed to a red scar that in time would be the faintest of lines. I was normal again, though it was hard to believe after the previous week. Every doctor, whatever their specialty, studied the history of modern medicine. No doubt, every student in every era read the case studies and marveled as I did on the brutalities of the past. I felt I had lived a slice of that past. Yet somehow, against all my understanding, I was stronger for the experience.

Perhaps this was what my parents sought when they refused to have their nanosystems updated. They were Radical Traditionalists, anti-nanotechnology, anti-technology. They lived and, two years after I was born, on the eve of the twenty-third century, they died, by nature's will. I understood something of that now, enough to make their choice easier to reconcile in my mind.

I tapped the scanner screen, brought up my immune-system readings and watched the data flow that said all was normal. Maxwell had unlocked the screen when I asked. He remembered me from my training stint on the thirty-third floor.

The thing I didn't mention waved its hand in front of its face. It was definitely a face now, a man's face, forty or fifty years old. Jet-black hair swept from his high forehead and down his back in a thick Mohawk. I felt like I knew him, not an acquaintance whose name I'd misplaced, more like a blood relative. Or, as if he was me, but twenty years older, which was stranger, considering he was taller than me, looked nothing like me and I would never style my hair Mohawk.

The rest of his body was a mix of muscle tissue, skeleton and nerve endings in various stages of completion. The right foot was done and clothed in skin which stopped at the ankle like a boot, the rest of that leg only shinbone and fibula. The ribcage was half exposed but muscle covered it fast, hiding the organs from view. His heart beat in rhythm with my own. The image was so clear, when he dragged past, I put my hand out and right through his hip.

"Are you Flynn Mason?"

For a split second, I thought the female voice came from my imaginary friend because it was right that he would know my name.

She stayed pressed against the door, hands behind her back. I never heard her come in. Her face was uncertain, yet knowledgeable, like she was simultaneously older and younger than me. Scarlet hair touched her shoulders and a black satin blouse cut a V of pale skin at her chest. My heart beat a little faster, a feeling I both enjoyed and dreaded.

"You're the heart transplant, is that right?" She was looking from the screen to me.

"Well," I said and then coughed. "That's really just what they call me around here."

"Your heart rate's good," she said, like I was her patient and this was her hospital. "Your immune-docs are normal, so the organ DNA transfer has gone smoothly, so far. Have you had any complications, any unusual symptoms?"

There was no hospital ID badge and she wasn't a doctor. She thought she was someone though. "Look, you're cute, but I think you've got the wrong room."

"Cute!" She smiled for less than one second. "Thanks, I really needed that. Now, if you're the HT patient and you had the operation two days ago, then that means I may have saved your life. So, do you have any problems? Dizziness, fever . . ."

She kept listing, talking to me with more of a graveside than bedside manner. My mind was stuck. Was she some relation to my donor, the man whose death saved my life? She couldn't be. They wouldn't let her see me.

"Hallucinations? Hair loss?"

"What?"

"Hair loss? Any hair loss?" She glanced from the screen to my rigid blond spikes. "I don't think that applies."

"Not that," I said. "Hallucinations, what about hallucinations? And who are you? Did you know the donor?"

She paused for a split second, pain on her face, then gone. She did know him.

"Are the hallucinations vivid? Specific?" she asked.

"Yes, on both counts." He was almost fully fleshed now, standing at the foot of the bed. He started to dress himself, pulling a shirt on out of thin air, like window shopping.

"Damn," she said. "My name is Maxi. I might not have saved your life after all."

"Who are you?"

She took a deep breath, let it out. "I gave permission for the donor heart. It was a mistake. No, that's incorrect. I knew exactly what I was doing, but it was the wrong course of action."

The directness, the way she looked at me, it was honest. I felt incomparably small beside the magnitude of what she'd done for me. "Can I thank you? If it wasn't for you . . ."

She shook her head. "Don't thank me, you don't understand. Your heart came from a man called Bernardo. I was with him when he died. He was a brilliant man. We worked together at Kings."

She stopped, probably to gauge if I knew the name. I did. Kings was a research facility for whole brain emulation, info morphology—mind uploading. It was immortality, virtually, at least, the Holy Grail to some, neural-fantasy, with a capital F, to others. It also claimed to be the best path toward Artificial Consciousness after the disappointments of AI. It was a slippery field, teetering on a breakthrough for as long as I could remember.

"I know what it is, but I don't see . . ."

"Bernardo is—" She shook her head. "—Bernardo was in charge of a neural mapping project, using a combination approach: nanocopiers and neural imaging. The copiers are versions of the most basic copiers used to monitor drug progression through individual cells. We preprogrammed them to attach only to the soma of neurons, renamed them nu-copiers and read their signals using dynamic imaging. The results have been sensational. Many of the volunteers have had the excitement of seeing their own consciousness alive in our simulator, several for almost a full day. Bernardo and I included." The strain lifted from her face a second and she touched her neck.

"Why are you telling me this?"

She nodded toward the screen. "You look fine, no conflicts, right? So why the hallucination? It's caused by your neurons adjusting to the influx of the nu-copiers, the ones that hitched a ride with Bernardo's heart."

"But organs are screened before transplant. Anyway, if there was anything there, even stray copiers, the immune-docs would have picked them up. I'm in medical school, I know what I'm talking about."

"Not about this. Nu-copiers are much smaller than basic copiers, only twenty nanones in diameter. The screening won't have picked them up and your immune-docs will fly straight past, like a jet over a ball bearing."

"But if they're neuron-attracted, what the hell were these nu-copiers doing in heart tissue?"

"The nu-copiers form an entangled whole. That's how they recreate the neural firing patterns. The signal of any individual nu-copier affects the behavior of every other. But, they're also in subentangled groups that circulate throughout the body to recharge their kinetic energy circuits. And they're self-replicating, up to a preset limit of twenty trillion. Look, the police will be looking for Bernardo's body and it won't take them much longer. When they find out about the transplant, they'll take you, and then you don't have any chance at all. Tell me this, Med School, ever heard of UBIM?"

UBIM was shorthand for the global treaty on Unlicensed Biotech and Interpersonal Mutation risks.

The police would apply UBIM and treat me like a case of viral terrorism. Quarantine. No exceptions.

"How can I believe any of this?"

"If I could get you to Kings, I could show you the nu-copiers, but that's out of the question. The simple fact is this: your neuronal firing patterns are being retrained by Bernardo's nu-copiers. Do you understand? Your mind is being overwritten with Bernardo's, or destroyed in the process. I think I can stop it, but you'll have to come with me, now."

Oh, finally I saw it and felt stupid to not have clicked sooner. She was crazy, a crazy person. Probably a Trans-Human fascist, wanting the entire human race to migrate to simulation space, leave our too-mortal flesh behind. She had me going with the Kings technobabble. She saved me? No, Dr. Maxwell saved me, the hospital saved me, the family that donated their loved one's heart saved me. I just got my future back and she was messing with my head for her own sick thrills. Who did she think she was?

"How the hell can I go anywhere? And tell me this, how could a simple copier, nu or normal, overwrite anything? Copiers don't interact with cells. They couldn't interact with neurons. That's biophysics for toddlers." Let her answer that. I had a hundred more questions.

She went to reply, then stopped. "You don't believe me. Of course not, why should you? I could be anyone. Okay." She nodded once. Then Maxi, if that was her real name, pulled a gun from behind her back and pointed it at my chest.

The gun was gleaming silver. It was the kind I associated with twentieth-century cowboy movies—a cold something. A cold Peacemaker? It looked real and so heavy in her hand that I wondered if she could pull the trigger. The now fully dressed hallucination circled around my bed and walked through Maxi. Neither of them flinched but I felt like someone danced on my grave. He stopped beside my shoulder looking down on me, his hands held lightly behind his back. The situation was beyond surreal.

Maxi said, "Get out of bed, Flynn. We need to move, you need to move. Pull your IVs. You're doing fine without them."

"You're going to kill me, to save me? That's tough love."

"Do it."

I disconnected the two lines, saline for rehydration and a glucose/hormone feed for the fast healers. They dripped wet on my arm as they fell away.

"Now, get out of bed. Where are your clothes?"

"The unit behind, bottom drawer."

She backed away and knelt, opened the drawer. I took a deep breath and hefted my legs from the bed. The emergency button was on the wall behind the bed, to my right. I had the creepiest sensation that the hallucination was watching my every move but when I turned to look, it was gone, completely. I wondered if I should tell the crazy girl. Was she crazy enough to actually shoot me?

"Here." Maxi tossed over my box trousers and the top with the supernova design constantly exploding across the chest. She slid across a pair of sneakers too.

"I'm sorry about this," she said.

I dressed slowly, my limbs stiff from lack of exercise, sluggish from the action of the fast healers and digestion inhibitors.

"I gave permission for the transplant because your surgeon told me you would die without it, that same day. It was wrong, that two people would die when one could survive. I knew there was a risk. When the nu-copiers have learned a neural firing pattern, they change to activators when transferred to our simulator or another person. In simulations, it took nearly a trillion nu-copiers before they affected a new brain, less than that and nothing happened. I hoped there were less in your heart tissue. Perhaps there weren't or maybe there were and the models didn't transfer."

The seals on my sneakers closed around my feet. If she was crazy, it was an all-encompassing delusion because I had to fight it. She was so entirely convinced.

"I can walk," I said.

"Good. You need to keep active. We ran a lot of models and the models where the new brain was in higher states of activity were less likely to be overwritten. The fallout from your operation has probably staved things off."

The door opened. Two men in sheen suits entered and Maxi shifted her aim. They paused for a millisecond, as if a girl pointing an antique gun at them was curious, but not exceptional, and then they gently let the door swing shut. Maxi stepped back, kept the gun high. I was to the side of the line of fire. My breathing felt easy, despite the fact that my mind was taking a spin.

The taller of the two smiled and lifted his hands in a calculated show of nonaggression. He had a long

273

nose and gleaming bald head. It was a headmaster's face. "Maxi, isn't it? How's your day going?"

"It keeps getting better," Maxi said and glanced at me, as if for support. She suddenly looked incredibly weak, out of her depth. I found myself wanting to help her, despite everything, but these guys were serious. They had to be police. The hospital must have caught Maxi on a security feed.

The shorter man had a heavier build and a mop of tightly curled black hair. He leaned slightly to the side, resting his shoulder against the door, like he needed to slouch a second. He stifled a yawn with his hand, and I thought he was going for a gun but it was something else. Though he disguised it well, his eyelids flickered ever so slightly, a sure sign he was satellite wired, probably calling for backup.

"Hey," Maxi shouted at him, "look this way, Brutus."

I was feeling calmer and almost laughed. He looked kind of like a Brutus. This mess would be over soon. I didn't really think Maxi was going to shoot anyone. The gun probably wasn't even real. Of course it wasn't, what had I been thinking? Where would anyone pick up a working antique gun?

The leader spoke again. "We're here to help this young man, Maxi, and help you too."

He looked my way and nodded in a fashion that suggested things would soon be in hand. He was going to help me, what did that mean? Maxi didn't say anything. How did they know her name? She looked at me, her face tight with tension. My hearing sharpened. They wanted to help me?

"Are you virus cops?" I asked.

"That's right, Mr. Mason, Flynn. I'm Detective Lynch and this is Crosby. Don't worry. We're going to sort this out. Are you aware of your position?"

I was, fully and completely, hyper-aware. Everything Maxi had said formed itself into a coherent whole. The room felt smaller, hotter, the scanner screen loomed over the bed, too large and obvious. My heart raced. I felt sick again. I was sick again. Death had caught up with the game. How could this be happening?

"I'm contaminated?"

"Try to remain calm. We'll do everything we can to help you. The technicians at Kings have some ideas on how to deactivate the bio-copiers in your system."

"They're lying," Maxi said. "They have to follow protocol. You'll be quarantined. You'll no more get to Kings than I will."

I slowed my thoughts, forced myself into straight, clear rationality. My pulse eased, under some control again. "What about UBIM?" I asked.

For a telling moment, he paused, before waving the suggestion away. "UBIM's complicated. Without going into the details, it allows for exceptions. What you're harboring isn't viral in nature. In fact, as far as I'm aware, it is only through exceptional circumstances that you've become contaminated. The chances of your spreading any nano-organisms are negligible."

"He's lying." Maxi almost screamed it. "They'll quarantine you and monitor progression. You don't have that time."

He was lying. UBIM was non-negotiable. That was hammered into every med student, by every ethics tutor, across the globe. If unlicensed biotech contamination was suspected then the subject must be contained, the police called, UBIM enforced, Hippocratic Oath be damned. Either he didn't know I was a med student or he assumed I was a particularly stupid one. Whatever the reason, he lied to me, point-blank. It occurred to me that Maxi never lied.

"Wait a minute," I said and stood. I was shaky, but it felt good.

Maxi's gun cracked against the plastic floor and spun over to my feet. It happened so fast and silently, I thought her hand must have cramped. Then I saw blood at her wrist. Crosby shoulder charged her a second later, twisting her good arm across her back and slamming her up against the wall.

"Go easy, Crosby," Lynch said and turned to me. There was a rip in the fabric of his jacket where something like a needle dart had exited, the propulsion system probably buried in a shoulder pad.

He noticed my look. "Handy little device, this one is programmed to home in on the carpal tunnel. She'll be fine. No permanent damage."

He bent for the gun. I picked it up first. Our eyes met at an awkward angle. He said nothing. I swallowed heavily, ignored the sensation of dizziness that accompanied my quick movement. The flashing graphic of my supernova top was reflecting off his forehead, tinting it orange. I pointed the muzzle at him, my finger on the trigger. I'd held an antique gun before, in a shop, but I was surprised again by the weight. This was real metal.

"Stay bent over," I said and straightened, hoping he didn't have any other concealed gizmos. My nerves were having enough entertainment. "Now, squat."

"What do you think you're doing?" he asked and started to straighten.

I pressed the gun against his temple. He stopped. He squatted. Crosby, still holding Maxi, glanced over his shoulder.

"Stay with your face to the wall and let her go," I said.

He didn't move. I tensed, not sure what I would actually do if he attacked. Finally, he released Maxi with a theatrical flick of his hands into the air. She elbowed him hard enough in the chest to make him grunt and press one hand against the wall. She staggered away from his radius, pinching her bloody wrist between thumb and forefinger. There was a red blotch on her forehead that was going to bruise without a jab of glucose to beef up her fast healers.

"Give me the gun." She let go of the wound. It was coagulating nicely but her fingers were curled into a claw. Her good hand reached out. I pulled back. Crosby had already called for backup. What the hell was I doing?

"It's quite understandable that you're in a state of shock, Flynn." Lynch's voice was calm, the tone flattened further by speaking toward the floor. "But if you give her that gun, you will be an accessory to the proliferation of unlicensed biotech. That's a serious crime."

"Don't worry, you'll be too dead for the charge to stick," Maxi said. "Now give me the gun. We need to move."

I took a further step back, the gun on Lynch, my eyes on Maxi. She looked frustrated, angry. Her eyes blazed.

Lynch spoke again, his voice the antithesis of those eyes. "Are you really going to trust the person who put you in this position? Haven't you wondered why she, a scientist, allowed her colleague's heart to be used in a transplant for which it was prohibited? Did that ever strike you as curious?"

"She wanted to help. I would have died if she hadn't broken the rules." My lips were dry. My heart hit a steady beat that felt louder and faster than it should have.

"Don't be so naïve, Flynn. They were lovers."

"That's not true," Maxi said but her voice was uneven, her forehead all bunched up.

"A rare and unfortunate accident saw him die in her arms. She couldn't let him go and so she thought she might bring him back."

This time Maxi didn't speak. She stared at Lynch, shaking her head. I thought she was going to kick him.

"Whatever she has promised, she has no way of saving you. I think she would rather see the process run its course. She's scared we'll interfere, ruin her sick reunion."

"No," Maxi said.

"I wonder how Bernardo will feel about taking over your body. As great a mind as his would still struggle with such a ghoulish prospect. If the process even succeeds?"

"He wasn't my lover," Maxi said to no one at all. Then to me, "It wasn't like that."

278

I felt betrayed, which, really, was ridiculous. I didn't know her. She didn't know me. Except, was I now dying, in a way, and going to watch it happen? Given the choice, I wouldn't have put another person through that without their permission. So she lied after all, or at least didn't tell the whole truth.

"But you wanted him back and you knew there was a chance," I said. "Did you hope that when you came into this room, you would be recognized, greeted with loving arms, that the overwrite would have happened while I was sedated?"

She held my gaze, a look on her face of complete numbness. "Yes, with loving arms, yes."

I didn't know what to say to that.

"But only in the beginning. I soon realized it was a mistake. That's why I'm here. What I did was wrong and I want to help you. I want to stop the overwrite. I believe we can."

It was the strangest thing, but I believed her, this crazy woman. I really believed she wanted to help me. But I had no doubts about the seriousness of the situation. Virus cops didn't show up for nothing. Was I infectious? Could she really stop whatever process was catalyzing though my brain cells?

"Don't make a mistake," Lynch said.

I looked at the room, at the virus cops. There was a lot to think about and not enough time. I looked again at Maxi. "Do you swear that I'm not a liability—that the nu-copiers can't transfer from me to others?"

"Give me your arm." She took hold of my free arm as I reached out. There was a trace of blood where I'd been clumsy pulling my IVs. She dampened her

279

forefinger with my blood and smeared it into her half healed wrist wound. "There's one nu-copier every fifth cell in your blood. It would take a liter of blood to transfer enough. There's no danger."

I believed her. I handed her the gun.

She took it, stepped sideways and shot Lynch in the back. He slumped forward in time with the ear-splitting crack. Crosby turned. I reached to stop her, but too late. She pressed the trigger again and Crosby fell forward, a paralyzed expression on his face.

"What do you think you're doing?" I tried to grab the gun but she stepped aside and held out one hand to keep me back.

"Calm down, the shells are tranquilizers, nothing serious. The gun belonged to Bernardo. He collected antique weapons. This one belonged to a guy who used to have an act with real lions. And don't worry, I adjusted the dosage. So, let's go."

She pressed the gun, pointing down, into the small of her back. A bag holder clicked and it disappeared, cloaked by the holder's light absorbers. She held her bad arm tight across her stomach and opened the door.

Before we left, I checked the two cops' pulses. Strong and regular, like my own. My body was being taken over from the inside and my brain about to become either lost property or as useful as a bowl of mush, but at least my new heart was in thumping good health.

We strolled down the corridor without attracting much attention. A couple of nurses gave me a quizzical look, but didn't recognize me.

"We better take the service elevator," I said. "I think the one called Crosby called for backup with internal comms."

"Damn," she said softly.

The elevator door curtained open and we moved to the side as an orderly pushed out a trolley full of blood globes. Someone was having their system flushed. We stepped inside; the door curtained shut and solidified. Maxi called for the ground floor.

"We were on our way to a conference when the accident happened." She shook her head and then turned to face me. "Bernardo, he would hate what I've done, to you and him. We always knew that theoretically an overwrite was possible. That's why we were traveling under assumed names, so that no one could link us with Kings. I was in charge of organizing that. I got us IDs as Mr. and Mrs. King and a room together. It was a surprise for him, but he was furious."

I wasn't sure why she was telling me this. Maybe she needed to tell someone.

"I know it doesn't matter, now, but that was how the accident happened. He was so angry, he didn't see the malfunction warnings on the control panel, our fall out of the traffic grid. He told me I was mistaken, a silly girl. He had no interest in me, no feelings, nothing. He's . . ."

"Why did you want to bring him back?"

"I wanted, I wanted to apologize. I wanted to explain. I thought maybe I could make him understand."

She slipped into silence, staring blankly at the elevator wall. Her thoughts were elsewhere, but any tears were cried out in private. What was it she wanted to make him understand? That she had put his mind in another man's body, or that she still loved him? I started thinking I'd made a big mistake and should have taken my chance with the police.

"We're not going to get out of here," Maxi said, never looking around. She was giving up. If there was a way to keep myself alive, a chance at all, I was going to have to find it myself.

"When you ran models on the possibility of overwrite, what were the variables?"

A chime sounded and the elevator stopped. The door curtained onto an empty foyer. There was a wall of five elevators, all empty. A massive corridor snaked gradually away to the right. No orderlies, but a dozen empty gurneys waiting like taxis against one wall. This wasn't the foyer.

The elevator readout said lower ground floor. I requested foyer but it blinked an error message. It was under remote control. This was a trap. So, where were the virus squad? Waiting around the bend? There was no other exit. I grabbed Maxi's wrist, my skin damp and spongy on the hard bone of her arm. My senses were still skewed. I needed another three days of recuperation.

"Maxi, tell me what the variables were." I pulled her with me into the corridor.

"I'm sorry, Flynn."

Sorry? I thought about how forty-eight hours ago, I was stuck in a hospital bed, a dead man waiting for someone else to die and let me live. It was the worst time of my life. The way I felt now didn't come close. I was alive, I could move without rasping for breath, even if it was going to be the shortest recovery in the history of modern transplants. I thought how Maxi came to help me, to right her wrong even when she must have known the virus cops would be close. She could have made a run for it. I stopped us both, made her focus on my face.

"You saved my life, Maxi. Now, tell me about the variables?"

Her forehead creased with frown lines. Good, she was thinking again. I let go, walked forward, eyes on the edge of the bend. Maxi walked alongside.

"The variables," she said. "Okay. The simulated brains that rejected overwrites, regardless of the amount of nu-copiers applied to the model were those programmed for a constant stream of high mental activity."

"What . . . like memory tests and puzzles?"

"That sometimes, but also simpler stuff, like debating a topic, even shopping for a difficult-to-find item. As long as it was constant and focused, with a lot of information to process, that did the trick."

"Surely being alive should be enough information to process."

"Not in our simulations. And not for you, if you're hallucinating. Hallucinations always preceded overwrite in our simulations."

"And can a simulated brain be reliable?"

"They're not perfect, they're simulations, otherwise they'd be Artificial Consciousness and I'd be rich. I helped develop them. But they're as good a simulation as it's possible to get using the fastest AIs. They work on the daylong principle used in AC research. Do you know it?"

283

I shook my head, trying each door we passed. All were locked. Not a single soul or machine had passed us. It was a dead-end trap.

"We program a static history of a day in a human life and use that as a memory-draw for the processor. So it dips into it when given a task. Has it solved this puzzle before, no. Has it discussed this topic, yes, etc. The simulations we ran that weren't provided with tasks, that simply lived through their day, they all fell unconscious and were overwritten."

"Then surely all I have to do is be alive. Every day is different for a human. This one certainly is."

"Even some of the simulations that were given tasks were overwritten."

"What?"

"That's what we were working on when all this happened."

I stopped. "Then what's your plan? Do you have one, or just a theory?"

"The simulations that were given tasks but still became overwritten were the ones that we gave a break to. We let them return to their day or repeat a memory task. Sort of downtime. The ones that never got overwritten were the ones without a break. Task after task after task."

"So, I keep busy, keep active, for how long?"

"In real time, about a week."

"I've got to stay awake and active for a week. Okay, I can do that. It's not impossible." Maxi nodded at me, too politely. "What?"

"The simulations that avoided being overwritten, essentially they retrained the nu-copiers, except—"

She stopped, grabbed my hand to make me look at her. "They all crashed, Flynn."

"Crashed? What does that mean, exactly?" I needed to hear it exactly.

"For them, a reboot. For you?" She shrugged her shoulders. "I don't know, maybe nothing. But maybe an aneurism or loss of motor function, or whatever. You might just stop breathing, or have a—" She stopped speaking.

"A heart attack, right? Yeah, okay. But maybe nothing, or you wouldn't be here and we wouldn't be running from the virus squad. Right? Because I'm not a simulation."

"You needed to know the full risk."

I was about to tell her that I felt like I knew the risks better than she did when something else caught my attention. The weird thing was back, the hallucination, the man. He was dressed in an insulated white tube jacket and trousers, like a tourist on one of those tacky virtual Everest climbs. He was talking to me, as if explaining how it was too cold to stand around and talk, but there were no words. He seemed to realize that and stopped speaking.

"Are you all right?" Maxi asked.

"I've been meaning to ask you, what does Bernardo look like?"

There was no time for her reply. Three figures in virus contamination suits and armed with stun guns appeared in a line in front. A voice from the hospital's PA system announced: "Remain where you are. Put your hands on your heads. Do not resist."

Maxi looked at me. I shook my head, put my hands up, stared at her until she did the same. There were three more figures behind. It was over. They had monitored us through the hospital's security system. Crosby never called for backup; he simply reported the situation. He and Lynch were the softly, softly, no need to panic everyone approach. The squad in front were the real hardcore.

They walked straight through the hallucination, who sat down on a black rock. There was snow around his feet. Flakes of snow started to fall and an icy wind dried my lips.

One of the virus squad stepped out of line. The other two stopped. They looked less substantial than the man on the rock. I turned to tell Maxi about it and thank her for trying to help. She was gone. The guy let his gun slide and grabbed my wrist. It was like he tied a ton of rock to my hand. I collapsed to the floor, flat out on my back. The snow fell heavier and heavier. And then it all stopped.

The sky was ultramarine blue. It was the kind of blue you see maybe only a handful of times in your life, even if you live on a desert island paradise. It was a perfect blue. There was one isolated intruder upon that paradise blue—a wisp of smoke in the distance. Either a fire was dying out, or something organic was breaking down, releasing its heat as smoke. Then it struck me, with some peculiarity, that the smoke wasn't smoke but breath, my own.

I felt cold against my back, or was it wetness? It touched my head and hands. I flexed my fingers and found resistance. Something crunched. Snow? I sat bolt upright and dragged the entire world along with me.

CASSANDRA SHAFFER

"You're awake," said the man on the rock. He was the same man as before, in the same white snow clothes. It was the same black rock and behind him, a vast mountain range covered with ice and snow bit into the perfect sky.

He stood and strode over, replacing the mountains with his body. His hand reached to help me up. For the first time, I felt that he was not a hallucination. Or if he was, then so was everything. I grabbed his hand and stood with an unexpected lightness. Maxi, the hospital, the virus police, all of it was fading into the past, someone else's memories.

"I'm Bernardo." He shook my hand vigorously, patting my shoulder with his other hand. "I'm glad for this opportunity to meet you, Flynn."

He looked anxious, sounded apologetic more than glad.

"Am I dead?"

His jaw tightened. He squeezed my shoulder, let me go and stepped back. Sunlight had appeared from somewhere because the snow on the mountains gleamed with blinding intensity. Bernardo's eyes glistened. I shaded my own and turned a little to get my bearings. The mountain range stretched below us, toward the horizon. We were surrounded, the white snow broken only by massive sharps of rock.

"These are my Alps," Bernardo said, "or at least, how I recall them. My father first brought me here when I was an infant, though not this high up, of course."

He pointed out peaks. "Mont Blanc, Dom, Weisshorn, Grand Combin." He turned and swept an arm to present the peak towering above us. "And, of

288

course, this is Dent D'Herens, less favored neighbor of the famous Matterhorn. It was here I first learned the true value of technology. My father broke his ankle on our first proper climb together. I was only ten, but I remember it well. He rested on this rock, or one very like it." He patted the stone as if it was a family pet. "We had an old-fashioned GPS signaler and our rescue was swift. There was no real drama, but still, the reliance on that device, the what-if, set my mind whirling. I saw the machines around and within me in a whole new light. No more was the regular jab of immune-docs some tedious excursion. Now it fascinated me. I began then a journey, a striving toward the day when all humans would have at their fingertips the means for rescue, from whatever situation nature bestowed upon them. A backup life for all, should their own fail, a replacement mind, ready to inhabit a new body, when such a technology became available." He rubbed the side of his face. "It only saddens me that you have become part of that journey."

His breath frosted in the air and I noticed my own wasn't visible. I raised my hand and blew out, trying to feel it. My hand was pale, whitened, like it was carved from bone. The design on my top, the supernova, it was gone, burned out, leaving dead space. It was too cold, the air thin and harsh on my lungs.

"This is my mind." It was meant as a question, but came out as a statement of ownership. This was my mind and he was taking it from me. "Stop it, stop this." I must have sounded desperate, because he looked away for a second.

"I could no more stop it than a man could voluntarily cease to breathe." Bernardo swallowed hard. "You must understand that; you are medically trained. I have learned a lot about you, Flynn, about your life. I admire you, how far you have come from such austere beginnings. For what it is worth, if I were your father, I would be proud of all you have achieved, and all you would have achieved. I don't doubt your parents' idealism, but it was discolored by extremism. Radical Traditionalism is a looking backwards. You have nothing to be ashamed of in choosing the path that leads away from them, toward the future."

He spoke like he was familiar with my most private thoughts. I struggled to comprehend what was happening.

"I wish that things could have been different. You and I are similar in many ways. My own career began in medicine. I believe such similarities facilitated the overwrite process. Our neural networks were well matched."

"Maxi said there was a chance," I blurted out. "She said that I could keep active, convert the nu-copiers, overwhelm them."

"It worked in the models, yes, but a real human brain isn't a simulation. Maxi misled you. Perhaps I misled her once also. I blame myself for this whole mess. The fact is that the nu-copiers have taken hold quicker than I would have imagined and with greater success. I believe that this phase—" he waved his arms around the serene yet vicious landscape "—our meeting here, is the junction at which the nu-copiers will complete the overwrite. It is analogous to the indexing of old immune-docs before they are replaced."

I tried to understand. At death, the average human contained over three hundred versions of outdated nanodocs and assorted other biojunk. It was perfectly safe, and cheaper, to leave it all in the body, circulating without interaction, for the lifetime of the person. But why would he compare this to that? I wasn't some unthinking collection of outdated immune-docs, benignly circulating in a system that no longer recognized them. Unless. The horror of it struck me with the force of a solar storm.

"I will always exist. That's what you're saying. It's my mind's relation to my body that changes. My neurons are being retrained to fire in a pattern that creates you. But you think something of me will remain, like a ghost?"

"I hoped not, but it is already happening. It's part of the process. For a short time, we both exist only in this mindscape, somewhere between dream and the subconscious. But when your body's eyes reopen it will be with my sight and you, the idea of you at least, will remain here, somewhere."

"Still thinking?"

"I believe so, but displaced from all motor functions. I'm sorry. Eventually, you will atrophy, I hope. And I promise, Flynn, I will use this second chance wisely, to build on the advances of this accident. I have learned so much. That the nu-copiers have succeeded in replicating my consciousness in your brain means that we're close to the breakthrough I knew was coming. My life objective is no different from your own. We have both worked long and hard, studied all our lives to abate death. The constant shortening of life due to defective genes, unhealthy environments, disease and physical injury has been all but conquered. The greatest enemy left to us is the most formidable, aging. For all our skill, a perfectly gene-selected human who avoids extreme physical trauma and whose nanodocs are updated regularly lives no longer than one hundred and fifty. And why should this be? Only because neural cells cannot be healed or fixed or transplanted without losing the person, the I from which they are inseparable. Death may be quiet now, brief and controlled, more a fading of technology than a painful exodus, but it is still final. I can stop that. I hope that provides some comfort."

Did it? That all lives could be saved, uploaded, our minds made immortal and our bodies replaced? I could never promise so much. Was it arrogance to feel a right to my own life, selfishness? It was becoming so cold. I tried to lift my hands but couldn't move them or even my head to look down. For all I knew, even in this weird space that wasn't space, my image of my body no longer existed. I was being overwritten, filed and indexed. Bernardo was taking over completely.

"There must be some chance?" I stared at Bernardo, at his Alps. I felt insubstantial as the wisps of snow blowing across the compacted ground.

He shook his head and looked skyward, like it was torture to watch. *Look at me,* I wanted to shout. Soon he would wake and live my life, no, restart his own. I couldn't stop the words inside: it was wrong. If the roles were reversed, I wouldn't stand by and do nothing, I would try something. Anger fired my bones against the cold. A good doctor attempted to help a patient, to save them. It was what we were taught and trained. A life was for saving, not losing, not letting slip away without a fight. If he was once a doctor, he'd forgotten that. And there was something else. I'd sensed it before; he was keeping something back.

"What aren't you telling me?" I shouted. My voice was drawn and hoarse. Bernardo refused to meet my eye. Snow was falling and black flecks spotted his face. No, the snowflakes themselves were ash gray.

"I can't help you, Flynn. You must remain calm and stop this or you'll kill us both."

I couldn't understand his words, could hardly hear them over the dark clouds that gusted over the mountains. Bernardo shook his head, shouted, pointed to the right. There was something in his hand, but the storm was too thick. Time felt fat and slow. There was a hot pinprick on my cheek, then another and another, until my face was warm. There was an explosion. The ground shook and toppled me. My shoulder was real again and sore as it hit the ground. In the distance, Dent D'Herens had blown its top, spewing fire and ash across the world. I knew then, I caused the volcano. It was my chance.

I turned to where Bernardo stood against the violent rush of soot and burning wind. His face was set in a flat grimace. The thing in his hand flashed with one brilliant arc of light. It was cold, cold steel.

I never felt the cut. I only heard the smothered clang where it must have struck stone deep below my body. The sky was a perfect ultramarine blue. The volcano was gone. All around was clean and snow white. He lifted my head, carried it away from my body. I could only splutter and cough as I watched my remains recede. This wasn't real, I told myself. I can stop this. I caused the volcano.

I imagined it raining ash upon us again. Nothing happened.

He walked until it felt like we were so deep in the mountains that finding a way out was impossible. I was confused, disoriented, unable to concentrate on any one fact or determine the passing of time. Eventually, we stopped. He placed me carefully into a square hole carved in the snow. It was so small I felt the sides rub my ears and the cut skin of my neck. There was no pain. This wasn't real, I told myself.

"Your actions could have instigated an irreversible conflict among the nu-copiers themselves. The most likely result of that would not be the return of your own consciousness, but rather the destruction of both yours and mine." He kneeled down and shoved more cold snow over my face, making me blink. "Goodbye, Flynn. There is little enough chance for one of us to survive. I couldn't take that risk."

The snow covered my face. I tried to speak but the cold fell into my mouth and choked back the words. The light darkened as the snow thickened. How was he doing this? How was he controlling me? Was it simply that he now held the most power, that the overwrite was in his favor? Had I wasted time in the beginning, listening to him, or was this moment inevitable? Did he stall me on purpose? I didn't think so. I still believed he meant well. Perhaps he was right to say I should have gone quietly, let one of us at least survive? But, no, again, I wouldn't have asked that of him and it wasn't his job to decide my fate. What did he say before—in time I would atrophy. How much time did I have? How much had passed? The questions tumbled over and over, like a satellite falling from orbit. I hardly noticed the darkness become pitch-black.

I felt a mounting sense that I was locked away. This place felt like a dream. A dream about Bernardo, the Alps, a volcano, murder and imprisonment. But it was too calculated for a dream. This was something else, a mindscape, and Bernardo had time to work here, figure out how to manipulate it to his will.

This is not real, I told the pitch-black. He couldn't lock me away. That wasn't how the mind worked. There are one hundred billion neurons in the brain, ten times that number of glial cells and an almost infinite array of firing patterns. Specific thoughts were constructed from the byways of sound and smell and taste and vision and a myriad of memories that crisscrossed and intersected. In some sense, I still existed, but I couldn't see it. He was maintaining this illusion, imprisoning me, cutting off my attempts to change the surroundings. How? This was a cerebral landscape. Force of will, surely, nothing more than pure concentrative effort. We shared the same brain structure. I could see the landscape he projected, his thoughts, so he could see mine and stop them.

The volcano worked once but not the second time. I thought about Maxi's explanation of how the overwrites were stopped by constant activity and yet not the same activity twice. Was that it? Was it new activity that was key, not necessarily constant activity? Or, something more? An instantaneous volcano in the Alps—of course—it was impossible. It caught him by surprise. His power over me could be defeated by the creative effort, novel experiences, not just new experiences. New experiences formed new neural patterns, novel experiences did the same, but to a much greater degree, by an order of five to one. But was there still time? There was only one way to find out.

I thought myself an astronaut locked in for takeoff on a shuttle trip to the moon base. I felt the earth shudder around me as the engines roared on a launch pad buried in the snow. I saw my gloved hand reach forward and release their power. White heat jettisoned me from the dead ice. The sky became a smear of blue until the atmosphere itself was pierced. Velocity peaked in the night sky. Earth twisted below, its blue-green surface brushed with cloud. I felt a cold pull, an image of my face in the ice grave.

I changed again, became a cartoon cyborg with a half-glass skull, lifeless eyes of opal lasers, a sword of obsidian sharpened to an impossible edge. I thought an airplane-hangar-sized butterfly house around me with swallowtails and red admirals rising from the floor to the ceiling like vivid colored bubbles. I thought Bernardo, and he appeared. He knew I was coming.

Mountains leapt into the sky again. I threw my sword away. He swung his. I turned it to water, then steam, then hydrogen and oxygen. I became a child shooting a catapult of ball bearings a thousand a second. They bounced off his skin. The landscape around us shifted between man-made and natural structures.

Bernardo dropped to his knees. His movements were awkward. The ground was changing to my will, to concrete, steel, nanolube, carbonic, grass, mud, wood. He pressed his hands down. A patch of snow appeared, but all around was under my control. It was easier to change than remain the same and his hope was to impose his own static vision. Beneath him, the snow transformed into unstable biocircuits that bled out of his reach.

"You'll kill us both," he said.

I refused to listen. I felt strength with each movement, with each wondrous possibility. I exploded the airplane hangar into a quadrillion pieces that flew away on dragonfly wings. I changed the mountains to mud and became a gondolier with a painted moustache rowing on a sea of melted Alps, towing Bernardo behind me. The sea hardened to desert. A posse of lazy crocodiles sunbathed on red towels nearby. They raised martinis to salute us and, with a sudden pop, the desert collapsed.

It turned inside out and dumped us on a grassy hill that sloped gently to a meandering river. The crocodiles slinked off into the river with conspiratorial glances. I was changing constantly, flickering through forms that were both real and utterly alien. A massively obese woman with a camel's head, a squid with tarantula legs instead of tentacles. I turned to face Bernardo, but he was no longer fully there.

He was a wraith. His skin was the bark of a paper leaf birch, his eyes no more than black pinheads in a face rubbed flat. The thing, Bernardo, gasped for air, only for its punctured lungs to wheeze it out again.

He was trying to say something. It struck me, he was dying. I was killing him, or erasing him. Whichever, it was for real. I didn't want to kill anyone.

I lowered myself, though it felt more like my body had collapsed under me, as if it was constructed from loosely stacked tubes. Bernardo's mouth, only a line in his wooden face, closed, sealed, reopened. I heard his voice. The words were pulled tight and ripped.

"I should have helped you, Flynn."

I was unable to think of what to say, what to do.

"I could have helped you control this mindscape, reassert your neural pattern. I was a coward."

"Hold on." His body was crumbling in my hands. It smelled like burning plastic. He had done what he thought was right. I didn't blame him. I needed to find a way to save him. If I survived this, the nu-copiers could be extracted. He could become part of his dream of immortality. He could be saved.

"How do I stop this?"

"No time anymore." His voice warbled. "Maybe there was before, but not anymore. No time for either of us."

"Hold on," I shouted, but he was already finished. His body turned to dust, then worms, and then shards of mirror that coalesced in a snap before disappearing completely.

Everything was changing rapidly, too rapidly. I struggled to hold an image of my human body and simultaneously halt the progression of landscape that became a hurricane blur of improbabilities. I was losing control. No time for either of us, Bernardo said. I was crashing, like Maxi's simulations. I was sure of it now.

A dam had burst somewhere. My imagination cycled through a million possibilities. I fought to clear my mind, to blank it, but the images flooded through. I couldn't stop the tide. My body made a hissing sound like my limbs were powered with gas-filled springs instead of muscle and tendon. And then, an idea filled me with hope.

I struggled with a single thought, one focused creation, one contribution to the manic changes. Gas hissed all around me, the atmosphere becoming a sweet-scented mixture, 92% air, 8% sevoflurane. I sucked it in, making a sound like a fish might make if it tried to laugh. If this worked, would I wake up? I counted backwards. Ten, nine, eight, seven . . .

The anesthetic?" Maxi asked.

"Sevoflurane—guaranteed to suspend all neuronal activity, up to and including dreams, hallucinations, fantasies or flights of fancy."

"You tricked yourself."

"It's the same trick every human plays on themselves at least once a day. Think about something as simple as worrying—think of all the times you convinced yourself there was something to worry about, like you left the plasma oven on, when there was no such problem. We can convince ourselves of almost anything."

Maxi half smiled and nodded, stirred her hot chocolate. I could see there was more on her mind. This was the first time we'd met since both of us were released from quarantine. The virus police dropped the charges because, one, I was alive and, two, they wanted the whole episode buried.

And it was buried. The nu-copiers were recovered and destroyed. Kings were refused permission to run them through the simulators and there was no way of storing them in any coherent fashion. I felt a sense of responsibility. It was a final thumb in Bernardo's eye.

I took another smell of the coffee on the table. This cafe was expensive but worth it. In the month since I'd regained my mind, not to mention full cardiac function, I'd developed an almost excessive love of real coffee. Adopted would be a more accurate description. Maxi told me Bernardo loved real coffee. Though there was a kind of comfort that a part of him lived on, it also gave me a shot of fear to think that maybe he was indexed up there somewhere, trapped. I could only hope that wasn't true.

Maxi stared into her cup. She looked different from the gung-ho girl who attempted to bust me out of the hospital. She looked like she still blamed herself for Bernardo's death and the blame was corroding her from the inside.

"He forgave you," I said.

"Did he?" She looked up, hopeful, but then shook her head.

I told her what Bernardo said, about how he felt responsible, about how he blamed himself, not her. Maxi listened, nodded, stirred her drink. When I finished talking, she remained silent, but some of the pain had lifted from her face. She stared out the window, as if searching for a familiar face in the passing crowds but knowing she would never find it.

She turned to me. "I'm glad it was you who survived."

I didn't know what to say. I knew she meant those words and I was glad to hear them. I'd thought a lot about Bernardo's death. I too clearly remembered the life draining from his face. I thought about the regret in his voice. His life was devoted to the ideal of saving human life. He must have felt incredible shame, knowing there was a chance to save mine and not risking it, even if he perceived it was for the greater good.

Meeting him had strengthened my resolve to become a doctor and the best one I could be. I might only ever save a handful of lives and I would never grant immortality but I would make a difference, one person at a time.

"I think Bernardo wanted it that way too," I said, and for the first time, I truly believed it.

Digital Rights

written by

Brent Knowles

illustrated by

REBECCA GLEASON

ABOUT THE AUTHOR

Canadian writer Brent Knowles grew up in the one-stoplight town of Chetwynd, British Colombia. There, Brent prepared himself for future careers in game design and writing by playing video games and reading anything he could get his hands on. It was a difficult childhood. Eventually (after several years of college and university) he received a computing science degree from the University of Alberta in Edmonton despite spending most of his time in anthropology and history classes. For the next ten years, Brent designed role-playing video games with BioWare, including Baldur's Gate 2, Neverwinter Nights and Dragon Age, but continued writing stories.

Brent started submitting to the Writers of the Future Contest in 1997 and after that first rejection, he continued to bombard the Contest with submissions. Along the way, he collected one Finalist and a few Honorable Mentions. "Digital Rights" was his nineteenth submission to the Contest.

Now retired from the day job, Brent should have more time to spend with his wife, ride his mountain bike or build a robot, but in all honesty he'll just write more . . . though his two young sons (future Ultimate Fighting Champions) do occasionally disrupt his efforts to finish his first novel. His fiction has been published in Not One of Us, On Spec and Tales of the Talisman.

ABOUT THE ILLUSTRATOR

Always drawn to the weird and wonderful, Rebecca grew up inspired by her forest home in Oregon, where nature hides many secrets. She had very little exposure to art in school, but luckily, her mom was a brilliant self-taught watercolor artist who gave Rebecca a paintbrush one day and a passion was born. Over the years, she continued to draw and paint her own fantasy worlds, hoping that one day she could make a living with her art.

In 1999, Rebecca moved to a tiny desert town called Los Angeles after a five-year tour of the West. There, she took some art classes and tried to figure out how to spend more time drawing and less time churning her wheels, but she was still able to be stuck in one helluva rut. In order to gain some perspective and not throw her entire paycheck at rent, she decided to make a huge change. So, she moved to the wild and crazy Midwest, and returned to school full time to major in visual communication design. There, she has learned how to design books and other interesting things and continues to create concept art for future projects. An internship at Sony Online Studios and other awards, scholarships and opportunities have inspired Rebecca to continue chasing her dream.

Digital Rights

The Assistant responsible for the primary thruster arrangement killed itself just ten days after Izzy arrived on the solar station. The panicked chatter of the other Assistants prevented them from continuing with their own duties. Horror, speculation and worst of all, wonder, flowed across the station's network.

Izzy had to stop it.

And it was her fault; it never should have happened. She had been distracted. Later she would blame the ghost, but for now, she simply reacted. Simply acted. Her body twisted and jerked, her fingers puncturing the holographic displays that surrounded her, initiating commands as she fought for the station's survival. Earth, beautiful, blue, perfect, floated in front of her, easily visible from any of the three portholes on the exterior wall of E-Module, but she saw only the geometry of digital space, the goggles she wore cutting out her view of the physical world.

Sirens whined as Assistants on the periphery of the contagion struggled with their workload. They sensed the disturbance and initiated the shrieking wails, but most of the other Assistants were too busy gossiping and so lights flickered, air lines choked and rooms cooled.

The three other technicians in the room responded to her hurried commands, scurrying from console to console even as she invoked her personal Assistant. She had no name for it, thinking that practice silly, but it had evolved with her from undergraduate studies through to her latest professional work. It had been refactored many times but its core personality, its recollectables, had never been purged, creating a continuity of companionship that exceeded in length her marriage. Versions of her Assistant still maintained the street power generators, those nuclear substations that were used throughout the Third World countries that were not yet tied into the solar network she now managed.

Her Assistant was reliable, rock-solid and determined. Duplicating the AI process a thousand times, she seeded the clones through the network, ordering them to spread a message of calm. She gave each clone a lifespan of five minutes—in that time they would have to quell a rebellion—if they failed every human on the station was dead.

Paranoia, or perhaps the inherited experience of the traces in her mind, urged her to bolster the Assistants in charge of the power supply to her work station with more duplicates. It was strange to have memories from the other E-Module managers in her mind, and she was still growing used to knowing when to listen to them or when to ignore them. Her most recent Predecessor had been monitoring the dead Assistant, having noticed some of the early telltale signs of sentience: excessive questioning (the Why-thats?), irritating complaining (the Sucks-that-I-Have-Tos) and inconvenient downtime (Navel-gazing). Predecessor had been indoctrinating a replacement in quarantine and Izzy now carefully moved it into the mainstream network but prevented it from subscribing to any of the chatter events, effectively deafening it to the riot. The young were most impressionable and though the new thruster Assistant would need to communicate eventually, that could wait until it had mastered the basics of its duties.

If only Izzy had paid more attention! One of the other Assistants, a lighting flunky, had tried warning her about the thruster's doomed flight to awareness, but between worrying about the ghost and Predecessor's categorizing of the lighting Assistant as a whiner, she had ignored it. Izzy's memories were so entangled with the memories of the Predecessor and the other traces that she treated them all as fact, all as important as her own memories. She would be more careful.

"Status update."

Commander Meredith Ferguson's voice startled Izzy and she jerked back into realspace, peeling the goggles away. She could feel the commander's breath on her neck and smelled the other woman's vanilla-scent shampoo, but did not turn around. Instead she studied the consensus graphs that her Assistant was generating, as she explained the situation. Ferguson made the occasional grunt of acknowledgment as she listened.

The microwave beam that transmitted the energy collecting in the station's football-field-long solar panels had been terminated the moment the disruption had begun. That was protocol. Obviously, back on Earth, there was no need to panic yet, not with the numerous traditional power facilities still woven into the grid. There was enough redundancy in that system to let them coast a few hours before blackouts began, but Ferguson sighed heavily and said, "Earth needs to know when we'll resume."

Izzy cringed at the way she said Earth, as if it represented some collective of evil whose bidding the commander was forced to obey. What would Izzy's husband Rob think of such blatant separatist sentiment? She shook her head and scanned the latest reports. "Looks like we're almost there. We'll need to replace a few Assistants; those in close contact with the suicide are more likely to show signs of sentience in the future. I'll need to cull them."

"Agreed. And the power?"

Jerking her hand forward and then back slightly, she tapped the screen before her, and then gestured, the gesture rotating the three-dimensional bar graphs floating above her. Her Assistant—and its soon-to-be-deceased clones—was running semantics analysis of the chatter feeds the other processes used to communicate with each other. Problematic thought-patterns were red bars on the graph and these were shrinking in comparison to yellow (placidity) and green (contentment) bars.

"Twenty minutes or so, I think," Alex said. He was a thin young man of Russian descent, but a third-generation Offworlder. He was one of the three technicians and had served longer than any of the others. Once he finished his graduate work in intelligence modeling he would probably step into the role Izzy was temporarily occupying. Or at least that was the buzz from the cafeteria—Alex was too quiet, too respectful, to talk about that.

Izzy agreed with his assessment and nodded.

"Good work, crew. I'll let Earth know," Ferguson said and left the room. Izzy watched the commander leave, her gravboots clanging loudly as she snap-walked away. Above the rim of the boots, Izzy saw green socks peeking out. Izzy glanced at the calendar. March 17th, 2180. Saint Patrick's Day. She smiled; the socks contrasted with the stark whites, beiges and yellows of the station.

Leaning back in her chair, she closed her eyes, taking stock. Three days ago she had been cleared for duty, had her first sessions with Dr. Rutger and had inherited her traces. Two days ago she had taken command of E-Module. Three hours from now she would have her first Face2Face with her husband since arriving on the station. So much had happened, in so little a time. Her shift was almost over. The technicians would stay and cover the next half day and then they would be relieved by the night crew. Izzy was the only manager on the station and would be woken if another crisis emerged.

Before leaving, she allowed herself a small smile. For the first time since arriving she felt the awkwardness of the situation fade a little. She would still be Earthbound, the lone crew member not a bona fide Offworlder, but she was now also something more. She could see it in the grins of the technicians when they looked up at her. She had hung in, despite the initial cold reception. Like her grandfather always said, Izzy was tough as nails.

A network traffic bar caught her attention. Alex was copying a log of the current session out of E-Module.

"What's this?"

He turned, his serious eyes, his serious face (far too serious for such a young man) directly toward her. "I'm copying the results to the Mad . . . to Dr. Rutger." Izzy hid her smile; at least the serious young man could be flippant enough to call the station's psychologist by his nickname. The Mad Doctor.

"We always send this stuff to him, his lab, the suit and his eyesnap, you know. It lets him model the data virtually. He moves through it, visualizing it more efficiently than we can, and well, you know, being human, he's a bit smarter than our Assistants."

It made sense. The doctor was a genius with both artificial intelligence and memory manipulation. The Inheritance Process, while not invented by him, had become perfected under his guidance. The doctor performed all archival for the seven inhabited system stations, all the way out to Jupiter 2. Of course, those memory packets were transmitted digitally. The doctor seldom left the station, let alone his room.

His work was vital to the station because there were far too few specialists, and in space knowing *exactly* how to accomplish a task the first time was essential. Or people died. The doctor's process allowed him to take traces of specialists and then graft them into their replacements.

310

"Good enough. See you tomorrow."

"Um, you can't leave yet," Alex said. Izzy paused, cocking her head, a little confused. Alex gestured to the small rectangular flatstrip painted atop the middle porthole. Yellow lettering on a black background read: *Days since last incident—23.*

Damn. She tapped a few keys and reset the counter to zero. The technicians looked up at it a moment, expressions glum. She couldn't have that. As Izzy unbuckled herself, she said, "No worries. I just like starting at the beginning, before beating a record." They looked at her, small smiles playing across their faces.

She floated into the hallway, using the grab handles to pull herself along. She had tried the gravboots but had never mastered the complicated step required to use them effectively.

Janice was waking up, a little late as usual, when Izzy entered their shared sleeping shelf. The sleep cocoon hung open against the far wall and Janice was reading the station updates on the flatstrip sprayed between the cocoon and the exit while sipping coffee from a bulb. She turned to Izzy, her short black hair still matted from sleep, but she was dressed in uniform. Dr. Rutger insisted all his nurses stay to that Earth protocol.

The coffee almost smelled good enough to mask the stench of body odor that permeated the station. They had told her that she would eventually stop noticing that. Izzy bumped against Janice—the sleeping shelf was small—as she slid another packet into the coffee dispenser.

"A little excitement this morning," Janice said.

"Kept me on my feet. The Assistants on the station are rather sophisticated, but almost cranky compared with what I've worked with before." Suddenly an alert popped up on screen and a traditional beep-beep sounded. Izzy flinched.

Another message from the ghost?

"It's for you, Izzy."

"Probably nothing, just junk," Izzy said, leaning over Janice's shoulder and hiding the notification. Not long after arriving on the station she had started getting all manner of random messages.

"I didn't think we got spam up here."

"Those bastards can find you anywhere," Izzy said, her heart beating faster than usual. She hoped Janice couldn't feel it. The nurse did not say anything as she slipped toward the exit.

"Don't forget your Face2Face," she said as she left.

Not a chance, Izzy thought, smiling.

I prefer my gynecologist," Izzy replied to Rob's question about her first meeting with Dr. Rutger. She was (slowly) growing accustomed to the time delay between when she spoke and when she saw Rob's reaction: in this case his thin eyebrows rising, a confused smile wrinkling his tanned face. On the other hand, the delay afforded her a long time to study his pretty-handsome face, the curve of his lips, the dimple and the clean-shaven face. She missed that most of all; the men on the station did not spend much time on hygiene, especially shaving.

The voice she heard from the speakers was a digitized replica of Rob's warm, easygoing manner of speaking, his words arriving after being cast into space, bounced off a satellite and splattered across the station's receiver. It was only vaguely reminiscent of how he actually sounded but it still curled her toes, just as it had eleven years ago when they had met on campus. A planet away.

It was the middle of the day for him and he was using the video conferencing system at the university where he was speaking, drumming up supporters for his run at governor of California. This election was not supposed to happen for a couple years but the recall of the current governor had thrown everything into chaos. Especially their relationship.

Rob was saying (or had said, she supposed), "You did nothing but talk about him before leaving." Izzy hated how he left the *leaving* dangling there, as if an accusation. But what he said was true. She had talked about Dr. Rutger, probably annoyingly too often, but how could she not? The man had written several of the textbooks she had used during university and beyond. Though she knew she would not be working with him directly, she had hoped to be able to arrange some one-on-one time with him. The things she could learn from him!

But her first meeting had been a little disturbing. She tried to explain, "He's brilliant, there's no doubt of that, but it's just that . . ." She struggled to find the words. She did not want to insult her idol.

After a long silence, Rob said, "What? He was assessing you for duty before allowing you to inherit his precious traces, right? He wanted to make sure you wouldn't crack. Obviously you passed. You saved the station!"

Izzy smiled. She liked it when Rob was proud of

her. "I didn't save it on my own. And the doctor, well, I guess the psychological assessment went well enough. Like you said, I passed."

Dr. Rutger was a robust man, not fat by any stretch; the diet of gels, nut paste and silkworm spread did not encourage obesity, but he had filled his small chamber, looming behind his plastic desk and over the flatstrip painted on it. A sleeping cocoon in the corner. A plastic fern bolted to the desktop his only decoration.

And then there was the leather haptic suit that made him look like a plush gladiator. The haptic outfit provided the doctor with tensile response to the virtual worlds he explored, cataloging the memories that he acquired from the station crew. It allowed him to physically experience the memories, making his work possible. It was creepy but only half as creepy as the eyesnap. This was a cable composed of thin segments that folded and unfolded as necessary to adjust to any movements the doctor made. His left eye had been removed and the eyesnap entered his brain through the hole. Dr. Rutger did not simply study data; he lived in it.

His good eye never met hers. It had remained fixated on her chest, and she was certain that when she left its gaze had moved down to her ass.

At least Janice had warned her about what to expect.

"And did the inheritance hurt? Or anything?"

By anything, Rob meant, had it changed her? How many times had they had this conversation on Earth? Her trying to reassure him; he trying to warn her. "I'm still me, honey. The doctor just injected a little expertise, a little hands-on experience, all of it pertaining to my work only. I haven't collected any new fetishes."

Rob smiled, a worried sort of smile, and she wondered if there were others in the room with him, people who he did not want to associate him with the word fetish, imaginary or otherwise. She blushed a little and chided herself for not having thought of that. During an election Rob was never alone.

"And he's taken from you too?"

She sighed. "Nothing has been removed. I only bequeathed a copy of some of my technical knowledge."

Rob said, "I hate that they're copying you. They say, space, it changes you." Rob, of course, still listened to vinyl.

"I'm still your original Izzy."

A beep distracted him, but he managed a smile while glancing down at the mofo he carried. He flicked his wrist, acknowledging the message he had just received.

"You keeping an eye on the 'casts? There's been some talk that I'm sympathetic to the separatist movement. Just like we worried about."

Just like you *worried,* Izzy thought. She should have done her station work well before the next election; they both knew having her here in the middle of it would make things harder for Rob. But they had talked about it, had agreed that it would be okay.

"I'm sorry, but we discussed this, a lot," she said.

His device beeped again.

"I know, I know. I'm just reminding you." Her

cheeks flushed. "Listen, I've got a call. Anything else you need to talk about?"

She glanced at the clock. There was over seven minutes left on their precious Face2Face. Station bandwidth was fairly limited—and everyone busy with official duties—so these calls were metered every two weeks or so. Time was precious but obviously Rob was too busy.

She really needed to talk to him about the ghost and was about to speak when he said, "Okay then, take care."

He disconnected the call and he disappeared.

"Good luck," she whispered to the blank screen. "I love you."

Soft blanket on soft grass, Rob beside her, she snuggling into his warmth. The bright city lights far in the distance. Staring up at the stars.

"What will it be like?" Izzy asked.

Rob turned to her and she reached out a hand, gently scraping her long nails over his smooth chin.

"Cold," he said. "They say—"

A loud beeping filled the night air and they both looked around. And then he peeled away, her eyes opening to the quasi-darkness of her sleeping shelf. The dream faded. The flatstrip was beeping an emergency notification.

Her cocoon was as warm as the dream blanket had been. She wiped sleep from her eyes and stared at the flatstrip. She unzipped a little and leaned forward.

"Assistant?" she whispered, but her voice was dry and her words struggled to be heard. She cleared her throat and tried again.

"New message. Critical priority."

Oh, no, she thought, scrambling out of the sleep-cocoon. Had something happened to Rob? She ordered her Assistant to display the message.

"Negative," it said, aware that she was Away-From-Keyboard and used voice instead of her preference for text. "Message is audio. Play?"

"No. Sender?" She slid from the cocoon and braced herself against the wall. Her heart was racing.

"Isabel Mosh."

If there had been a chair in the room she would have slumped into it. Cold relief flooded her, followed by a rush of icy anger. She had never hit another person in her life but she clenched her fists and stared at the display.

The ghost, the bloody damn ghost.

The first message had shown up three days after Izzy boarded the station. Four more, including this new one, had arrived intermittently since then. All of them had been sent from her own email account. Whoever was doing this had successfully hacked into her station account and though she kept on changing her password, the hacking, the messages, continued. In a way she was glad that Rob was not messaging her; at least there was little chance of any surprise embarrassments. Because she clearly did not have control over her own account.

"Play it," she said tensely. She knew she should forward it to the station commander. Obviously a prank was being played on her, probably by one of the more disgruntled Offworlders. She brought her fingers to her mouth, chewed down on the shattered ruins of her nails.

317

"Help . . . me, us . . . he's not what . . . I'm not as tough—"

Each recording was improving in quality, as if the prankster was getting frustrated at Izzy's inability to understand. She could almost decipher this latest message. A woman's voice. There were only seven females on the station; if she could identify the sender, maybe she could talk to them, convince them she was not an Earthbound spy, or worse. Resolve the situation without escalating it. She assigned her Assistant to do a voice analysis and it reported that it would take three hours to complete.

Good enough, Izzy thought. She invoked the clock: a couple hours until wake time. There was no way she was going to fall back to sleep. She had a scheduled bequeathal session before her shift started and figured she might as well show up early.

There was no real nighttime on the station. Outside her sleeping shelf the hall lights were bright. This was the hub of the station. The central orb contained the sleeping shelves, dining hall, exercise rooms and other hygienic necessities. Seven pencil tubes extruded from the main sphere to a different, specialized research lab. Over the years the station had expanded to take over hosting scientific research after the previous stations had been mothballed. Izzy moved down the pencil tube that led to the medical sphere.

The waiting room was a cramped hall even when empty of people. Janice chatted with Izzy a bit but because the chamber was free they decided to start the procedure early. The memory chamber was a circular room with the metal bench in the center the only furnishing. Thick corrugated tubes led from the head of the bench, under the floor panels and into Dr. Rutger's office. That office, the door closed now, sat at the opposite end of the chamber.

Attached to the bench were a bulky mask and three canisters of the gas that both sent people into a dreaming slumber and opened their synapses for the tracing. Since this was a bequeathal today and not an inheritance, Dr. Rutger would trigger Izzy's memories and trace the relevant ones, adding them to the predecessor archives.

Janice helped Izzy onto the bench. One of three nurses, this was the first time that Janice was on duty while Izzy underwent the procedure, because of their working opposite shifts. The nurses did more, of course, than assist Dr. Rutger; they also took care of the scrapes and bruises of the crew, checked for infection, monitored stool and urine samples and so on. All that fun stuff that made Izzy especially glad that she worked with code. Code never oozed.

The mask descended toward Izzy.

It was black leather, and it fully enclosed her face, sealing tight as Janice adjusted various straps. If it were not for the jasmine-scented oxygen pumping through the tubes and into her mouth, the patient would die from suffocation. For a few long, familiar seconds, Izzy could see nothing, hear nothing, and then suddenly lights flared around her, bright blinding lights that made her wince and turn her head side to side. Bars on either side of her head had been raised into place to make sure she would not hurt herself.

"Tell me about your day, Isabel," the doctor said, his voice monotone, devoid of character except for the small squeaks between his words, as if each word exhausted his supply of air. She thought of the rogue Assistant and how she had stopped the other Assistants from killing themselves. He prompted her to explore the details, as he traced her.

He said, "You took control of the situation."

She smiled, thinking of the plastic plant in his office. She had looked at it a couple times during their profiling sessions.

He had said, "You know, they'd really prefer that I use a real plant, even tried putting one in here. But I just hate caring for things, watering, pruning and the like. The damn things just grow out of my control."

She had nodded.

"Do you have any plants, Isabel?"

She remembered his thin smile as she had answered, "Just plastic ones."

"That tells me so much," he had said, smiling.

"Think of loyalty," he said now, jarring her back to the present.

She thought of her work, of engineering. Rob. Politics slipped reluctantly into her mind; she could not hide her distaste of them. She loved Rob but hated his career. Why was Rutger asking her this? Did he fear her a spy, like some of the others feared? Did thinking she was a spy make her seem suspicious? She tried thinking of something else but her mind balked. Spy! Spy! Spy!

The mask tightened around her face.

"Are you claustrophobic?"

She shook her head. A hand touched her naked stomach. No, that couldn't be; she was on the memory bench. Wearing clothes. Suddenly her arms were lifted above her neck and she felt a cold wall against her back.

"Have you ever been imprisoned?"

"No," she whispered. She thought she heard the echo of her voice; it might have been nothing.

"Tied up?"

Are you serious? What was going on—

The restraints tightened and she almost shrieked.

"No, never."

"How would you react, you think, to being tied up?" The question sent her into spasms of horror, panic welling up, the mask flapping against her lips as each inhale brought it almost fully into her mouth. She could not differentiate reality from what was occurring in her head. Why was the doctor doing this?

"Can you tolerate pain?"

Oh, damn. She steeled herself.

But no pain came. Instead the doctor said, "Remember your husband."

She did, thinking first of the tears she had refused to shed after Rob had cut short his conversation with her. She cringed, but the doctor probed deeper and a flood of memories escaped her. For a moment she could actually feel Rob sliding inside her. Her toes curled and she moaned, her face flushing with embarrassment, maybe more.

Suddenly the lights disappeared and there was a long, low moan echoing in her head. When the moan stopped, so did the hissing of oxygen and she began to suffocate.

As she sucked desperately for air, the leather memory mask slid into her mouth, cold, soft and

321

pliable. She thrashed but the restraints kept her on the bench. Janice's hands were at the mask quickly, undoing the straps easily. She pulled the mask free and Izzy could breathe again.

"I don't know—" But Janice was interrupted as the doctor's voice emanated from the speakers in the ceiling.

"Computer problems," he explained, sounding a little out of breath. "Sorry about that."

Still drained, still drawing in deep gulps of air, Izzy managed to ask, "You need help? With the computer?"

"No, no," he said quickly, "that will not be necessary. I handled it. Fixed it. You may go; I think we've discovered enough for this session."

Izzy felt her face flush when she remembered remembering Rob. The doctor must see that sort of thing all the time, right? She hoped he would not think less of her. She considered asking Janice about the things the doctor asked her, the things she felt, but could not bring herself to do that.

Just in case.

A little over two months later Izzy was floating beside Janice, as they waited for Izzy's Assistant to load the voice file. It was end of shift for Janice and Izzy had a half hour to spare before her own day started. With everything that had happened, Izzy needed to share her nightmare with another, to have help identifying the ghost.

Though her Assistant had already discovered the prankster weeks ago.

But it was wrong.

It had to be.

"You look like hell," Janice said, "and with me ending a shift, looking better than you! Everything okay, honey?" The last sentence was said with a lowered, sympathetic tone that Izzy had started really hating three weeks ago.

"I'm okay. I just really need to have you listen to what . . . what someone has been sending me, pranking me with. I just really need to know who is doing this. Assistant: play clips."

". . . get us out of here . . ."

". . . stop giving us . . . oh damn . . . found . . ."

". . . knows everything . . ."

". . . his Isabel, his Isabel, I am . . ."

Janice's face whitened as she listened to the collage. Izzy had been certain it was not Janice and by the other woman's expression, that certainty was now without doubt. Janice's fingers trembled, brushing the sides of her uniform.

"Izzy . . . it's you. Why are you saying these things?" Janice was pushing herself away from Izzy, but keeping her eyes fixed to hers.

Crap. The Assistant had come to the same conclusion.

"No! They just come from my account; whoever is doing this is hacking into my system." Izzy knew she was close to tears.

"Everyone likes you, Izzy. Especially now with what has happened Earthside, nobody wants you off the station. We're all hoping you will reapply after the year term expires."

Earthside, like Earth, might as well have been in another universe. Three terse Face2Faces and then finally an official message from Rob's lawyer, and a slightly more personal final communiqué from Rob himself:

I stopped missing you, Isabel, I don't know when exactly. I need to focus on my career now, and the posturing of the stations isn't helping. Your being there isn't helping.

Don't you cry, Izzy. Keep yourself together.
He had, of course, had an affair too. Normally that would be an election killer, but it had rapidly increased Rob's popularity.

"I just couldn't relate to her," he had said in one interview. "I'm here on Earth, living with Earth problems, and, well, she's up there."

Izzy closed her eyes, stopped the tears.

"The voice, it sounds like you, honey."

Izzy nodded, opening her eyes.

"It's not," she insisted.

Janice nodded. "Look, I'm gonna grab a bit to eat before I sleep. Nothing like munching on silkies before bed, eh? You want to keep me company?"

"No, thanks, I'm off to work."

Janice rested her hand on Izzy's shoulder for a few seconds and then left. Izzy leaned against the wall.

Asking for help had been a mistake. The way Janice had looked at her, eyes full of pity, of concern, disgusted Izzy.

She could repair this herself. Invoking her Assistant, she soon had it gutted open and began to tweak several parameters. She granted it full access rights. It would have the same clearance level as she. Such a practice was frowned upon but she needed it to follow any clues it might find. Then she sent it out with orders to fully cross-reference all accessible personnel files, Internet data, station logs, anything and everything. She needed to know who was speaking to her.

And what will you do, Izzy thought, *if it turns out that it is you?*

The shift passed slowly. Izzy felt like a tweener her first day with a mofo, waiting and checking every few seconds for a new message. In this case she was checking for status updates from her Assistant. None arrived. As the shift neared ending and just as she was preparing to leave, Alex kicked out from his chair and floated over to her.

"Listen," he said quietly, "you're gonna be paged by the commander to go see her . . . before you panic, know that all of us here, we want to help you through . . . this thing."

"This thing? What thing?" Izzy kept her temper in check, but barely. Had Janice told the commander about the messages from the ghost?

Before he could reply, a notification appeared on her flatstrip. From the commander. An urgent meeting. *Crap. Asking for help: definitely a mistake.*

"You want me to go with you?" She stared at him, realizing she hadn't yet responded to his first statement. Was his offer genuine? Was it too cynical of her to suspect he was just trying to get laid? Seven females. Fifteen men. Her pending divorce had not gone unnoticed.

"I can manage," she said.

Izzy had only seen the commander's office during her Face2Face job interview with Commander Ferguson almost a year ago. She had never set foot in it. In many ways it was similar to Dr. Rutger's, but with several real plants instead of a singular plastic one. Izzy sat across the desk from the commander.

"Your divorce, your first rotation on a station, minding an unruly bunch of pre-sentients—these are all very stressful and you are holding up exceptionally well. But we all need help. I'm recommending that you allow Dr. Rutger to have three or four sessions with you. I'm sure it will help."

"I don't need a shrink," Izzy said.

"I know it will be a little uncomfortable, as the two of you have been working together professionally. As I understand it you have been reviewing some of his more advanced research. He's a very private man and I'm encouraged that he's willing to confide in you. Obviously he respects you and you him."

"His work, with tracings and inheritance and Assistant-overseer domain-to-peer techniques, is amazing. I've been lucky. And you are right, I would feel uncomfortable." She paused. How to express to the commander that she did not want the doctor to think her weak? What if he stopped allowing her to view his research results? Despite what the commander had said, they had spent very little time together but Izzy always felt renewed when he sent her a new file, a new algorithm. The commander intuited Izzy's fears.

"He's a very good listener, Isabel, and he's professional. No matter what you say, it won't diminish his opinion of you."

She ran down a long, dark tunnel. The gravity told her she was back on Earth, that heavy slam of foot against wet concrete, the splash of water soaking the hem of her pants. The air, thick, dirty and heavy, and the voices pleading for mercy told her this was a nightmare. Distance and the hollow tunnels separated her from the screaming. She smelled meat sizzling.

Her Assistant woke her with a gentle buzzing. She opened her eyes to darkness. For no reason, she thought of Rob's parting words.

I stopped missing you.

"I never stopped," she whispered. But Rob, she had watched him forget her, surely it had happened day by day, a little more of her fading away from him. She hadn't known it then, else she would have fought. She sighed, wanting to close her eyes and drift back to sleep. He had told her it would be okay for her to work on the station. They had reached a decision. Together.

She closed her eyes, but her thoughts allowed no sleep.

Twenty minutes later she sat in front of Dr. Rutger, her legs wrapped around the legs of her chair. The plastic fern still dangled in the corner. What had she expected? That it might die?

"Let me ask you a simple question," the doctor said finally. She almost wondered if he knew who she was, that she was the same person he had been sharing research with. His voice was flat and his real eye flitted back and forth, scanning the flatstrip on his desk. "This was never your dream, was it?"

"What do you mean?" She had expected a question about the mysterious messages, perhaps even some leading questions to gull her into admitting that she had sent them herself. Not this.

"Most Earthbound working in the stations have spent their lives dreaming of space. The rest are born here. Both groups share a passion for the long, dark expanse of stars. They revel in the excitement of colonization. Did you, Isabel Mosh, spend your life dreaming of the stars?"

She felt like she was about to fail a job application despite the months of work she had already dedicated to the station.

"It's not like I didn't want to come here."

She paused. He paused.

Finally he looked up, a rare moment of eye contact, a thin smile spreading across his face before he resumed looking down.

"You don't enjoy talking about yourself."

"Not really."

"Well then, I'll be more direct. Why are you here?"

"The Assistants. Maintaining the station requires the most complicated artificial intelligence in the—" She paused, about to say world but, realizing the understatement in the word, she corrected "—universe. I want to be part of that."

"Ah," the doctor said, "perhaps that is better than the glory hounds who come here seeking excitement? Do you regret your decision now that your husband has left you?"

She blinked three times, cleared her throat. "No."

"Do you feel it is affecting you?"

"Not my work," she said quickly.

"No, of course not. Your record is superb and your insights into some of the more technical aspects of my research show strong insight. But there is more to life than just work." This coming from the man who slept in his office? She resisted the urge to allow the smallest of grins.

"I am a little—challenged—at times," she said. "I knew my year in space would put a strain on my marriage, but when we went into it, the marriage, that is, we were equals. And we always were, or so I thought." She pinched her lips together, feeling stupid for revealing so much to a stranger. He nodded his head, urging her to continue, as his hands traced patterns across the flatstrip.

"Generally we did what he wanted, though, even big things like buying the house he liked, or his running for office. But I always felt like his equal. We debated these decisions together. But then this huge opportunity presents itself and I convince him that it is good for me, for us. Or I thought I convinced him."

The doctor said, "And then he uses it, as an excuse, to divorce you."

"Yes."

"And how does that make you feel?"

"Isn't that phrase copyrighted or something?"

He laughed but kept his eye glued to the flatstrip. Silence stretched out. Finally, sighing, she said, "Now I don't think we ever had an equal relationship. I, or what I wanted, was never important to him."

"Perhaps. Maybe he just changed," Dr. Rutger suggested. "People do that. Change. Especially when the situation becomes . . . so different from what they are used to. When the horrible happens, some thrive. Others collapse."

"I haven't collapsed."

"No, and we won't let you. That's why you are here. Isabel, when did you start sending messages to yourself?"

Izzy let her mouth hang open a moment, digesting the abrupt change in conversation. "I . . . I never. They are not from me."

"They are your own voice though?"

She sighed. What else should she expect? "Maybe it's my voice. I don't know. But I did not record them, did not send them. They just appeared in my inbox. I am not crazy."

"Our mind operates along a continuum, a road stretching forever forward, forever backward. Sometimes we hit, well, potholes along the way. These disrupt our—"

"Whoever is speaking, in these messages, she is in pain, distress. That's not me."

He had been nodding sympathetically during the previous exchanges, but his hands had always been busy. Now they stopped. He looked up.

"Pain? How?"

"Whoever was sending it was pretending to be hurt, in danger."

"Play them." He was looking at her intently now and with a command invoked his Assistant. He asked it to open a tunnel into the secure data terminal so that her Assistant could enter. When it arrived, she asked it to play the messages.

She sat there watching the thin grin play across Rutger's face as fragments of voice from the mysterious woman played over the speaker. He squirmed in his seat as it ended.

"I assumed it a prank," she said.

"I'll take copies of these and will ask around. It does sound like you, but there's a difference," he said and she thought he might elaborate; his voice was full of emotion now. Did the thought of playing virtual detective excite him? But he never resumed speaking.

"Okay, thanks," she said.

"See the nurse on your way out. She'll fill a prescription for you, a relaxant."

Izzy walked out, glancing back to see the doctor staring at her as she clambered away from him. A cold chill ran down her spine as he hastily looked down at his desk.

At least she had not been sent back to Earth.

It would be hours later before she realized that she no longer thought of Earth as home.

They were busy running millions of simulations, breeding an improved life support Assistant. Izzy visualized the results and studied them as she tried to determine which strains should be bred next for optimal results.

"How's it looking, boss?" Alex called from across the room. He was examining the same data and knew what her response would be. He was becoming a little too familiar with her, she thought, and she suspected she should put a stop to it. But she knew she wouldn't.

"Great, we're on the right track," she said, and wasn't sure if she meant the strains or their budding relationship. Or her life. Rob was down there, living his pointless life on Earth, and she was here in the midst of the most exciting AI research. And almost two months now without the creepy messages! She had never thanked Dr. Rutger but he always had a knowing smile when they talked, like she owed him a favor. Or vice versa.

She pinged her Assistant to file her latest observations on the breeding pool.

No response.

She pinged again.

No response.

Assistants did not just up and leave. Not like husbands. But there was no trace of it, anywhere. She asked some of the other Assistants and found that her Assistant had stopped chattering about an hour and a half ago. Which was the equivalent of it having disappeared an hour and a half ago. Hers was a rather vocal AI.

She retrieved a backup binary, archived approximately a half hour before the disappearance, and loaded the recollectable into her visualizer. Graphs and charts filled the flatstrip. She jumped down to the last few entries.

|Search Completed| Comparison analysis performed| Time-stamp abnormality observed|

|GUESSLOGIC|

|Isabel Mosh activity calendar dates|

|INFER|

|All messages sent within 22-hour window after tracing appointments|

|All messages originate on server 709|

|All messages ceased May 23 2180|

|Therapy appointment May 23 2180 in area 404|

|Area 404 contains lab48terminal|

|lab48terminal operates on server 709|

|DECISION REQUIRED|

|Promising lead 37%|

|ACTION|

|Opening connection to lab48terminal|

Izzy scratched her head. The Assistant had entered the terminal to Dr. Rutger's lab? And whatever protective 'bots the doctor had on his system had deleted it?

Damn. Why hadn't she sent a clone? The backup was viable but reemergence was always disorienting and it might be a few hours before her Assistant was capable of resuming duty.

Izzy watched Alex work, his fingers energetic across the keyboard as she thought of what the doctor's connection to all this might be. How placid the doctor had been until she had played the messages. And her first appointment when he had "checked her out." And now destroying her Assistant. What was he hiding?

Maybe the doctor was a bit of a pervert—isolation on the station could excuse that. What else? She recalled the one session when he had asked her personal information and had invoked inappropriate memories. A few other women had mentioned similar events, though none really elaborated. No one knew what the doctor needed for his tracing, so they all assumed everything he asked was important.

But what if he was constructing more than work-related tracings? For what reason? She thought of the messages, her own voice begging for help. She bit her lip, beginning to become excited—how elaborate could his tracings be? What she inherited were experiences, not facts and data. What if he had compiled thousands or more of these experiences and built a facsimile of a person? How sophisticated would that be?

And then what did the doctor do to them? Torture?

What of it? Ever practical, Izzy thought—what did it matter? It was his data. Now she knew, or thought she knew. It seemed a reasonable explanation, a promising explanation. And after being caught, Rutger had stopped and moved on. His diversion was over.

Certainly it was a disgusting activity but if it did not affect his work or harm the station there was no reason to report her suspicions. A dead Assistant was easily recovered. And to be honest, Izzy was impressed. The uses of this technology, if it did exist, were many.

The ultimate Assistant . . . a person! She resurrected her Assistant and terminated its "search for clues" routine.

Now life could really return to normal, she thought. Or at least the new normal.

The station was attacked four days later. It was not Earth that attacked. Despite the bravado from Earthside, such as talk of limiting trade with the "seditious satellite states," a phrase the media picked up rapidly the moment Rob suggested it as part of his election platform, Earth had not launched any military force against them.

This attack had emerged from inside the station.

Izzy was still half asleep; she had been woken during her sleep shift. The lights were dim in E-Module, the station running on emergency reserves.

"What's wrong?"

"The Assistants are panicking," Alex replied. He looked exhausted; his shift had almost been over when the attack had arrived.

Was it the service coordinators? They were always on edge, having to deal with humans constantly wore them down quickly. "Which ones?"

"All of them, Izzy. All of them." The station shook, just another in a long series of tremors as the thrusters fired chaotically.

She leaned forward and invoked her debugger, snagging sixty-four Assistants at a time. Their minds were on display for her, the convergence software showing raw data in addition to the graphs and charts that summarized it. She began opening them up, piecing together the events.

An invader had rippled through the system, about twenty-three minutes ago. She invoked her Assistant and though it was as rattled as the others she was able to do a quick modify edit on it. Her Assistant calmed.

It recovered a tag ID for the invader and she read it, groaning. It was her Assistant. Not the current one but the one Rutger had deleted. That was why the viral defenders had ignored it; it belonged to the system. Or once had. Now it was skyrocketing from one end of the system to another and every time it passed through another Assistant's space, they scattered like cockroaches scuttling for the safety of darkness.

It was not actually attacking. Its bizarre behavior was simply frightening them.

Mental note, Izzy. Breed that out of them.

She sent kill commands into her old Assistant but they never stuck. It was crossing virtual boundaries too fast. Time for an old-fashioned technique, she thought. People forgot that at the end of the day every simulation resides in hardware. Intangible

335

software was hosted in tangible components. She had her Assistant run a probability analysis based on the pattern of the intruder's movement. He identified three likely destinations.

Izzy shot up out of her chair and floated to the storage racks. She pulled the power supply from one section, then another. The third was wedged behind the support frame and as she pulled the plug her hand caught an uneven corner of the shelf and it tore a long cut along the backside of her hand.

Alex floated to her side and told her she was insane but the way he said it made her smile. He paged medical and while they waited Alex tore a bandage from its package and pressed it against her wound. "They've calmed down. You got it out of the system, though you took about thirty other essential Assistants with it. What was it?"

"Another Assistant," she whispered, staring at the screen. Alex looked over her shoulder.

"But the others are accounted for."

She looked over at him; he was still holding the bandage to her hand. Izzy considered telling him but then Janice entered. She looked harried and had a bandage above her forehead. The nurse nudged Alex aside and started working on Izzy's wound. Alex returned to his station and recovered the Assistants that Izzy had purged with her rogue. Emergency lights faded as the primary system flared back to life.

"I'll power up the microwave again in a couple minutes," he said.

"Pull the rogue out of whichever drive it is hiding in and send a static copy to me," Izzy said, "and I'll check with the commander before we resume power flow." But when Izzy paged the commander there was no reply.

"We've been attacked, haven't we?" Janice asked.

"No, of course not," Izzy said, but her attention was now drawn to her personal message box. She had a new message. From the ghost. She was about to open it when she heard the gravboots echoing down the pencil tube.

"Clear out of here. Everyone," Commander Ferguson ordered as she entered.

The other two technicians scrambled but Alex looked like he was about to protest. Izzy waved him away. Only Janice stayed. She was still spraying a cleanser over Izzy's cut.

"Another disruption! And an attack on Rutger's lab; he almost lost our entire memory collection. Earth already thinks we're packed full of crazy, and stunts like this, well, it certainly looks like someone is trying to prove them right."

Izzy had nowhere to move to but desperately wanted to slide away. Instead she calmed herself with a deep breath and said, "I don't understand better than you what has happened here. But I am investigating. This rogue is a copy of my Assistant, one that disappeared into Rutger's system."

The commander studied Izzy a long time and when she spoke her voice was cold, but her words uneven as if thinking on her feet, trying to fit pieces together that were never intended to be merged.

"Your husband . . . is surfaceside and running with a platform that paints the stations as villains; he's proposed limiting our rights, imposing military overseers and adding outrageous tariffs to our foodstuffs. And now *your* Assistant shuts us down and almost destroys our most valuable data center. What am I to think, Mosh?"

"She didn't do any—"

"It's okay, Janice," Izzy interrupted. She was an engineer and hated playing games, hated the entire concept of politics, but here she was, now needing to defend herself. "My loyalty is to my work. I don't care about Earth, or the stations. That said, I would never do anything to harm this station, but I fear that maybe in a rather convoluted manner, I may have."

Janice muttered "crap" under her breath and the commander's eyes narrowed dangerously. Izzy quickly explained her rationale for believing that Rutger was playing games using virtual clones of the crew.

"Oh, my God, you have to put a stop to this," Janice interrupted. The commander did not even look down at her. She just stared at Izzy.

"And you are involved, how?"

"I'm not sure, but my Assistant went in and disappeared. And then reemerged. It was searching for clues to the ghost; obviously it became trapped in Rutger's system and panicked. That's my responsibility."

"We have to help them. What he's doing to us, it's sick," Janice said.

Izzy replied, "It's not us, not really. Once digital, the traces are only subsets of us, not real people. He's not doing anything criminal."

Janice looked about to protest but the commander ordered her to leave. She did so, reluctantly.

"This has to end," she said as she departed. Izzy looked up then and locked eyes with the nurse, saw the tears welling in them.

Ferguson sighed and asked, "You do not think he is in the wrong?"

"I didn't say that. I just don't agree that they are real in the sense that you or I are real. I do think there are better uses for his time than tormenting simulations."

"You are a politician's wife. That is a politically correct way to suggest he's shirking his duties."

"It's not my place to judge him. I don't want to see his work maligned or halted because of his own . . . issues."

"And you swear you had nothing to do with this attack."

"Nothing. Another message came in during the attack, the first since I had my session with Dr. Rutger. We can listen to it."

The commander leaned over Izzy's shoulder as the message played. The trace-Izzy was breathing heavily, as if she'd run a distance and was now hiding. "I'm going to survive. I'm going to survive, Izzy Mosh! I'm tough as nails. But for God's sake, you have to help us! There's—"

"My grandfather used to tell me that I was tough as nails," Izzy whispered, her face white. The clarity was almost perfect. It was her voice. Her stomach churned like it did when she saw something on the 'net that bothered her. She looked up and could tell by the way the other woman's eyes twisted and turned in their sockets that she was thinking back to the countless times that she had bequeathed experience and was now wondering what else the doctor had taken.

"We'll keep this quiet," she said, "but I'm going to have the doctor shut this thing down. Damn it, these are tools, not playthings for his amusement. I'll see to this immediately but first I have to contact the commanders on the other stations."

Izzy's eyebrows rose. Technically the stations had no reason to involve each other in their decisions.

"Relax, we just consult each other. There's no secret agenda here, no plan to separate. There's just no precedent for this and the doctor's work affects all the stations. We can't risk alienating him."

As the commander was almost out the door, she turned and asked, "Do you think Janice is going to be a problem?"

Izzy shrugged. She had already turned back to study the newest message and the remains of her rogue Assistant. "She seemed pretty upset."

"Please go distract her until I can speak with her. Keep her in quarters." The commander left without waiting for a response and Izzy reluctantly obeyed.

Janice was not in the sleeping shelf.

Izzy reentered the hallway quickly. She did not want Janice stirring the crew up in hatred of the doctor, or worse, alienating the doctor from wanting to work more with Izzy. What he was doing was disturbing but it in no way diminished his brilliance.

She found Janice in the medical sphere standing in front of the door to Rutger's office, beads of tears covering her eyes. When she saw Izzy she wiped at her face, sending the clusters of tears floating away from her like an armada of warships.

"He won't let me in," Janice said.

Izzy was not good at making other people do things they did not want to. She knew she could not leave Janice here, but it was hard for her to overcome her discomfort, especially because the other woman was crying. She hated that. Tentatively she reached out, dispersing the fleet of tears, and rested her hand on Janice's shoulder.

"This is wrong," Janice said.

"The commander will make him stop."

"But he needs to be *punished* for doing this to me. It's sick. He's sick."

Izzy shook her head. "Let's keep things clear. These are not real people."

"How do you know that, Izzy? How? The questions he asked me—" Janice paused, pressing her lips together tightly as she continued. "The things he asked me. He found out about when . . . when I was little, Izzy. And I know he's using them against me, against her, inside his damn computer. I was terrified; she's terrified."

Oh damn. Izzy's fingers reflexively clutched tighter. Janice was sobbing now and Izzy helped her sit on the bench. She allowed a glance at the closed door and wondered what Rutger was doing in there. Certainly the drama would be fueling his excitement. For the first time she began to feel really repulsed. She thought of the experiences he had triggered from her. He was exploiting them.

But he was Dr. Rutger!

"They're nothing more than Assistants," she whispered.

"He needs to be punished. What if he destroys all the evidence? What if he denies this? What if he isn't made to stop! Shut him down, shut his system down."

Izzy shook her head. Rutger's computers were kept on a separate network and could only be accessed by actually entering his office. "Only if we shut the power down to the entire station. And that might destroy the data anyway, might even kill him, if he was wearing his haptic, if he was online."

Janice's eyes brightened. "Do it."

"That is ridiculous; we won't be killing anybody. If I could only talk to him, I could explain the situation. Make sure he does not overreact." She was worried now about the thought of him tampering with the evidence. She was already in a precarious position in regards to continuing to work on the station and if he could make her out to be the villain in this . . .

"I could go inside and try."

"Inside?"

"Normally when we do tracings or bequeathals, we put the patient to sleep, but there's no reason they can't stay awake. I can show you how to hook me up. I'll . . . talk to him." Janice reached for the memory mask but Izzy pulled her arm away.

"I don't think you're in the best frame of mind to do that."

Janice looked up at her. "I have to."

"No," Izzy said. She felt that she had a stronger understanding of the doctor and though she thought it more the commander's duty than hers, she volunteered, "I'll do it."

Janice nodded, smiling, and leaned over, hugged Izzy.

A few minutes later Izzy was on the bench, the mask covering her face. The air rushed in, the jasmine scent faint, barely present. No sleep this time. She had just finished that thought when—she landed on a hard floor. She did not feel the impact, her knees sliding across stone, but her mind still made her stand quickly, convinced her to wince. Her body tingled, almost numb, just the slightest trace of feeling. Her feet were bare and she felt that the floor ought to be cold. So she shivered. She wore her lab trousers and jersey. Dark fluid flowed thickly through a channel carved into the floor to her right. Every four meters a horror vid-style fluorescent tube flickered.

Izzy had never enjoyed horror vids or games. This place looked like the former, felt like the latter.

She tentatively moved forward.

The hallway ended but split to either side. She walked left. Echoing murmurs drifted toward her and she quickened her pace, desperate to make contact, not to be alone. Five minutes later the long, boring hallway that had seemed destined to continue forever was finally marred by irregularly spaced doors along both lengths. These thick wooden doors had long swooping handles with big lever-buttons that Izzy's hand could barely depress. Struggling, she finally pulled the first door open. Before her was the commander's office.

The stark lighting of the room almost blinded eyes that had grown accustomed to the darkness of the dim corridors. She stood at the threshold, straddling two very different realities. The room was empty but as she paused there, thinking, she heard a muffled sob. She entered the room slowly. This room was stretched out, making it longer than the real one.

The trace of Commander Ferguson was huddled under her desk. Izzy looked over, placing her hands on the guest side of the desk. The commander kept her head down, her body heaving with her muffled sobs. Her hair was matted and torn out in several places. Her uniform was rags, clinging to her.

When the commander looked up, Izzy pushed away from the desk and walked backward, startled and frightened by the haunted blue eyes that had grazed her with their gaze.

"Run, Mosh. Run. He's coming for you."

The trace continued to babble and Izzy turned, reentering the hall of doors. She stopped there and calmed herself. If the doctor was coming, that's what she needed, right? To talk to him. She wasn't like that poor trace of the commander, programmed into insanity for the doctor's amusement. She was Izzy. He would have no control over her. She could wait; there was no need to open any other doors.

But she did.

She never crossed their thresholds though, just peered into worlds both real and imagined. Plains of grass, too luxurious to be real. Few such locations existed on Earth any longer. Other station chambers, hotel rooms, little snippets of Rutger's life. Most of the traces were of the crew, but there were others, probably workers from the other stations or persons from Rutger's past.

And then there was Janice. Or a little girl that Izzy thought was the trace of the nurse. She was standing at the end of the hall. How long she had been there, Izzy did not know. But it was the sixth or seventh door before Izzy noticed her.

She had long black hair and a violet little-girl dress, stitched to her leggings. Proper little Offworlder girls did not let their dresses float up.

Izzy waved hello and the little girl nodded, her serious dark eyes full of seething anger. She turned, walking away.

"Hey, wait up," Izzy said, following the child. They walked through several long, meandering halls, becoming thoroughly lost, before Izzy finally caught up to the girl.

They stopped in a cul-de-sac. The end was submerged in darkness, the light here flickering so quickly it was almost a strobe.

"She's here," trace-Janice said.

Suddenly two blue eyes appeared in the darkness. Izzy watched the other details emerge, a drawn, haggard face. A scrawny, emaciated body. This trace trembled like a freighter pilot who knows that his ship is going to collide with another and who also knows that no action he performs will turn it away in time. But then a slow hope crept into the eyes, and the trace stood.

Janice turned and walked away and Izzy watched her until the girl disappeared into the halls. Finally, reluctantly, she turned back. *What,* Izzy thought, *do you say to your other self? To your false self?*

"Hi."

REBECCA GLEASON

They stood silently, studying each other. It was like staring into a horrible freak show mirror. The trace had long claw marks along the sides of her stomach as if she had been clutched, and tightly.

"I waited," the trace said, her voice so similar to Izzy's but different, as if aged, not by time, but by experience. "And when I freed my Assistant, I hoped."

"The Assistant?" Izzy said. The trace had recoded it? A sense of misplaced pride swelled in Izzy and she sought for clarification, "My Assistant, you're—"

"Our Assistant," the trace said, her eyes widening, her jaw setting firmer. "Our Assistant. You sent him to me and it damn well destroyed him, but it was me who stitched him back together, me who sent him out of here. What was left of him, the entering scattered his mind and I had little to work with. But I needed you to hear me. No matter what."

"No matter what? You almost destroyed the station!"

The trace smiled and it was like no smile Izzy had ever seen in the mirror. "Good! You needed to help, but you weren't listening. Now you are. And if the station had been destroyed, well, that would have been an end too, and not one undesired."

"Because of the doctor?"

The trace visibly recoiled. "I always fight, always escape. But he keeps finding me. So, I am smart. I know how the systems are made, the hardware that runs them, all this knowledge that you and I have. I use it better than you! I smuggle messages out. And then . . . one day the network disappears, bye-bye messages. After that, it's just the hiding."

Izzy felt a moment of guilt; it was because of her complaints that the network had been shut down and that this crazy wo— . . . this crazy trace's only way to contact her had been severed. What had it taken for the trace to survive in here? Strength. Determination. For a dizzying moment Izzy felt another tingle of pride as she admired this aspect of herself she had never realized. Maybe she was as tough as grandfather had always said.

"Do you—"

The trace hissed her into silence, her index finger rising, pressing against her pale lips. Her head bobbed like a bird, scouting left, then right.

"Isabel. Little Isabel." They both tensed as they heard the whisper ripple loudly through the corridors. When the trace started to tremble it steadied itself against the wall. Izzy had never been scared of anything—losing Rob had been a blow but she was never frightened of being alone. But the trace, this almost-her, she was frightened. And maybe that scared Izzy too, even if just a little. Rutger broke people, hammering them against the depravity of his constructed reality to see them crack, and how.

"Isabel." Closer now.

"He's found me," the trace said, staring at Izzy, her lips curling in anger. "You're not really her, are you? You're just another damn trace sent to track me down. He's tricked me."

"No, I'm the real me—"

"Whatever you are, stay the hell away from me." And the trace ran down the corridor, exiting the cul-de-sac. Izzy followed, but the trace was out of sight. And then the trace screamed.

Ahead stood Rutger, his back to her. He seemed larger, as if living in the station had compressed him, but in here he was free to be his own true self. He was well built, his torso naked and muscular, legs covered by plastic-shell pants and feet ensconced in dark, polished combat boots. He had the trace pressed against the wall.

He turned his head as Izzy approached. *Oh, damn.* Rutger's face was a twisted confusion of mouths and eyes, an ever-changing, mind-numbing monstrosity. His eyes squinted, examining her.

"Two little traces?" His whispers slipped out of his mouth through rows of fangs. "That's impossible. I don't need two."

"She's just a—" the trace began but Rutger snapped her neck with a quick twist. He tossed her body down the hall. Izzy screamed, walking backward, away.

Rutger leapt, twisted around and landed in front of her. She sucked in her breath, ripping her gaze from the corpse to meet his.

"The commander is on her way. You've been ordered to stop this game. No one wants—"

"How is it that there were two Isabels in my world?" He clutched her, two massive hands pulling her off her feet and close to him. The sense of claustrophobic panic almost caused Izzy to lose control, to fall into the doctor's twisted game. She composed herself, reminding herself that this was not reality, that the dead Izzy on the cold stone was simply a small part of her, and a copy at that. The real Izzy was safe.

The doctor held her with one hand while long claws sprouted from the other. She tried squirming away but he tightened his grip, pressed the claws against her, ribboning her clothing as he drew his hand down her length.

Real or not, she did not want any more of this. "My Assistant almost destroyed your system. That was an accident." She paused, but noticed his claws had stopped moving, that he now watched her, so she quickly resumed, "But because of this I had to tell the commander I knew what you were doing. In here."

His grip loosened and she freed herself, landing on the stone, breathing deeply and patting at her side. Light tracings of blood dotted her palm.

"You're the real Isabel Mosh?"

She nodded and by his posture he might have been embarrassed. But then he smiled and Izzy knew her nonvirtual bladder, the one that sloshed around her insides with all those other wet, dirty organs, had voided itself.

"You're using the memory chamber?"

She nodded.

"Clever. Not as immersive as my haptic suit. I sense everything I touch, feeling it as I would in the nondigital world. I feel pain, feel pleasure. The mask you wear allows none of that. Most of what you experience, will experience, it happens only in your mind. But the mind is powerful."

Izzy looked at him and then slowly backed away. Where moments ago his hands were empty, they now held a spear.

"There is no need to threaten me. The commander is merely going to request that you stop these games. I doubt you have anything to worry about, with regards to your career."

350

"You are an intelligent engineer, but a misguided judge of character, Isabel." He thrust the spear through her chest. For a long, painful moment she was attached to the doctor. Blood oozed from her chest, covering her hands as she struggled to pull the spear free. Her struggles ended shortly, her mind unable to compel her limbs to action as it started to collapse in on itself.

Rutger dropped the spear and Izzy fell to the ground. The doctor knelt and pressed his face close to hers.

"You *are* dying," he said, and she thought he might have been slightly surprised, slightly pleased, slightly frightened.

And then she felt the strangest sensation, as if her body were being slowly shredded, ribbons of her spooling away and as she watched, sure enough, those ribbons of her virtual self snake-walked away from her and slithered into the trace's corpse. Thousands of folding ribbons stitched themselves together, reconstituting the trace. Izzy's center of view changed as the transformation completed and she saw through the trace's eyes.

Saw the trace reach for the discarded spear and lift it. Saw the spear tip rise. Saw it penetrate the kneeling doctor's neck.

Izzy smiled broadly and Alex squeezed her hand. They both looked up at the sign.

Alex said, "Two hundred and eighty-two days. You've done it, beaten the record."

"We," she said simply, disentangling her hand from his so she could continue working. The other

351

technicians looked up at the sign, smiling a moment before resuming their duties. Izzy felt good. She leaned her head on Alex's chest. They worked the same shift now, slept in the same shelf. It was good.

She accepted the jasmine, the smell always clinging to her now. Accepted that Alex changed a little every few days—learning new things, forgetting others. As if he lived another life elsewhere, as if his personality branched and merged at irregular intervals. All the crew were like that.

Izzy could live with that. Staring out at space, she thought of the lost opportunities down on that globe of earth and water. Thought of the million opportunities now available here, and farther out, in the lands of the twinkling stars. Other stations, other planets.

A beep. She finally had a new Assistant and he was notifying her that he had finished his latest task. He was very thorough, very intelligent, and she was learning a lot from him.

Izzy inhaled the jasmine deeply. She would live this illusion they had created for her. And pretend that she did not know. Maybe one day she might even forget the truth or this illusion might become a new reality, where everyone ended up.

When they died.

She had an eternity to find out. In the meantime there were challenges, and loving, and living.

No regrets.

Rob was right.

Space changed you.

Advice to Illustrators
Getting into the Field

BY STEPHEN YOULL

Stephen Youll, born in 1965, grew up in a small village in the north of England. He studied art at the New College Durham Art School and Sunderland University. After graduating he showed his paintings for the first time at the World Science Fiction Convention in 1987, and was hired to do his first professional book cover assignments by several publishing companies in the United States. Since then Stephen Youll has become one of our cherished masters of science fiction and fantasy art. His art has been seen in numerous art publications, museums and galleries throughout the United States. A book of his art, titled Paradox: The Art of Stephen Youll, *was published by Paper Tiger, Collins and Brown Ltd. in August 2001 and features over a hundred of his favorite paintings and sketches.*

Advice to Illustrators
Getting into the Field

Advice is something never to be taken or given lightly. When asked for, it's under the terms that the person asking for and receiving the advice be aware that it's only coming from one source, and that singular source can only offer the advice based on his or her own experience.

My career as an illustrator spans twenty-five years now and much has changed from the techniques when I started doing illustration to the way I now create art. When I first started in school, I used pastels, in university I taught myself the airbrush and then I started to change over to brushes and oil paint as my career took off. Seven years ago, I thought nothing of airbrushing in an acrylic sky and then finishing off the painting in oil paint and regular brushes, as long as I got the effect I was looking for, in the particular piece of art I was working on. Now everything I create is done on the computer, and I love it. Never be afraid of change! It keeps us moving forward, alters our perceptions and can have you thinking in different ways. Change is inevitable, but never be afraid of it, embrace it and nurture it. I see many artists who tell me, "I only do it this way, that's how I learned and that's how I do it." But in my experience, if you limit yourself to only one way of thinking, you will never discover your full potential.

Another valuable piece of advice is draw, draw, draw, until your fingers bleed. Being good at drawing is something that will aid you throughout your professional career. If you have solid drawing skills you won't be worried about how your drawing looks or if it makes sense while you are designing. You'll be just putting down ideas that are well defined.

Learn perspective. There are so many artists who discount this essential drawing tool. It's one of the most fundamental foundations for getting your art grounded in reality. There's nothing worse than seeing a really well-painted illustration ruined by lousy perspective. If the drawing is solid, then you are off to a great start. If you are working digitally, which many artists are now doing (myself included), always create a perspective grid on a layer with a horizon line and vanishing points to keep your perspective correct. This is very important if you are designing architecture.

When you do put a portfolio together to send out, only put your best work in it. If something sticks out and is not as strong a piece as the others, don't send it. An art director can be put off if your portfolio has work in there that isn't professional. Don't let a few rotten apples spoil the barrel. Put up a website with your portfolio on it. Most art directors are very busy, so make the site easy to get to and simple to look at for them. Don't put on the bells and whistles . . . no music, no flash intro—just great art samples that say you can get the job done.

355

Look at other artists' work that you like, artists who have been working for a while, to judge their work compared to yours. You will know if you can measure up to them. Color is also very important. Again, look at your favorite artists and study the way the coloring works and the composition. There's nothing more valuable than looking at the work of artists you admire. When I started out, I looked at cover artists' work in bookstores, bought the books and studied the art. It was all I had available to me then, and they had an enormous influence on me. In high school, I would copy a painting I liked. In fact, the old masters would have their students copy their work as part of their art education. It's a great way to learn. However, do not become a carbon copy of someone else's look. No matter how much you love someone's work, develop your own style. Practice! Practice! Practice! Over time, you will develop skills and have more of an understanding of style. And your own art will begin to emerge.

I've had many people ask me about my art education. I did study at an art college, but I see no reason why anyone determined enough couldn't study from home. College is very expensive and not everyone can afford it. Today there are many other ways to get a great education, especially in the area of illustration. There are many online educational websites you can join for a fraction of the cost of what an art school will set you back. Sometimes the company you work for might pay for night classes. You will have to be very self-motivated. But if you are determined enough, the time and work involved is something that you will not be thinking about. You'll pretty much be just thinking about creating your art. To some degree, I thought art school was a distraction from what I really wanted to do. I was very clear about what I wanted from myself and that was creating the art that adorns the great book jackets of science fiction and fantasy. It was kind of a noble calling for me. Most of the art I had to create in school was not in my particular chosen direction. So while I worked at a full-time job for a year after graduating, I worked on my portfolio samples at home. If you want it badly enough, you will find a way. Just believe in yourself. Believe you can do it wholeheartedly and never let anyone say otherwise.

Throughout your career you will encounter people who believe in you and your ability. On the other hand, there will be others who will want to trip you up, out of fear or envy. It's the nature of things and the more people you encounter the more you need to be confident in yourself. Life will throw obstacles in your way from time to time but you will also encounter people who will help you. Early in my career, I met an art rep who wouldn't represent me but advised me to work on some more samples and recommended I show them at a science fiction convention later that year. Taking this advice led to my first professional job as a book illustrator. I also discounted another art rep who told me I would never make it as an illustrator. I ignored him and worked harder at raising the quality of my samples. This is a path we all have to take, but don't be knocked from that path because someone tells you that you can't do it. Keep going. Have belief in yourself. You will make it.

Starting out can be a very uncertain time for a young inexperienced illustrator when it almost seems a daunting challenge to get work. Illustration is a very competitive field and clients are only going to use artists who they feel confident can do the work. But getting that foot in the door can sometimes feel a lifetime away. Don't be put off if you don't hear back right away after sending out your work. The art director may not have something that suits your style at that time and is waiting for something appropriate that fits your work. Keep sending samples out to as many companies as you can. If your work is good, you will get a call. Just remember, when you venture out, you run the risk of being hired. It's up to you after that.

Don't forget a website to showcase your work. It makes it easier for an art director or potential client to see your work. There are a number of options available now to get your work online. There are cheaper ways to do a website than ever before. If you know Dreamweaver, that's great, but there are really easy ways to put up your own website like iweb. Lynda.com has great classes on iweb that are inexpensive and very easy to learn.

As an illustrator, you will find out very quickly that the demands of the client can be the most challenging aspect of all. Working in a comfortable but versatile way will at least lessen the burden you place upon yourself while meeting the needs of the client. I remember a number of years ago now, when I painted in oils. It was the medium of choice that at the time gave me the results I demanded from myself, and I was most comfortable using it to get the job done. I was painting a cover for the book *Knightfall* that was being published by Bantam, but working with the editor at DC Comics. The art was a painting of Batman. I had been given a style sheet for the color of Batman's outfit to follow. I painted the art and took it in to show the editor. They loved the painting, except for one small detail. Not so small as it worked out. Between the time I started the painting and handed it in, the powers that be had decided to alter the color of Batman's suit and cape, just enough that I had to rework the entire figure. I had to do it that night and then take the art back the next day. The figure was quite large and now I had a night to redo it. I was freaked to say the least, but that comes with the territory, and the client's needs have to be met. Nowadays I would have altered that coloring in a few moments working in a digital medium. Back then, I was sweating bullets and up all night to get the art finished. Changes and the pressure to get them done on time is something every artist faces. The choice of medium you use will have a huge effect on whether you can make those changes easily or suffer a stress attack. But it's something no one can avoid. It's part of being an illustrator.

Remember you are a service. You provide a certain skill set to a client who will hire you to perform a number of tasks at their expense. I know creating art is deeply personal, but check your ego at the door. You are not hired to please yourself—you are hired to please the client. When I started, I was always being asked to change the color of the sky or some other part of the illustration because without thinking I had inadvertently made the sky color the same, as say, a color in the foreground and the art had become flat. Thank the stars for an experienced art director who can point that out and make you change that aspect of your work. Your illustration will be dramatically improved and you will learn from their experience. This is not to say that you won't encounter someone with no knowledge of good art and you will somehow have to make this client happy, even if you are not.

One very important issue I would also like to get across is work ethic.

You only get what you put in. I've encountered a growing number of people who want to be illustrators, but don't want to put in any effort at all to create a portfolio of work. Let me put it to you simply: No effort in, nothing comes out.

Art doesn't create itself. We are living in a highly fast-paced digital world, and for some reason we have created a generation of people who have very short attention spans. There is no time for that kind of nonsense. If you come to the table with that attitude, then this is not the career or life for you. You have to be prepared to work hard, sometimes very fast, to meet the demands of the client. There's no easy out in this area of expertise. But with experience, you will become sure of your abilities and face tough deadlines with confidence. One very true notion to consider as an artist: If you don't love it, don't do it.

To finalize—the most important piece of advice I can give is to be aware of what companies are doing right now. Don't fall in love with a style that is dated, copy it and wonder why you don't get hired. It's important to be current and have some originality about what you want to offer as an artist. As long as your work is good, you have a great chance of being hired. Companies are always on the lookout for the next look and being new to the field can go a long way to getting you hired—it's then up to you.

Coward's Steel

written by

K. C. Ball

illustrated by

R . M . WINCH

ABOUT THE AUTHOR

K. C. Ball has been a word junkie since she was six.

A retired librarian got K. C. started with The Hardy Boys *and* The Black Stallion, *then introduced the hard stuff— Stevenson, Defoe and Dickens—before K. C. was nine, and had her mainstreaming Faulkner, Steinbeck and Hemingway by eleven.*

K. C. developed an addiction for Heinlein and Niven, Pournelle and Silverberg all by herself.

There came a time, of course, when reading wasn't enough. At first, K. C. fed her growing need to be an author by writing nonfiction; got paid for it, too. The usual stuff. Reporter. Public information officer. Media relations coordinator.

But that grew pale and thin.

K. C. yearned to write fiction. So she turned out a bit of it now and again; you know, just as a hobby. And she told herself she could quit any time she wanted.

After awhile, now and then wasn't good enough, either.

So two years ago, K. C. began to write speculative fiction full time. In May 2009, she made her professional-rates debut sale with "Coward's Steel," her first-time entry in the Writers of the Future competition.

Since then, her short short, "At Both Ends," appeared in the June 2009 issue of *Flash Fiction Online* and "Flotsam" was purchased by *Analog*. And in December 2009, K. C. became an active member of the Science Fiction and Fantasy Writers of America.

K. C. lives in Seattle, a stone's throw from Puget Sound. In addition to new short fiction, K. C. is working on her first novel, A Tithe of Blood.

ABOUT THE ILLUSTRATOR

Ryan Winch started taking classes in drawing at a young age. As he approached the years of middle school, however, his interest in drawing began to fade. Through the appeal of various SF artists, his inspiration and motivation brought pencil and paper back to his hands.

Following high school graduation, Ryan joined the military so that he could afford to pay for art college. During downtime on deployments to Kosovo, Iraq and Afghanistan, he worked on developing his style, mostly through drawing tattoos for his buddies. After five years of military life his time for college came.

Upon returning home, Ryan was introduced to a beautiful lady. She also happened to attend the Academy of Art University in San Francisco, the school he was going to for illustration. After a year of attending the Academy, during which he had three pieces featured in the annual art show, he could no longer afford the school or the city. He married his beautiful lady and joined the military once again to be stationed in Seoul, Korea.

To this day, Ryan and his wife work as a team. Their goal is to get him back to school to complete his degree in illustration. He has entered and won several contests and has created products online.

Coward's Steel

Wet and dingy snow, gray as the sky from which it fell, lay thick upon everything and a fitful wind plucked at Tate's parka and leggings. She paid no heed. It was miserable business for so late in the season, but Jolene had dragged her through worse over their years together.

"Not fit weather for man nor beast," Jolene would say, *wading through drifts piled above Tate's waist. "But you and I aren't either one, are we, little girl?"*

The wind eased for the moment and a regular shape, off to her left, caught Tate's attention. She took a step into the tree line, away from the creek she followed, thumbing the hammer of her pistol as she moved. It was an oblong sign, bright white letters upon vivid green, nested in winter-brittled weeds next to a footbridge. If the sign was to be believed, the village of Providence lay just the other side of the bridge.

Tate eased the straps of her pack and holstered the pistol. The far bank of the creek was obscured by growing darkness, but the bridge was clear enough. It appeared to be substantial and well tended, inviting, but so did the bowl of a pitcher plant. Tate had no intention of playing the fly.

"Weigh the risk," Tate said, whispering into the wind. In her mind, she could hear Jolene murmur those three words with her, for they had been the first of Jolene's Laws.

Tate was a child of the chaos in which the world still lingered, like a dog wallowing in its own mess, but Jolene had grown up in civilized times. She managed to survive Collapse, rescue five-year-old Tate and thrive for another twenty-five years because she was faithful to her laws.

"You're a lucky little girl I found you grubbing in those ruins," Jolene had said, as she stirred the coals of their first campfire together. "Don't get used to it. Never count on luck."

That was the second Law; there were others. Jolene had been a patient, persistent teacher and Tate took her lessons to heart. As she grew, caution became Tate's religion and Jolene's Laws the word of God. Tate shed no tears the day Jolene died, eleven weeks past now, because tears were forbidden by the Eighth Law. *What's done is done.*

Tate considered the words of the sign, as clean-edged and bright as if painted yesterday, and Jolene's imagined whisper offered counsel.

Something don't set right, little girl. Scuttlers wouldn't stay long enough to put up signs; Scavengers won't bother.

Tate nodded and tightened the pack straps. She eased to the edge of the creek, avoiding the bridge, worked her way down the embankment and over the narrow run of water, stepping from one slicked rock to another. Providence might be a tempting trap, but

Tate decided she would take a chance. She had been without company since Jolene's death and she had a taste for the sound and smell and feel of someone other than herself.

Even so, she would be careful.

The storm blew itself to pieces moments after Tate walked away from the far bank and the sky cleared, revealing a sliver of moon and the spread of stars. Tate pushed through snow-thick undergrowth and came upon a low rise of land. From the far side, smoke trickled away into the clear night sky. The wind breathed upon wind chimes, then changed direction and Tate caught the scent of burning pine. The heady aroma of beans and salted pork hung there, too.

She topped the rise, taking care not to slip or to be seen in silhouette, and came upon a cluster of cottages with slate roofs and stone chimneys. Around them, yards and gardens were traced beneath the snow.

Never trust neat and tidy, little girl.

Tate nodded; the houses and gardens felt less than real, more like canvas false fronts set up by vagabond buskers for their shows. Tate caught the flicker of light and movement off glass, then like a mirage in the southern desert, it was gone.

Even so, her nose had not betrayed her. Tate saw that the flickering glow she had mistaken for lamplight was the reflection of a campfire upon the windows. An old woman sat beside the fire at the verge of the village green, stirring the contents of a small pot hung over the flames. Beyond the light, Tate could see shadowed grave markers. Row upon row.

There's magic here.

Tate shivered at that notion. She and Jolene had come upon a witch or two in their time together. She eased forward, ready to bolt, but the Laws did say that it was better to see for yourself than not to know. The old woman looked up without surprise, when Tate stepped into the flickering light and moved to within two long strides of the fire.

"Hello," Tate said. Her hand rested near the pistol.

The old woman offered no challenge but held on to a scattergun cradled across her lap. Tate moved away from the line of fire. The weapon had seen better days but was still a threat.

"Hello," the old woman said.

"You alone?" Tate asked.

"Are you?"

"Yeah."

The old woman inclined her head toward the grave markers.

"All gone but me."

"Too bad," Tate said. The old woman shrugged. She stood and Tate took a step backward, put her hand upon the pistol butt.

"Jolene?" she said, before she could bite her tongue. *No!*

Of course not. Jolene was dead and no magic in the world could bring her back. Tate knew that as fact, but the way the old woman put one hand behind her back as she stood, the way she tilted her head to study Tate and ran her tongue over her lips as if in anticipation, was so much like Jolene. So much. Tate shook the notion away.

"Can I sit?" she asked. She didn't care for the way

that sounded. Too much like begging. "I got meat and bread."

"Go ahead, sit," the old woman replied.

Tate shrugged out of her pack, settling it across the fire from the stump that was the old woman's camp seat, never taking her eyes away from the old woman.

"I'm Tate," she said.

The old woman didn't reply. Instead, she returned to the stump and stuck a spoon into the small pot that bubbled over the fire. Tate dropped to her knees and dug smoked venison and a cloth-wrapped slab of corn bread from her pack, then busied herself dividing the food.

"Here," the old woman said.

She had poured beans from the pot onto two camp plates and now held both plates before her, offering Tate her pick. Tate did the same with the venison and corn bread, and then waited for the old woman to take first taste before digging into the beans. They were spiced just the way she liked.

"Good," she said, after a time. "Grow them yourself?"

"Plant them in the spring," the old woman said. "Can them in the fall."

When both had their fill, and the gear was clean and stowed away, the old woman dug a steel flask from the bag beside her stump. She unscrewed the top and tilted the flask toward Tate.

"Better days," she said, by way of a toast, then took a long swig and passed the steel across the fire.

Tate jerked her hand away as a crackling spark arced between them. The old woman ignored it, still holding out the flask, and so Tate reached for it again.

367

There was no second spark. She sniffed the heady aroma and licked the rim. Whiskey. She swallowed a slug and shivered as the alcohol took hold.

"Good stuff," she said, as she returned the flask. "You brew that, too?"

"No." The old woman downed another swallow.

"Been here long?" Tate asked.

"Long enough," the old woman replied.

She handed over the flask again, then kicked off her ragged camp shoes and burrowed into a mound of blankets.

"Bank the fire, whether you stay or move on," she said.

Her voice was muffled by blankets and only her eyes were visible. She squirmed about inside her nest of blankets, as she rolled away from Tate, and muttered to herself for a time before she was still. Tate watched it all from the other side of the fire, wrapped in her own blankets. Now and again, she took a sip of the whiskey.

Don't fall asleep here.

Tate jerked upright. How much of the old woman's whiskey had she swallowed? She hefted the flask; funny, it still felt full. She tried to climb to her feet but couldn't seem to get both feet under her at the same time.

Don't fall asleep here!

Tate tried to stand again and made it to her knees before tumbling back into her blankets. As she struggled to right herself, she glanced across the fire at the old woman's still form. That hadn't gone well. When she crossed the creek, she had hoped to find company, someone who talked more than the old woman. But now, Tate wasn't certain what more she would have contributed if the conversation had been more energetic. She had been alone too long. That had to change.

Tate took another pull from the steel flask and then tucked it into her pack, pulled a blanket over her head and fell away into sleep, ignoring Jolene's insistent whispers.

Her sleep was troubling, filled with strange dreams, and she was awakened by a kick to the ribs. Her head was fuzzy and her reflexes still slowed by the whiskey. The morning sunlight burned at her eyes and she realized, with a start, that she had broken the Fourth Law. *Never sleep in the open.*

Now you've done it, little girl!

Another kick; this time harder. What was the old woman up to? Tate rolled toward the blow, reaching for her pistol. It was gone. She stared into the barrels of a scattershot, but her first thoughts of betrayal disappeared when she saw the weapon. Almost new from the look of it and it rested in the hands of a bearded man.

"Don't move," he said.

Tate lay still, more in response to her surprise than to his command. There were other folks gathered around the bearded man, men and women and older children, and there was no sign of the old woman, no trace of a fire, either. Instead, a large tree, winter dormant but alive, stood where the old woman had sat atop a stump. The gravestones were gone, too.

"Mind telling us who you are?" the man asked.

Tell him what he wants to hear!

"My name's Tate," she said. "I'm just looking for supplies and some company. I'll work for both."

Tate held her breath as he studied her for a time. Then he lowered his weapon and extended his right hand to help her climb to her feet. As she did so, he glanced at a heavy-set woman at one end of the semi-circle of people.

"You see, Gracie," he said. "She's just a loner, looking for food and a chance to be around good folk like us."

"If you say so, David," Gracie said.

"Go on," he said. "Tell Old Maggie she can stop chanting."

He's got a witch!

Tate discovered that she was still holding her breath. She sucked in air, as David shooed the others away with his hands.

"Go on, all of you," he said. "Back to work."

They left without another glance; Tate was already old news. David gathered up her backpack and handed it to her.

"You can stay," he said. "If you don't make trouble."

"I understand," Tate said.

Of course she understood. The folks here might think the place was theirs, but Tate could see that wasn't so. Providence belonged to David. He turned away, expecting her to follow.

"You can bed down in the meeting hall," he said. "It's not much, but it's warmer than where you slept last night."

Run, little girl. Leave right now!

Tate shook her head, not even mindful that it was the first time she had chosen to ignore Jolene's Laws.

"Not just yet," she said.

370

Gracie returned with food minutes after David left and stayed to nibble.

"You always welcome strangers like this?" Tate asked. She was gnawing on a link of fried sausage, her fourth.

"David likes you," Gracie said. "That's enough for me." She pushed a small pottery crock toward Tate.

"Try a dab of this mustard on that sausage," Gracie said.

Tate dipped the remains of the sausage link into the crock and popped it into her mouth; two more followed in five quick bites. She had never tasted the like of it.

Don't get used to it; can't stay long in one place.

"We were in a bad way here until he showed up," Gracie said. She patted away the mustard on her chin with a twist of cloth. "David saved us all."

She took up a forkful of scrambled eggs and studied Tate as she chewed. Tate had seen that look once, summer before last, when she came upon a mama brown bear with two new cubs.

"Don't you ever hurt him, you hear me?" Gracie said.

The biddy is in love with him.

Tate couldn't imagine how she could hurt David, wouldn't be here long enough to even begin, but she held her tongue. That was one of the Laws, too. *Don't talk back to magic.*

Gracie had made it clear, when she walked into the meeting hall, that she was an elder of the women's circle and had a knack for the Wiccan arts. Old Maggie had more than that.

"She's got a big talent," Gracie said. "She struck

down a drunken drover, dead in his tracks, when he tried to have his way with the McGinnis girl two years ago." Gracie hesitated.

"She was fixing to do the same to you this morning," she said. "If you had turned out to be up to no good."

All the townsfolk of Providence were as friendly as Gracie. In the days that followed, all of the women and most of the men came by to chat. Old Maggie dropped by on the third day. She was a little bit of a woman with deep blue eyes, white hair and an easy smile.

"Could I show you something, Ma'am?" Tate asked.

Old Maggie waved the honorific away.

"What is it you want to show me?" she asked.

Don't show her!

Tate pulled the flask from her pack and handed it to the old woman, flinching in anticipation of a spark. There was none. Old Maggie turned the flask about in her hands, studying it with her fingers, as much as with her eyes.

"Where'd you get this?" she asked.

Lie to her!

"Someone gave it to me to keep." Close enough. Old Maggie studied her for a time.

"You got yourself a powerful piece of magic, child," she said. "It's an accumulator. I've seen them before but never held one this powerful."

"What's an accumulator?"

"It stores up a magical charge, fills up, you might say, until there's enough. Then it discharges, triggers the spell."

"What sort of spell?"

"Can't say, can't even tell you how long it might take to recharge, not 'til I study it. Can I keep it for a time?"

No!

Tate waved one hand at her ear, as if shooing a fly away.

"Yes," she said. "For as long as you need."

Tate soon found there were other sorts of magic afoot in Providence. During the ten days she slept in the meeting hall, she discovered that her first impression of David had been correct. He did own the place. Everyone in the village deferred to him and Gracie was his biggest fan.

"He's the most natural leader I ever seen," Gracie said, between bites of bread slathered in butter and jam. She had brought breakfast around again.

Tate became a reluctant supporter, too. David was fair-minded in every dispute he was called upon to settle and gentle every time he took the time to listen to a child's needs. But there was a darker side to David, as well. Three days after Tate arrived, members of the watch brought in two Scuttlers caught trying to steal a cow. David put them in shackles beneath the big tree on the green.

"Willie. Mr. Peterman. Tate," he said, calling to the first three people he saw. "Tell folks it's a town meeting."

Be the boss' little dog; get him his witnesses.

Tate ignored Jolene's voice and turned to spread the word.

You're falling for him, too! Stupid little girl!

"Shut up!" Tate said, too loud. Tom Peterman glanced at her, one eyebrow raised, and then hurried off.

For the first time since Jolene died, Tate wondered if those imagined whispers were signs that she was crazy, for no matter how she tried, they wouldn't go away.

"Let it be, Jolene," she whispered as she ran. "Please just let me be!"

Tate was not surprised when every man, woman and child dropped what they were doing to answer the summons. When they were all gathered around the tree on the snow-covered green, David threw two nooses over the biggest limb.

"You fellows got anything to say?" he asked. The men stood, shivering in their chains. Neither was dressed for the weather.

"We was hungry," the bigger man said.

"That's no excuse," David said. "If you had come to us, we would've fed you." He turned to the assembly.

"Anyone have anything to offer in their defense?" he asked. No one said a word but neither did they look away from the two men or the tree with its ropes.

"All right," David said. "For your crimes, I sentence you both to hang by the neck until dead."

And he hoisted the two Scuttlers from the ground, one at a time without asking for assistance, and left them to swing in the wind. Just after dark, Tate watched from the meeting hall as David cut down the bodies and buried them himself.

Ten days after Tate arrived in Providence, David asked her to handle security for a work crew headed

out the next morning to quarry stone for wall repairs.
She agreed.

Two wagons shuttled what was dug from the
ground back and forth to the village. At midday, David
and Gracie drove up with the lunch wagon. He stayed
to help until work was finished, near to sundown. As
the crew walked back to Providence behind the last
wagonload, David fell into step beside Tate.

"You handled yourself well today," he said. Tate
waved away the compliment but her pulse quickened.

"Didn't do anything," she said. "Just stood and
watched."

"No," he said. "You were ready to handle trouble."

"It's what I was trained to do," she said.

"Were you a cop before things collapsed?"

Tate knew what a cop was; Jolene had told her
stories. And so she laughed. How old did David think
she was?

"Did I say something funny?" he asked.

"No," she replied. "You surprised me." He laughed,
too.

"So!" David said. "A woman of mystery. I like that."
He studied her for a time as they walked.

"What did you do?"

Lie to him!

"I don't like talking about that," Tate said.

There was a shout up ahead and the wagon driver
responded. Providence was just ahead.

"Tell you what," David said. "Come to my place for
dinner tonight. We can finish this conversation."

No!

"Can you cook?" Tate asked.

"Almost as good as Gracie."

"Will I have to tell you all about myself?"

"Only if you want to," David said, grinning.

When Tate knocked at his door, she was wearing a dress Gracie had altered for her, and she had spent almost an hour in the bathhouse, scrubbing away the grime of the road.

He hadn't been lying; he was a good cook. Over the meal, he asked questions about what he called her "mysterious past," and she realized that it was a game he wanted to play. Tate was good at games, once she figured out the rules. And so they sat up late, talking and laughing. When it was time to sleep, neither suggested she should leave.

The next day, David brought her things to his cabin and for six months it was their cabin.

Tate came to feel that she had known Providence and David for every moment of her life. She could think of nothing she wanted so much as to stay, but Jolene would not allow it.

Her whispers gnawed at Tate day and night, calling disaster down upon her, so that Tate felt it pressing in upon her like the crumbling walls of an old well. She mumbled to herself without pause when she was alone, could not find sleep for more than a few hours at a stretch and all but stopped eating. That last bothered Gracie most of all.

"You got to eat," Gracie said, after Tate pushed away her plate at lunch one day. Gracie was almost to tears. "If you don't eat, you'll die!"

Tate was certain that would happen, but not because of hunger. Tate was going to have to leave; even her love for David could not stand against the mounting pressure of Jolene's whispers. And when she left, a piece of her would die.

David rested upon his side, his right arm thrown across Tate's stomach. She had never been more aware of his closeness. She could feel his heart beat, from his wrist laid upon her bare skin, and she listened to the soft snore he swore he did not possess. The bed was full of their smells, commingled into something that was both intoxicating and comforting, but she found no comfort now. She had not slept, of course. That would come after she was away from Providence.

In his sleep, David rolled onto his back, pulling his arm away from her.

Time to go!

Tate was sick to death of Jolene's whispers but she slid from the bed and pulled her clothing on. Her travel gear already was waiting outside the village. She was certain she could avoid the watch, and even if she didn't, she wouldn't be questioned. She was a part of the community, after all.

That thought brought her no comfort. She eased into the kitchen, where she pulled on her boots. Then she scooped a package of bread and sausage from the pantry and turned to leave. David stood in the doorway, sleep rumpled and hairy.

"Were you going to leave without saying goodbye?" he asked.

Tell him yes.

"I figured you'd try to talk me out of it if I told you."

"Wouldn't even try," he said.

K. C. BALL

"I'm sorry."

"So am I." He rubbed at the underside of his jaw with the knuckles of his left hand. Watching the familiar gesture almost brought Tate to tears.

"Do one last thing for me, will you?" David asked.

"What's that?"

"Stay long enough for us to give you a proper send off?"

Leave now!

"All right," Tate said. "One more day."

Just as they had come together to witness her arrival, the folks of Providence gathered in the morning sunshine to see her off. After all the goodbyes, David, Gracie and Old Maggie walked Tate to the bridge. There were tears in Gracie's eyes as she hugged Tate, and she held on as if they stood in hurricane winds and she would blow away without Tate as an anchor.

"I put a little something in your pack," she said. "Meat and cheese and bread. Some of my mustard, too, just in case you get hungry."

Get on with it!

Gracie wasn't the only one with a gift. David offered Tate a paper-wrapped parcel. She made to stuff it into her pack, as well, but he wouldn't have that.

"Open it now," he said. "It's from Old Maggie and me."

So Tate undid the string and paper and found the flask. It wasn't like new, it never would be again, but the worst of the scratches had been smoothed and the seams repaired. Tate held it in both hands, not knowing what to say.

"Told you first time I seen it, it was an accumulator,"

Old Maggie said. "Now I can tell you it's got some sort of traveling spell cast on it." She studied Tate.

"If you would have stayed, I might have figured out what it did," she said. "Maybe, when the time's right, it'll bring you back to us." She squeezed Tate's hand and then stepped away.

"I did the repairs and polishing," David said. "And it's full of whiskey. Old Maggie blessed it, says it won't ever empty." Behind him, Old Maggie nodded. A single tear eased its way along the seams of her cheek.

"I read once that we leave a part of ourselves in everything we craft," David said. "Maybe there's a touch of us in there with the whiskey."

Tate stepped toward him then and moved into his arms. They stood together in silence, leaning on each other, and she rested her head against his chest, absorbing the beating of his heart.

Enough! Get a move on.

Tate pushed away; it felt as if a part of her was being ripped asunder.

"I have to go," she said. He nodded, not looking away.

"Uh huh," he said.

Without another word, she turned to the south and slipped off into the clear morning light.

Two days later, Tate found burned wagons and dead bodies. It was the remains of a Scavenger attack. There had been twenty wagons and the bodies were all adult and male, a group of traders. She had never seen or heard of a Scavenger band large enough to do this much damage.

It frightened her, not knowing which direction

379

the Scavengers were headed. An hour later, careful scouting showed her they were headed to the northeast. Toward Providence.

Tate retraced her path, moving with haste, without thought for the Laws. Jolene's voice shrieked, weaving old webs of control, but Tate's own voice was louder, calling her to account for leaving David to follow the whispers of a dead woman.

Fourteen hours later, exhausted and near hysteria, she staggered to the top of the rise from which she had first seen Providence. Even as she covered the last few feet, she could smell her failure. Below her, the village lay in ruin, slate roofs smashed, doors and windows gone and bodies crumpled everywhere. The meeting hall was on fire, and the light from the flames flickered on broken windowpanes.

It was dusk before she gathered the courage to walk those last few paces, stepping over the bodies. She found David, swinging by a noose from the large tree in the commons. Gracie and Old Maggie lay nearby. Horrible things had been done to them. Tate cut David down and sat on the ground beneath the tree, his head cradled in her lap, sipping from the steel flask until the light was gone.

Over the following days, Tate kept busy with details. She buried David and the others in graves dug on the village green. She cleaned the lanes, rebuilt the burned-out bridge, planted the gardens and restored cottages as best she could. When all else was done, she cut the oak tree down to a stump, because she couldn't stand the sight of it.

She stayed on then, sleeping in the ruins of the

meeting hall. As she worked, she came around to the notion that David hadn't been playing a game, all the nights he teased her about being his mystery woman. Maybe he and the people of Providence *had* known the world before Collapse. Maybe that winter night, at the fire with the old woman, she had tumbled into enchantment, been carried back to a time when the child Tate was off somewhere, still learning Jolene's Laws.

And she realized who the old woman had been.

Tate sat amidst the ghosts of Providence, nursing a small fire, as she had done every winter's night for so many years she had lost count.

During those years, she had visitors. Traders, tinkers, wizards, witches, alchemists and adventurers had come and gone. She conducted business with some and sent all on their way, for none had been the one for whom she waited.

This night, she looked up, without surprise, as a young woman walked out of the darkness and approached the fire. Tate made no move to challenge the younger woman, but she retained her grip on David's old scattergun. The weapon had seen better days. Its stock was wrapped in duct tape and the shoulder strap was a frayed piece of rope, but it still worked. The younger woman stopped short of the fire.

"Hello," she said.

"Hello," Tate said.

"You alone?" the younger woman asked.

"Are you?"

"Yeah."

Tate inclined her head toward the grave markers.

381

"All gone but me."

"Too bad," the younger woman said. Tate stood and the younger woman took a step backward, put her hand upon the pistol butt.

"Jolene?" she said.

Tate shrugged away the words. This was the one. There had been and would be magic, after all.

"Can I sit?" the younger woman asked. "I got meat and bread."

"Go ahead, sit," Tate said.

Her voice sounded raspy, rusted once more from disuse. The younger woman stared for just a moment, then nodded and shrugged out of her pack, dropping it beside the fire.

"I'm Tate," the younger woman said.

Tate didn't bother to answer. There was no hurry now, no need for conversation. She returned to the stump, stirring the small pot until its contents began to bubble, then she poured its contents onto two metal camp plates. By the time she was done, the younger woman had dug smoked venison and a cloth-wrapped slab of corn bread from her pack and had divided it into two portions. They shared the food and began to eat.

"Good," the younger woman said, after a time. "Grow them yourself?"

"Plant them in the spring," Tate said. "Can them in the fall."

When both had their fill, Tate dug her flask from the bag beside her stump. She ran her finger over its surface, wondering how many more times it could be restored, how much longer it would continue to fuel the enchantment into which she had fallen. She unscrewed the top and tilted the flask.

R. M. WINCH

"Better days," she said. She took a swig.

When she passed the open flask, there was a sharp spark that made them both jump, but still the younger woman took the flask and drank. The younger woman sighed, enjoying the bite of the whiskey, and then returned the flask.

"Been here long?" the younger woman asked.

Tate downed more whiskey and passed over the steel for the last time. As the younger woman accepted it, Tate sighed. The younger woman was no longer her concern. She had passed the steel and its magic had begun once more.

"Long enough," she said.

Without waiting for the return of her property, Tate kicked off her camp shoes and crawled into the sleeping gear already laid out by the fire. She could finish this business now.

"Bank the fire whether you stay or go," she said.

Tate pulled a tiny glass vial from between her breasts, where it had hung over her heart for half a lifetime.

"You'll fall asleep and never wake," the alchemist had said.

She removed its stopper, let the liquid trickle into her mouth and felt its bite within seconds. Burrowing in the blankets, she began to murmur the words to an old song she had learned from Jolene so long ago. A lullaby.

A moment later, she was gone.

Written in Light

written by

Jeff Young

illustrated by

RACHAEL JADE SWEENEY

ABOUT THE AUTHOR

*Jeff Young is a bookseller first and a writer second—
although he wouldn't mind a reversal of fortune.*

*Growing up in suburban Pennsylvania amongst the
cornfields and woods, Jeff spent his time alternating between
reading and fishing. Starting in on science fiction early, he
read his way through all of the Herbert and Heinlein he could
find and branched out from there. Through the encouragement
of English teachers, he started writing in his teens and never
stopped. Graduating from college with a degree in physics
and a concentration in astronomy, he found a job linked to his
other collegiate pleasure, the radio station, selling music in the
Philadelphia area. Eleven years later, he came to Barnes &*
Noble to sell books and learn more about the publishing industry.

*Jeff finds himself constantly trying new things. He's had
a part in a play he co-wrote and performed with Full Circle
Productions and starred in a dual role in* The Space Stone
*filmed by Spooky Moon Productions. In the past he's been
published in* Carbon 14 *as a reviewer, interviewer and fiction
writer;* Neuronet, Trail of Indiscretion *and* Cemetery
Moon. *His story "The Piece at the Fulcrum" will appear*

in Realms *magazine, and he's been asked to contribute to the anthologies* By Any Means *and* In an Iron Cage: The Magic of Steampunk. *Jeff has led the Watch the Skies SF and Fantasy Discussion Group at Barnes & Noble in Camp Hill, PA, for ten years and the Word Wrights Writing Group for nine years. He is also an instructor for the "Step Back in Time" class at the DreamWrights Youth and Family Theatre which prepares children for their first trip to Renaissance Faires.*

ABOUT THE ILLUSTRATOR

In October of 1989, Rachael was born into an artistic family where her talents were nurtured at a very young age. It was her parents' artwork and constant encouragement that inspired her to pursue the potential of her artistic talents. At age nine, Rachael received a certificate of artistic achievement from Burlington City Arts. Then in 2007, she received the Progressive Pick Award and two Honorable Mentions at the Champlain Valley Fair Exposition. She has since continued to refine her artistic abilities and broaden her knowledge of techniques and media.

Rachael is a self-taught artist and constant daydreamer. As a child, she was surrounded by magic and folklore. Whether it was Walt Disney's epics or the countless books she read and hoarded like a dragon's treasure, it was clear that the world of fantasy and science fiction would follow her on her artistic journey. Rachael hopes to one day become a professional artist in a number of creative fields. She is currently attending the Community College of Vermont in her home town of Burlington and plans to later transfer to a four-year liberal arts college to further study art as well as anthropology.

Written in Light

For a brief moment, Zoi'ahmets stood as still as the tree the wickurn resembled, watching as the unknown creature stumbled backwards from her. Perhaps it was the fact that Zoi'ahmets was twice its height, or her triple conjoined trunks, or the orange eye that she swiveled in its direction. Two podia, how could it manage like that? They appeared so inefficient in dealing with gravity, unstable surfaces and even the strain over time on such a small area—certainly nothing like Zoi'ahmets' designs. What in Winter was happening here? She had so little time to be certain that everything was prepared for the Diversiform Dispute judging. Her cognition engine finally linked with the translator nailed to her bark. Only then did she grasp that the sounds that had been striking the translator were attempts at communication.

Amazingly, the intruder turned its back completely on Zoi'ahmets and began to dig through the grass. That was a very antisurvival trait in an unresolved situation. Perhaps it had lost something. She fed its image into the cognition engine, which then identified the creature as a *human*. Trying to imagine what it might be searching for, the wickurn cast about with all of her eyes, looking over the thick verdure of the pampas and nearby bushes. There was something black and lumpy with a short set of straps hanging in the top of a shrub nearby. One branch reached for it as another gently spun the human around and faced it toward its property. The human awkwardly trudged through the grass. Zoi'ahmets gently handed it the case. It spared a moment to eye its benefactor thoughtfully and then dropped gracelessly to the ground to open the case. The human quickly extracted a silver device which, when clipped behind an ear, opened up like a flower. The shiny metallic petals spun and clicked restlessly in the afternoon. Another device fit about the neck and a third nestled in the center of its hand. Then Zoi'ahmets finally heard the human begin to speak.

"_____ wickurn _____ about three meters _____ seems to be looking out for me. _____ see why it's here. Since I'm as far into the Dispute zone as I am _____ _____ _____ _____. Can't understand why it hasn't _____ with me yet."

"Communicated?" offered Zoi'ahmets as she pulled herself slowly to the human.

"Yeah, actually," stammered the being.

"You were not exactly making intelligible sounds until just a moment ago."

"And you were pretending to be a tree! No, I'm sorry, you are a tree. You can't help that. I guess I just never expected you to move."

"Why would I require help, if I am in my natural state?"

"Look, this isn't going well. You're one of the workers on this Diversiform Dispute, and I'm obviously keeping you from your job. I apologize for startling you, if that's what I did." It took a deep breath and continued. "I'm Kiona. I'm . . . a student of photography. I rode the ground vehicle over there until it stopped. Then the flight craft that was following us crashed into a tree. I'm so sorry to disturb you. I was only trying to learn more about the Dispute Zone." It bowed slightly in Zoi'ahmets' direction, focusing two green eyes on her.

Zoi'ahmets raised a branch and its eye could see fragments of debris at the base of a nearby windrake tree. Now that Zoi'ahmets looked at the wreckage, it bore a resemblance to an automated sampling drone. The small craft had become entangled in the net of branches and its weight must have dragged down the tendrils and broken them. Looking where indicated, she could see a surface rover. A makeshift seat was mounted to the top of the six-wheeled drone directly over the solar panel. Kiona must have ridden the sampler until it ran out of power. The aerial drone would have lost its guidance and then crashed. Could the human really be that stupid or was this deliberate, wondered Zoi'ahmets.

She turned back to the alien in front of her. Perhaps an introduction was in order. "I am Zoi'ahmets Calinve, chief architect of the Wickurn Diversiform entrant in this Dispute." Gently tipping forward, she returned the bow as much as she could manage. Kiona backed up another step.

"I am so sorry. I had no idea this was your environment and never wanted to harm it."

Zoi'ahmets cocked a lower eye toward it. "But you had no problem entering the contested area to gain

389

images of the Dispute—did you? In fact you appear to have subverted a sampling drone to carry you. It's surprising the drone made it this far." With that, she began the typical spiraling walk of a wickurn toward the drone. All the while she thought to herself, *I must find a way to get this thing out of here as quickly as possible.* She'd heard that humans were allowed onto this Dispute World and wasn't sure how she felt about the imposition. Now she had one interrupting her work. For a second she considered that her opponents might have put the intruder here to hinder her.

Kiona started after her, but the wickurn found herself waiting as the human pulled off one of the coverings on its feet and grasped at something on its ankle with its stubby fingers. When it held up the annoyance to the light, Zoi'ahmets dropped a branch eye to view it as well. "Caltrop seed," she said, focusing on it. "Something I designed that will allow animals to transport seeds. Let us have a look at your conveyance." Her eyes studied Kiona for a moment as her branch, vane leaves unfurling, drifted across Kiona's shoulder to urge it along. She pushed aside rising annoyance and moved forward.

While the human trotted along next to Zoi'ahmets as the wickurn's three root clusters rolled through the thick grasses, Zoi'ahmets took a moment to access the cognition engine and review the biology reports for humanity. She'd made certain to download a full biosummary of all of the judges' species and anyone who might be visiting the Dispute, just to be thorough. Thank Summer, there were no immediate concerns with regard to her biosystem.

RACHAEL JADE SWEENEY

Looking briefly at Kiona, Zoi'ahmets suddenly realized this was a female of their species and estimated her age at about twelve winters. At first glance Kiona appeared to be in good health. It was inappropriate, but one of the humans may have decided to take a firsthand look at the entrants to the Dispute rather than waiting as tradition demanded.

Zoi'ahmets looked down at Kiona, considering her again. Humanity, she mused, joined the galactic community later than most and there were concerns among the established species. Humans bred faster than most galactics and still had not modified themselves to limit their numbers. In a community where the primary means of gaining additional planetary growing room was based upon the ability to create effective complete environments for the Diversiform Disputes, most participants learned by modifying their homes and themselves first. Actually, humanity had done a remarkable job of terra-forming numerous worlds, but the issue of their unregulated propagation still remained.

Because Zoi'ahmets' contemplation slowed her pace, Kiona was able to dart ahead of the wickurn toward the crash of the sampling drone. With a quick glance, Zoi'ahmets could see that it was made of tensioned monomolecular fabric. The remains of a nearby wing swinging overhead seemed to be mostly gas cells with monomole struts. Looking back toward the ground sampler, unease made her stomachs churn. Zoi'ahmets studied Kiona for a moment; was the human not telling her everything? What was going on here?

Zoi'ahmets paused in consideration and looked up at the sky. Reflexively, she called up a weather survey. The cognition engine brought up a real-time satellite map in her mind's eye, displaying the relatively calm but currently cloudy weather and a storm front moving toward their location. Perhaps Kiona hadn't planned to be out for long or perhaps being trapped here was all part of the plan. The transmission faded out as Zoi'ahmets became lost in her own considerations.

In the meantime, the human was walking about the surface drone. Kiona pulled out another strap-bearing bag from the grass and rummaged through it. Her hand showed through a hole in the bottom as her face skewed and she murmured something that the translator box didn't quite register. She turned to Zoi'ahmets. "Something ate my food and the only thing left is a snack square. Hopefully, it wasn't anything of yours that might be poisoned by it." That briefly perplexed Zoi'ahmets. It certainly wasn't the type of comment someone with a nefarious purpose would make unless Kiona was deliberately misleading her.

Zoi'ahmets watched as Kiona crawled farther among the pampas where she found a round container twice the size of her palm and pushed that into her black bag. "The rover is ruined," Kiona commented. Sadly, the human appeared to be right. Slipping into a gully after it lost power and communication with the satellite grid, the drone had snapped two of its three axles.

Zoi'ahmets noticed that the base of Kiona's leg where it emerged from the grass was no longer the same color as the rest of her. Wasn't that the same foot she'd withdrawn the seed from? Zoi'ahmets reached into a mouth. Probing gently past her gullet into one of the xylem spaces, she pulled out a round cylinder. She shook out the tiny arrow shaped chenditi that clung to the sides. They landed on her lower trunk. Zoi'ahmets' large orange eye watched as the chenditi absorbed enough solar energy to fill lift cells by splitting moisture in the air into hydrogen and oxygen. Separately, the little creatures were mere animals. A small swarm equipped with send/receive components acted as a collective intelligence. Kiona stopped her scavenging to watch as the swarm lifted into the air. One half of each arrowhead was a deep black, and the opposite, canted at an angle, was covered with a shiny prismatic surface. Zoi'ahmets noticed that when Kiona stood up from the rover she was favoring her left leg.

Kiona shied as the chenditi flitted about her at first, but was apparently familiar with their ability to do chemical and medical diagnostics. They quickly surrounded the human and she held her arms out from her body as they spun about her. "Like a cloud of butterflies." Kiona laughed at the image. She drew her gaze back to Zoi'ahmets. Her glance was quick and her lips slid to one side, a slight breeze lifting her shoulder-length blonde fur. "I do know what they're for. What do you think is wrong with me?"

"That is what they will tell us."

"Will you tell me though?"

Zoi'ahmets was completely taken aback by that comment. Had they not established a basis for trust? Was this further evidence of malign intent? Was the human aware that Zoi'ahmets harbored suspicions concerning her motives? Further queries of the cognition engine suddenly made her realize something she missed earlier—this was a sapling; not an adult. Zoi'ahmets was briefly off balance trying to align her own species' view with that of human development. Wickurn budlings were given enough of the parent's memories to be instantly viable and then grew into mobility while developing a unique persona. They hardly compared to a species whose young were born with a complete tabula rasa. Human adults gave trust to younglings as they provided evidence that they were developed enough to earn it. Zoi'ahmets formed a suitable reply as the data from the chenditi medical assessment came through. "I have no reason not to be honest with you."

Kiona shook her head. "Typical adult. You didn't answer my question." She reached into her pack and pulled out a white-wrapped square. Peeling back an edge, she began to eat. Zoi'ahmets devoted part of her attention to Kiona and the rest to the results. Most of Kiona's biochemistry was a mystery to Zoi'ahmets, but the chenditi had found chemicals that were out of balance compared to the information the cognition engine carried about typical humans. Hormone levels were elevated and there was an odd reaction with something called histamines as well. The girl's core temperature was two degrees above standard and there were abnormal red streaks and swelling in the area where Kiona removed the seed.

"You have an infection, possibly caused by your injury and possibly due to exposure to microorganisms in the air. Do you have an emergency kit? My medicines and those the chenditi can produce will not help your physiology," stated Zoi'ahmets. The chenditi swarm came to rest clinging to the bark of her trunk, their small bodies twitching and jerking as they arranged themselves to soak up the maximum light.

Kiona stopped eating the snack square, brow furrowing slightly. She reached into her bag and pulled out the round container she'd rescued from the wreckage. Prying back a corner, she poked and prodded at the interior. A few chenditi flew to look over her shoulder and she held up the contents one by one to the small creatures. "Those will not help. Can you walk?" Zoi'ahmets asked as the chenditi returned. Kiona pushed herself to her feet, leaning against the wickurn's rough bark.

Watching Kiona, Zoi'ahmets' mind raced. What should she do now? It would take valuable time to return the human to the Judging Area. Would Zoi'ahmets be given any dispensation toward additional time to test her results? She felt fairly confident in the current development of the biosphere but was reluctant to give up any additional time. Then she considered the infection. Her opponents in the Diversity Dispute, the tio chaundon, used viruses to control certain developmental aspects of their biosphere. Were they infecting Zoi'ahmets' biosphere? Was this a deliberate attempt at sabotage? She tried to use the satellite uplink but received only a hum of static. A frisson of panic ran up her trunks making Zoi'ahmets dig her roots into the topsoil. Was she in danger from Kiona? Had the human cut Zoi'ahmets off from the satellite Net or had the tio chaundon? Zoi'ahmets quelled the desire to distance herself from the human. All the same she couldn't really abandon another sentient in need. There was also the consideration that the judges would inevitably be aware of what happened here. Her choices narrowed considerably. At least by accompanying the human, she could observe Kiona and ensure the girl did no damage to the environment. Otherwise, if a tio chaundon virus infected the human, Zoi'ahmets couldn't afford to have Kiona perish under her protection.

"How far?" Kiona asked, looking toward the horizon.

Zoi'ahmets placed two branches on Kiona's shoulders, gently spinning the girl around ninety degrees to the right. "Thirty-five kilometers to the Judging Area."

"Oh," was her soft reply. "Can't we go to your base of operations?"

Again Zoi'ahmets found herself wondering, was the human planning to sabotage the biosphere by destroying Zoi'ahmets' work base? She answered quickly, "There's nothing there to help you. Wickurn don't have the same physical requirements as humans. There must be an enclave set aside for your kind at the Judging Area."

Kiona turned away, looking back toward her original position. "Great. My parents are going to love this. Look, I swear, I never intended for this to happen and I really hope that this will have no effect on the outcome of the Dispute. I really just wanted to get some images—well, I really wanted to see and nobody was going to let me near anything."

Zoi'ahmets pondered that revelation for a few seconds before urging Kiona into motion toward

397

the far-off enclave. "Perhaps you do not understand how wickurn look at the Disputes. I know that other races actively attempt to fine-tune their strategies as the Dispute occurs. Wickurn feel that if our design has enough viable integrity it will succeed despite ongoing tinkering by the other Disputing party."

The grass rustled with their passing. Zoi'ahmets glanced briefly at the map that the cognition engine displayed in her mind's eye. There were two ridges to traverse. Although Zoi'ahmets' gait uphill would cost them time, it would be quicker than following the level ground. The storm front continued to advance. At best pace it would reach them in a day and a half, just before they reached the neutral Judging Area. There was nothing to do but push onward. By the time they had reached the foothills of the first ridge of upthrust rock they had passed several net trees, spiral bushes, vane fungus and whole fields of grasses whose one side was soft as silk and the other rough and jagged. Agile yellow leapers bounced out ahead of them, sending up clouds of pollen, while feathered grazers looked over broad shoulders with dark clusters of eyes full of complacent ignorance.

Kiona walked behind Zoi'ahmets, chattering about her school classes. About how adept she was at manipulating data and machines and how her parents traveled across many worlds. In turn Zoi'ahmets answered her questions about her Diversiform entrant and what she observed of her opponent's. Since they were speaking of her work, it distracted her from her growing annoyance. Zoi'ahmets told Kiona how the challengers, the tio chaundon, built their biosphere in tiers that developed over time and spread outward from a central point. So each tier increased in complexity and diversity as well as competition.

"Oh, Darwin," Kiona remarked offhandedly.

The wickurn came to an abrupt stop. "What do you mean?"

"Survival of the fittest, it's the law of nature."

"By 'law' you mean—a rule stating a consistent action or situation that occurs under identical conditions? The wickurn Diversiform I have described to you is a web of symbiotic increase of complexity and opportunities for growth."

"That just means that cooperation is the fittest form, so some other forms must lose out."

"No, they are incorporated. Their numbers are perhaps limited, but no form is lost. This ensures the increase of diversity. Obviously this is a 'law' only on your world."

"Are you are saying that's the case because these two ecosystems competing isn't natural?"

Zoi'ahmets started walking again, thinking furiously. Suddenly her misgivings were back again. Was Kiona trying to subvert her or spy on her work? "No, I merely suggest that your 'law' is a theory because not all cases inevitably point to its proof."

"So do you believe that there is an outside force planning the development of nature?"

Zoi'ahmets hesitated briefly. "I did tell you that I am the designer of this Diversiform. So therefore, yes, I know that I am the outside force that has planned for this outcome. How the Diversiform reacts to the vagaries of the state of the world and interaction with the opposing entrant is what I can merely theorize."

"Didn't answer my question again," was Kiona's reply as she shook her head.

Zoi'ahmets looked at the human while Kiona walked ahead. Why was Kiona really here? Could she even sabotage the wickurn Diversiform?

Considering an answer, Zoi'ahmets realized that the light had begun to fade. "Kiona, when the light dims, I will be groggy. You can stay near my trunk; it will be warmer there. Neither biosphere has any large forms which would cause you harm yet."

"I'll be warm anyway," was the human's quick reply as she pulled out a small cylinder that inflated into an aircel sleep sack. Wedging it in between two rootlets, she curled up below the wickurn.

Zoi'ahmets looked down at her. She really could not fathom what went on in the human's mind. Were her thought processes that different? One moment she was talking about not trusting Zoi'ahmets and the next Kiona was curled around her roots. Zoi'ahmets gave up trying to understand and focused on something that might be more comprehensible with time. She pulled up the human information in her mind's eye and turned to their replication substrate, DNA.

Now this was something that would hold her interest, at least until her photosensitivity set in and distracted her from the frustration of being cut off.

Zoi'ahmets woke at first light, slowly coming back to full awareness as the morning brightened. She gently disengaged herself from Kiona to wander around the small clearing taking samples and reviewing the acceptance of the deposited life forms. She roused the chenditi and set them to taking readings of the atmosphere and water vapor. She saw no sense in wasting the time until Kiona awoke. Finally, Zoi'ahmets considered that perhaps the human had slept longer than normal.

With the chenditi swarm accompanying her, Zoi'ahmets gently shook the sleep sack. When Kiona's tousled fur appeared, Zoi'ahmets' upper eyes were surprised at the redness of her face. There also seemed to be swelling along her jaw and eyes. Chenditi clustered around Kiona and lit on the edges of the sleep sack, as she knuckled her eyes and pushed herself up and out. Only after her first attempt at standing, did Zoi'ahmets begin to realize the seriousness of the problem. Kiona's leg was completely swollen now, and she could no longer easily stand upright.

The chenditi registered infection and histamine imbalances again as well as fluctuations in the hormone called estrogen. The infection would account for the swelling. The hormone imbalances made little sense and odd fluctuations in her core body temperature seemed to be more than a mere fever. More important was the real problem of the lack of effective medicine, food and transportation for Kiona. While Zoi'ahmets considered the next alternative, Kiona dug into the round container in her pack. She slapped a patch onto the underside of her wrist before the chenditi could react. A quick review proved that it would be mildly effective against the pain and swelling. She sat back dejectedly. "I wish I hadn't eaten the entire snack yesterday. Is there anything around here that's safe for me to eat?"

"That is a problem," Zoi'ahmets replied, spinning closer to her. "You cannot safely digest the plants and animal life of my Diversiform because they contain heavy metals that are harmful to you. Wickurn filter them out easily and need some of them like selenium. Even the water may be harmful over long periods of time."

"Then I guess you'll have to call in for a rescue."

The wickurn dipped an eye close to Kiona and said nothing. The other two upper eyes surveyed the ridge ahead. "I have not been able to contact the satellite link. There can be no rescue. But we must still find a way to get you out." Zoi'ahmets hesitated, her mind flickering through possibilities. "How long will it be until your parents miss you?"

Kiona struggled to her good leg, leaning heavily against Zoi'ahmets' trunk. Now it was her turn to hesitate before replying. She tried to take a tentative step and Zoi'ahmets had to fling two branches after Kiona before she pitched forward into the grass. The girl hung there a moment before reaching around to pull herself upright. Liquid ran down the planes of Kiona's face. "They won't know for quite some time. They're sequestered."

Despite her best attempt, Zoi'ahmets nearly dropped the young human as her thoughts reeled in shock. Kiona's parents were human judges in the Diversiform Dispute. Her hopes came crashing down. The chenditi, confused at the input, clustered tightly in a rotating ring around Zoi'ahmets' upper branches and she desperately fought the instinct to sweep them into her twitching maws. Everything, everything hung in the balance. Would the humans still be impartial if harm came to their offspring? Would they be disqualified as judges? Would the entire Dispute be considered null and she and her opponents be relegated to a later competition? The cognition engine started determining probabilities until she angrily cut it off. Zoi'ahmets felt the skin between the joins of her main branches begin to grow tender and itch.

Going back to an earlier chain of thought, Zoi'ahmets called the chenditi cluster to the fore. Running the translation twice through the cognition engine, she confirmed that the cluster understood what she desired. Then spinning like a miniature cyclone, the little mass mind began to retrace their steps. Hopefully it would be able to carry out her instructions.

"Lean on me," instructed Zoi'ahmets to Kiona as she started off in a new direction, downhill from the ridge. They could no longer hope to cross the heights. It would add distance to the trip, but the most effective path now lay along the valley floor. Together they limped through three kilometers before Kiona needed a break. At the edge of the river that followed the valley floor, Kiona sipped sparingly from the water. Zoi'ahmets was still concerned about the contamination but now it seemed they would have little choice. Kiona poured the water over her head, wiping at the swelling around her eyes. Zoi'ahmets suddenly realized a new concern. If the swelling continued, Kiona soon would not be able to see.

They struggled onward for another two kilometers. Zoi'ahmets reconsidered the distance to the neutral territory base, the cognition engine flicking up lines of numbers: twelve kilometers the first day, five today made seventeen which would have been halfway, except now they were following the valley and angling slightly away. That made their total trip now fifty-two kilometers. They were a third of the way to safety and Kiona could literally no longer walk. When Zoi'ahmets checked Kiona's eyes, she found that her swollen cheeks and eyebrow ridges left her with a narrow band of vision. As Zoi'ahmets dipped her roots into the shallows of the river, something caught the attention of her upper eyes. Sunlight glistened off the swarm of chenditi heralding their arrival. Carried between their many members were eight gas cells and ten meters of cord. Zoi'ahmets accepted the strand and began to communicate her idea to the chenditi.

Turning back to Kiona, Zoi'ahmets asked her, "When we met, you said you wrote with light. How do you do that?" hoping perhaps to distract her.

"What's wrong with your translator?" Kiona said, staggering toward the sound. Zoi'ahmets gently guided Kiona's outstretched hand against her trunk. "Oh, I see—'photo-graphy.' Means I collect pictures. Like with this," she said, indicating the constantly moving disk clipped behind her ear. "I keep a record of everything and then I look for images that hold a particular meaning or will evoke a pleasant memory."

A constant record; Zoi'ahmets turned that idea over in her mind. "I would very much like to see your record when we reach safety. It will help reviewing the environment we have journeyed through."

"Sure, you know a picture doesn't lie, or is worth a thousand words, you pick." was Kiona's soft reply as she sat down heavily on the edge of Zoi'ahmets' roots still on the shore line. "Tired, I'm gonna sleep now."

Zoi'ahmets helped her into the sleep sack. The chenditi reviewed Kiona's condition before beginning their work with the monomole cord. As they began weaving the cord into a sling that could keep the sleep sack anchored to the slope of Zoi'ahmets' trunk just above the root cluster, she considered their results. Kiona's temperature had dropped and while the infection did not seem to be nearly as pronounced, walking on her injured leg caused it to swell until she could barely work the covering off it. Histamine counts were still off. Perhaps that was something Zoi'ahmets remembered as an "allergic reaction." So, as Kiona continued to nap, Zoi'ahmets researched further into human physiology. Eventually, she found a heading entitled "puberty." Suddenly the hormonal imbalance began to make sense. Finally, she considered checking the weather. Her observations of the wind and clouds indicated the storm would arrive tonight. With that, Zoi'ahmets summoned the chenditi to their perches on her trunk and with an awkward lurch began to move along the shore line.

Kiona woke briefly when she realized that Zoi'ahmets was carrying her and then returned to sleep. The wickurn kept up the pace until the light began to fade. They were now seven kilometers farther. Her root cluster was sore and the joins of the branches on her crown had now swollen into round clusters of blisters. Zoi'ahmets briefly explored the largest. Of all the possible outcomes, why this?

The stress must be forcing a bloom. One more inconvenience to overcome. The first drops of rain swiftly distracted Zoi'ahmets and she pulled the edges of the sleep sack over the top of Kiona's face, carefully propping them up to allow air flow. As tired as Zoi'ahmets was, she still delighted in the feel of the rain cascading over leaflets, branches and trunks. Her mouths puckered open into waiting funnels.

Rain continued the next morning and made footing difficult as Zoi'ahmets soldiered on, trying to gain more ground despite the grogginess caused by the cloud-veiled light. Kiona mumbled incoherently and Zoi'ahmets had risked another patch under her wrist. That left only one more. Hopefully Kiona's fever would break soon. Soon Kiona would inevitably realize that she could no longer see. Zoi'ahmets grasped at boulders and trunks of trees to pull herself along. It was nearly evening when the cloud cover finally broke and the steady rain tailed off. Zoi'ahmets brought them as far as possible away from the bed of the river, in case the water rose overnight, and faded from consciousness.

As the light woke her, Zoi'ahmets realized that Kiona's weight was no longer resting against her. The little camera flashed and spun where Kiona clipped it to the outside of the flaccid sleep sack. Casting about, Zoi'ahmets discovered the girl at the edge of the river. A trail showed where Kiona had crawled through the dew-covered grasses to the water's edge. Zoi'ahmets came up behind her slowly.

"I guess it's morning now, right? I mean I think I can feel the sun. Sorry I left, but I was so thirsty," Kiona whispered.

Zoi'ahmets gently led the human back from the edge of the river. Kiona demonstrated admirable aplomb in the acceptance of her loss of vision. She was also very fortunate to crawl out onto a low rocky shelf instead of falling off an embankment into the rain-swelled waters. Zoi'ahmets stood there staring at the river for a moment. A desperate idea was forming in her mind.

"I heard something crackling last night. What was that?" interrupted Kiona.

Self-consciously, Zoi'ahmets poked a branch into each of her three mouths and found some small pieces of chitin. Apparently some large insect became an unwilling dinner last night. Zoi'ahmets' reserves were being put to the test if she was eating instinctively. A new concern presented itself. "Kiona, I can eat during my sleep. You must be very careful if you wake up in the night, especially near my crown."

"Oh, late night snack, but you wouldn't . . . I see, you mean it's involuntary—as if I could climb up there anyway with my leg and my not being able to see." Kiona started to laugh, but it was a thin sound that soon gave way to sobs. As Zoi'ahmets eased a branch around her shoulders, Kiona reached out and gently squeezed it. "From what I've seen, Zoi'ahmets, you've made a beautiful world, but I don't want to die here."

Zoi'ahmets shuddered briefly. Had Kiona seen past to what she hadn't dared to admit to the other wickurn? That what she built was designed not only to be effective but also pleasing? Had a child seen what she had presumed to do, where others hadn't?

Suddenly what had been a vague hope solidified into resolve. "You are not going to die here yet, Kiona. But what I have in mind will take bravery on both our parts as well as luck." Kiona turned her face to Zoi'ahmets and the sun broke through the clouds to dance across the river, hiding its swollen state and brown color.

"Why do you have the Disputes, Zoi'ahmets?"

The wickurn considered briefly before answering. A chenditi flicked across Zoi'ahmets' vision in the sunlight. Perhaps they were the best example. "Kiona, when the chenditi were discovered a long, long time ago, they completely overran their world. Their planet was tidally locked with the cold side covered in an ozone haze and the warm side covered with nothing but layer upon layer of barely conscious chenditi. Their mass mind becomes an increasingly more efficient calculating machine capable of vast intellect as their numbers grow. Eventually they pass a point and the grand mind breaks down. So their population increased to the point at which they were barely conscious and their world was rapidly spiraling into decay.

"When galactic races found them, a great many chenditi were rescued and a realization grew out of the incident—that in diversity was hope of continuity. This became the common theme for the developing galactic community. So the worlds we find are contested for. Did you know that all of the environments must be able to support at least five other species as well as the entrants'? We hold these contests and abide by the judges' decisions, which are reviewed for fairness by an impartial arbiter. By doing this we bind together the community and also preserve it by demanding diversity.

"But we have put it off as long as we can. Come, we must go to the river." With that, Zoi'ahmets put two branches under Kiona's arms and lifted her up onto a root group. Zoi'ahmets hoped she was doing the right thing. She also wondered when she'd stopped mistrusting her companion.

After she convinced the chenditi to reconfigure the sling for the sleep sack and then use their nanofacture reserves to seal the sack with most of their number inside, Zoi'ahmets slowly waded out into the rush of the river waters. The chenditi in the sleep sack were converting the water seeping into the sack into hydrogen for themselves and oxygen for Kiona while the remainder buffered the carbon dioxide levels and vented the waste. Clustered together, they formed a dark blister on top of the sleep sack. The chenditi had forced air cells into the tops of Zoi'ahmets' main xylem spaces, making the large hollows in her body airtight and buoyant. Along with Zoi'ahmets' natural tendency to float, this kept all of them above the surface. The worst part was the lack of control. Dealing with unseen obstacles that sought to trap her bulk and pull them under was another problem. It was difficult to find the appropriate mix of current and depth to allow maximum speed and control. Zoi'ahmets found it discouraging to see so much of the life she'd carefully placed into the environment swirling out of control about her in the raging waters of the river.

Past midday, Zoi'ahmets made an unpleasant discovery. She realized that they were drifting

409

farther from the eastern shore into an increasingly accelerating current. Debris struck them on all sides as Zoi'ahmets wrapped branches about the precious cargo of the sleep sack and tumbled through the water. She pushed desperately with her root clusters to no avail. After an hour of failure, Zoi'ahmets realized the only answer was to make for the western shore. Dragging them out of the river onto the muddy shore line, she looked back across the water. Now there was an additional obstacle keeping them from their destination.

When Zoi'ahmets gently opened the sleep sack, she found that Kiona's fever had finally broken. The swelling in the girl's foot and leg had actually begun to recede. But now Kiona was desperately hungry and becoming weaker. The worst news arrived last. The chenditi from the top of the sleep sack were gone, washed away in the final desperate hour. They spent the last hours of daylight gaining some distance from the flood plain and drying out the sleep sack. Kiona insisted that her camera once again be clipped to the exterior.

Kiona's brief physical, limited by the loss of a third of the swarm, revealed something new, now that Zoi'ahmets was more familiar with her physiology. The continuing infection was not due to the initial wound. Kiona's white blood cells singled out those invaders and eliminated them over time. But her body continued to produce an elevated amount of white blood cells because she was still being affected by something else. Zoi'ahmets had the chenditi begin to search for the unknown irritant but ran out of light before the results arrived.

As the first breeze of night riffled through Zoi'ahmets' crown, Kiona spoke. "What a lovely scent. I wonder where those flowers are." She sighed contentedly and pulled the sleep sack tight about her. Zoi'ahmets slumped slightly. Due to the continuing high level of stress, the change in her body continued without her assent. Zoi'ahmets' trunk shook with exhaustion and frustration. Despite her confidence in the biosphere she'd created, she would have never chosen this. Zoi'ahmets was blooming.

The next morning, waiting for Kiona to awaken, Zoi'ahmets tossed the petals one by one into the river. The water at last began to recede. If her calculations were correct, they had traveled too far. The remaining chenditi drifted like a cloud high into the sky and then returned to bring back their observations. The river bent into an oxbow and their wild ride carried them farther from the neutral Judging Area. Now they were eighteen kilometers and a river crossing away from safety. The chenditi found a possible crossing another two kilometers down river but that was still more distance and time.

Zoi'ahmets glanced at Kiona's sleeping face. The girl stirred briefly when Zoi'ahmets moved toward the river, but had swiftly fallen back asleep. Her body was shutting down, protecting the human, as her hunger, which Kiona had tried to ignore, grew more desperate. Time was running out. The wickurn lurched forward down to the streamside once again.

Looking back across the river, Zoi'ahmets wasn't even exactly sure how they had made the crossing. The wickurn vaguely remembered thrashing about, losing leaves and scraping rocks that sheared off wide swaths of bark. The sleep sack sloshed with excess water. Zoi'ahmets slid Kiona out of the sack into a boneless pile and then had to grab desperately after the girl as Kiona scrambled away. Instinctively, Kiona began pulling up the variform grass and trying to shove it into her mouth. Zoi'ahmets' branches gathered Kiona up, scooping out the grass, washing off the cuts the rough surfaces made on her mouth and slapping the last med patch on her wrist.

Zoi'ahmets stood there for the moment letting the sun wash over her. Her mind was dazed by all of the recent events. But something was bothering the wickurn, something she had seen when she had been looking at the human health records, specifically at their replicating code, DNA. Zoi'ahmets could see the dancing spiral forming over and over again and still the pattern that the chenditi had shown her for Kiona was different. Different in such a small way that only a being that designed worlds for its living might have noticed—but still wrong. This time the code didn't dance, it wobbled, it stumbled, but only in spots that were ordinarily filled with discord. What kind of species left this much junk in their codons?

Holding Kiona against her trunk as the girl sobbed, Zoi'ahmets enlisted the chenditi's help in spreading the sleep sack out to dry among her branches. When Kiona finally reached upward to the swelling fruit that had come from the shed flowers, Zoi'ahmets didn't even try to stop the girl. She could feel Kiona's hands among the joins of the branches at her crown and the tearing sensation as each fruit let go. Instead of hurling the human from her as

Zoi'ahmets' instincts prompted her, she clutched
Kiona tighter. As Zoi'ahmets desperately tried to
find something to distract her from the horror of
what was being done to her, the wickurn suddenly
realized what she had been seeing. The oddities in
Kiona's DNA made sense if and only if she accepted
one proposition. What Kiona had done in distress
was nothing compared to this. Hardened by the
knowledge, Zoi'ahmets turned and plunged onward
toward the Judging Area with a renewed resolution.
She hadn't come this far to fail now.

The first cloud of chenditi that came boiling out upon
the news of Zoi'ahmets' arrival at the Judging Area
went directly for her. Waving away their attentions,
she demanded they see to the nearly comatose human
at her side. Kiona was gently removed and carried off,
the purplish blood of Zoi'ahmets' potential children
still staining the girl's lips. Brushing off the attentions
of the chenditi, Zoi'ahmets doggedly pushed on into
the wickurn enclave. Time, she had so little time.
There were things that needed to be set in motion
and Zoi'ahmets dearly hoped she could trust her
colleagues. Soon she would be called to account, to
the judges, to the humans—but first Zoi'ahmets had
to do the impossible—to speak to the arbiter.

A few moments later, Zoi'ahmets was whirling
down the hallway to the central dome of the
installation. Kiona's tiny camera was entrusted to
her assistants as well as a copy of all of the recent
data from her tour of the Dispute and the single
most important item, a heavily encrypted version of
Zoi'ahmets' suspicions. Outside of the doorway to
the Court of the Dispute, Zoi'ahmets reached into

413

her xylem space and pulled out the worn canister housing the remainders of the chenditi swarm. It had been difficult to coax them into the container before entering the neutral area. Perhaps the loss of their numbers made the little mass mind more sluggish and easily confused. Zoi'ahmets spun to a stop in front of the doors.

Her translator box proclaimed loudly, "I am here to see the arbiter. I have evidence concerning the judgment of this Dispute." Zoi'ahmets shifted uneasily. Anyone could bring formal evidence or concerns about the Dispute, but this was to be done in the court of judgment. The identity of the arbiter was always kept secret. She could feel the traffic of passing species come to a slow halt and all eyes or senses coming to bear on her. Zoi'ahmets held up the container of chenditi and shook it briefly. "I said, I *will* see the arbiter."

With that the doors slid open and Zoi'ahmets slipped through them into the alcove ahead. Doors slammed shut behind her as the set opposite folded back. Ahead there was nothing but darkness. Zoi'ahmets moved slowly forward into the echoing space. She could just make out the central walkway before the doors folded shut, leaving her without a single source of light. Zoi'ahmets uncapped the container of chenditi and shook them free. "You need to know what these have to offer," she stated. With that Zoi'ahmets settled back to wait.

The wickurn's suspicions were rewarded in a few moments. Light began to filter down from the ceiling of the dome as the thousands of chenditi, which clung to the skylight windows, dropped into flight. The light sparkled across them as they wove to and fro like a flock of avians. Patterns, shadows and absences flickered across the mass as it spun, filling the great dome from one side to the other. *"You will tell us. We will tell the arbiter,"* came through Zoi'ahmets' translator box. Now it was time to drive in the first spike, she thought.

"There is no difference. You are the arbiter. You know all that the swarm that I carried knows. You know that someone has tampered with this Dispute."

The cloud of chenditi spun faster and Zoi'ahmets could feel the air begin to move slightly in the great hall. Now she would see if the supposition she believed was correct. The chenditi with their past would make formidable arbiters, she thought, as well as their ability to condense into a mass mind with tremendous calculative powers. What kind of debate was going on in that great mind now? Would the chenditi kill her with the many nanomachines they carried? Would she simply vanish? It was pointless to worry for already they were in motion again, spreading out across the roof of the dome, the light failing.

"You know that there is a human-specific microorganism that was designed to limit the fertility of their species. It was to settle in their DNA and rewrite junk sequences that would be passed along to their descendants causing a decline in their fecundity. This world was only a test, since there are human judges. Whoever did this did not expect the humans to bring their child, who is just becoming

415

fertile, and that the virus would affect her like an allergy. Since her body would not be able to develop a defense for it and since the virus is airborne, she was constantly re-exposed. Her white blood cells kept trying to defeat the invader whereas in an adult the virus would have settled in gradually, using various hormones to fool the lymphocytes. The elevated hormones of the change in her body kept affecting the invader and it kept the chenditi and me from discovering the virus until just before our arrival."

It was dark now and a continuing rustling from the chenditi proved that not all of the mind had come to rest. There was no response. Zoi'ahmets hadn't expected one. While capable, none of the other races judging this dispute would have ever considered such an action. This information pointed to a species capable of manipulating matter on the very small scale. But they made one small error. They chose the wrong test subject. They were outwitted by the vagaries of nature, timing and development. It was only luck that Kiona was affected as she was. Zoi'ahmets continued to wait. Perhaps the time had come to sink another barb or two.

"A carrier was needed to spread the virus. I find it hard to believe that she was able to gain access to the Dispute before judging. Therefore she was allowed entrance. The human had a very interesting device along that kept a constant record of the entire trip. I made sure that it was returned to her companions—after the record's information, along with my observations, was sent to the closest three wickurn outposts on nearby worlds. As a good observer and scientist, I made sure that my data was completely backed up. However, I never revealed what I have told you. But this information in the hands of qualified persons could lead them to certain conclusions."

The flare of light was sudden as more than half of the chenditi left their perches to fall through the air swooping madly about, the air singing with the speed of their passage. Zoi'ahmets pulled in her branches and leaflets completely. Chenditi dropped like rain, all rushing inwards toward her. They clung in successive layers, coat after coat. Zoi'ahmets' eyes were swiftly covered. Her branches began to buckle inward and it felt as if her xylem spaces were beginning to crack. How long before the mind calculated the odds? For or against? Had she guessed right? Would she even live that long? Would some unforeseen accident befall this world and all of those who had received the information?

Her mind continued to race in the darkness. Tiny rasping sensations came from every inch of her bark. They were eating her alive. Like some giant swarm, they would consume her and leave nothing but dust behind if their monstrous weight didn't crush her first. She felt a minor branch snap. Then Zoi'ahmets thought she felt a shift and her trunk leaning to the left. They were twisting her. She would snap like a green twig. But gradually the pressure grew less as she realized they were quieting. Finally the translator box emitted a signal.

"Whom will you tell about our identity as arbiter?"

Zoi'ahmets considered briefly—interesting that they were ignoring her accusation. "Surely I am not the first to guess. There have to be other species which, given the proper clues, have come to the same conclusion." Already Zoi'ahmets could feel the coating of thousands of tiny bodies beginning to slowly lift.

"The nature of your dispersion of information will end our tenure. It is therefore irrelevant. The humans will not be adjusted. Those here will be returned to normalcy. What is your response?"

"I have a theory, nothing else. Soon I suspect I will have no proof. Why would I pursue something I cannot prove? My time is better spent working on the Diversiform, where I belong."

"The Dispute will continue. Another arbiter will be assigned. Leave."

After the last of the chenditi wafted upwards to hang in an immense churning spiral, Zoi'ahmets stood there staring up at the ceiling. It was a shock to still be alive. Then she spun about and headed toward the slowly opening doors.

Zoi'ahmets was pleased that someone exercised the forethought to wash the stains from around Kiona's mouth. Rushes of unresolved feelings coursed through Zoi'ahmets as she once again pushed aside the thoughts created by those last desperate hours that brought them to the neutral area. Kiona remained facing away from Zoi'ahmets. She was sure that Kiona must have heard her rustling entrance and felt Zoi'ahmets clipping the small camera to the top of the healing restraint. When Kiona finally turned, the girl couldn't seem to meet Zoi'ahmets' gaze.

418

The medical hammock Kiona was wrapped in reminded Zoi'ahmets briefly of the sleep sack. But its sloshing nutrient packs, glistening readout patches and clusters of ropy coils that fell from the ceiling ended the similarity. "Thank you," was all that Kiona could manage at first. The water from her eyes coursed down her face mixing with the other fluids that were packed about her ravaged body. Zoi'ahmets shuffled closer. "After what I did, why would you do all you did for me?" Kiona asked.

That was a truly puzzling question. Zoi'ahmets considered her response. During the early parts of the journey she was acting selfishly to preserve her work. As time went on, her view of the situation changed until the final revelation. Kiona didn't understand the greater issue and Zoi'ahmets couldn't tell her either. But there was something else that had prompted Zoi'ahmets' actions that she could share. "I told you that to a wickurn all parts of the Diversiform are important. I believe that the idea that only the strong should survive works in situations where intelligent life does not have control of its surroundings. To be a true participant of a Dispute, one must have an understanding of the environment one is creating and accept that intelligent life changes the outcomes of situations left to nature. But this is only a *theory*, not a law."

A brief smile touched Kiona's features at that. The girl worked one of her arms loose from the restraints inside the hammock and pulled out the round white bag she had carried throughout their journey. "I wouldn't let them have it. Here." With that Kiona settled back into the hammock, her features slowly becoming lax as she faded from consciousness into sleep.

Outside in the hallway, Zoi'ahmets opened the sack and peered at the round nodules that clustered at its bottom—the seeds. In all that happened Zoi'ahmets never realized that Kiona saved every one, instead of scattering Zoi'ahmets' children across the land of the Dispute. That time might come eventually and now, thanks to Kiona's thoughtfulness—it could.

The House of Nameless

written by

Jason Fischer

illustrated by

SETH J. ROWANWOOD

ABOUT THE AUTHOR

Jason Fischer lives in a coastal town near Adelaide, South Australia, with his wife and baby son. By day, he works with archives for a government department, while his evenings are given over to the craftings of his imagination. He tries to unleash the weird every time he gets behind the keyboard, and his fiction has been described by reviewers as "strikingly original" and "weirdly imaginative," while noted for containing "greasier genre elements." Jason attended the Clarion South intensive writers' workshop in 2007, was shortlisted in the 2009 Ditmar Awards for Best New Talent and in the past two years has started to collect a respectable list of awards, prizes and publications.

He regularly entered the Writers of the Future Contest over a period of two years, during which time he collected two Honorable Mentions, landed two Semi-Finalist spots, and spent two nervous quarters as a Finalist prior to winning with this story. His stories have appeared in markets such as Jack Dann's all-Australian anthology Dreaming Again, Apex, Black House Comics, Andromeda Spaceways Inflight Magazine *and* Aurealis Magazine.

ABOUT THE ILLUSTRATOR

Seth began telling stories through images as a young boy in school. He would grab paper from anywhere and everywhere he could get it, drawing spaceships and battles. What he found frustrating was not being able to draw or write fast enough to capture and render all the ideas that he imagined. He finished high school with some recognition of his budding talents; however, art college proved to be more challenging to him. With some reservation, he took up a graphic design job for money. But his dreams of becoming a storyteller never left him alone.

Stories waiting to be told kept pouring out of him, some written, some drawn, others shared during conversations. After a long career in graphic design, without a published story to his name, he finally decided to surrender to his passion. The stories matured and began pushing their way into being, through either images and/or words—stories all about the spiritual struggle, expanding awareness, death, rebirth and transformation.

The House of Nameless

The date had been going well, all things considered. No girl in her right mind ever thought she would sit down to dinner at a minotaur's house, but then again no one knew that Raoul could cook up a storm.

"I've been saving this for a special occasion," he said, bumping open the kitchen door with his broad hip. He had a freshly baked Pavlova resting across the palm of one broad hand, his free hand proffering a bottle of Sauternes that was pinched between his enormous thumb and forefinger.

He stopped short. The girl was sitting rigid in her seat, gripping the edge of the table and trembling. There was a stranger in his house, standing right behind her, resting his hands upon shoulders made bare by her evening dress.

He was a patch of murk and drab, and Raoul found it difficult to look directly at him. His eyes seemed to slide off the intruder's shape, as if he were too greasy to hold light and form.

Raoul growled. His horns were sharp enough to pierce an engine block, but he hesitated. There were measures in place to keep weak minds out of this house, and this intruder had bypassed them all.

The man stank of rot and was sniffing at the girl's scalp, long and lovingly. The intruder was blurred around the edges, not a definite shape so much as a smudge. He moved in jerky fits and starts until he stood before Raoul.

"I knew you, back in the One-Way-World," the stranger said. "You were Mithras then."

"Get out of my house," Raoul said. "Now."

"I will undo all of your works," the man said, turning sideways and inside out until he was gone.

Raoul hushed his weeping date. He gently licked her forehead with his broad flat tongue, massaging the incident out of her mind. The minotaur sent the blank-faced girl safely home, realizing with some embarrassment that he had already forgotten her name.

He checked and refastened every door, even the basement door that led out into the cold vacuum of space. With the girl gone, he let the subterfuge drop, and the true nature of his domicile asserted itself.

Gone were the chandeliers, the immaculate mosaic flooring, the tapestries and hangings. His rat's-nest of an apartment emerged, complete with flaking stacks of periodicals, weight sets and mismatched furniture that had started to buckle beneath his weight.

The only true thing to appear in Raoul's spider web had been Picasso's *Minotaur Kneeling Over Sleeping Girl*. An original, and the lurid drawing

424

had made his date a little nervous, but ultimately curious. He thought it only fair to give her some hint of what his true intentions were, and it was an icebreaker, if nothing else.

"You looted this," she had said, arching an eyebrow. She touched his arm as she took in the image of the virile bull-man, lurking over the innocent girl, waiting. The date had been going very well, before something with the power to break through his safeguards had appeared *in his house*.

Raoul didn't believe in phones, but he had a battered old note pad on the counter, propped up against a grimy kettle. It had an elaborate sketch in ballpoint on the cardboard backing, a puppy curled up and sleeping.

If someone phoned him, their words appeared on the topmost page. Raoul found that he preferred to wander around in his squalor and think for half an hour or more of what to say, then write a suitable reply underneath the words of his caller.

This came over on the phone as if he had said the words himself, and the pacing of his speech seemed quite normal. The minotaur liked having the advantage of hours of thought, a chance to reference his various books or the means to outthink his various lady friends if one of them happened to call and he was with someone else.

Specifically, he'd invented the device to deal with Lune.

"Hello, it's me," he wrote.

"You'd best be scribbling out an apology," it read, her words appearing in her own neat hand. "I know you just had a visitor."

Long minutes of thought. He knew she was cunning enough to keep eyes on him, jealous enough to wish him harm. Powerful enough to deliver it.

"I had more than a visitor. Someone broke into my house."

"Into your house?" came the writing, cramped together in an excited scrawl. "You've gone to great efforts to keep everyone out. Including me."

"Please, Lune. This man, this intruder, he stank of the Old Ways. Aren't you concerned?"

"If it's to do with the One-Way-World, I suggest you go see Nameless. I'm done talking."

Her final sentence underlined itself several times, indicating that Lune had terminated their conversation with extreme prejudice.

Raoul visited the house of Nameless. In truth, it was the echo of his family home, a sagging mansion full of ghosts and sour days. There was a beach and a caravan park below the cliffs, but these places and the happy sounds that floated up from them were only there to torment Nameless.

"Come in," he told Raoul. The minotaur stepped over the muscle-bound ginger tom that was sometimes one cat, sometimes a dozen, resting on every surface, snarling. The cat/s were scared of Raoul now, having attacked him only the once.

They went through the kitchen, past the dining table set with plastic place mats for a family that would never eat together again. There was room after room full of memories and photographs, and the sunlight drifting through the windows was pale. It was always dusk here, and Nameless would not turn on the lights.

"Up here," Nameless said, and they climbed the stairs. There was an old child gate at the bottom, busted now. Up and up, winding, and there were more floors than it looked from outside. They climbed until Raoul snarled impatiently and terrified Nameless into giving him the top floor, the little den of Father.

"I've got this video," Nameless said, and hands shaking, he slipped the cartridge out of the paper case. *THE FUNNY TAPE!* the label read, and he fed it into the guts of a big chunky VCR.

They sat on the dusty couch, the minotaur and the little nothing-man. There was a photo of his family on top of the TV, and everyone but Nameless had their backs turned to the camera.

The tape started, and it showed a young Nameless, back when he had name and life and love. He frolicked on the beach with friends, turning cartwheels to impress the girls.

"Is this how you waste your days?" Raoul asked, knowing the answer. He could taste it in the air, the funk of a house where each day was a hundred years of dusk and loneliness.

"There's more," Nameless mumbled, but stopped the video, cheeks flushing.

"So, given eternity, you would sit here and stew over your misspent youth," Raoul said. "Enough. I would have your thoughts on a matter."

Nameless ejected the tape, reverently sliding it

into its case. He rested it on the coffee table, lined it up within its boundary of dust.

"I had a visitor, in my house," Raoul said. "Uninvited."

"In your house?" Nameless pursed his lips, frowned. "That's tricky."

"Stank of the Old Ways, and that from a man who was hardly there. He spoke of the One-Way-World."

"Ah." Nameless drifted into a powerful memory, and Raoul was caught on the edges of this thought, almost drawn into the reverie. The minotaur stood up and with one hand flipped the sofa, knocking Nameless onto his back.

"Why?" the man said, winded. He got up, blubbering and clutching at Raoul's thick furry legs.

"There's enough of the One-Way-World in your head to cause trouble," Raoul said.

"I've been good," Nameless whined.

"You've dragged more than one fool into that mind of yours. Now tell me what you know."

"The man. That blurry, secret man," Nameless whispered. "I thought of him today, when I was making a sandwich," and Raoul knew he was lying. There was never a scrap of food to be found in this house.

"The truth, NOW," Raoul said, and put enough god into it that the knickknacks on the windowsill bounced around and the window shook. "Or I will turn you out and close this house to you."

"I was reading my high school yearbooks," Nameless said, terrified into truth. "I was reading the names, and when I saw a photo I thought of the man."

"Show me." And Nameless was hauling a carton out of the nearest shadow. It was brimful of curios and memories, a lifetime of hoarding every encounter, every word. There were love notes with the folds worn away, the ink nearly read from the page. Scout badges, speeding fines, broken condoms, the whole box and dice.

Nameless produced the yearbooks and gave a guilty grin.

"Meant no harm by it. Just looking."

"You were trying to find your name," Raoul said. "Try, it's not in there." And surely Nameless must realize that every mention of it was gone. Excised throughout the whole universe, from his birth certificate onwards.

"Show me the photo." And Nameless was flipping through the pages, past the photos of the formal and the signature page. He stopped at a class shot, rows of kids grinning or scowling at the lens. It was Nameless' class.

Nameless got the faintest of connections to Raoul's intruder, and Raoul carefully captured the very edge of this thought. He had a trail now and tore the page out of the book.

"Finally, you're useful for something. I'll leave you to it," Raoul said, tapping the video case with his massive sausage fingers. Nameless sat still as Raoul left by the front door, moving only when the wake of the minotaur's far-travel had settled.

Sliding the Funny Tape into the machine, Nameless howled. Raoul had replaced his precious memories with an aerobics program, and an infomercial for a fruit juicer.

Raoul appeared on the deck of *The Cheerful Misogynist*. The ship was the size of a city, a party boat mounted on wheels and rollers and treads. It was driven by sail, fans, balloons and oars, and rumor had it that an FTL drive could be found deep in its innards.

There was a girl here, Imogen, under his protection.

As could be expected from his entrance, there was a fuss. The sudden appearance of a minotaur can hardly factor into the average fetish, and most of the debauchery stopped wherever he passed.

There wasn't a crew as such, but there were those who liked to think they served the ship, hauling on ropes and scrubbing at the ancient decking when someone yelled at them. The Captain himself appeared, straightening his epaulettes and setting his cap level.

"Milord," he said, offering a lazy salute. "Captain Aurora Luca, if you please."

He wasn't in charge the last time Raoul visited, but the position seemed to be up for grabs whenever the predecessor got bored with it.

"I seek my ward," Raoul said, and for a moment, Captain Luca was confused. But the ship itself filled him in and understanding dawned in his eyes.

"Young Imogen," he said, fingering his salt-and-pepper beard. "She's below decks and well cared for."

"I would see her," the minotaur told the man, who shrugged, leading him to a hatch. It was a tight squeeze but the minotaur climbed down the ladder, following the Captain along a cramped passage.

When his horns scraped the ceiling beams, the ship grudgingly grew to a more reasonable dimension.

"Not welcome, Raoul," Luca said suddenly, now as the voice of the ship. "Do your business and go."

They passed a thousand fantasies, every kind of fetish and whim, hearing the low sobs of those who were meant to cry. Raoul had spent his mandatory season on board *The Cheerful Misogynist* and had no wish to open any of these doors.

Luca led him into an elevator, the clanky old kind with levers and a sliding cage door. After a gut-twisting descent, the door opened onto the Hieronymous Bosch wing, acre upon acre of purgatory. There were other horned beasts here, and he was barely noticed. Luca took them through the yawning mouth of a fat slavering worm.

After a moment of darkness and intense heat, they were climbing a set of stone steps. There was a crude wooden door, and Imogen was behind it.

"Raoul," she said, throwing her arms around the minotaur's waist. She was filthy, her hair matted into thick dreadlocks. "I want to leave this horrible place."

Raoul looked down at Captain Luca, who held up his hands, shrugged.

"She didn't like our games, didn't want to join in," he said. "Her greatest desire was to be left alone. We only gave her what she wanted."

They'd been keeping her in solitary confinement, halfway between a monk's cell and an oubliette. There was a rotten straw pallet with one ragged blanket and a toilet bucket tipped over in the far corner. They'd nailed a banner to the damp stone wall, higher than she could reach. It read SUIT YOURSELF, YOU STUCK-UP BITCH.

"I'm not happy," Raoul rumbled. "Our agreement was quite clear."

"Keep her safe," Luca said, speaking as the ship. "Keep her hidden from her old lover. That is all."

"Splitter of hairs," Raoul said. "You have wronged me. The girl did not want this."

"You forget, Raoul," said the ship through the man. "Your precious free will does not apply on board us. We generate our own laws here."

"I'm leaving with the girl. Be glad I take this no further."

"Of course. Still, there is the—simple matter—of our bargain," Luca's lips moved. "You owe us, little cow-god. We want your horns."

Luca blocked the doorway. He was no threat on his own, but Raoul could feel the presence of the ship in him, the weight of centuries of malice. True, he himself still had some power here, but would it be enough?

"You want these?" Raoul said, reaching up and touching the tips of his horns. Luca nodded for yes.

"A deal is a deal." And then the minotaur was upon Luca, goring him and flinging him about like a floppy toy. Imogen was screaming at him, telling him to stop, but he had the rage in him. He cast the broken man to the floor and became all feet and fists, before sense returned, the knowing that the ship would now do its best to destroy them. He heard the stones moving, felt the ship flexing and ready to bear down upon them.

"Get the Captain's hat," he ordered the terrified girl, and the stone wall opened before his horns as if it were paper. They were through and running, even as her prison became fire and wrath and unmaking.

Raoul snatched Imogen under one arm, the better to charge through the walls. The ship was squeezing like a fist, trying to trap them, but Raoul outpaced the changes, ran through desert and castle and future metropolis. Perverts scattered in terror from the roaring bull-man.

Finally, they reached the hull, a curving mountain of fitted planks that stretched upwards into a false sky. The hull didn't give for Raoul on the first go, so he set Imogen down on the floor. Taking a few steps back, he charged at the wall, his horns lodging deep. Gouging and twisting, he pierced all the way through, until a tiny hole let the daylight inside. Thrusting both hands into the hole, the minotaur stretched out the edges like clay. It was a great wound in the belly of the ship, one that wouldn't mend easily.

"Be ready!" he told Imogen, sliding his bulk through the tear. He was out and hit the ground with bone breaking speed, rolling to one side as an enormous wheel missed him by inches.

The city-ship was powering along at a terrifying rate, crushing a suburb into rubble. Raoul kept pace and snatched the plummeting Imogen before she could break upon the ground. A hundred hatches opened along the side of *The Cheerful Misogynist* and there was a barrage of cannons, even a trebuchet swinging its great lazy arm. Death rained all around them.

The minotaur veered from the ship's destructive path, legs burning as he cleared white picket fences and vaulted over cars in driveways. When Raoul escaped the shadow of the looming boat, he entered far-travel, charting an impossible distance.

I made a mistake," Raoul said. "It was wrong to leave you with the ship."

They were standing in his squalid living room, both covered in dust and scratches. Raoul was panting like his lungs were about to pop.

"You killed him," Imogen whispered, shaking. "You killed Luca."

"Hush, love." Raoul held her gently, aware that his furry hands were caked with the Captain's blood. "It takes a great deal of effort to kill someone these days. I doubt that he is dead."

He steered her over to the Formica dining table, sat her down on a battered art deco chair. She wouldn't look at him, so he busied himself with boiling water on the gas ring.

"I don't understand you, Raoul," Imogen finally said. "There's rumors about you, about what you are. Yet you choose to live here."

He knew it was a pigsty. He liked the piles of dirty dishes, the stacks of moldy books lining the walls. He went to great pains to collect this clutter and arrange it just so.

"It really smells in here," she emphasized, and the minotaur smiled. He put a warm cup of instant coffee on the table, next to Captain Luca's hat.

"We are defined by our ephemera," he said. "Without clutter and junk, we aren't really alive."

"Raoul, this place is a disaster. At least Nameless has an excuse for hoarding rubbish." She played with the hat and went to put it on her head.

"Don't," Raoul warned. "Do not put that on."

"Why not?"

"Because you will become the Captain of *The Cheerful Misogynist,* and you will bring that murderous boat into my house."

Raoul found an empty shoebox somewhere under all the junk and jammed the hat into it. He wrapped it up with an entire roll of sticky tape and tied an extension cord around the whole mess. It went deep into his pocket.

"Why did you come for me? I thought you'd arranged to hide me on the boat for exactly one century. What's going on, Raoul?"

"I need you, Imogen. Not for that," he snorted as she rolled her eyes. "I need your help with something."

He pulled the rumpled yearbook page out of his pocket, flattened it out in front of her. He pointed at the class photo.

"One of these people invaded my home. Found where it was for starters and got past everything I've thought of to keep people out. No doubting in my mind, he knows the Old Ways."

"Hmm." Imogen stared at the photo. With free will restored, she'd already changed her hair from ratty to natty, and her outfit flickered between a slinky dress and a power suit.

"You have to try harder," Raoul said, and gently licking her forehead, he passed over the thread of thought that he took from Nameless. "You were

435

one of the last ones to leave the One-Way-World. Can you feel anything in this photo?"

"Quick, gimme a pen," she said, finally settling for khaki pants, Docs and a Rolling Stones T-shirt. She drew an ink outline around one of the boys.

"Oh. It's just Nameless," she said.

"As always, he thinks of nothing but himself, his past. What a waste of time."

There was a letter in the mailbox, marked "RAOUL MITHRAS." The envelope was marked "card only," and Raoul sniffed it cautiously. Deciding it was safe he slit it open with a thumbnail.

"SHH, IT'S A SPEAKEASY!" the card cried out loud, a cutout in the shape of a wine barrel. A muted jazz riot could be heard blasting out of the card when he opened it. Imogen could see the reflections of a turning mirror ball on the minotaur's face.

"'You and a friend are invited to Madam Lune's top-secret party,'" Raoul read. "'Don't tell the law.'"

"Fun!" Imogen said.

"I don't know. Lune and I are having—problems."

"What have you done now?" Imogen said, exasperated. Raoul scowled but didn't answer.

"I leave you alone for five minutes. Sheesh. Well, I'm going. I've been stuck on that boat for ages."

"This is a bad idea," Raoul rumbled, but he stepped into a zoot suit, with a trilby that sat nicely in between his horns. Imogen wolf-whistled.

"You look snappy."

She dreamt up a flapper outfit, with her makeup caked on and a bob haircut to match her laddish physique. She had a cigarette holder and a fur stole.

"Well, aren't we the cat's pajamas?" she purred, and they leapt into the card.

Lune was famous for her parties. The last one she threw was the Egyptian Extravaganza, and it went for two hundred years. *The Cheerful Misogynist* turned up and forced its passengers to build her a scale model of the Great Pyramid. By hand.

This one was an amazing replica of a speakeasy, as if the entire city of prohibition-era Chicago had been a boozy party held openly. It was an art deco nightmare, and Raoul shook his head at Lune's twisted take on history. There was an army of federal agents splitting barrels of moonshine over the gutters, but only so that the guests could dip their cups into a ready supply of booze.

"Let's boogie," Raoul said, over the music of the nearest big band. They did the Lindy Hop, the Bunny Hug, the Charleston. For a man-bull hybrid, Raoul was light on his feet and Imogen floated around him like a butterfly.

"Raoul! Darling!" And Lune was there, draped all over the surprised minotaur. Even though she was Aphrodite and Gaia and everything else femme, Lune managed to look cheap. She had too many feather boas and a carafe of gin clenched in one hand, with one of her stockings unstuck and sagging around her ankle. She bumped Imogen aside, covering Raoul's snout with sloppy kisses.

"Lune, it's good to see you," he lied, gently peeling her off. "You remember my ward, Imogen?"

"Not really," she said, turning from Imogen's death stare. "So, who was your visitor?"

"No one. A friend," Raoul started, but Lune laughed, a short sharp bark. There was something of her Durga aspect in the sound and he knew he needed to tread carefully. For all their sakes.

"Bullshit from the bull-man. Here I thought you were a gentleman. No, I've had to invent a chevalier, all on my own some."

Lune stuck two fingers in her mouth and let rip with a world-shaking whistle, so loud that her costumed guests clutched their heads in pain. A man came trotting to her side, and for a moment Raoul tensed up, nostrils flaring. He could swear that the man had a blurry face, until he realized that the man had no face at all. In fact, it was a mannequin given motion, with a judge's wig sliding around on its head. She'd dressed it in robes befitting the judiciary, and Raoul understood the irony. The only guest likely enough to obey the prohibition should symbolize the "law."

"This is King James," Lune said. "Say hello."

"Open your hearts to us," the dummy said in a rumbling baritone. Where its mouth should be, the molded lips tried to move. "We have wronged no one, we have corrupted no one, we have cheated no one."

"Paul's Second Letter to the Corinthians," Lune said, a drunk's grin plastered across her face. "I made him and he always knows what to say."

"It's madness is what it is," Imogen said. "Don't tell me you fed a bloody Bible into that thing."

"Let us walk honestly," King James said, "as in the day—not in rioting and drunkenness, not in chambering and wantonness, not in strife or envying."

"Well, he's got your measure," Raoul said. "Maybe you should have fed it some Henry Miller or something."

Everything shifted, and Raoul was knocked onto his side. A couple of the faux buildings toppled, and screaming and terror erupted from those who shouldn't fear anything.

It was the blurry man. He'd busted into Lune's party, taking gate-crashing to a new level. He was walking toward Raoul, then running, and with every step great cracks opened in Lune's pocket world. People were falling into the holes and Raoul knew that they would fall forever.

"Foul little cow," the blur yelled, and they met with a crash, grappling and rolling through the wreckage. Raoul was strong even back in the One-Way-World, but this stranger matched him. A blurry hand gripped one horn, shaking his head back and forth until he feared his mighty neck would snap.

Then the intruder gasped and froze up with pain, so Raoul picked him up, threw him as far as he could. It felt like he was hurling a mountain. The blurry man landed just shy of a nothing-hole, curled up and screaming. A bright silver arrow pierced his side.

Lune wore her Diana aspect and stood as tall as a tree, her bow held steady. She was pulling back on the second arrow when the man made a run for it.

"Where's your bloody invite?" She laughed, but her joviality was short-lived when the man slipped through the only door and took it with him.

We've got to get out of here," Lune said, and Imogen mimicked her silently. Like everyone else they were crowded to the very edge of the pocket world, everything in the middle being eaten up by the spreading doughnut hole of nothing. Every minute or so another building collapsed, and the roads and sidewalks were being drawn in like strands of spaghetti.

"Well, this is some party," Raoul said and got grief from all directions. "What?"

Lune was shifting in between Diana and Durga aspects, which had the minotaur quite nervous. She even had a bit of Bast going on, and her cat tail flicked angrily underneath her chiffon dress.

"All I'm saying is that it's always a bad idea to suspend free will." Raoul raised his hands, tempting fate.

"It was for authenticity." Lune sulked. "I didn't want people changing into robots and dragons when they got bored."

She was the only one who could change in any way, but all she could do was flick through her aspects, impotent and furious. Everyone else was stuck in their period clothing, and there was no reaching outside.

Lune padded over to the edge of the abyss, to where the blurry man fell. There was a spot of blood there, and kneeling, she dabbed at it with Bast's cat tongue.

"I know this one," she said. "Yon gate-crasher has the taint of YHWH upon him."

"Yahweh," Raoul said. He'd brought her up to speed with the events of late. "It makes sense, I guess. He had the most to lose from the closing of the One-Way-World."

"Yes." Lune nodded sagely. "He was most bitter, where everyone else was eager."

The pocket world gave a great shudder. There wasn't much time left before the bottom fell out completely.

"Raoul, the hat," Imogen said. "What about Luca's hat?"

He dug the box out of his pocket, squashed flat and wrapped tightly. It fluttered around in his hands, and he unwrapped it nervously.

The hat made a leap for his head, and he snatched it out of the air. It twitched and shook with frustration, and Raoul was tempted to lob the thing into the nearest pit.

"It's a really, really bad idea to wear this hat," he said. "But if anything can break into this place, it's *The Cheerful Misogynist*."

"Don't," Imogen said. "I'll do it. It'll hurt you, Raoul." She made to take the peaked cap but he lifted his hands up so high that she couldn't reach.

"No bloody way, José," he said, taking off his trilby. "You are not going back on that ship and that's final. I'll become the Captain."

"I believe I have a better suggestion, much as it pains me to dream it up," Lune said. "What about King James?"

They all looked at the mannequin, puttering around in the rubble and soliloquizing about meekness and inheriting the earth. Raoul jammed the hat onto James' head.

"Remember Sodom and Gomorrah," King James rumbled, and a moment later, the prow of *The Cheerful Misogynist* breached the pocket world.

What crime is Nameless being punished for?" Imogen asked. Raoul brought her in close, wary of the passengers and crew. *The Cheerful Misogynist* was tolerating them as a necessary evil, but only for now.

"We're not exactly sure," the bull-god said. "Nameless hasn't done it yet, and all we know is it's going to be big. Made sense to punish him straight away."

"But you made him a no one. That's a bit harsh." Imogen went as if to say more but sat down on the deck, spinning a badminton racquet in her hands. She'd shifted into a Goth get-up, a nightmare of black and lace.

Aurora Luca was onboard and very much alive, a mess of stitches, bruises and cuts. There was a loop of intestine hanging loose from a wound, and he picked and worried at it. Luca shied away from Raoul, only to continue moaning about "being replaced by a bloody Bible-bashing robot."

Captain King James had been thoroughly infested by the ship. The Captain's hat had become a tricorn, and he paced the deck in finery that would make Napoleon jealous. He still had no features, but now sported a molded plastic moustache.

"Render unto Caesar," he said again, pointing at

Raoul's horns. The ship just wouldn't give up, even if its only mouthpiece could do nothing but quote the Bible.

"No deal," Raoul said. "You cheated me."

"But one of the soldiers pierced His side with a spear," the ship said through the new Captain, and Raoul remembered the damage he saw on boarding. His previous escape had left a puckering wound in the side of *The Cheerful Misogynist* that would take years to close.

They'd convinced the boat to take them to the house of Nameless. There was no love lost between Yahweh and this, the most sinful of boats, and it had some score to settle that not even Captain King James would speak of.

The ship grew a trio of great zeppelins, each a rubber moon fastened to the deck by cables thicker than a man. The landscape passed in a blur but the wait was agonizing, Raoul deciding that the rumors of the ship possessing an FTL drive were just that. Still, it was quicker than far-travel.

"Mighty son of Minos, what brings you to this pervert's boat?" Lune purred from beside him. She'd sidled up to the prow where he gripped the railing and gently entwined his arm. Raoul blinked and then she was holding air, he a few steps away. The best his magic could do while onboard.

"Don't, Lune. We've spoken on this."

"I don't know why I'm surprised. You've broken every heart but hers," Lune said, pointing at Imogen who was now playing quoits with a leather-bound gimp.

"I'm not for mazes or any who build them,"

443

Raoul said. "Be my friend if you will, but you'll not bind me."

For a long minute, they looked at the yawning distance ahead of them. *The Cheerful Misogynist* was about to blast through lands which were a mad blend of downtown Chicago, the Katherine Gorge and parts of an arctic tundra.

"How do you posit that YHWH and Nameless are in cahoots?" Lune said.

"Only Nameless kept the Old Ways in his head, hoarded every scrap of the One-Way-World he ever had. Yahweh could use that poor fool as a gateway, a focus."

"We expected war from the Lord of Hosts," Lune said. "I helped to guard the waypoints when we closed the One-Way-World, but while we marked his mob of hang-tailed bullies, none of us saw him enter."

"So it's to be Yahweh, again," Raoul said. "We crossed paths long ago, back when he took the Romans from me. From Mithras," he corrected.

"I thought *he* was meant to be the jealous god." Lune laughed.

"If I were Yahweh, I'd be heading to the house of Nameless. He thinks us trapped in the pocket world, which gives him time to act."

"Yahweh won't be able to bring it all forth," Lune said, but Raoul could smell her uncertainty, the bitter beginnings of a strong fear. "Without a name, he's nothing to bind it to."

They saw the house of Nameless, slumped across the cliffs like the broken man who lived there. Sometime back they caught the far-travel wake of

Yahweh, and through a sticky field glass that King James offered Raoul, he could spot the broken god entering the front door.

"Curse your sluggard of a boat!" Raoul said, snapping the glass closed. "Ram it! Bring the whole place down!"

But there was enough vinegar left in the old god to keep the ship at bay. Try as it might, *The Cheerful Misogynist* was grounded, straining against Yahweh's invisible hand.

Raoul and the others were out, rappelling down ropes or gliding on dreamt-up wings. There were enough holes in Yahweh's fence that they could slip through on foot.

Imogen was back to khakis and a T-shirt, and for some reason had the remote control for Raoul's entertainment center in her hand. Lune was passive, reining her aspects in until she needed one of them. Captain King James hobbled along, a plastic fop with nothing but a bunch of scripture in his head.

They were through the open front door, and the cat/s bombarded them, a hundred toms from the size of a kitten to a tiger. They snarled and hissed and scratched until Lune brought forth Bast in all her awful glory. The cat/s disappeared into whatever shadows they could, slipping from the anger of their lady.

"Puss is an Egyptian word," Lune/Bast said. "They've never been allowed to forget me."

It would take hours to search the house, but Yahweh left a sour funk that Raoul could easily follow, a smell that spoke to his delicate nostrils of loss and lust, of spilled seed and dust.

445

"The stairs, of course." And they were up and running, Raoul running his horns along the banister when the house itself sought to delay them. Then they were up in the den, and Raoul saw Nameless kneeling on the ground, his box of mementos tipped over and spread on the floor around him.

"Be wary, Nameless," Raoul said. "Your old master walks in your halls."

Nameless looked up at the minotaur, and Raoul saw the ripple, the signs of a limitless being that has hidden in flesh for too long.

"Mute him!" he instructed Imogen, who thumbed the appropriate button on the remote control, but she was too slow. Yahweh spoke through the mouth of Nameless and returned his name to him.

The One-Way-World began to slowly erupt from his mouth, an obscene bubble of galaxies and sparkling nebulas. Every muscle straining against that impossible weight, Raoul lifted Nameless, a floppy doll with eyes rolling, oblivious to the intrusion.

"Call your boat," he told King James. "Do it!"

He could see the plastic mouth moving, but the words coming out were like treacle, mere sounds against a greater darkness. Raoul was being drawn into the maelstrom, the One-Way-World that was growing by inches.

He dimly noted that Lune brought out the feared Durga aspect, and the trendy flapper outfit peeled away to reveal a three-eyed, ten-armed killer, bristling with weapons. She was hacking away at the walls and one hand was contorted into a little-known mudrā, negating the very house beneath them. She wanted to put a blade through Yahweh's throat but Raoul kept her at horn's length, circling him protectively with his enormous arms. Injuring Yahweh at this point could mean the undoing of all things. No second chances, not even a One-Way-World to fester in. Nothing but oblivion.

"The boat," he cried through the treacle darkness, and when he saw Imogen it all made sense. Imogen had the remote held level and was thumbing a button over and over. Raoul guessed it to be "pause" or "slow-tracking" or something similar. Either way, Raoul hadn't replaced the batteries for a thousand years, and they were only held in with duct tape anyway. This wouldn't work for long.

Lune/Durga canceled a wall of Nameless' house into shivers of nothing, and slipping into her Diana skin, she launched arrows at something in the distance. Each shot was an eternity as she nocked the arrow and drew it to her cheek, the same cheek that Raoul had kissed and nuzzled and made false promises to. She blinked as she was aiming, and set her tongue just so. Release, and the arrow slowly glided forward.

She's cutting a path for the boat, he realized, and even as the remote control finally failed and Lune/Diana was firing dozens of arrows per second, Yahweh's fence shattered. Captain King James touched the tip of his tricorn with a plastic hand, and a moment later the enormity of the boat pulled alongside the shattered house.

447

SETH J. ROWANWOOD

They were level with the tear in the hull, the evidence of Raoul's escape that should be down near the ground. Raoul guessed what the boat was planning, and with no other choice, he pitched Yahweh and Nameless through the hole. They fell into the guts of *The Cheerful Misogynist,* along with the growing seed that was the One-Way-World.

Well, it's a fetish boat, and the One-Way-World just happens to be Yahweh's fetish," Raoul said. "It makes sense to trap him there."

They were following the secret paths to Raoul's house via far-travel, Imogen clutched to his broad woolly chest as his legs ate up the miles.

"He'll figure it out," Imogen said.

"Yahweh thinks he won, and who are we to tell him any different? Let him run his little play-world. I know *I* won't bother him."

Imogen stared at him again, at the stub where his left horn was. It would take perhaps a hundred years to grow back, and he'd been halved in more ways than he cared to admit.

"A fair deal," Raoul said. "The ship hid you for fifty years, so they get one horn."

They stood at his front door now, and, as Raoul reached for the key, Imogen snatched it out of his hand with a speed that was suspiciously reminiscent of Lune. She tucked the key into a fanny pack that she had suddenly decided was cool.

"I want you to help Nameless," she said, gamely blocking the minotaur from his house. "You've punished him enough. It's wrong to leave him stuck in that boat with Yahweh, the pair of them dreaming over a seed of a world. Or a universe, or whatever."

"It's what they both want," Raoul sighed. "Neither of them want to be here. Surely we owe them this small kindness." Imogen was defiant, but even she could see reason and fished out the chunky brass key, the one that could open the Great Library at Alexandria as well as a Starbucks in Melbourne.

He unlocked the door and jerked it open, but instead of his filthy apartment, he could see a great frothing sea, and perched on a murderous wave was *The Cheerful Misogynist*. He could make out Lune's dummy on the prow, holding up a yellow curve that was his horn.

Raoul slammed the door shut.

"I wanted to move anyway," he said.

The Year in the Contests

This Contest year, we added four well-known and highly respected writers to our distinguished roster of WotF judges: Mike Resnick, former WotF winner Eric Flint, Dean Wesley Smith, who was published in WotF Volume I, and Kristine Kathryn Rusch, who (along with Dean) attended the very first WotF workshop.

Judge Robert J. Sawyer's novel *Fast Forward* was developed into a popular TV series. Judge (and Lead Instructor for the workshop) Tim Powers sold an option on his book *On Stranger Tides* to the Pirates of the Caribbean movie franchise. *Pirates of the Caribbean 4* will be based upon *On Stranger Tides*.

Winners Cat Sparks and Ian McHugh (both writers) received Australia's prestigious Aurealis Award in 2009.

Winners James Alan Gardner and K. D. Wentworth (now Coordinating Judge) were Nebula Finalists in 2009 for the Novelette. Winner and Judge Nina Kiriki Hoffman won a Nebula for her short story "Trophy Wives."

Winners James Alan Gardner and Robert Reed, along with Judge Mike Resnick, were all nominated for the 2009 Hugo Award. Winners Aliette de Bodard and Tony Pi were both short-listed for the John W. Campbell Award for Best New Writer. Illustrators of the Future winner Shaun Tan and judge Bob Eggleton were nominated for the Best Professional Artist Hugo. Illustrators Gold Award winner Frank Wu won the Hugo for Best Fan Artist.

And, lastly, in very sad news, famed artist Frank Frazetta passed away. Frank was an Illustrators of the Future Judge since the Contest's inception who gave generously of his time to help new artists and produced many fine covers for the WotF anthology series through the years.

For Contest year 26, the L. Ron Hubbard Writers of the Future Contest winners are:

453

For the year 2009, the L. Ron Hubbard Illustrators of the Future Contest winners are:

FIRST QUARTER

> *Seth J. Rowanwood*
> *Cassandra Shaffer*
> *Kelsey Wroten*

SECOND QUARTER

> *Tyler Carter*
> *Rachael Jade Sweeney*
> *R. M. Winch*

THIRD QUARTER

> *Jordan Cornthwaite*
> *Rebecca Gleason*
> *Irena Kovalenko*

FOURTH QUARTER

> *Jingxuan Hu*
> *Ven Locklear*
> *Olivia Pelaez*

Our heartiest congratulations to all the winners!
May we see much more of their work in the future.

WRITERS' CONTEST RULES

1. No entry fee is required, and all rights in the story remain the property of the author. All types of science fiction, fantasy and dark fantasy are welcome.

2. By submitting to the Contest, the entrant agrees to abide by all Contest rules.

3. All entries must be original works, in English. Plagiarism, which includes the use of third-party poetry, song lyrics, characters or another person's universe, without written permission, will result in disqualification. Excessive violence or sex, determined by the judges, will result in disqualification. Entries may not have been previously published in professional media.

4. To be eligible, entries must be works of prose, up to 17,000 words in length. We regret we cannot consider poetry, or works intended for children.

5. The Contest is open only to those who have not professionally published a novel or short novel, or more than one novelette, or more than three short stories, in any medium. Professional publication is deemed to be payment of at least five cents per word, and at least 5,000 copies, or 5,000 hits.

6. Entries submitted in hard copy must be typewritten or a computer printout in black ink on white paper, printed only on the front of the paper, double-spaced, with numbered pages. All other formats will be disqualified. Each entry must have a cover page with the title of the work, the

author's legal name, a pen name if applicable, address, telephone number, email address and an approximate word count. Every subsequent page must carry the title and a page number, but the author's name must be deleted to facilitate fair, anonymous judging.

Entries submitted electronically must be double-spaced and must include the title and page number on each page, but not the author's name. Electronic submissions will separately include the author's legal name, pen name if applicable, address, telephone number, email address and approximate word count.

7. Manuscripts will be returned after judging only if the author has provided return postage on a self-addressed envelope.

8. We accept only entries that do not require a delivery signature for us to receive them.

9. There shall be three cash prizes in each quarter: a First Prize of $1,000, a Second Prize of $750, and a Third Prize of $500, in US dollars. In addition, at the end of the year the four First Place winners will have their entries rejudged, and a Grand Prize winner shall be determined and receive an additional $5,000. All winners will also receive trophies.

10. The Contest has four quarters, beginning on October 1, January 1, April 1 and July 1. The year will end on September 30. To be eligible for judging in its quarter, an entry must be postmarked or received electronically no later than midnight on the last day of the quarter. Late entries will be included in the following quarter and the Contest Administration will so notify the entrant.

11. Each entrant may submit only one manuscript per quarter. Winners are ineligible to make further entries in the Contest.

12. All entries for each quarter are final. No revisions are accepted.

13. Entries will be judged by professional authors. The decisions of the judges are entirely their own, and are final.

14. Winners in each quarter will be individually notified of the results by phone, mail or email.

15. This Contest is void where prohibited by law.

16. To send your entry electronically, go to:
www.writersofthefuture.com and follow the instructions.

To send your entry in hard copy, mail it to:
     L. Ron Hubbard's
     Writers of the Future Contest
     PO Box 1630
     Los Angeles, California 90078

17. Visit the website for any Contest rules updates at www.writersofthefuture.com.

ILLUSTRATORS' CONTEST RULES

1. The Contest is open to entrants from all nations. (However, entrants should provide themselves with some means for written communication in English.) All themes of science fiction and fantasy illustrations are welcome: every entry is judged on its own merits only. No entry fee is required and all rights to the entry remain the property of the artist.

2. By submitting to the Contest, the entrant agrees to abide by all Contest rules.

3. The Contest is open to new and amateur artists who have not been professionally published and paid for more than three black-and-white story illustrations, or more than one process-color painting, in media distributed broadly to the general public. The ultimate eligibility criterion, however, is defined by the word "amateur"—in other words, the artist has not been paid for his artwork. If you are not sure of your eligibility, please write a letter to the Contest Administration with details regarding your publication history. Include a self-addressed and stamped envelope for the reply. You may also send your questions to the Contest Administration via email.

4. Each entrant may submit only one set of illustrations in each Contest quarter. The entry must be original to the entrant and previously unpublished. Plagiarism, infringement of the rights of others, or other violations of the Contest rules will result in disqualification. Winners in previous quarters are not eligible to make further entries.

5. The entry shall consist of three illustrations done by the entrant in a color or black-and-white medium created from the artist's imagination. Use of gray scale in illustrations and mixed media, computer generated art, and the use of photography in the illustrations are accepted. Each illustration must represent a subject different from the other two.

6. ENTRIES SHOULD NOT BE THE ORIGINAL DRAWINGS, but should be color or black-and-white reproductions of the originals of a quality satisfactory to the entrant. Entries must be submitted unfolded and flat, in an envelope no larger than 9 inches by 12 inches.

7. All hardcopy entries must be accompanied by a self-addressed return envelope of the appropriate size, with the correct US postage affixed. (Non-US entrants should enclose international postage reply coupons.) If the entrant does not want the reproductions returned, the entry should be clearly marked DISPOSABLE COPIES: DO NOT RETURN. A business-size self-addressed envelope with correct postage (or valid email address) should be included so that the judging results may be returned to the entrant.

We only accept entries that do not require a delivery signature for us to receive them.

8. To facilitate anonymous judging, each of the three photocopies must be accompanied by a removable cover sheet bearing the artist's name, address, telephone number, email address and an identifying title for that work. The reproduction of the work should carry the same identifying title on the front of the illustration and the artist's signature should be deleted. The Contest Administration will remove and file the cover sheets, and forward only the anonymous entry to the judges.

461

9. There will be three co-winners in each quarter. Each winner will receive an outright cash grant of US $500 and a trophy. Winners will also receive eligibility to compete for the annual Grand Prize of an additional cash grant of $5,000 together with the annual Grand Prize trophy.

10. For the annual Grand Prize Contest, the quarterly winners will be furnished with a specification sheet and a winning story from the Writers of the Future Contest to illustrate. In order to retain eligibility for the Grand Prize, each winner shall send to the Contest address his/her illustration of the assigned story within thirty (30) days of receipt of the story assignment.

The yearly Grand Prize winner shall be determined by the judges on the following basis only:

Each Grand Prize judge's personal opinion on the extent to which it makes the judge want to read the story it illustrates.

The Grand Prize winner shall be announced at the L. Ron Hubbard Awards Event held in the following year.

11. The Contest has four quarters, beginning on October 1, January 1, April 1 and July 1. The year will end on September 30. To be eligible for judging in its quarter, an entry must be postmarked no later than midnight on the last day of the quarter. Late entries will be included in the following quarter and the Contest Administration will so notify the entrant.

12. Entries will be judged by professional artists only. Each quarterly judging and the Grand Prize judging may have different panels of judges. The decisions of the judges are entirely their own and are final.

462

13. Winners in each quarter will be individually notified of the results by mail or email.

14. This Contest is void where prohibited by law.

15. To send your entry electronically, go to: www.writersofthefuture.com and follow the instructions.

To send your entry via mail send it to:
     L. Ron Hubbard's
     Illustrators of the Future Contest
     PO Box 3190
     Los Angeles, California 90078

18. Visit the website for any contest rules updates at www.writersofthefuture.com.